# DARKNESS DESCENDING

# Darkness Descending

*A Novel*

Bethann Korsmit

iUniverse, Inc.

New York  Lincoln  Shanghai

## Darkness Descending

iUniverse books may be ordered through booksellers or by contacting:

iUniverse
2021 Pine Lake Road, Suite 100
Lincoln, NE 68512
www.iuniverse.com
1-800-Authors (1-800-288-4677)

This is a work of fiction. All of the characters, names, incidents, organizations, and dialogue in this novel are either the products of the author's imagination or are used fictitiously.

ISBN: 978-0-595-44405-2 (pbk)
ISBN: 978-0-595-88735-4 (ebk)

Printed in the United States of America

To my husband, Michiel Korsmit, who stands by me and supports me in everything that I do. Together we can take on anything that gets in our way. Forever and for always—Ik hou van jou.

To my parents—I cannot thank you enough for all that you do. I love you.

To my best friend, Calin Pirvu, who always supported me and encouraged me to write. Your enthusiasm for writing and for life have always inspired me. We are the flip-side of the same coin, my friend. You are, and always will be, my dearest friend.

# CHAPTER 1

▼

Quiet contentment mixed with the faint smell of a Cuban cigar filled the intricately decorated, majestic master bedroom and made it's main occupant smile a wide smile. The day had been long and overly stressful, but the evening held great promise, thought the tall, athletically thin, distinguished Robert Petrovic as he took a long drag on his cigar. Anticipation burned brightly behind his piercing mahogany eyes. It had been a long time. Too long since he had been in the arms of the one he loved, and in the arms that loved him back.

Great attention to detail was displayed in Robert's choice of clothing. Charcoal gabardine, pleated trousers with a black cashmere sweater. He cut quite a dashing figure, a swashbuckling, debonair mixture of worldly diplomat and a Casanova spy. It was quite an accomplishment for a founder/owner of a construction company.

Robert looked down at his Rolex, glanced a quick glimpse into the mirror with a smile, and started to walk down to the main part of the house. The house was not as ostentatious as it could have been, but Robert preferred to simply call it a house, not a mansion like it really was. He had overseen every aspect of the construction and made sure every minute detail was constructed to perfection. The beauty of the exterior, and inside the home, was for him alone, for it was his sanctuary from life and the stresses of business. The three-story, twenty-six room brick home was shared with no one, with the exception of his lover when his lover wanted to stay over. There were servants who came to cook, clean, wash and do small errands for Mr. P., as they called him, but no one stayed on as live-in servants.

Robert came into the dining room and smiled at the lovely table setting. His cook had even remembered to put out the candles for his intended, romantic candlelight dinner. He called out for his cook, but no one answered. As he was walking toward the kitchen, he noticed a small piece of stationary lying at the far end of the table. He nodded with understanding as he read the note …

Dear Mr. P.,

I had to leave early, but the meal is prepared and is warming in the oven.

All you have to do is serve. Enjoy your evening.

Robert folded the note and placed it aside. Everything was perfect. The food was prepared; the ambiance was warm and romantic. The only thing missing was the guest of honor. The doorbell rang as if Robert willed his guest to the front door. With a spring in his step and a glint in his eye, Robert gracefully opened the door. The smile quickly dissipated from Robert's face as he spoke with unsuppressed annoyance. "What are you doing here, George?"

"I want to talk to you," George uttered with equal annoyance.

"Now's not a good time. I'm having someone over for dinner."

"Someone?" George said with mock surprise. "Please! Your queer friend can wait. I can't," George said with undisguised hostility.

Rage and anger spread like wildfire through Robert's veins causing him to involuntarily squeeze his long, thin fingers in taut fists. "Get out of my house," he shouted. "Nobody comes here and insults me or my friends."

"I'll leave after I've said what I came to say."

"Say it and then get the hell out of my house," yelled Robert as his blood pressure continued to skyrocket.

George nonchalantly walked into the living room and sat down, all the while knowing that his actions were pushing Robert toward the breaking point. George glanced at the dinner table and back at Robert with venomous eyes, "Who the hell do you think you are?"

"State your business, George, before I have you removed," answered an annoyed Robert.

"You can't stand to see your mother happy, can you?"

"I love my mother, but she'll never be happy with you."

"What is it Petrovic, you jealous? Can't leave your mommy's apron strings?"

"I have no problem leaving mama's apron strings as long as someone else's hand isn't on her pocketbook."

George jumped out of his chair and stood face-to-face with Robert, glaring into Robert's unblinking eyes. "I don't want anything from your mother except her love and companionship."

Robert chimed in without missing a beat, "And access to her bank account." George looked as if he was going to choke Robert, but Robert continued, "Isn't that your M.O.? Get an elderly lady with a nice bank account to fall in love with you?"

George struck out at Robert, but only caught hold of his collar as Robert, sensing an attack, moved out of the way. Robert grabbed George's hands and removed them from his cashmere collar. "I know all about you George. I know you never married until you were in your sixties. Wasn't that about the same time you started having financial problems … from gambling?"

"I didn't get married until I was in my sixties because I was a content bachelor enjoying my career."

"Did you say bachelor? More like gigolo from what I heard."

With hatred emanating from his eyes and dripping from his every word, George responded, "You don't know anything about me."

Confidently and calmly, Robert replied, "I know that when you ran into money problems, you took an instant liking to a well-off elderly widow in your neighborhood, but that you didn't marry her until she was diagnosed with a terminal illness."

This time the blow found it's mark on Robert's chin. Robert's head snapped back as he fell to one knee, but the blow only encouraged the verbal assault that Robert had launched upon his mother's boyfriend. George came for a fight; Robert obliged. "Truth hurt, does it George?"

"You bastard. I loved Grace and I took care of her until the day she died."

"You took care of her bank account and life savings too, didn't you?" Robert slowly stood and straightened his clothing, "Bottom line, George. How much will it take to get you out of my mother's life?"

"You little faggot! You can cook your little dinners for that other little queer, but you can't stand to see your mother happy."

"You speak to me like that again and I'll forget my manners and destroy you." Robert was now shouting, "Do you hear me?"

George started walking toward the front door, but turned toward Robert with sarcasm dripping from his words, "I'll tell your mother you said hello!"

Robert's eyes, totally devoid of all emotion, glared at George as he spoke with cold determination, "My mother lives very comfortably, but I'm the one with the money. Her lifestyle is provided by me, remember that." Robert walked up to George and got in his face, "You may end up in my mother's will, but I control everything. Good day, Mr. Pennington. Give my regards to my mother." With that, Robert opened the door and escorted George out, just as Robert's guest was pulling into the driveway.

# CHAPTER 2

▼

As Robert's lover walked up the long sidewalk to the opulent front door, he looked questioningly from the car angrily leaving the driveway to Robert's feigned look of happiness. He stopped before crossing the threshold, "Robert, what's going on?" When Robert failed to answer, Mitchell asked tenderly, "Are you all right?"

A sad smile eclipsed on Robert's distinguished face, making him look several years older than his fifty years. "I'm fine now that you're here."

Mitchell Rains, a tall, athletically built gentleman of early middle-age, with stunning blue eyes and short blonde hair, reached out and took Robert's hand gently into his own and led him into the house and onto the large sofa. Still holding onto Robert's hand, he looked deeply into Robert's deep brown eyes and inquired about what had just transpired before his arrival. "Robert, what did George want?"

Trying overtly to avoid discussing what had just happened, Robert replied calmly, "Nothing really."

Disbelieving, Mitchell spoke more tenderly, melting Robert's already fragile facade. "I know you don't want to discuss George for fear you'll ruin our evening, but Robert it's okay. Nothing or nobody is going to ruin our evening together. If George is causing you problems, I want to know about it, okay?"

Robert turned away to hide the tears that glistened unshed in his eyes, but Mitchell slowly turned Robert's face back to him. Robert closed his eyes tightly and replied calmly and steadily. "He just showed up unannounced ranting about how I had no business checking out his past."

"What else? You shouldn't be this upset if he was just ranting and raving. You deal with people like him all the time."

Robert bowed his head and Mitchell caught on, "He said something about me and you, didn't he?"

Robert turned away again and started to rise, but Mitchell caught his hand and stopped him. "Please Mitchell, can't we just forget about George and everyone else in this world for tonight?" Robert asked pleadingly.

Mitchell cupped Robert's face with his soft hands, tilted his head from side to side as he studied Robert's expressive eyes, and smiled, "Sure. What's for dinner?"

A smile crossed Robert's tired face and Mitchell smiled reassuringly at him as the two walked into the dining room. The aromatic smell of fettuccini alfredo filled the dining room. A bottle of red wine and two tall, thin candles accented the elegant setting that Robert's staff cook created.

Mitchell sat down, spreading his napkin over his lap as Robert opened the aged wine and poured a glass for Mitchell and himself. They raised their glasses heavenward "To life, love and happiness."

The two lingered over dinner for almost three hours, discussing everything under the sun. Robert, the more conservative of the two, never disagreed openly with Mitchell's opinion, but always agreed to keep an open mind. The idealist in Mitchell made him see what was wrong in the world, and sometimes the way to conquer prejudices so that everyone would have the same opportunities as anyone else.

After dinner the conversation moved into Robert's living room, where the two lit up Cuban cigars and poured themselves some Brandy. Mitchell sat down next to Robert and put his arm around Robert's shoulders and playfully pulled him close. "Thank you for a wonderful evening."

Robert backed out of Mitchell's grasp to look him in the eyes, "I'm glad you came. You know I would do anything to make you happy."

Mitchell smiled mischievously at Robert's words, "Do you mean ANYTHING?"

Robert's face blushed an amazing shade of red, "Almost anything."

Mitchell laughed and Robert responded in kind. It had been such a long time since they both were able to laugh.

Taking a long drag on his cigar, Mitchell inquired, "Do you have your tuxedo out and ready to go for tomorrow?"

Confused, Robert asked, "What's tomorrow?"

Mitchell was amused, "Tomorrow is the 4th of July."

"Why do I need a tuxedo?"

"I accepted an invitation from one of my friends to attend a cookout and then an evening in the city dancing."

"That's great Mitchell. I'm sure you'll have a wonderful time," Robert added sincerely.

"I'm sure we'll both have a wonderful time. We were both invited, so I accepted for both of us," Mitchell said enthusiastically.

Robert stood up and walked over to the table where the alcohol was placed. He poured himself a shot of whiskey and downed it as soon as he poured it. Gathering his courage, he replied to Mitchell, "I wish you hadn't done that. You know I can't go."

Mitchell answered in a controlled tone of anger, "Yes, you can go. There is no good reason for you to stay home."

"I'm sorry Mitchell, but I can't jeopardize his career."

"Screw his career! He wouldn't help you if you were lying at his feet gasping for air."

Robert shook his head sadly in agreement, "I know he wouldn't, but he's still my son and I love him."

"You love him more than me." It was more a statement than a question.

"Please Mitchell, try to understand."

"I understand perfectly. You are willing to give up happiness for yourself so that your ungrateful son can get ahead in his career. Am I right?"

"I just don't want to jeopardize his career and his future."

Mitchell sat down and shook his head back and forth disbelieving. Robert, on the verge of tears, sat down next to Mitchell and put his arm around Mitchell's shoulder. Robert tried to speak gracefully and steadily, but his voice cracked as he said to Mitchell, "I love you too."

Mitchell looked Robert in the face and replied softly, "I love you too, Robert, but I can't keep doing this. I want to go out and enjoy life. I want to take you to parties, to dinner and dancing in the city." Mitchell took a deep breath, and continued, "You always said you wanted to travel, but when I ask you to go somewhere you won't go."

"I know I upset you with my indecisions, but he's my son, regardless of whether he admits that or not. I don't want to be the reason he fails."

"Trust me, Robert. He will fail, and it won't be any fault of yours."

"I promise we'll go somewhere soon, just the two of us."

"I'm sorry Robert, but I've heard that one before."

"Please believe me," Robert pleaded shyly.

Mitchell stood up and paced back and forth in front of Robert. "I'm sorry Robert, but I can't go on like this. It's a long weekend with the 4th tomorrow. I assumed we would spend time together with friends, but I guess I was wrong. I'm a sociable person, Robert. I can't live in isolation like you do."

Stunned, but sensing what was occurring, Robert inquired, "What are you saying?"

"I'm saying that I think it best we break up."

"Best for whom?"

"Best for me. I'm still a relatively young guy, and I want to do so many things in this lifetime. Things that I want to share with another person."

"You don't love me, do you?" asked Robert with an unsteady, cracking voice.

"Yes I love you, but that doesn't change the fact that we don't have a life together. We get together for dinners on special occasions, and sometimes I spend the night, but none of that is considered a life."

"Please Mitchell. Please don't leave me. I love you," pleaded Robert.

"I'm sorry Robert, but it's for the best. For both of us."

With tears glistening in his eyes, Robert replied calmly, "You lied to me."

Caught off guard, Mitchell responded, "I have never lied to you."

"Yes you did. You told me tonight that no one would ruin our evening together."

Mitchell, realizing the hurt that he was causing, sighed deeply. "I'm sorry Robert. Please believe that. Seeing you in pain is ripping my heart out, but I can't go on like this. In time you'll see that it was for the best."

"Your leaving will never be good for me."

"Everything will work out." Mitchell took one last gulp of his Brandy and started for the door. Robert jumped up and caught him, pulling him into an embrace.

"I love you Mitchell. Please don't go," sobbed Robert into Mitchell's shoulder.

"This isn't goodbye, Robert. We'll still be friends." As Mitchell was pulling away from Robert's embrace, Mitchell leaned in and kissed him delicately on the cheek. "I love you Robert."

Before Robert could regain his composure, Mitchell was out the door and racing out of the driveway.

# CHAPTER 3

▼

Anna Petrovic, a plain, gray-haired, conservatively dressed, soft-spoken lady in her mid-70's, sat on the freshly cut lawn as she weeded her prized garden. She had always had a green thumb, but these days she spent in the garden were for enjoyment, not survival. Delicately, she plucked several yellow tomatoes and a handful of green onions. As she walked slowly into the house, careful not to drop her vegetables, she watched George pull into her small driveway.

Waiting for George to exit his vehicle, Anna laid the vegetables down on the patio table. She went to greet George with her customary hug and peck on the cheek, but something in his eyes told Anna that something was terribly wrong.

"What's wrong, George?" asked an anxious Anna.

"Nothing. I just had a bad day. That's all."

"Don't lie to me, Honey. I can read you like a book. Now tell me, what's wrong?"

"I went to see your son," answered George with bitterness.

"What did you and Robert argue about this time?" inquired a relieved Anna.

"We didn't argue. I went there to tell him to stay out of our lives."

"George, he's my son. We can't throw him out of our lives."

"Anna," said George softly, "Robert had a private investigator dig into my past."

"That sounds like one of Robert's tactics," offered Anna still without concern.

"He's going to talk you into getting rid of me."

"Why would I do that? You don't have anything horrible in your past, do you?

"No, of course not, but Robert will stop at nothing. He'll make up stories bout me just so that we will break up."

"I'm stronger than you think, George. I can handle my own son. I'm an adult, and I sure as hell can determine who I want to spend the rest of my life with."

George took Anna into his arms and held her tightly against him for several long moments. Anna finally broke the embrace and lightened the somber mood that had transcended the garden when George arrived. "What do you think of my tomatoes and onions?"

"I think they look delicious! How would you like it if I made you and me a tomato and onion sandwich?"

"I would love it," Anna said with a huge smile. "Anytime anyone offers to make me something to eat, I can't refuse."

"Well Madame, please step inside and I will wow you with my culinary expertise," said George with a silly French accent.

"Do you know that my grandson, Alex, always told me that a tomato sandwich was a Depression-era sandwich? He'd say, 'Grandma, the Depression ended a long time ago,'" related Anna.

"You don't see your grandson very much these days, do you?"

Sadly Anna replied, "Not as often as I would like. He has a very important position working as a political consultant and Party official. I talk to him a few times a month on the phone." A tiny smile turned the corner of her lips upward, "He wants me to get email. Can you imagine me with email?"

"Hey, a lot of grandmas and grandpas use email to keep in touch with family members who are far away. Besides, you could be a surfin' grandma."

Anna laughed out loud at that proposition, "I don't think so."

George laughed for a moment and then got serious, "Why doesn't Alex come home to visit?"

"It's a long story, but the basic reason is that he disapproves of his father's lifestyle."

"I can understand that," George stated sarcastically.

"Why? Robert's lifestyle has not changed who he is on the inside," offered an irritated Anna.

"I wouldn't know because I didn't know Robert before, but I'm sure that it was hard on Alex finding out that his father is a homo."

"Can we change the subject please?"

"Absolutely … what do you want to talk about?" asked George.

"What did Robert say when you confronted him?"

"He said that I was only after your money and entry into your Will. He also said that you had poor judgment and that is the reason he controls the finances." George looked for a reaction from Anna and found her vulnerable spot. Inwardl

George smiled devilishly, "When I asked him if he thought you deserved happiness in your life, he said NO, not with a person like me."

Anna looked around the room to find a focal point to distract her from her anger. "He actually said that I don't deserve to be happy if I'm with you?"

"I wish I could tell you he didn't say it, but he did. He'd rather see you live the rest of your life in loneliness instead of in happiness with me."

"How could he be so cruel? I never rejected Mitchell or tried to deny Robert of any happiness, wherever he found it."

"I think Robert's problem is that he can't let go of you. He doesn't want to cut the apron strings."

"For Christ's sake, he's fifty years old. It's time he grows up." Anna walked to the refrigerator and poured two glasses of ice tea. The anger coursed through Anna's veins as she drank the ice tea slowly, but she could not stop the rage that was threatening to get out of control.

"George, can you stay here for awhile? I have to run an errand, but it will only take a few minutes."

"Do you want me to come with you?"

"No, I just want you to be here when I get back, so that we can plan what we are going to do tomorrow."

"No problem, I'll stay right here."

"Thanks Sweetie. I love you," she uttered as she was walking out the door.

A mischievous smile crept onto George's slightly wrinkled face. The plan had worked, and Anna could not have cooperated any better if he had written the script himself. "We'll see who wins in the end, Robert," stated George out loud but to himself. "I hold the key to your mother's heart. What will you do when your mother marries me?"

George went to the refrigerator and poured himself another glass of ice tea before retiring into the living room to watch the Yankees play the Red Sox. Laughing at the thought that Robert was getting a verbal beating from his mother, George spoke aloud once more, "One bad decision could affect you for the rest of your life. Keep your assault up on me, Robert, and you'll end up with nothing."

# CHAPTER 4

▼

Robert paced back and forth in front of his telephone hoping against hope that Mitchell would call and say that he really did not mean what he had said. The stress of the evening created black circles under Robert's smoldering brown eyes, and left his cheeks flushed from all the tears that he had shed. Sitting down in front of the telephone, Robert stared at it intensely and decided to take the first step and call Mitchell. As he was dialing Mitchell's number, the doorbell rang loudly in Robert's study, frightening him for a split second and causing him to hang up the telephone.

Robert sprinted to the front door with anxious anticipation that the person who rang the doorbell would be Mitchell. As he yanked the door open, welcome disbelief spread throughout his tense body. "Mom," he said with surprise. "Come in."

Anna walked through the door and past Robert in her path to the living room. A mixture of anger and hurt illuminated her beautiful face. She sat down, but did not say a word.

"I'm so glad you're here Mom. I've had the worst day of my life."

Anna looked at Robert up and down, and side to side before she spoke. Her usual soft-spoken voice turned harsh and unforgiving. "You poor thing! How do you think my day went after I found out that my only child thinks I'm an idiot?"

Surprised, Robert inquired, "What are you talking about? I've never thought of you as anything but the greatest mom a child could have."

Anna jumped all over his statement, "That's right Robert, the greatest mom a child could have. Not a grown man."

"Mom, what's happened? I don't know what you're talking about."

Angry words spilled from Anna lips as she continued, "I know what you did to George. He told me all about your conversation. How come you can't let me enjoy the last years of my life?"

"Mom, he's using you. All he wants is your money."

"Oh, I guess he couldn't be interested in me for just being me. Am I that unattractive that my own son couldn't believe that someone was interested in me for anything other than my money?"

"Mom, you're beautiful, but you can do better than George Pennington."

"Maybe I can, but it is George that I love, and nothing is going to change that, not even you."

"Mom, please think this through. The only reason I had George's past checked out is because I don't want to see you hurt. I don't think I could bear seeing you with a broken heart," said Robert sincerely.

Still unrelenting, "No, you'd rather see me alone for the rest of my life."

"You'll never be alone, Mom. You'll always have me."

"Damn it, Robert. I think it's time to cut the apron strings."

"Fine, if that's the way you want it, go be with that swindler, but the finances will still be run by me."

"Money and power are the only things that you care about, aren't they? You just want me to be dependent on you for the rest of my life."

"I've taken care of you financially for 35 years, but I guess that doesn't matter to you. You'd let some stranger with a history of stealing money from elderly women come into your life and take everything that I spent a lifetime earning," Robert replied angrily.

"Well I apologize if I was such a burden to you for the past 35 years. Here I thought you did it because you loved me."

"I do love you, Mom. That's why I don't want to see you get hurt."

"Tell the truth for once, Bobby. You don't want me to have any man come into my life."

"That's not true. I would welcome any man who was honest and had the proper intentions when it came to you."

"Can't you see how wrong this is? I'm your mother, and you're interrogating me about the man I love. Since when did you become the parent in our relationship?"

"Come on, Mom. I just don't want George to hurt you," Robert offered sincerely.

"George is a big part of my life. I love him, and nothing or no one is going to change that, and no one is going to stop me from seeing him whenever I want. Do you understand?" Anna asked stubbornly.

"No, I won't stop until I expose George for what he is … a con man."

"Then you leave me no choice," she said matter-of-factly.

"What do you mean by that?" asked Robert curiously.

"From this moment on, I don't have a son," she stated coldly.

Robert stared at Anna with his mouth agape. He turned from her to catch his breath. Those few words struck him like a baseball bat to the chest and left him gasping for air. "You don't mean that?"

"Yes I do. With all your petty resentments toward George, you made me pick between the two of you. I love George and want to spend the rest of my life with him. It's a shame that you can't see that I am a lonely old woman starved for companionship from a man who is part of the same generation as me."

"I understand that Mom, but you can do a lot better," Robert pleaded.

"I don't want to do any better. Why can't you see that?" Anna asked annoyed.

"Mom, I love you, but I can't sit back and watch that swindler steal every dime you have."

"If that's your final choice, from this moment on I have no son," Anna stated without emotion.

"Please Mom, don't say that. I know you still love me," Robert said with a tear in his eye.

"Goodbye Robert. If you come to your senses, George and I would be glad to have you over for dinner. If not, I hope life treats you well." With her pain hidden from Robert, Anna walked proudly to the door and left, leaving Robert to relive what had just happened.

Robert stood in the exact spot where Anna had just told him he was no longer a part of her life. He stared at the television program that was on in the living room, but he did not see it or hear it, for his senses were working overtime after being blindsided by his mother's comments. As he replayed the scene that had just played out before him, tears fell in torrents down his cheeks. Nothing had prepared him for such an attack from his own mother.

Robert sat down and let his mind wonder back to where he grew up, before his father died. Suddenly he was 15 years old and sitting at the bottom of his father's bed the morning his father died. Stefan Petrovic could barely hold his head up from weakness related to his disease, but he found enough strength to address his only child, Robert. Stefan spoke slowly and softly, "Bobby, you have to take care of your mother now. When I'm gone, you'll be the man of the house, and it will be your duty to care for your mother." Stefan coughed uncontrollably, but regained his composure to speak once again to his son, "It's your duty to obey your father, right?"

Robert answered shyly, "Yes father."

"Then you'll swear to me that you'll always look after your mother?"

"I swear, father." Robert said softly.

After receiving Robert's promise to look after Anna, Stefan closed his eyes peacefully and never woke up. Anna cried and sobbed, but Robert reacted stoically, for he knew that he had a rough road ahead of him.

As if awakening from a nightmare, Robert snapped out of reliving his past. Realizing that he had failed and had broken his promise to his father, Robert suddenly grabbed his car keys and headed for the garage.

With no particular destination in mind, Robert drove around the city for hours, reliving everything that had happened to him that day. Losing Mitchell pained him tremendously, but losing his mother was like sticking a dagger through his heart. No matter what had happened in their lives, Robert and Anna were always there for each other. Now their relationship was gone because of some hustler that seduced Anna into believing that Robert was the bad guy. The part that hurt him the most was that Anna believed George over her own son.

With the pain of the evening choking the life out of Robert, he stopped at a local bar to drown his sorrows. As he sat down at the bar and ordered a scotch, he knew that there were eyes watching him from everywhere in the bar. Choosing to ignore the stares, Robert downed his scotch and ordered another. After several drinks, the bartender refused to serve Robert anymore. As Robert started to verbally abuse the bartender, several bar patrons came over and told Robert to leave. Robert did not budge.

"Get out of here. We don't want your kind in here," spewed one patron.

As Robert prepared to do physical battle, the bartender stepped in and addressed Robert, "Sir, I must ask you to leave the premises, or I'm going to call the police."

"Do what you want," Robert defied. "But I'm not going anywhere. I'm a paying customer, and I want another drink."

"Go get it somewhere else," came a voice from the crowd of patrons.

As Robert sat defiantly on the bar stool, the bartender called the police. Two police officers responded within five minutes, and immediately escorted Robert out of the bar.

As the officers led Robert out the door, the one officer recognized him. "Be careful, he's some big time black belt."

"How do you know that?" asked the other officer.

"My nephew used to take classes where he used to practice sparring."

"Your nephew quit, didn't he?"

"My sister made him quit. She didn't want her boy anywhere near 'his kind', if you know what I mean?"

Robert listened intently as he staggered toward his car. The one officer reached out and grabbed Robert by the arm to stop him.

"Don't come back here queer. Understand?" the officer said in a low tone so that nobody could hear him. "Don't your kind have their own bar?" the officer asked sarcastically.

The pent up anger that had been building like a volcano, from earlier in the evening to the ignorant comments just espoused by the redneck policemen, got the better of him as he swore at the officers. The one officer pushed Robert roughly, and the other hit him with the billy club on the back of his left leg. Robert fought back, and in his drunken condition, he back-handed the nearest officer. For his troubles, the officers sprayed him with pepper spray, cuffed him and threw him into the back of the patrol car. Robert writhed in pain as the tears poured out of his eyes and the choking feeling made him cough violently until he succumbed to the welcome oblivion of intoxication. When they arrived at the county jail, Robert had already passed out.

Early the next morning, Robert awakened with a horrendous headache and demanded to know why he was behind bars. The guard assigned to the holding cell contacted the officer who had arrested Robert, and the officer explained what had happened. Robert did not believe any of the story, but he knew he had to get out of there. Speaking with authority, Robert asked, "I do get a phone call, don't I?"

The officer unlocked the cell and handcuffed Robert for the short walk to the office. Robert dialed his attorney, but there was no answer, only an answering machine that stated that the attorney and his staff were on vacation for the next two weeks. Robert's heart sank as the officer re-handcuffed him and led him back to the holding cell.

"You can call again after your bail hearing," stated the officer politely.

Robert laid down on the cot and tried to relive what had happened that landed him in the county jail. Nothing came to him, only replays of the events that led to Mitchell and Anna leaving him. He tried to remain calm to alleviate the headache, but nothing was helping.

Two hours after Robert made his first telephone call, the officers came to escort him to the magistrate's office for a bail hearing. The magistrate looked over the facts in the case and granted bail in the amount of five thousand dollars straight bond. The amount didn't trouble Robert, for he had more money than he could ever spend. What troubled him was how he was going to get someone to bring five thousand dollars to the county jail on a holiday.

After arriving back at the holding cell, Robert demanded to make a phone call. Frantically trying to think of someone to call, Robert forgot his pride and dialed Mitchell's number. After the third ring, a woman's voice answered the phone, "Hello, Rain's residence."

"Yes, hello. I need to speak to Mitchell. Tell him it's an emergency," Robert offered desperately.

"Sir, Mr. Rains is not here at the moment. Can I take a message?" asked the woman nervously.

"Listen, I know he's there. Please ask him to come to the phone. I'm in trouble," Robert offered more desperately.

"Sir, he's not here," the woman answered as Mitchell listened in the background.

"Fine," Robert shouted with frightened anger and hung up. Quickly dialing the phone again, he waited for a friendly voice, but none came. The answering machine at Anna's house picked up the message, as Robert desperately pleaded for his mother to pick up the phone, "Mom, please pick up. I'm in trouble. I need you to bring five thousand dollars to the county jail. Please Mom. Please hurry!"

As the officer led Robert back to the holding cell, he offered some advice to the new inmate, "If you have the money, why don't you call the bank and have them send over a cashier's check for your bail?"

Robert stared at the guard with disbelief. How could he have not thought of that himself? Escorted once more back to the phone a few hours later, Robert dialed the number for the bank, but there was no answer. He tried again, and this time a message was played stating that the bank would be closed for the 4th of July and would not reopen until July 7th. All of the color quickly drained from Robert's tired face. "How can I wait until Monday?" thought Robert. Despondently, he walked back to his cell handcuffed, and after the cuffs were released, he collapsed onto his cot with stress and the pain of a hangover threatening to render him unconscious.

# CHAPTER 5

▼

Anna sat anxiously by the telephone and replayed the message from Robert over and over again. "What kind of trouble could he be in?" she thought to herself. Anna agonized over whether she should take the money to Robert or allow him to stay in jail where he could possibly learn a lesson. Robert had always had a forceful personality, but maybe this turn of events could teach him how to treat others, or more importantly, teach him that he is not the most important person in this world.

George walked in and saw the distress on Anna's face. "Anna, he's a man. He shouldn't need to rely on his Mommy like he does with you," George said with sincerity. "Plus, this is probably just a ploy to get you back into his life."

"I don't know, George. He sounded desperate on the answering machine."

"Anna, your son is a millionaire. I'm sure he has people on his payroll that can take bail money to him."

"I know George, but I can't help but feel responsible for him landing in jail."

"My God, Anna, you can't be responsible for his actions. Whatever he did, he'll have to suffer the consequences. Maybe that will take the cockiness out of him," George stated annoyed.

"George, you don't know anything about Robert. If it weren't for him, I would not have survived after Stefan's death. He went to school all day long, and then he worked afternoon shift at the steel mills. He always put me first, no matter what. That's a hard life for a fifteen year old, to have to take care of yourself and your mother. I don't know how he did it. He worked forty hours a week and attended school full-time, always achieving highest honors." Anna stated proudly.

"I would think that any son would do that for his mother if the circumstances were the same." George stated arrogantly.

"I don't think so. Even after he graduated from high school, he continued working full time at the steel mills, and he also took a job working construction during the day. He worked the second job so that he would have money to attend college."

"Whatever he has done in the past, it doesn't give him the right to control your life," George stated matter-of-factly.

"I know that George, but I can't help but feel responsible," added Anna.

"Anna, I think it's time you stand up to him. If you don't, he's going to keep relying on you. You'll always be a puppet on a string for him."

"I know," Anna said as tears began to run down her pale cheeks, "But that doesn't make it any easier sitting back and doing nothing."

"What do you say we go into the kitchen and I'll make you pancakes for breakfast," George smiled as he took Anna's hand.

"That sounds good. At least it will keep my mind off of what's going on."

"Great, one stack of pancakes coming up," stated a delighted George.

*     *     *     *

Relaxing in a corner office in the nation's capital, Alex Petrovic perused the daily newspaper and drank his strong, black coffee. His assistant, Danielle, brought Alex the Saturday morning newspaper from his hometown. "Good morning, Danielle," Alex said with a smile.

"Good morning, Sir," she hesitantly said.

"What's wrong?"

"Sir, there is an article in your local hometown newspaper that I think you should read."

"Why, did the one horse town lose its only horse," laughed Alex with his ridiculous sense of humor.

"Sir, there is an article in there about your father."

"Really! Did he win the Chamber of Commerce's good citizen award?" he asked sarcastically.

"Sir, he's in jail."

Stunned, Alex replied, "What? Why?"

"I didn't read the article, but I do know that he's been there since Thursday night."

"Why? Was he denied bail?" asked Alex questioningly.

"I don't know, Sir," responded a caring Danielle.

"Danielle, can you cancel any appointments I have today."

"Sure."

"And can you call the airport and tell them to have the private jet ready for takeoff in about an hour?"

"Where are you going, Sir?"

"I'm going home for damage control. All I need is the media to find out about this," stated Alex with no emotion.

"Do you want me to call your wife and tell her you're going out of town?

"No, I'll call her from the plane. If something important comes up, call me on my cell phone, okay?"

"I will. Don't worry about things here. I'll hold down the fort," Danielle said with a reassuring smile.

"I know you will. I have complete trust in you."

"Good luck at home, Sir."

Picking up a bag from his closet, Alex started packing clothing for a few days stay. "Thanks, Danielle."

✳       ✳       ✳       ✳

Late Saturday afternoon, Alex was relaxing on the private jet, reading over some early poll numbers regarding the possibility of him running for Congress. There was over a year to the election, but Alex poured over the numbers for some sign that he would be liked, and more importantly, elected to Congress.

A deep voice came over the intercom, "Sir, we will be landing in about an hour."

"Thank you," Alex replied without looking up from his poll numbers. After studying the numbers since takeoff, Alex set the papers aside and picked up his cell phone to call his wife. As he was about to dial the phone, it rang. Startled, Alex answered, "Hello."

"Sir, this is Danielle."

"Yes, I know who it is. What's wrong?"

"Sir, you just received a call from a George Pennington."

Scratching his head, Alex responded, "I don't know any George Pennington's."

"Sir, he said he is a friend of your Grandmother's."

"Oh, yeah. I remember the name now. What did he want?

"Sir, he said that your Grandmother had a massive stroke earlier today."

Shocked, Alex replied, "What? Where is she? Is she okay?"

"He said that she's in the ICU at Memorial Hospital."

"Did he say she was okay?" Alex asked desperately.

"Sir, he didn't say, but I gathered it was very serious."

"Thanks, Danielle. Can you call my wife and tell her what happened and that I'll call her later tonight?"

"Absolutely. Is there anything I can do for you or your family?"

"Thanks Danielle. The best thing you can do is pray for my grandmother."

"I already have, Sir," she said softly.

Turning off his cell phone, Alex could not wait until he landed to find out any information on his grandmother. He punched in 411 on his cell phone, and when the operator answered, he quickly spoke as if by doing so would get him on the ground quicker. "Hello, I need the number for Memorial Hospital."

The operator answered in a monotone, "One moment, Sir."

The few seconds that it took to retrieve the requested information set Alex on pins and needles, as he desperately tried to fight off the anxiety. "Come on," he whispered.

"Sir, would you like me to put you through to Memorial Hospital?" replied the monotone.

"Yes please. Thank you," Alex answered hurriedly.

The phone rang twice before anyone answered. The voice that came across the cell phone was warm and reassuring, "Hello, can I help you?"

"Yes," answered Alex quickly. "Can you tell me what room Anna Petrovic is in?"

"Sure, do you know when she was admitted?"

"Today, but I don't know when today."

"That's okay, let me just pull up the admissions screen, and I'll get you that information."

There was a few seconds pause as the hospital computer revealed the correct screen. "Sir, we don't have any Anna Petrovic listed in the admissions. How do you spell the last name ... P E T R"

Alex jumped in, "P E T R O V I C," as he spelled it out letter by letter.

"That's how I spelled it. Sometimes if the person was just brought in today, the information doesn't appear on the admissions form until later in the day."

"I don't know when she was brought in, but her friend called and said that she was in the intensive care unit," Alex responded sternly and matter-of-factly, although he did not intend to yell at the nice woman who was trying to help him."

"Okay, let me check the ICU admissions for today. It will just take a second," the lady said politely.

Alex sat nervously on the edge of his seat, repeatedly trying to will the woman into hurrying up the search.

"Sir, there is no Anna Petrovic listed on the ICU admission form."

Frustrated and frightened, Alex snapped, "Are you sure?"

"Yes Sir. The only Anna is a Anna Pennington."

Alex's brain leapt to attention. "Wait. Did you say Anna Pennington?"

"Yes Sir. She was admitted today."

"What room is she in," he demanded unintentionally.

"ICU 3."

"Thank you ma'am. I apologize for my rude behavior."

"That's okay. I hope your friend or family member is going to be okay," she answered sincerely.

Relieved to have the information, Alex responded, "From your mouth to God's ear." Alex turned off his cell phone and sat back in his seat. "Damn," he said out loud. "Now how do I get Robert out?"

Alex stood up and stretched before walking the short distance to the cockpit. "How long before we land, captain?"

"About 35 minutes, sir," responded the plane's pilot without looking back at Alex.

"Thank you." Alex rushed back to his seat and hurriedly dialed 411 on his cell phone again. The same operator answered with the monotone voice, but before she could get out the customary greeting, Alex interrupted, "I need the number for an Antonio Daniels. He's an attorney."

"One moment, sir."

Again the one moment seemed like an eternity. Alex planned another course of action if he couldn't get in touch with his friend, Antonio. As he was about to write another name down on a small tablet next to the reclining seat where he was conducting these infernal question and answer sessions with telephone operators, the monotone voice spoke loudly.

"Sir, do you want to be connected to Antonio Daniels?"

"Yes, thank you." The phone rang several times before a young voice answered the phone.

"Hello," Alex said quickly, "Is your daddy home?"

The young voice dropped the phone as Alex heard the child scream, "Daaaaddddd"

A few moments passed, and Alex wished he could reach through the phone line to grab someone by the throat. As he was about to hang up, a fluid voice came on the line, "Hello, Antonio Daniels speaking."

"Antonio, hi, it's Alex Petrovic."

"Hey, Alex. What's going on? What did I do to receive a call from the next newly elected Congressman?" Antonio stated tongue-in-cheek.

"I don't have much time Antonio, but I need you to go to the county jail and bail out my father. His bail was set at $5,000 straight cash, so I'll call a wire service and have the money ready for you to pick up," Alex said quickly.

"Whoa, slow down. Why can't you go and bail out your father?"

"I'm on my way there, but I just got a call that my grandmother had a massive stroke and is in the ICU at Memorial Hospital."

"I'm sorry to hear that. As soon as I take a shower, I'll go down to the jail and bail out your father. Don't worry about the money. I'll pay the bail, and then you can write me a check."

"Thanks Antonio. I'll owe you one."

Laughing, "You owe me about 100 by now."

"I know. You're a great friend," Alex paused, "Tell Robert about his mom if you think he can handle the news."

"Sure, no problem. Hey, I better get going. I'll talk to you later, okay? I'll say a prayer for your grandmother."

"Thanks Antonio," Alex answered with relief.

Leaning back in the recliner, Alex ran his fingers through his thick, dark hair. In an instance, he became alert to the fact that his grandmother was listed at the hospital as Anna Pennington. "What is going on?" he said aloud. "I should have stayed in bed this morning," he thought.

# CHAPTER 6

▼

Robert paced frantically back and forth in the holding cell that he had accommodated since his arrest. He grabbed hold of the bars with both hands and started to lightly hit his head back and forth on the steel bars that separated him from freedom. As Robert continued his odd behavior, the slightly overweight guard that had been working the 4$^{th}$ of July holiday and so far the weekend came to stand in front of Robert's cell with a menacing smile.

"It seems that you're leaving us," the guard said mockingly, "But I'm sure it will only be temporary."

"Has my bail been posted?" asked a cautiously optimistic Robert.

No answer emanated from the fat lips of the portly guard as he unlocked Robert's cell. The guard stood aside and motioned for Robert to exit the cell. "This way," the guard grumbled.

Robert cautiously walked to the front office of the county jail, and there he found a finely dressed young man in a navy blue silk suit, white shirt and red tie, capped off with black, neatly shined wing-tips and a black leather attaché case.

Antonio Daniels, with his smoldering good looks and his brilliant legal mind, spoke clearly and slowly to Robert, "Mr. Petrovic, my name is Antonio Daniels. I have been retained to provide you with legal representation if you so choose."

Robert looked skeptically at the neatly dressed young man, but Antonio continued, "Your bail has been posted, so you are free to go as soon as these fine gentlemen retrieve your personal affects." Antonio shot a disdainful look at the jail guards, and the overweight guard retrieved Robert's personal items with a grumble and harsh words that were barely audible under his breath. Antonio glared at the guard and the guard responded by handing the items to Robert to inspect.

Robert quickly looked through his items to make sure they were all there, and as he did so he stated in a barely constrained, joyous voice, "I knew mama would come through for me. She gets mad at me, but I know that she ..." Antonio interrupted.

"Mr. Petrovic, your mother did not post your bail or hire me to represent you," he said politely.

"Then Mitchell must have heard my plea and hired you?" questioned a slightly confused Robert.

"No sir, I was hired by your son."

"Alexander hired you to bail me out and represent me?" Robert asked disbelieving.

"Yes Mr. Petrovic, Alex called me just a little while ago and asked me to help you out."

"I don't believe you," Robert said angrily, slightly raising his voice, "You're lying to me!"

"Mr. Petrovic, I assure you I am not lying to you. Alex and I have been friends since high school. He called me about 45 minutes ago from his plane. He was planning to come and bail you out himself, but something came up."

"Something always comes up," Robert stated cynically.

"Sir, something did come up, and I don't know how to tell you this, but your mother is in the ICU at Memorial. She had a massive stroke earlier today, and Alex found out about his grandmother on his way here, so he rightly diverted his attention to his ailing grandmother" Antonio said sternly.

"Oh my God," Robert uttered with despair, "Is she all right?"

"Mr. Petrovic, I don't know."

"Am I free to go?" Robert snapped at the guards.

"Yes. It appears your paperwork is all in order," the guard answered with blatant disrespect.

"Thank you," Robert stated hurriedly as he raced toward the door.

"Mr. Petrovic, wait! Do you have a way to the hospital?" Antonio asked with concern.

"No, I'll get a cab, or I'll hitchhike if I have to," he answered with total grief registering on his distinguished face.

"Never mind that. I'll take you," Antonio said as he walked past Robert and out the door, "Come on."

Robert obeyed as they rushed out of the jail and into Antonio's red BMW. Robert sat grimly in the passenger seat and never uttered a word as he stared out the black-tinted windows, but a stifled sob occasionally broke the silence in the car. Antonio searched for words to comfort the man he had just bailed out of jail, the man that his good friend Alex could not stand to be around, but no words emerged from his lips.

*     *     *     *

Alex stared through the glass window into the intensive care room that his grandmother was lying in, unconscious. A nurse, donning purple scrubs, walked by Alex on her way to the nurse's station, but Alex stopped her with his soft, pleading voice, "Excuse me, nurse."

"Can I help you?" answered the nurse without turning around to look at Alex.

"Yes ma'am. Can you tell me how my grandmother is doing?"

"Is Anna Pennington your grandmother?"

"Her name is Anna Petrovic. I have no idea why she is listed here in the hospital as Anna Pennington," Alex stated harshly.

"Because that's her name," George stated matter-of-factly to the strange young man looking into Anna's room.

"Who are you?" snapped Alex.

"I'm George Pennington, and that woman is my wife," George answered nastily. "Now, who the hell are you?"

"I'm Alex Petrovic, and she's my grandmother," Alex answered angrily.

"Oh, I'm so sorry Alex. I had no idea who you were," George replied apologetically as he reached to shake Alex's hand.

Hesitatingly, Alex extended his hand, "How is my grandmother?"

"She had a major stroke, Alex," George responded with no hint of emotion.

"What have the doctors said about her prognosis? Is she going to be okay?"

"They haven't said anything to me. They just admitted her into the ICU."

Alex, starting to feel total frustration from this man who married his grandmother without any word to anyone, spoke with controlled anger, "Well I'm going to find her doctors and get answers from them about her prognosis. I won't sit back and do nothing," Alex added to intentionally offend the opportunistic older gentleman.

Before George could reply, or more likely protest Alex's statements, Alex had turned and quickly walked down the hospital corridor to the main nursing station. George looked through the window at Anna for a brief moment and then left. As he strolled down the corridor toward the cafeteria, George thought about the exchange he had just had with his new step-grandson, and frowned at the thought that Alex was possibly an even bigger threat to his relationship with

Anna than Robert was. "How can I handle someone that I don't know nothing about?" George mentally asked himself.

As George sat down with his tray filled with a hamburger, fries, a salad and an ice tea, Antonio and Robert pulled under the underpass and Robert jumped out of the car before it even came to a complete stop. Robert sprinted to the front desk and asked what floor the ICU was on before dashing off to the elevators. After only a few seconds of waiting, Robert ran for the steps and took them two at a time until he reached the proper floor. Forcefully throwing the doors open, Robert ran to the nurses' station and asked where Anna was.

"What is your mother's name?" asked the same nurse that had been stopped and questioned by Alex.

"Anna Petrovic," he blurted out quickly.

Without mentioning to him that Anna was listed as Anna Pennington, and not Anna Petrovic, the nurse gave Robert the room number and showed him the correct corridor to follow to get to Anna's room. Robert rushed down the hallway and stopped at the glass window before entering. He stood there, motionless, like a child that had been lost and separated from his mother. Gathering his courage, Robert opened the door and immediately sat down beside his mother, taking her hand in his. He studied her face as tears borne from his soul trickled down his unwashed face. Robert reached up and smoothed Anna's hair on her forehead, hoping for some sign that she was okay. None came. He leaned in close to her and spoke softly, almost with a whisper, "I'm so sorry, mama. Please be okay" The tears ran down Robert's cheek in torrents, "Please mama, just get better and I promise I'll do anything you ask. Don't leave me mama." Robert buried his head on the sheet rumpled beside Anna, "I'm so sorry mama. I never meant to hurt you. Please be okay"

A sudden thump from the door forced Robert to jump out of his seat next to Anna's bed. Standing in the doorway, George barked orders for Robert to leave the room. Hearing the commotion, a nurse came running and forced the men to leave Anna's room. "What is wrong with you?" the nurse snapped as she glared at George and Robert.

"This man is not permitted in that room," George said hatefully.

"You can't stop me," yelled Robert.

"Oh yes I can. Nurse, call security," demanded George arrogantly.

"I don't give a damn if you call the President. That's my mother in there, and no one is going to stop me from seeing her."

Before the altercation between Robert and George turned physical, security arrived and stepped between the two, demanding to know what was going on.

"Officer, I don't want this man anywhere near this patient," stated George.

"Officer, that is my mother, and this man is nothing to her," offered Robert.

"Officer, that woman in there is my wife," George replied with an evil grin.

"The hell she is. Stop your lying," snapped Robert.

"Officer, I have proof that this woman is my wife." George reached into his pocket and pulled out a document. "We were married yesterday, on the 4th of July."

The security officer carefully analyzed the document and stated to Robert that the document showed that George Pennington and Anna Petrovic were married on the 4th of July. Robert stated incredulously, "It has to be fake."

"It's not fake. We were married yesterday while you were sitting in a jail cell," George retorted mockingly. "Now Officer, I don't want this man anywhere near my wife. He's the reason she is in there."

"Sir, you are going to have to leave," stated the security officer with growing annoyance for them both.

"Officer, I did not cause my mother to have a stroke. I wasn't even near her," Robert responded desperately. "You can't make me leave. I love her and she needs me." Robert now verged on the edge of tears.

"Tell the truth for once in your life, Robert. You don't love her. You want to control her," George replied.

The security officer gently grabbed Robert by the shoulder, "Sir, you are going to have to leave."

Shrugging away from the security officer's firm grasp, Robert pleaded, "but I didn't do this. I can't leave my mama. She needs me."

"Dammit Robert! That call you left on the answering machine ate Anna up. She couldn't bear to think of you in jail, and you knew that, that's why you called. But Anna finally had to make her stand and show you you aren't the boss," George snapped.

With utter, agonizing despair and rejection, Robert unknowingly allowed the security officer escort him out of the hospital. Robert, in a mental fog, kept hearing his mother repeating the words 'you are no longer my son'. Without a word, his mother was going to leave him forever and there was nothing he could do about it. All his money, power and assets couldn't buy him what he most desired at the moment … his mother's forgiveness.

# CHAPTER 7

▼

Alex returned to the area outside of his grandmother's room, and immediately the nurse that he had stopped on arrival to learn his grandmother's condition, stopped him. She pulled him aside and spoke softly, "Sir, your grandmother does not need to be witness to family squabbles. She needs her family to be supportive, not combative."

Alex looked at her with confusion, "What are you talking about?"

"Your grandmother's husband and her son just got into a heated mess."

"What?" Alex asked angrily.

"Your grandmother's husband had her son removed by security and banned from seeing the patient. Is that man your father?"

"Yes," he replied with building anger. "Damn him! What right does he have to ban anyone from seeing my grandmother? My father is her only child."

"I don't know the legality of the situation, but I do know that this type of behavior can be detrimental to the patient's recovery," the nurse continued with genuine kindness.

"Nurse," Alex said more civilly, "Where did my father go? Do you know?"

"Security escorted him out of the building."

"Was he fighting with them?" Alex asked with concern.

"No sir, he looked like he was lost. I don't even think he realized that he had been escorted out."

"What the hell is going on?" Alex thought to himself. "Thank you, nurse. I promise you that nothing or no one will impede my grandmother's recovery," Alex offered sincerely.

"Thank you," replied the nurse as she went about her duties.

Alex desperately wanted to confront George about his spiteful actions concerning visitation, but all he could think about was the words spoken by the nurse "… he looked lost. I don't even think he realized that he had been escorted out." Alex knew Robert would fight George to the death if need be to see his mother, but for some reason Robert allowed himself to be removed and forbidden to see his mother by a man that Robert despised. Alex knew about the tensions between George and Robert from the conversations that he had with his grandmother, but nothing had prepared Alex for the actions, or the inactions, of his father. Something desperately was wrong, and the only one with answers would be Robert. Even though Alex kicked Robert out of his life years before, he still cared, if for no other reason than the happiness of his grandmother. With more questions than answers, Alex jogged down the hallway to the elevator.

*     *     *     *

Robert handed the taxi driver fifty dollars and walked away. The fare totaled fifteen dollars, but in his present state, Robert just pulled out the money and handed it to the cabby without even looking at the denomination. He walked in his front door, not even realizing that it was unlocked. Walking through the hallway, Mrs. Butler, the dry cleaning lady, stopped a few feet from Robert and smiled at him as she greeted him, "Hello, Mr. P. How are you today?"

Continuing on his path to the master bedroom, Robert walked by Mrs. Butler without acknowledging her presence. Not seeing his favorite household staff member, Robert mumbled, "I didn't mean it. I'm so sorry, mama."

Concerned, Mrs. Butler started to follow her boss through the hallway and into his bedroom, but decided against it as he started to undress. Robert ripped at the three buttons on his black cashmere sweater in an attempt to yank it off his body. Mrs. Butler watched from a distance, but softly closed the door as Robert unzipped his charcoal gabardine trousers. Throwing the recently, over-worn clothing into a pile in the far corner of his room, Robert entered his bathroom and turned on the hot water in his white marble shower. Standing under the penetrating hot water, Robert broke down and sobbed uncontrollably. His legs crumbled underneath him, and he sank down onto the hard marble floor. The falling water equaled the tears that raced down his sunken, suddenly old, cheeks. Robert sat on the marble floor, pulling his legs up, wrapping his arms tightly around his knees, and burying his face between his knees. The hot water continued to run down over his head as one wracking sob was replaced by another one. "I'm so sorry, father. I never meant to let you down," he cried as the anguish swept over him. Suddenly reliving the image of his mother lying in the ICU unconscious, Robert fell over onto his side as he cried, "Please forgive me, mama. I love you."

After lying in the shower for a few moments, the events of the past few days came rushing back as the last words of this mother echoed in his head, "… from this moment on, I don't have a son."

Completely exhausted from his grief, Robert slowly sat up and heard the last words of his mother again, only this time louder, "… I don't have a son." Entirely out of tears, Robert gradually picked himself up and turned the water off. Standing there in silence, he rested his head against the shower wall. "I've failed everyone," Robert said aloud and totally devoid of emotion. After a moment of reflection and rest, Robert dried himself off and went to his closet.

In the back of the closet hung his clothes from a lifetime ago, the clothes of a poor working boy trying desperately to take care of his mother and himself. He pulled out a pair of worn denim jeans and a plain white tee shirt. Nobody in the past several decades had seen him in such attire, for he dressed the part of a successful businessman. Without thought, he grabbed a pair of white athletic socks, pulled on his jeans and tee shirt, and searched for his favorite running shoes.

Dressed and clean, Robert looked in the mirror and stared at his swollen eyes and the red blotches that his grief had caused to appear on his face. He picked up a comb and slicked back his short, salt-and-pepper hair. He sighed deeply as he took one last look into the mirror. Suddenly, an eerie calm had descended on him as he walked out of his bedroom and down the hallway to the side entrance.

# CHAPTER 8

▼

Alex jammed on the brakes of his rental car in front of Robert's house and ran inside without taking the keys out of the ignition. He looked intently around the living room and foyer, but with no luck. As he started jogging down the hallway toward Robert's room, Mrs. Butler appeared. Startled, she asked, "Excuse me, what are you doing here?"

"I'm looking for Robert."

"Oh, I'm sorry. You're Mr. P.'s son, Alex," she said happily as she touched him lovingly on the shoulder.

"Yes, I'm Alex. How did you know who I am?"

"From Mr. P.'s pictures in his bedroom."

"Oh," he paused to collect his thoughts. "Have you seen Robert?"

"Yes, he was just here, but I think there is something wrong," she said as a frown crept onto her fair-colored face.

"Why do you think something is wrong?" Alex asked with apprehension.

"He came in a little while ago, and he looked right at me, but didn't say a word. I said hello, but he kept walking, mumbling something. He just wasn't himself."

"Do you know where he went?"

"I was about to call his mother for her to come over, but then I saw Mr. P. outside walking toward the barn."

"Why were you calling his mother?"

"Because I was worried about Mr. P. He came in and went straight for his bedroom. He was in there a really long time, but when I went to check on him, he wasn't there, so I was going to call Ms. Anna to come over to find out what was wrong."

"But you didn't when you saw him going to the barn?" Alex inquired worriedly.

"That's right. He was dressed like he was going to go riding," she said softly.

"How was he dressed?"

"He had on blue jeans and a tee shirt."

"Okay, thank you for the information," Alex stated as he started for the door.

"Alex, should I call Ms. Anna?"

"I'm sorry," he paused as he tried to recall her name, even though she never mentioned it. "What is your name again?" Alex asked politely.

"Mrs. Butler."

"I'm sorry Mrs. Butler, but my grandmother had a massive stroke this morning."

Mrs. Butler's hand flew to her mouth as she sighed, "Is she all right?"

"The doctors say it's too early to tell," he said in a voice slightly louder than a whisper.

"Is there anything I can do?"

"Pray," Alex said with a slight smile. "Can you stay here until I find Robert?"

"Sure, I'll just finish up with the clothing and I'll be here if you need me."

"Thank you, Mrs. Butler. Robert is lucky to have a loyal friend like you," Alex stated as he ran toward the door.

As Alex reached the door, the cell phone that he had in a pouch on his belt rang its familiar tune. Alex turned it on and found a familiar voice. "Hi Danielle. Has something happened?"

"No sir. I just wanted to check in. Everything okay?"

"No, Danielle, things are crazy here. Did you call my wife?"

"Yes, Emily said to call her when you get a free minute. What's going on there? Is there anything I can do?" Danielle asked with concern.

"No, just hold down the fort for me. I'll call when I can."

"Okay, take care of yourself and don't worry about things here."

"Thanks Danielle." Alex threw the phone onto the couch in the living room and ran out the door.

Mrs. Butler stood in the living room with an incredulous look about all the things that had happened. She looked heavenward and said a prayer for the lovely lady that she had come to be friends with through her benevolent boss, Mr. P. A single tear trickled down her face as she asked her God for the recovery of Ms. Anna, and the peace that Mr. P. so desperately needed. The tear wiped away,

Mrs. Butler gathered the remaining clothing that needed to be taken for dry cleaning, and set it aside as she waited for Mr. P. and Alex to return to the main house.

*          *          *          *

Quickly running from barn to barn on the vast expanse of land where Robert made his home, Alex peered into each barn hoping to find some evidence that would lead him to Robert's whereabouts. As he approached the last barn on the edge of a lush line of maple trees, Alex stopped in his tracks when he heard a thunderous crashing sound. He bolted toward the door and ripped it open, stopping dead as he stared in shock.

Paralyzed, Alex gawked at the scene in front of him. A heavy wooden chair lay broken in a heap on the floor. Above the broken chair was Robert, hanging from a thick piece of rope from a ceiling rafter in the barn. His body hung limply, as it twisted slowly.

Alex, with lightning fast quickness, threw a hay bale under his father and jumped on top of it so that he could reach him. He grabbed Robert around the thighs and lifted him so that the rope would loosen around his neck. Reaching the rope with only one hand, Alex desperately pulled at it so that he could undo the knot.

Frantic, Alex pleaded as he worked the knot, "Don't you die on me. Please don't die. Wake up, Robert."

With a powerful yank on the knot, it loosened and Robert's body went limp in Alex's arms. Alex jumped off the hay bale and laid Robert on the ground as he desperately checked for a pulse. "Dammit Dad! Don't you die!"

Alex frantically felt for a pulse, first in Robert's right wrist, and then in Robert's left wrist with no success. "Dammit!" Placing his index and middle fingers on Robert's carotid artery, Alex heaved a sigh of relief as he felt a faint pulse weakly beating above the crimson ligature mark on Robert's neck.

Grabbing for his cell phone, Alex screamed in frustration, realizing that he had left his cell phone lying in Robert's living room. He yelled out for Mrs. Butler, but the barn was too far from the house for her to hear him. Not wanting to leave Robert in his condition, and throwing caution to the wind with regard to any possible neck injuries, Alex scooped Robert up in his arms and rushed toward the house to call an ambulance. As he lifted Robert into his arms, Robert unconsciously laid his head gently against Alex's shoulder.

As Alex and Robert got closer to the house, Mrs. Butler witnessed Robert lying limp in Alex's strong arms. She ran to the door and flung it open as Alex rushed in and laid Robert on the couch.

Hysterical, Mrs. Butler stammered, "What happened?" Oh, God. Please let him be okay!"

"Where's my phone?" Alex screamed with panic wearing on his face.

Mrs. Butler picked up the phone and threw it to Alex, who frantically dialed 911.

"Emergency dispatch," came the calm voice over the phone, "What is your emergency?"

"We need an ambulance at 1400 Carnegie Street," stammered Alex.

"What's the emergency, Sir?" stated the dispatcher with a smooth, patient voice.

"There was an accident. My father isn't breathing. Hurry!"

"What type of accident?"

"Why the hell does that matter! Just send an ambulance."

"An ambulance is on the way. What is your name Sir?"

"Why does it matter?" Alex snapped with growing annoyance, "What the hell, my name is Alex Petrovic."

"Okay Mr. Petrovic, please stay on the line until the ambulance arrives. Is your father breathing at all?"

"It is very irregular and erratic. He has a faint pulse."

"What happened to him?"

Angered, Alex replied, "I told you there was an accident."

"I understand that, but what type of accident was it? What type of injuries does your father have?"

Hearing the faint echoes of the ambulance sirens, Alex disconnected with the dispatcher and turned off his cell phone.

"Mrs. Butler, please go out and show the paramedics in, and tell them to please hurry," Alex ordered gently. Without a word, Mrs. Butler obeyed and quickly disappeared from the living room.

Leaning close to Robert's ear, Alex demanded softly, "Don't you dare die on me, Dad. You hear me?" Alex gently took Robert's hand into his own and held it lovingly.

Robert stirred slightly and started mumbling incoherently. He opened his eyes slightly, but with an unfocused gaze he whispered slowly and almost inaudibly, "I'm sorry, daddy. Mama, please forgive me. I can't do …" he paused, "… anything right."

The front doors swung open and in rushed the paramedics with several large duffle-type bags full of medical supplies. The first paramedic to enter the room was a tall, lanky suntanned fellow, and his partner was a rather short, portly, balding man of middle age. The portly man gave the orders, and the lanky man started to do several medical procedures on Robert all at once.

"What happened?" asked the portly paramedic.

"I heard a loud crash in the barn, and when I looked in I saw him hanging from the rafters," Alex answered emotionally.

"How long was he hanging?"

"Only about a minute. As soon as I heard the noise, I ran in and jumped on a hay bale so that I could take the tension off the rope as I untied it."

"How did he get in here?" the portly paramedic asked without looking up from the notes he was taking.

"I carried him," Alex responded as the scene flashed back in his mind. The image of his father hanging from the rafters dug into his brain.

"You shouldn't have moved him," the portly paramedic stated mat-ter-of-factly.

"I didn't want to leave him, and I didn't have my cell phone with me, so I carefully carried him in here."

The other paramedic, looking away from Robert for a brief second, addressed his partner, "We need to get going. His pulse is weak and his breathing is irregu-lar."

"Let me grab the stretcher," the portly paramedic stated as he grabbed the stretcher and started to unfasten the belts. "Keep your gloves on with him."

The lanky paramedic looked at his partner with a perplexed look on his face as he asked, "Why?"

"Because he's one of them," the portly paramedic answered with disgust. "You don't want to risk catching anything."

Alex went ballistic, "What the hell are you talking about?" He grabbed the portly paramedic by the collar as he threatened, "Just treat him and shut up."

Quickly changing the subject, the lanky paramedic asked as he looked at Alex and Mrs. Butler, "Was he conscious at any time before we arrived?"

"He opened his eyes slightly and mumbled something that I couldn't under-stand," Alex answered.

The portly paramedic rolled the stretcher over beside Robert's lifeless body and he and the other paramedic applied a cervical collar and slid a spinal board under Robert. Carefully lifting the backboard, they placed Robert on the stretcher and gently secured him and the portable oxygen that the lanky paramedic placed over Robert's nose and mouth. Guiding the stretcher out the door and into the waiting ambulance that was left running, Alex followed behind and quickly took a seat in the passenger side of the ambulance without asking if he was permitted to ride along to the hospital.

Mrs. Butler watched the ambulance exit the driveway, and said a quick prayer as she locked the front door of Robert's stately mansion.

# CHAPTER 9

▼

As the paramedics pushed the stretcher into the emergency room, Alex rushed in behind him and was met by a team of medical personnel. A handsome, olive-skinned resident led the questioning of the paramedics. The portly paramedic answered the doctor's questions; "Fifty year old male found hanging from a rafter in his barn. He was cut down and carried into his residence, without spinal precautions, where emergency dispatch was called."

"Thank you," answered the doctor as the paramedics turned and pushed out their stretcher after transferring Robert onto the emergency room table.

With several medical personnel performing medical tasks on Robert, the doctor turned to Alex and asked, "Are you the one who found him?"

"Yes," Alex paused, "I found him in the barn."

"How long do you think he was hanging there?"

"No more than a minute," Alex answered with slight emotion as he remembered the image of finding his father hanging from a rafter. "I heard a crash and went running to the source. I found him hanging there, so I grabbed a hay bale to climb on and lifted him to take the pressure off his neck as I untied the knot."

"Are you a relative?" asked the resident without looking away from his patient.

"Yes, I'm his son."

"Is your father taking any medications?"

"I don't know," replied Alex.

"Is he allergic to any medications?"

"I don't know."

"Has your father been depressed?"

"I don't know," answered a slightly ashamed Alex. As he looked from Robert to the doctor, he replied, "We aren't close."

After several moments of examining Robert, the doctor walked over to Alex and led him to the hallway outside the examining room. He put his hand on Alex's shoulder as he spoke, "I'm sending your father to x-ray to make sure that nothing is damaged in his neck. After that he will be taken to the psychiatric ward to be admitted."

With deep concern, Alex asked, "Is he going to be okay?"

After he is admitted, a psychiatrist will talk with him and hopefully find out what caused him to do this."

"Thank you doctor. Can I go with him?"

"You can go up to the second floor where he'll be admitted. He'll be taken there after being x-rayed."

"Thanks again, doctor."

Standing alone in the elevator to the second floor, Alex rested his head against the elevator wall as it ascended to the psychiatric ward. He could not get the sight of his father hanging from the rafter out of his mind. Hitting his head lightly on the elevator wall, the door swung open and a group of several young doctors were waiting to enter the elevator. Alex stepped out and went immediately to the nurse's station to find out what room would be Robert's. The nurse pointed Alex in the direction of the waiting room and promised to come get him when Robert was settled in a room.

An hour passed and Alex could not wait any longer. He went back to the nurse's station and asked a different nurse for information about Robert. She looked at the computer monitor and responded with a room number. As he was walking toward the room, the nurse called him back. "The resident wants to talk to you about your father," she said.

"Where can I find him?" asked Alex.

"He should be out in a moment if you just want to wait here," she answered politely.

"That would be fine," Alex replied.

Within five minutes a young, blurry-eyed resident in light blue scrubs approached Alex. He inquired, "Are you Mr. Petrovic's son?"

"Yes, how is he?"

"Well I just spoke with the ER doctor who treated your father when you first came in, and he said that the x-rays were negative, so that's good news. Right now, we are just going to wait for him to wake up on his own."

"When do you think he'll wake up?" inquired Alex.

"It's hard to tell, but the chief psychiatrist will be in the first thing in the morning. Sooner if he's needed, but I don't foresee anything other than a quiet night with regards to your father," the young doctor answered confidently.

"Thank you doctor. Can I see him now?"

"Sure, but you should know that we have him restrained. I don't want you to go in there and be surprised to see him in restraints."

"Is that necessary?"

"Absolutely. Obviously he's a harm to himself at this point."

"Okay, if it's for the best."

"It is. You can stay as long as you want, and if you have any questions, have me paged. My name is Stan Hollings."

"Thank you Dr. Hollings," Alex answered with appreciation.

Alex walked to the door and stopped momentarily to look through the tiny window that provided a view of Robert lying very still in his hospital bed. As he opened the door and walked over to his father's bedside, he looked down with genuine concern for the man whom he had thought to be indestructible. Never could Alex imagine a scenario of Robert trying to end his own life. Alex reached down and gently tried to hold Robert's hand, but a restraint prevented him from lifting Robert's hand off of the bed. Alex pulled up a chair to sit down before a sudden feeling of nausea made his knees buckle. "How could this happen?" Alex mentally asked himself.

Alex, feeling better from his unusual bout of nausea, lifted his chair quietly and pushed it back into a dark corner. He found a pillow in an adjacent corner and contorted his body into a semi-comfortable position to rest.

Several hours after sitting down in the corner, Alex awakened to a hushed noise. He looked over at Robert to see him stirring. Alex rushed over to the side of the bed and spoke gently to his father, "Robert, can you hear me?"

Robert's eyes fluttered open with a hollow gaze as they looked at Alex. Alex leaned in closer as he continued to speak to Robert, "Can you hear me, Robert?"

Robert slowly focused his eyes on Alex, and Alex momentarily breathed a sigh of relief when Robert looked at him. Robert started mumbling something incoherent, so Alex moved in even closer to try to understand what Robert was trying to say. Robert took a deep breath and spoke more clearly as he realized that his hands were immobilized. Robert looked pleadingly at Alex as he spoke, "I'm so sorry."

Alex brushed Robert's hair back off his forehead as he always wore it, as he reassured his father, "There's nothing for you to be sorry for."

Robert continued as the hollow gaze returned to his eyes, "I'm so sorry father. I can't do anything right."

Alex went quickly to the door and called for a nurse. Robert, becoming more agitated, started to pull at the restraints and twist from side to side as he continued speaking, "Mama, please forgive me. I didn't mean it."

As the nurse came running in with Dr. Hollings only a few steps behind, they witnessed Robert's agitation and his apologies. Robert pulled hard on the restraints as tears poured out of his eyes as he screamed, "MAMA." He paused to take a deep breath, "PLEASE, MAMA!"

Dr. Hollings yelled for an orderly and instructed the nurse to retrieve certain medication. The orderly, a broad-shouldered, stocky man in his early thirties, wearing a crew cut and a bulldog tattoo on his forearm, charged in and got his instructions from the doctor.

As the nurse opened the syringe, the doctor ordered her to retrieve the needed medication. The orderly strongly held Robert's right hand to the bed as he removed the restraint. When the restraint was removed, the orderly, still fiercely holding Robert's wrist, rolled Robert over almost onto his stomach and pulled the hospital gown open to reveal Robert's bare buttocks. The doctor grabbed the syringe from the nurse and plunged it into Robert's buttocks as far as it would go as Robert screamed in pain. When the needle was removed, the orderly rolled Robert back over and reapplied the restraint onto Robert's right wrist.

"I'm going to call the doctor-on-call to see what he wants us to do," replied the doctor to a scared Alex, who had stepped back into the corner to watch. Alex did not reply, and the doctor, nurse, and orderly started to leave. Robert lay very still and quiet in the bed, but the tears continued to fall unabated. As the nurse was halfway out the door, Alex called out to her to stop. "What did they give him?" asked a concerned Alex.

"A drug that will calm him down and make him sleep," the nurse answered quietly.

Alex allowed the nurse to leave before kneeling down next to Robert's bed. He gently spoke to Robert, "You're going to be all right. I promise."

Robert responded to the voice and turned his head slightly to where Alex was kneeling. "Sir, I have to leave. If I don't go to work, Mr. O'Brien will fire me, and then me and my mama won't be able to eat," Robert said in a child-like tone that almost made Alex cry.

Alex turned his head away from Robert to shield him from seeing Alex's tears. Alex was completely perplexed at Robert's statement. "Why did he call me 'sir'?"

Alex asked himself internally. He gathered his courage and responded, "Robert, it's okay. Mr. O'Brien knows you are sick and won't be in to work for a while."

In a drug-induced stupor, Robert replied, "But he'll fire me. How will I take care of my mama if I lose my job?"

As Robert was slowly drifting off to sleep, Alex spoke to him reassuringly, "He won't fire you Robert. I promise you."

As sleep started to envelop him, Robert nodded with child-like acceptance.

Alex continued to kneel at Robert's bedside for several minutes before moving back into the uncomfortable chair that he had placed in the corner. He looked out the window and into the darkness and prayed that Robert would be fine. He prayed that when Robert awakened in the morning that Robert would be his normal self, the self that Alex very comfortably disliked in his mind. He disliked Robert for the choices that Robert made, but the Robert that was lying in the hospital bed was a man that Alex did not even recognize. The always strong, self-assured, sometimes cocky Robert was now replaced by a vulnerable, child-like, scared shell of what Robert once was. It was easy for Alex to hate Robert for who he was, but now he was no longer that person. Now he was someone who did not even recognize his own son, and even called him 'sir'. Those words and the image of Robert hanging in the barn burned indelibly in Alex's fatigued brain as he set about to fall asleep in the shadows.

Several restful moments later, Alex was startled out of his relaxed state by the familiar ring of his cell phone. He quickly answered it for fear that it would awaken Robert, although he knew somewhere in the back of his brain that the drugs that Robert was given would knock him out for hours. Answering in a startled voice, he spoke in a deep whisper, "Hello."

"Alex? Is that you?" asked the melodic voice.

"Yeah, it's me, Emily. Oh my God," he stated as he took a deep, realizing breath, "I was supposed to call you, wasn't I?"

"Yes, that's what Danielle said when she called this afternoon. Is everything okay?" she asked with no hint of anger.

"No. Things couldn't be more wrong," he said with sadness in his voice.

"Isn't your grandmother doing well?"

"I truly don't know, Honey."

"What? What's going on? You're scaring me," Emily asked anxiously.

"I'm at the hospital right now. My father tried to kill himself today," Alex said as his emotions threatened to overcome him.

"What?" Emily asked fearfully.

"Yeah. I found him hanging in the barn. I managed to get the rope loose and then I carried him to the house and called 911."

Emily spoke with true concern, "Is he all right?" She paused for a brief second and asked with deeper concern, "Are you all right?"

"I'm all right. Robert was admitted to the psychiatric ward. That's where we are now."

"Did he say why he did it?"

"No, he's been unconscious most of the time. When he did come around, he kept mumbling something about his father."

"His father's been dead for years," she offered.

"Yeah, for almost 35 years." Alex paused and hesitated before speaking and Emily recognized her husband's slight hesitation and became concerned.

"What else, Honey?"

"It's nothing really. He was drugged and probably didn't know what he was saying."

"Saying what?"

"He looked right at me and called me sir. He didn't know who I was," Alex said regretfully.

Emily spoke without giving her husband a chance to continue. "I'm going to pack some things and I'll be there first thing in the morning."

"No, you don't have to do that. I'll be all right, and the kids need you."

"After what you've been through, you need me more right now. Are you going to stay at the hospital tonight?"

"Yeah. I want to talk to the head doctor in the morning."

"Okay, I'll take a taxi from the airport to the hospital."

"Emily, you really don't need to do this. I'll be fine," he offered with fake sincerity.

"I know I don't need to do it, but I don't want you to have to deal with all this by yourself. We're a team, remember," she said reassuringly.

"Yeah, we are. I love you, Emily."

"I love you too. I'll see you in the morning. Try to get some sleep."

"I will. Be careful. Tell the kids I love them."

"I will. Alex," she paused, "I hope your dad and grandma are going to be all right. They're both tough, so if anybody can get through this, they can."

"Thanks Honey. Have a safe flight. Good night."

"Good night."

# CHAPTER 10

▼

A hot, blinding glare of sunlight filtered through the small window in Robert's room and instantly brought Alex to a state of alertness, ending a night of restless sleep. As he gingerly climbed out of his makeshift recliner, he stretched his tired aching muscles as he stood at the foot of Robert's bed. Robert peacefully slept with his head turned slightly to the left, and Alex disdainfully frowned at the drool that slightly trickled out of Robert's open mouth. Alex gently touched the blankets that covered Robert's legs, and headed for the door.

The round white clock nearest to the nurse's station pointed its hands to indicate that it was 7 a.m. Alex waited in front of the large desk as a short, pale nurse of about twenty-seven years old carried a chart and placed it on the large desk. She looked up at Alex with a smile, "Can I help you Sir?"

"Yes, I'm Alex Petrovic, Robert's son. I was told last night that the chief doctor would be in this morning to treat my father."

"He's here. He came in about 45 minutes ago, and he took your father's chart, so he should be around pretty soon to check on Robert."

"Thank you. Could you tell me what his name is? I forgot to ask last night."

"Sure, he's Dr. Erik Hamilton. He's the best psychiatric doctor in the state," the nurse said proudly. As Alex was turning to leave, the nurse stopped him, "Mr. Petrovic, that's Dr. Hamilton coming down the hallway." She pointed down the corridor and Alex started in that direction.

Alex hurried down the hallway and stopped the doctor. "Hi. Are you Dr. Hamilton?"

"Yes, I'm Dr. Hamilton," he said with a smile.

Alex extended his hand to the doctor as he spoke, "I'm Alex Petrovic—Robert Petrovic's son."

"Ah, okay I just read over his chart."

"Doctor, is he going to be okay?"

"Let's go find a place to sit down and we'll talk, okay?"

Alex nodded as he followed the surprisingly young doctor down the hallway and into an empty waiting room. Dr. Hamilton motioned for Alex to sit down, and the doctor followed suit. The tall, thin, middle-aged doctor with a short goatee and dark hair opened the chart and looked at Alex, "I reviewed the x-rays that the ER doctor had taken of your father's neck and everything appeared to be normal.

"What about his mental state?"

"Well, I haven't had a chance to examine your father or talk with him," he replied as he looked again at the notes in the chart, "Well he hasn't been coherent yet to talk, so when he wakes up we'll see what goes on, and we'll go from there."

"When he woke up last night he was apologizing to his father and then he became really upset, and that's when the doctor gave him a shot to calm him down."

"Do you know what he was apologizing for to his father?"

"No. His father's been dead for 35 years."

"Did he say anything else?"

"After the doctor gave him the shot, he looked up at me and said that he had to get out of here so that he could go to work."

"What type of work does he do?"

"No, you don't understand. He said that he had to go to work or Mr. O'Brien would fire him and then he and my grandmother would go hungry."

"Have you talked to this Mr. O'Brien?"

"Doctor, my father owns his own company. He's his own boss. I remember him telling a story once that Mr. O'Brien was his first boss when he was fifteen."

"Did he respond in any way to you being there with him?"

"No," Alex replied sadly, "He didn't even know who I was. He actually called me 'sir.'"

"From what you tell me, it appears that your father had some type of mental breakdown that could have lead to him regressing back to his childhood, or even young adulthood. That may be the reason why he didn't know you. If he's living in the past, you weren't around yet, and his memory won't allow him to remember the present and what caused him to mentally collapse and try to end his own life."

"Will he recover from this and regain his memory?"

"If this scenario turns out to be his diagnosis, then I would say that he will regain his memory, but it will probably take time. You see, his mind is protecting him from some type of emotional trauma that he can't deal with right now. When he's able to deal with it, then his memory should return. We'll do a CT scan of his brain to make sure he didn't have a stroke or any other problems that could be causing his memory loss," Dr. Hamilton explained. "How long do you think your father was hanging before he was found?"

"Just a minute or two, I think," Alex answered. "I was the one who found him."

"Good thing you found him when you did," Dr. Hamilton stated. "If it was only a minute or two, he wasn't deprived very long of oxygen."

"So you don't think the hanging is causing him not to know me?" Alex questioned.

"We'll run some tests, and then I'll be able to give you a more definitive answer, okay? Dr. Hamilton replied.

"What type of treatment do you recommend?"

"Well, I have to first talk with your father, but I would probably say that we'll treat him medically at first. There are several different medications that we'll try, and then we'll probably start him in therapy."

"Thank you, doctor."

"I'm going to go look in on him now, but I suspect that he'll probably be out for a few more hours. After I've had a chance to examine him, I'll let you know what we're going to do with regards to treatment." The doctor stood up and extended his hand to Alex as he spoke, "Why don't you go home for a little while to rest, or at least go eat some breakfast."

"Thanks doctor. I'll be in the cafeteria."

Alex leaned back in his chair and watched as the middle-aged doctor walked down the hallway towards Robert's room. He gazed down at his wristwatch and jumped up. He ran toward an open elevator and punched in the 3 for the third floor. He quickly exited the elevator when it stopped and immediately went to the nurse's station where the first nurse that he encountered at the hospital met him. She smiled as she greeted him, "Good morning, Mr. Petrovic."

Surprised that she remembered his name, Alex smiled slightly and replied, "Good morning. How is my grandmother?"

"She is in stable condition. There is every reason to be optimistic."

Heaving a sigh of relief, Alex responded, "Thank you nurse. I'll be back later this morning to see her, okay?"

"I'm sure she will know you are here and appreciate your visit."

"Can you tell me what floor the cafeteria is on?"

"The fourth floor. As soon as you get off the elevator, make a right and it will take you right to it."

"Thank you," Alex answered as he headed for the elevator.

Alex solitarily sat in a far corner of the cafeteria as he ate a bowl of cereal and drank a large glass of orange juice. He remained there for almost an hour before his worrying got the better of him and caused him to return to the second floor room of his father. He opened the door and looked in, but Robert was still oblivious to his surroundings. He stepped back slowly and closed the door as he looked down the several long hallways that seemed to converge at the area right outside Robert's room.

Standing by a water fountain near the nurse's station, Dr. Hamilton spotted Alex and motioned for Alex to come toward him. Alex quickly strolled down the hallway to speak to Dr. Hamilton, "Doctor, have you had a chance to examine my father?"

"I've been in to see him, and he did awaken for a brief moment, but then he fell right back to sleep before I could ask him any questions."

"Do you think he'll wake up pretty soon?" Alex curiously asked.

"Yes, the grogginess is starting to wear off, so I'll be back to see him in about an hour."

"What if he wakes up? Should I tell him anything?" questioned Alex.

"If he wakes up, push the call button and tell the nurse that he's awake. Just go along with him and listen to what he says. Be vague, but keep him talking," informed Dr. Hamilton.

"Okay, I can do that. I'll see you later."

"Wait a second," the doctor called out politely as Alex started to leave.

"Yeah," Alex answered curiously as he turned to face the doctor.

"Do you have any idea what may have caused him to try to end his life? Or was it just a cry for help or attention?"

"It wasn't a cry for help, doctor," Alex answered with a flush of anger tinting his cheeks. "There was nobody home when he went out to the barn. There was no one to stop him. He didn't even know I was home. I flew in that morning, but I came directly here to the hospital to see my grandmother before going home. Robert had no idea I was home."

"Why did you come to the hospital to see your grandmother? Is she sick?"

"Yes, she had a massive stroke yesterday morning," Alex answered with an audible hint of anger in his voice.

"Could this have been a factor in your father's suicide attempt?"

"I don't know. He had an argument, according to the ICU nurse, with my grandmother's new husband and Robert was escorted out of the hospital by security.

"Why was that?" the doctor asked with intrigue. "Did Robert physically try to harm his stepfather?"

"No! And he's not his stepfather."

The doctor looked at Alex with confusion written over his entire face. Alex realized what the confusion was about and tried to clear it up, "He wasn't his stepfather. George just married my grandmother on Friday, and I know from recent conversations with my grandmother that George and Robert did not get along."

"So you think that is why Robert was escorted out of the hospital, because your grandmother's new husband and him didn't get along?"

"There was more going on even then. Robert would never have been taken away from his mother by anyone without a major fight," Alex replied more calmly.

"So you think there was something wrong even before he left the hospital?"

"Yes I do," Alex answered matter-of-factly.

"Is your father married or have someone that he is close to?" probed Dr. Hamilton.

"He's not married, but there is someone he's close to." Alex answered with slight disdain.

"I think maybe it would be a good idea to speak to her."

"Speak to who?" Alex answered confused.

"The lady he is close to."

Alex shook his head, "It's not a lady." The disapproval and shame forced Alex to turn from the doctor.

"Is your father a homosexual?"

"Yes," Alex answered quietly, trying to keep anyone in proximity from hearing the answer.

"I take it you disapprove of your father's lifestyle?" the doctor said with a hint of bitterness dripping from his words.

"Yes, I do, but I don't want to see him lying in that room either, tied to the bed," Alex answered annoyed.

"Well I assure you, Mr. Petrovic, that your father will get the best care possible, regardless of his sexual orientation," Dr. Hamilton answered with blatant sarcasm as he turned and walked away.

Alex walked back to his father's room and looked in the window. Still no movement. Alex paced back and forth for several minutes as Dr. Hamilton's sarcastic last words replayed over and over again in his mind. Reaching for his cell phone, he punched in the number 411 and waited. On the line came the familiar monotone from the previous day. Alex mentally questioned whether this was the only operator. "Yes, can you tell me the number for Mitchell Rains please?"

"One moment, Sir," came the monotone. "Do you want to be connected?"

"Please," he paused, and with a more pleasant voice he spoke, "Thank you, ma'am."

The phone rang several times before a lady's voice answered, "Hello."

"Hello, I need to speak to Mr. Rains right away."

"Who may I say is calling?"

"Tell him it's Alex Petrovic and it's an emergency," Alex answered stoically.

A moment passed before a deep voice came over the line, "Yes Alex, what is it? What's wrong?" Mitchell asked nonchalantly.

"My father is in Memorial Hospital. He was badly injured late yesterday, and I thought you would want to know."

"Is he going to be all right?" Mitchell asked trying to appear unaffected by the news.

"I don't know. He hasn't regained consciousness yet." Alex answered with subtle annoyance.

"I'll be there in a little while."

"Well, don't go out of your way or anything. For Christ's sake, the man you're supposed to love could be dying and you'll be here in a little while," Alex raised his voice as he continued, "Don't do him any favors."

Alex slammed his cell phone shut and slapped the wall in frustration. He leaned heavily against the wallpapered wall and sighed heavily. "Why do I even care if he comes? Robert's apparently better off without him," Alex thought to himself. After regaining his composure, Alex went back to Robert's room and pulled a chair up beside Robert's bed.

Robert stirred and pulled gently on the restraints, which brought him to full alertness. He stared at the restraints and futilely tried to free his wrists, but gave up after several unsuccessful attempts. He looked at Alex shyly, but alertly. Alex smiled, "How are you feeling?"

"Doctor, I need to find my mama," answered Robert, which immediately brought a frown to Alex's face.

"What makes you think I'm a doctor?"

"I'm in a hospital, right? Nobody else would be here with me except my mama or a doctor, and you're not my mama." Robert answered shyly but with a hint of humor.

"No, I'm not your mama, but that was a good observation," Alex answered with a smile. It had been a long time since he had smiled at his father. "I'm also not a doctor."

"Who are you then? And where's my mama?" Robert asked with urgency.

"I'm a friend of the family, Robert. My name is Alex. Do you know why you're in the hospital?"

"No, my head feels really fuzzy."

"You were hurt very badly."

With growing desperation, Robert asked, "Where's my mama? Is she all right? Was she hurt too?"

"No Robert, your mama is fine," Alex replied reassuringly. "I took your mama to stay with her sister until you get better and can go home."

"Aunt Mildred?" Robert asked disbelievingly.

"Yes, that's right. I didn't think you would want your mama to be alone …" Alex said soothingly as Robert shook his head from side to side to indicate that he would not want his mama to be alone. "So I took her to stay with her sister. I hope that is okay with you."

Robert shook his head in approval, "Yeah, that's fine."

"Good, let me just push this button here," Alex said as he pressed the nurse call button. "And the doctor will come down. He's been wanting to talk with you, but you've been sleeping quite a long time."

"I'm sorry," Robert answered apologetically.

"No, there's nothing to be sorry for. The doctor gave you something last night that made you sleepy. Don't you remember?"

"Nope," Robert answered as he looked down again at his restrained wrists, but he did not choose to ask why they were there.

Alex looked into Robert's blank eyes and became uneasy. "Nope," Alex said to himself, "Robert never talked like that." The puzzled look on Alex's face continued to grow and just as Robert was about to ask what was wrong, Dr. Hamilton entered the room.

"Hi Robert, I'm Dr. Hamilton."

"Hi," Robert answered shyly.

Dr. Hamilton looked at Alex and asked, "Sir, can you excuse us for a few minutes?"

"Sure, I'll be right outside."

Dr. Hamilton interrupted, "There's a man outside who said that you called him."

Alex shook his head indicating he knew whom the doctor was speaking about. Before he walked out of the room, Alex leaned in close to Robert and touched his hand, "Dr. Hamilton is a nice man. It's okay to talk to him, so don't be shy, all right?"

Robert nodded his head, "I'll try."

Alex smiled and walked out the door. Standing against a wall opposite Robert's room, Mitchell Rains cockily asked, "How is he? I just saw the doctor going in."

"Did the doctor tell you what happened?" Alex asked.

"No, he didn't say anything, so are you going to tell me what happened?"

"Yeah, I'll tell you what happened," Alex started angrily, "Late yesterday afternoon Robert tried to kill himself. I found him hanging in the barn."

Mitchell stepped back with surprise, "What?"

"Yeah, after I got the rope off the rafter, I carried him into the house and called 911."

"Why?" Mitchell asked with a genuine caring.

"I don't know. Something happened between Robert and George, but I don't know what."

"Robert had George investigated, and George came to the house on Thursday night and he and Robert had it out. Robert told him he was going to make sure George was never part of Anna's life," Mitchell explained.

"That explains some of what happened outside of my grandmother's hospital room," Alex stated more to himself than to Mitchell.

"Wait. What's wrong with Anna?" Mitchell asked sincerely.

"She had a massive stroke yesterday morning."

"Is that why you are here?"

"No, I was coming to bail Robert out of jail when I got a call that my grandmother had been rushed to the hospital."

"You mean Robert was in jail until yesterday?" Mitchell asked in horror.

"Yeah, he'd been in there since Thursday night. Why didn't you bail him out?"

"It's a long story," Mitchell said trying to change the subject. "Well what happened outside Anna's room?"

"According to the nurse who witnessed the argument, George had Robert escorted out of the hospital by security and banned from seeing Anna."

"What?" Mitchell said disbelieving, "How can he stop anyone from seeing Anna?"

"Because on Friday, while Robert was locked up, George convinced Anna to get married."

Mitchell shook his head in disbelief, "Wait a minute, you mean Robert didn't protest in any way? That doesn't sound like the Robert I know."

"Nor the one I know."

"Alex, is he going to be all right?"

"I don't know, but I do know that he's going to need you more than anyone since his mother is ill."

Mitchell turned away from Alex as he spoke, "I'm sorry Alex, but I can't be there for him. We broke up Thursday night."

"What? Who broke it off?" Alex questioned in anger.

"I did."

"Well why the hell did you do that?"

Raising his voice in anger, Mitchell responded, "I don't owe you any answer."

"The hell you don't! This is one of the things that could have led him to hang himself," Alex answered in a rising anger.

"Fine, if you want to know why I broke up with him, you don't have to look any further than yourself."

Alex looked puzzled, "What are you talking about? Up until yesterday, I hadn't seen my father in years."

"That's true, but you were always involved in our relationship. I had accepted an invitation for Robert and myself to go to a party, but he turned me down. Why? Because he didn't want to jeopardize his ungrateful son's career."

"You're lying."

"Robert always told me he wanted to go on vacations, and he really needed time off with all the stress he deals with, but when the time came, he always backed out because he didn't want the press to see him with me, and ultimately hurt you. He dreamed about us going to a tropical island together, but he wouldn't go. He denied himself happiness to protect you."

"I don't believe you. No matter what happened, he needs you right now. Are you going to walk away and not be there for him when he needs you the most?"

"Don't give me that guilt trip, boy. I was there with him when he found out from his mother that he had twin grandchildren. It ripped his heart out to never be able to see them. I was the one who picked up the pieces after he'd fall apart on the twins' birthday. No matter what, he would send cards with gifts at the off-chance you would tell them the gifts were from their grandfather and that he loved them, but the gifts always came back unopened."

Alex leaned heavily against the wall, suddenly feeling the exhaustion that had built up in his mind and body since the day before. He continued to stare at Mitchell with disbelief, and a touch of guilt.

"I love Robert, boy. That will never change, but I won't stop living my life because of you, you ungrateful bastard." Mitchell continued in anger and pain, "And I can't stand around and watch Robert live his life in pain. It hurts me too much. That's why I can't be part of his life. You say he needs someone? Well boy, you're it! He'd be the first one there for you, regardless of how you have treated him, if you needed someone."

"That may be true, but besides his mother, you know him better than anyone. He needs you!" Alex continued emphatically.

"I'll stop by to see him every once in a while, but I won't allow myself to become emotionally attached just because you want to back out of any responsibility," Mitchell stated defiantly.

"Fine!" Alex shouted. "I don't need your help, and Robert certainly is better off without you. Now, get the hell out of my sight," Alex yelled furiously.

Mitchell turned and walked away without even a look toward Robert's room. The head nurse on duty came running down the hallway and snapped at Alex, "What is the matter with you?"

"I'm sorry if we became a bit loud," Alex said sincerely.

"Loud?" the nurse repeated, "They could hear you all over the hospital."

"I apologize."

"Don't let it happen again or I'll have security remove you from the premises. Our patients need a quiet environment, not people screaming in the hallway."

"I promise. It will never happen again," Alex repeated apologetically.

"Good. Sir, your father is in a serious mental state right now, and the last thing he needs is for you to be yelling and carrying on right outside his room."

"I know. Robert's well-being is the most important thing right now," Alex stated.

With the rules and consequences properly explained, the nurse walked away and went about her business. Alex walked over to Robert's door and observed Dr. Hamilton writing in Robert's chart, as Robert appeared to be talking. Backing away, Alex went over to the far wall, opposite Robert's door, and slid down the wall wearily into a sitting position. The argument that he had just had with Mitchell was endlessly repeating in his mind. He tried to put the pieces together as to why Robert had tried to kill himself, but nothing was adding up. Breaking up with Mitchell, although Robert loved him, would not be a reason for Robert to try to hang himself, nor would a heated argument with George. There was one important piece missing. Alex shut his eyes tightly to try to concentrate on what could have possibly set Robert on such a destructive course. Robert could hold his own with anyone, and nothing Mitchell or George could do would ever make him try to end his own life.

Alex tried to clear his mind of all the heartbreaking images and sounds that he had witnessed throughout the previous day. Without Anna or Mitchell, Robert had no one who cared about him or who would look after him. Alex leaned his head back against the hard wall and exhaled loudly as he came to the realization that he was the only one Robert could rely on. Or could he? The past few years came flooding back as Alex acknowledged the feelings that had caused him to reject Robert and his way of life. "Has that all changed?" Alex asked himself quietly. "Will things be different if he regains his memory?" More confused than he had ever been, Alex clasped his knees and tried to forget the past few days. "If only I had not received the local paper that morning," he rationalized in his mind, "I would be home right now enjoying the weekend." At the thought of a relaxing weekend, Alex smiled involuntarily, but a frown quickly erased all happiness. "If I hadn't been here, Robert would be dead right now, and nobody would know why," Alex said to himself silently. As the turmoil threatened to overwhelm him, the doctor came out of Robert's room and motioned for Alex to follow him.

"How is he doctor?" Alex asked sincerely.

"He's confused about a lot of things, like what he is doing here. I'm afraid that your father has regressed back to when he was a teenager."

"You said earlier that he would eventually regain his memory?" Alex said more as a question than a statement.

"There is a good possibility that when he is mentally able to deal with the trauma that caused all of this, he will regain his memory."

"Is he going to be all right?"

"Physically he should recover quickly. Your father is in excellent physical condition. Mentally, though, I think it is going to be quite some time before he is ready to confront what happened to him. Right now he thinks he is only fifteen years old."

"What do I tell him if he asks me questions about why he is here?"

"I asked him if he remembered why he was here, but he couldn't remember anything. I alleviated his concerns momentarily by telling him that there had been an accident and he was badly injured."

"What do I tell him if he asks me why he's restrained?"

"Tell him that it is hospital policy, and that the restraints will allow him to heal faster."

"I'm sure he'll believe that?" Alex said sarcastically. "He's not stupid, doctor, nor was he stupid when he was a teenager."

"That's true, Mr. Petrovic, but your father is in a different mental state than he was when he was actually fifteen. Do you understand what I'm saying?"

"I'm not sure. Are you saying that his reasoning may not be as rational as it normally would be?"

"Yes."

"Well is he dangerous then? I mean if he's not rational, then he could possibly still be a danger to himself, right? Alex questioned intelligently.

"It's a possibility. That's why we're keeping him in restraints for a while longer, but I don't honestly think he's a danger to himself anymore."

"Why?" Alex asked intrigued.

"Because he keeps asking about his mother. Obviously he wants to see her, and from what you've told me, he has been responsible for your grandmother since he was fifteen, right?

"Yeah, everyday since my grandfather died when he was fifteen."

"That's why I don't think he's a danger to himself any longer, because he had a major responsibility of taking care of his mother when he was fifteen. Right now he believes he's fifteen, so I think he believes that he still has to take care of her."

"He wouldn't want to hurt himself with such a huge responsibility?" Alex stated with understanding. "Thanks, Dr. Hamilton. I appreciate everything that you are doing for Robert," Alex answered with genuine appreciation.

"We're just doing our jobs," Dr. Hamilton replied as he reached out to shake Alex's hand. "By the way, was that man the man we spoke of earlier?"

"Yes, it was, but unfortunately he's no longer a part of my father's life."

"Unfortunately?" the doctor repeated as he caught the change in attitude regarding Alex's feelings for Robert's significant other.

"Yeah, unfortunately. Besides my grandmother, Mitchell knew Robert better than anyone else, but they broke off their relationship, so I'm the only one that Robert has. The only problem is that I don't know him very well," Alex responded candidly.

"Trust me, Mr. Petrovic, you know him well enough, as long as you don't allow your feelings about his sexuality cloud your judgment."

"I guess I don't have that luxury any more, do I?" Alex replied with no hint of prejudice, only compassion.

"I'm not going to lie to you or mislead you, Mr. Petrovic. The next few months are going to be very stressful and difficult, but with your help I think Robert will get past this. And when he does, you both will be better off for it."

"I hope so," Alex stated, as he turned away from the doctor, but turned back to ask a final question, "Is it okay if I stay with him for a while?" Alex questioned with sad optimism.

"Yes, of course. Stay as long as you want. If you have any questions, have the nurse page me, okay?"

"Thank you again, doctor," Alex responded sincerely as he turned and walked back the long corridor to Robert's room. As he looked in, Robert was staring at the ceiling and tapping his fingers on the bed. The restraints prevented him from moving his arms, but his fingers were free to move about. As Alex gently opened the door, he heard Robert humming a soft tune.

"Hi Robert. Do you mind if I come in?"

"Please. It's very lonely in here."

"I know, so that's why I'm going to stick around for a while, if that's okay with you?"

"Yeah, I'd like that," Robert answered happily.

"Good. What was that tune you were humming?"

"I don't know its name. It's something mama always hums," Robert answered as the sad look returned to his tired eyes.

"You miss her, don't you?"

"Yeah. It's just me and her. It's been like that since my father died."

"Well hopefully soon you will be well enough and you can see her," Alex replied with fake optimism.

"I have to get well fast, or I'm gonna lose my job," Robert stated with great anxiety.

"I promise you, Robert, that you won't lose your job," Alex said with a smile.

"I can't lose it, or I don't know what we'll do."

"Robert, can I ask you a serious question?"

"Sure."

"Why do you feel so protective of your mother?" Alex asked tactfully.

"Because I promised my father that I would always protect her, no matter what," Robert answered without hesitation. "I love her, and besides, she takes care of me too."

"That's a good reason." Alex paused momentarily before continuing, "Your mama's okay Robert, I promise you that. Now the most important thing is for you to get better."

"I'll try, but I don't really know what's wrong with me," Robert answered with confusion.

"How do you feel right now?"

Robert moved his head from side to side slowly as he closed his eyes. "My head feels really fuzzy."

"Do you remember anything about what happened?" Alex quizzed.

"Nope. I've tried to concentrate, but I can't think straight."

Alex smiled inwardly at Robert's ironic statement. "Well, your memory will come back, but it might take some time. When that happens, you'll be better," Alex explained.

"Alex, why are my hands tied?" Robert asked with childlike timidity, "Did I do something wrong?"

"No, Robert, you did nothing wrong, and I don't want you to think that way, okay? Your hands are tied right now, but soon they will be free. The doctor said that you'll heal quicker if you have them on," answered Alex, hoping that Robert would accept his explanation.

Robert looked down at his right hand, and then his left, before speaking again, "If that's true then you can keep them tied until I get better."

Trying desperately to think of some way to reply, Alex rubbed Robert's right hand gently, "I think they just need to be on for a little while."

Robert accepted Alex's statement without question and closed his weary eyes.

# CHAPTER 11

▼

At 12:30 p.m., Alex's brief nap in the chair next to his sleeping father was interrupted by the stocky orderly that had physically restrained Robert the previous night as the resident painfully injected Robert with the drug that was still causing his drowsiness. The orderly wheeled in a tray and politely asked Alex to move.

Alex tapped gently on Robert's shoulder to wake him up. Robert wearily opened his eyes as Alex spoke, "Robert, your lunch is here. Are you hungry?"

"Not really," Robert mumbled.

"Robert, you have to eat or you're not going to get better."

Robert opened his eyes a bit wider, "All right, I'll try to eat a little bit."

Alex smiled, "Good."

The orderly stepped closer and pushed the remote control on the bed to raise the top of the bed higher. "Sir, can you excuse us for a while?" the orderly respectfully asked Alex.

"Are you going to help him?" Alex questioned.

"Yes. Until the doctor gives the order for the restraints to be removed, someone will help him eat," explained the orderly.

"Okay," Alex said as he got out of the orderly's way. Alex leaned in close to Robert's ear, "I'll be back in a little while. This man is going to help you eat. I know you can do it yourself, but it's hospital rules, so he's going to help you, okay? Everything will be all right, so try to eat a lot," Alex stated encouragingly.

"I'll try," came the soft reply as Robert watched the orderly cutting up the bland-looking food.

Alex walked out of the room and a wonderful surprise met his weary eyes. Emily jogged down the hallway and into her husband's waiting arms. She kissed him on the cheek and held him in a long embrace. Alex melted under her loving touch, causing his knees to go weak. The two stood there in the hallway outside Robert's room, relishing the reunion. Alex was the first to break the embrace, as the weakness continued flowing from his knees to the rest of his body.

Emily sensed her husband's pain, "Honey, what's wrong? Are you okay?"

"I'm wonderful now that you're here," he said smiling.

"Let's go sit down somewhere. You look exhausted."

Alex took her soft hand in his and led her to the waiting room. "I am tired. It's been a long night."

"Have you had any sleep at all?" Emily asked concerned.

"A few minutes here and there," Alex answered grimly.

"How's Robert?"

"Right now he's being fed by an orderly. The same orderly that held him down last night so that the doctor could stick a needle in his ass," Alex stated with a new anger.

"Honey, you need to get some sleep. Let me take you out of here so that you can rest for a while," Emily said with warm sincerity.

"I can't leave. I promised Robert that I would be back after he ate."

"Well," she paused. "Why don't we wait a few minutes and then go up there and tell Robert that we'll be back later? I'm sure he'll understand."

"You'd want to come back with me to visit with him?" Alex asked incredulously.

"Yeah. I feel bad for him, Alex, and he'd probably like the company. I'm sure that it gets lonely for him."

"Especially when you're tied to the bed and can't move," Alex responded matter-of-factly.

"He's still restrained? Why? Is he still a danger to himself?" Emily questioned anxiously.

"He's still restrained. The doctor said that the restraints would be left on for a little while longer. He doesn't believe that Robert's a threat to himself, but he wants to make sure."

"Well, I can see his reasoning. He's just looking out for what's best for Robert," Emily said with understanding.

"Yeah, I know, but seeing him like that is tough."

Emily pulled Alex into a loving embrace as she whispered in his ear, "He's going to be okay, baby. I promise you."

"I hope you're right."

"I'm always right. You just don't always see that," Emily teased.

Alex genuinely smiled as he gazed into his loving wife's eyes. "When we get back, we'll check on my grandmother again too, okay?"

"Definitely. I'd like to spend some time with her if that's okay?"

"I don't see why not, just as long as George doesn't have you removed," Alex stated with annoyance as he remembered the nurse telling him that George had Robert removed.

"What are you talking about?"

"I'll tell you when we get home."

"Where is home, by the way?"

"Robert's."

"Okay," she paused as she took Alex's hand. "Are you ready?"

"Yeah, I'm ready. The question is … are you ready?"

"What do you mean? Ready for what?" she said perplexed.

"Ready to see Robert like he is," Alex said sadly.

"Yeah, let's go."

Alex put his arm around Emily's shoulder as they walked down the long corridor to Robert's room. Alex looked in the small window on Robert's door, and hesitated briefly before pushing the door open. Holding Emily's hand, the two walked in as the orderly was preparing to leave.

"Hi Robert. Did you eat anything?"

The orderly glanced up at Alex as he pushed the tray toward the hallway to indicate that Robert did not eat. Robert, once again staring off into the distance, did not answer Alex's question.

Alex stepped beside the bed and pulled Emily closer. "Robert, I want you to meet someone."

Robert slowly turned his gaze back to Alex's voice. With unfocused eyes, he looked in Emily's direction, but did not say anything.

Concerned, Alex touched Robert's cheek gently as he spoke, "Robert, are you okay?"

Robert did not reply, but his eyes slowly brimmed with unshed tears that threatened to fall.

Alex let go of Emily's hand and sat down on the edge of Robert's bed. He leaned in close to Robert and spoke in a loving, tender voice that Emily had never heard before, "What happened Robert? Did that man do something to you?"

Robert lowered his head, frantically trying to hide his tears. When he felt the touch of Alex tenderly wiping his tears, Robert broke down and sobbed. "I don't like that man, Alex. He hurt me last night."

Desperately trying to stop his own tears from showing, Alex hugged Robert affectionately as he tried to alleviate his fears, "I'll make sure he doesn't come back, okay? Would that make you feel better?"

Robert nodded his head in approval, but the tears continued to cascade down Robert's cheeks and onto his blanket. Alex motioned for Emily to push the nurse call button as he held Robert in a warm embrace. As Alex continued to console him, a nurse opened the door.

"Nurse, can you get Dr. Hamilton? He told me to have him paged if I needed him," Alex stated without pulling away from Robert. Alex could feel the tension in Robert's body as Robert tried to free his hands to wrap around Alex.

Within two minutes, Dr. Hamilton came through the door. "Hi. The nurse had me paged," the doctor stated as he witnessed Alex holding Robert as Robert wept.

"Yeah doctor, we have a problem," Alex stated as he slowly pulled away, leaving Robert to hang his head as the tears continued.

"What happened?" The doctor asked with concern.

"The orderly who helped with feeding wasn't very nice to Robert, and Robert remembered him as the mean man who hurt him last night."

"Hurt him how?"

Alex turned away from Robert as he stood to face the doctor, "He's the one who held him down last night when that resident gave him that shot."

"Oh okay," the doctor said with understanding as he walked over to stand beside Robert. "Robert, I'll make sure that man never comes back in here again, okay?"

Robert failed to respond, but nodded his head slightly. Alex tapped the doctor on the sleeve to silently motion him outside. Emily remained with Robert, unable to think of any comforting words.

Outside the room, an alarmed Alex questioned the doctor, "What happened?"

"He associated the orderly with the physical restraint and the pain that he felt." Dr. Hamilton stated with reassurance, "That's a common response."

"So he's okay?"

"Well, I'll make sure that that particular orderly does not work with Robert any longer."

"What about now? Why's he so distraught?"

"It could be a lot of factors."

"Is he going to be all right? My wife and I were going to go home so that I could take a nap, but now I'm afraid to leave him."

"I'm going to give him a sedative to calm him down, so why don't you wait a few minutes until he falls asleep before you leave. That way he won't think that you left him, and he'll be asleep for hours."

"Okay."

"Good. I'm not going to call for an orderly, so do you think you can talk to him and keep him calm while I give him a shot?"

"I think so."

As Dr. Hamilton stepped away to get the medication, Alex politely asked Emily to wait outside. Emily willingly left the room as Alex came over to sit on Robert's left side. He turned Robert's face toward him to show him he was there.

As the doctor returned and was unloosening the right wrist restraint, Alex explained to Robert what the doctor was going to do, "Robert, Dr. Hamilton is going to give you a shot in the butt to make you feel better, okay?"

Robert gazed at Alex with fear in his eyes and with a shaky voice he spoke to him, "I don't want a shot, Alex. I'll be okay, I promise."

"I know you don't want a shot, Robert, but you need it," Alex spoke sympathetically and with understanding. "I know they hurt you last night, but Dr. Hamilton will be a lot gentler, I promise you," Alex said as he wiped the tears lovingly from Robert's eyes. "Is it okay if he gives it to you now?" Alex asked, trying to give Robert a feeling of some control.

"Will you stay here with me?" Robert asked with silent pleading in his voice.

"Of course I'll stay here with you," Alex smiled reassuringly.

"Okay. I'm ready then," Robert said as he braced himself inwardly.

Dr. Hamilton released the restraint and gently rolled Robert onto his side and placed Robert's hand in Alex's. He spoke to Robert calmly, "Robert, I want you to take a deep breath and hold it until I tell you to let it out, okay?

"Okay," Robert whispered.

"Take a deep breath."

Robert took a deep breath as instructed, and as Dr. Hamilton told him to release it, Dr. Hamilton gently pushed the needle in and pulled it back out without even a flinch from Robert.

"All done," stated the doctor.

Robert rolled slightly over to look at the doctor in disbelief. Dr. Hamilton disposed of the needle in the red bin on the wall and came back to stand at Robert's side.

"Did that hurt, Robert?" the doctor asked with a smile.

Robert shook his head from side to side as he responded with a grateful, "No."

"Good. Now I want you to get some rest, okay?"

"Okay," Robert responded as his eyes started to get heavy.

Dr. Hamilton waited until Robert was asleep before he rolled Robert back onto his back to have his right wrist re-restrained.

"Thank you so much doctor," Alex said gratefully as he stared at Robert's restraints.

"You're welcome. He didn't need to be restrained for those few moments."

"I'm sure he appreciates it, as do I."

"There are easier ways, but some doctors like the hard way," replied Dr. Hamilton.

"The way you gave him that shot was great. He didn't even flinch," Alex said with amazement as the two left the room.

"That's what I wanted. He had a bad experience, so I'll make sure that he doesn't have anymore."

"So what do we do now?" Alex asked.

"We're going to let him rest for awhile, and then I'll talk to him again," Dr. Hamilton explained.

"And what if his condition hasn't changed?" Alex questioned.

"It would then be very helpful if I could talk to someone who was close to your father prior to his suicide attempt," Dr. Hamilton explained.

"That may be a little difficult," Alex replied.

"Why?" Dr. Hamilton inquired.

"Because my grandma and Mitchell are the only people who are close to him, and as you already know, my grandma is clinging to life in the ICU—unable to speak," Alex explained.

"What about the other person you mentioned?" Dr. Hamilton asked.

"Mitchell? In case you forgot, I told you that he's no longer in Robert's life," Alex offered annoyed.

"You don't think he'd be willing to talk to me, even if it meant a possibly faster recovery for Robert?" Dr. Hamilton asked.

"I don't know," Alex admitted reluctantly.

"Is it you don't know, or you don't want to have to ask him?" Dr. Hamilton asked perceptively.

Alex's face slightly blushed as he answered honestly, "Both, I guess."

"It may be necessary for me to speak with him, Alex. He could provide valuable information that could help me better treat your father," Dr. Hamilton explained simply.

"If it comes to that, of course I'll ask him. I'll do anything to help Robert recover as quickly as possible," Alex stated.

"Good," Dr. Hamilton replied. "Like I said, we'll let your father rest for awhile and then I'll be back. In the meantime, if you have any questions, ask the nurse to page me."

Alex extended his hand and shook the doctor's hand firmly, "Thank you, Dr. Hamilton. I wish I could be more help to you."

"You saved your father's life, so you've already done the most important thing," Dr. Hamilton replied.

"Yeah, but I wish I knew more about Robert's life so that I could help you treat him more effectively," Alex continued.

Dr. Hamilton smiled genuinely as he patted Alex on the shoulder, "Remember that for the future."

Alex took the advice in stride, "I'll try."

"I truly hope so," Dr. Hamilton replied sincerely. "I have to go, but I'll be back a little later, and like I said, if you have any questions or you need me for anything, have the nurse page me."

"Thanks again," Alex offered as he watched Dr. Hamilton stop in front of Emily.

The doctor paused and looked at Emily, "I'm sorry, we haven't been introduced, I'm Dr. Hamilton."

"Hi Doctor, I'm Emily Petrovic, Alex's wife."

"It's nice to meet you Emily. Do you think you could do me a favor?" the doctor lightheartedly asked.

Emily looked at him questioningly, "Sure, what do you need?"

"Can you take this guy home and make sure he gets some sleep," replied the doctor as he pointed to Alex.

Emily smiled, "Yeah, I can do that."

"Good, now get going. Robert will be fine, so take some time for yourselves and get some rest. That's doctor's orders!" he said playfully.

"We're on our way," responded Alex as he led Emily down the hallway. As they stopped at the elevator, Alex turned around and said sincerely, "Thank you, Dr. Hamilton."

"You're welcome."

*     *     *     *

Robert awakened, bleary-eyed, and disoriented. He looked, unfocused, at the old-fashioned clock on the wall and realized that five hours had passed. Suddenly, he began to panic. He tried to sit up in the bed, but the restraints prevented him.

Robert began to tremble as he looked around the room. He was alone and restrained in an unknown place, and he could not form a coherent thought. As he was about to call out to someone for help, a flash of memory went through his mind. Robert closed his eyes tightly and concentrated on the flash of memory. His trembling started to ease as he recalled the last thing before falling asleep. He remembered the young man who sat beside his bed and calmed him with reassuring words as the doctor gave him medication. Robert remembered the doctor who skillfully and painlessly medicated him, and talked to him as if his feelings mattered. The anxiety of being alone and restrained disappeared and Robert started to relax, and even drifted off momentarily from the still present after-affects from the medication.

When Robert reawakened a few minutes later, a timid smile appeared on his face as he looked around the room.

"Hi Robert," Alex said amiably.

"Hi," Robert replied still a bit sleepily.

Alex moved his chair closer to Robert's bed, "Do you remember who I am?"

Robert answered confidently, "You said your name is Alex."

Alex smiled through his disappointment, "That's right, and do you remember who I said I was?"

Robert looked at Alex with confusion, "You said your name is Alex and that you are a friend."

Alex smiled to relieve Robert's anxiety, "That's absolutely correct. I am a friend."

"I knew you were a friend when you took Mama to be with Aunt Mildred while I'm here," Robert replied.

"I'm a friend of the family, and I'm someone you can trust Robert. I promise you that," Alex said sincerely, with all past resentments gone.

Robert's demeanor turned serious, "Alex?"

"Yeah," Alex responded.

"When can I go home?" Robert asked a little desperately.

"I don't know, Robert. You need time to heal," Alex answered honestly. "What's the rush?"

"I need to go back to work and back to school," Robert answered.

Alex smiled wryly, "You seem like a pretty smart guy, so unless I'm wrong about that, I don't think you go to school in the summertime."

Robert's stressed expression troubled Alex. Robert closed his eyes momentarily and took a deep breath before speaking, "It's summertime?"

"Yeah," Alex answered honestly. "It's July, so you don't have to worry about school."

"No," Robert replied with apprehension. "But I'm still worried about work."

"Don't be," Alex responded.

"Easy for you to say. If I don't work, my mother and I will get kicked out into the street and have nothing to eat," Robert explained. "How can I not be worried?"

"I told you last night, but you might not remember. I called your boss, Mr. O'Brien, and explained to him what's going on, and he said your job would be waiting for you when you're completely well," Alex explained as he patted Robert reassuringly on the leg.

Robert closed his eyes tightly again as he spoke, "Why can't I remember?"

Alex got up from his chair and sat down on the bottom of Robert's bed, "You had an accident, Robert. Your body needs time to recover from a trauma."

"But I don't feel like I'm hurt anywhere," Robert said with a hint of frustration.

"Do you remember anything that happened?" Alex asked delicately.

Robert's frustration was apparent, "No." He paused for a moment, "And from what you tell me, I don't even know what season it is."

Alex tried to calm Robert by speaking softly, "It's okay, Robert. You'll get your memory back. Dr. Hamilton is an excellent doctor, and he's going to help you remember things."

Robert's frustration and fear began to evaporate, "Do you really think so?"

"Yes I do," Alex answered with superficial confidence.

"I sure hope you're right," Robert replied with sadness evident in his eyes.

Alex tried to change the subject to get Robert's mind off of his memory problems, "You must be hungry. Would you like me to get you something from the cafeteria?"

"No, you don't have to," Robert answered, slowly beginning a descent into a world of despair.

"It's not a problem, Robert. Plus, you need to keep your strength up, so what's it going to be?" Alex asked.

"It really doesn't matter," Robert responded.

Alex began to worry about the sudden onset of Robert's apathy, so he tried to lighten the mood, "Would you care for the chicken or the beef?"

Robert stared momentarily at Alex before a smile turned up the corner of his lips. The goofiness of Alex's tone made Robert smile involuntarily, "What?"

Alex reiterated his question in the same goofy voice, "Would you care for the chicken or the beef?"

Robert pondered the question a moment before answering, "I guess if I have to pick, I'll pick the chicken."

"Good choice, my good man," Alex continued in his playful persona. "I'm sure you'll find the chicken to be a culinary delight."

"Are you okay?" Robert asked with a smile.

"Oh yes, my dear fellow, I am fine and I will return soon with your dinner," Alex answered as he strolled playfully toward the door. As Alex opened the door, his voice turned serious, "Just relax for a little while, and I'll be back soon from the cafeteria with your dinner."

Robert pulled lightly on the restraints, "I'm not going anywhere."

Alex quickly exited the room to conceal his sadness. He immediately went to the nurses' desk and addressed the nurse sitting there working on the computer, "Excuse me, nurse."

"How can I help you?" she asked amiably.

"Is Dr. Hamilton still here?" Alex asked.

"I can call his office and see, but I'm pretty sure he hasn't left for the day," the nurse answered.

"Thank you," Alex replied as he waited for the nurse to call Dr. Hamilton's office.

The nurse briefly covered the receiver as she addressed Alex, "Yes, Dr. Hamilton is still in his office. Would you like to leave a message with his secretary?"

"Yes. Tell the secretary that I'd like to talk to Dr. Hamilton before he leaves, if that's possible?" Alex replied.

The nurse relayed the message over the telephone, and then looked back to Alex, "What's your name, sir?"

"Alex Petrovic," Alex responded.

"And you'd like to talk to Dr. Hamilton concerning what?" the nurse questioned.

"My father—his patient, Robert Petrovic," Alex answered.

The nurse once again relayed the information, and hung up the phone, "Dr. Hamilton should be down in a few minutes."

"Thank you," Alex responded. "I'll be in the cafeteria."

"I'll let him know where he can find you if you're not back," the nurse said helpfully.

Alex offered his thanks and proceeded to absentmindedly walk to the cafeteria. When he arrived, the cafeteria was filled with the hustle and bustle of the dinner crowd—overworked residents in their baby-blue scrubs, relatives of hospitalized patients, and an assortment of other people sitting around chatting. Alex quickly jumped in line to try to avoid the inevitable long wait for Robert's dinner. Ten minutes later, with a chicken dinner in hand, Alex was grateful to be leaving the chaos and din of the cafeteria. As he exited the elevator, he spotted Dr. Hamilton standing at the nurses' desk reading a patient's chart. Alex immediately walked over to the desk, "Hi Doctor."

Dr. Hamilton turned to face Alex, "Hi, how are you?"

"I hope I didn't keep you waiting?" Alex apologized.

"No, not at all. I was just reviewing your father's chart," the doctor explained. "Have you been in to see him?"

"Yeah," Alex answered. "That's what I wanted to talk to you about."

"Did something happen?" Dr. Hamilton questioned.

"Not anything specific," Alex answered.

Dr. Hamilton motioned for Alex to follow him, "Let's go somewhere private to talk."

Alex walked through the waiting room door and proceeded to sit down on a large sofa near the window, "Thanks for staying to talk with me about Robert."

Dr. Hamilton smiled, "It's my job." He sat down on a recliner opposite Alex, "So what's going on?"

"When I got here a little while ago, Robert was still sleeping, but he soon awoke. I asked him if he remembered me—hoping he remembered me—and he said he did," Alex explained.

"He regained his memory?" Dr. Hamilton asked skeptically.

"Unfortunately, no. He said he remembered me telling him that my name is Alex and that I'm a friend of the family," Alex continued.

"I'm going to send him for some tests to rule out any problems with his brain," Dr. Hamilton explained.

"Do you think he has a brain injury?" Alex inquired.

"It's best to rule it out," Dr. Hamilton replied.

"But you think his memory problem is psychological?" Alex stated.

"It's a definite possibility. If the tests show no brain abnormalities, then yes, Robert's memory problems are psychological in nature," Dr. Hamilton explained.

Alex shifted uncomfortably on the couch, "You mentioned before that if Robert hadn't regained his memory that you'd like to speak to Mitchell. Does that still hold true?"

"Yes, I think that your father's significant other could give me valuable insight into the past few months," Dr. Hamilton stated as he looked sympathetically at Alex. "I know this is tough on you, but it could possibly help me treat your father more effectively."

"I'll do anything that you ask if it'll help Robert," Alex stated honestly.

"I'm glad you feel that way," Dr. Hamilton replied with apparent skepticism.

"I want Robert to get better," Alex said emphatically.

"I believe you," Dr. Hamilton stated softly. "Robert's going to need your support—now more than ever."

"What should I tell Mitchell when I call?" Alex inquired.

"Ask him if he'll come to the hospital tomorrow so that we can talk," Dr. Hamilton answered.

"Should I tell him to come to your office?" Alex asked.

"No, just have him stop at 'information' in the lobby, and tell the receptionist that I'm expecting him. She'll then call my office and I'll meet him in a conference room," Dr. Hamilton explained.

"Okay, I'll call him after I take Robert his dinner. I can't promise you he'll come, but I'll try," Alex stated.

"We won't know until you talk to him," Dr. Hamilton stated the obvious.

"Yeah. Hopefully his feelings for me won't cloud his judgment," Alex said matter-of-factly.

"I'm betting his feelings for your father, even though they've broken up, are stronger than his animosity towards you," Dr. Hamilton explained.

"I hope you're right," Alex stated before standing up. "I better take this to Robert before it gets cold."

"I'll come with you. I want to talk to Robert briefly before I leave," Dr. Hamilton informed.

"Should I wait here?" Alex asked.

"No, you can hear what I tell Robert," Dr. Hamilton answered as they walked out of the waiting room and down the corridor to Robert's room.

Alex opened Robert's door and found Robert staring absently at the wall. Alex walked over to the chair beside Robert's bed and sat down. "Hi Robert, I got you something good to eat, but first Dr. Hamilton wants to speak to you, Okay?"

Robert gazed pensively at Alex, "I guess so."

Dr. Hamilton went to stand on the opposite side of the bed from where Alex was seated, "How are you feeling, Robert?"

Robert answered plainly, "Okay."

"I'm glad to hear that," Dr. Hamilton said with a smile. "Later this evening I'm going to send you for some tests." Panic registered immediately on Robert's handsome, but tired face. "It's nothing to worry about. These tests are painless— I promise," Dr. Hamilton explained to calm his patient.

"Are you sure?" Robert asked skeptically.

"I promise you Robert that these tests are completely painless," Dr. Hamilton reassured.

"I hope so," Robert said with a hint of doubt in his tone.

"Now," Dr. Hamilton said with an upbeat demeanor as he started to undo Robert's one wrist restraint nearest him. "I think these can come off for awhile. How does that sound?"

Robert's smile lit up his face, "Great! Thank you."

"You're welcome, but this comes with a condition," Dr. Hamilton added.

"Anything," Robert replied.

"These can come off for now, and stay off until visiting hours are over, but when Alex leaves, the doctor on duty is going to have them put back on for overnight. Do you understand?" Dr. Hamilton explained simply.

"Yeah, I understand, but when can they go for good?" Robert inquired.

Dr. Hamilton went to the other side of the bed and undid the other restraint, "Well, the restraints can be off as long as Alex or myself or some other medical personnel is with you. We'll decide when they go for good at a later time. Okay?" Dr. Hamilton explained as he walked to the foot of the bed.

"Yeah, thank you," Robert replied, grateful that he was getting a short reprieve.

"You're welcome. One more thing before I go. I'm leaving orders for the nurse to give you some medication tonight to help you sleep," Dr. Hamilton stated in a calm voice.

"It's not gonna hurt, is it?" Robert asked nervously.

"No, it's just a little pill you have to swallow," Dr. Hamilton clarified.

"Okay," Robert responded with relief.

"Okay then, I'll be in to see you in the morning. Have a good evening," Dr. Hamilton said with a genuine smile.

"Good night, doctor," Alex said. "And thanks."

"See you tomorrow," Dr. Hamilton said as he walked toward the door.

"Good night, doc," Robert said.

"Good night," the doctor replied as he exited the room.

Alex smiled at Robert and started to open the bag of food from the cafeteria. "I hope you're hungry."

Robert gratefully stretched his arms out to take the bag, "A little."

Alex laughed, "Just a little? You have a lot of chicken in there to eat."

"I'll do the best I can," Robert replied with a smile.

Alex returned Robert's smile, "I know you will. I didn't know what you wanted to drink, so I just brought you a ginger ale. Is that all right?"

"That's fine," Robert replied before he turned serious. "Thank you, Alex."

Alex was taken off guard momentarily, "For what?"

"For buying me something to eat," Robert replied.

Alex's anxiety melted, "Oh, that? That's nothing."

"No it's not. Not for me at least. I couldn't afford to buy that type of dinner," Robert replied in a serious tone.

"Well, you needed a big meal. You haven't eaten all day, and like I said before, you need to keep your strength up, so dig in and enjoy!" Alex said trying to lighten the mood.

"Okay," Robert replied as he opened the bag and laid the food out on the table that Alex pushed up to Robert's bed. "This definitely looks better than the stuff they tried to give me for lunch."

Alex, realizing that Robert was feeling better, interjected, "Yeah, that was nasty looking."

"Alex?" Robert said as he pulled the chicken apart with his fingers, after realizing that he wasn't given any silverware.

"Yeah," Alex answered.

"I'm sorry about what happened after lunch," Robert stated sincerely.

"There's nothing to be sorry for," Alex said sternly, but affectionately. "You did nothing wrong, so forget about it, okay? Dr. Hamilton fixed that problem, so it won't happen again."

"I hope not," Robert said as he drifted momentarily back to the memory of his lunch time encounter with the orderly.

"Eat up!" Alex stated forcefully, but playfully. "You don't want it to get cold."

"Okay, okay, I'm eating," Robert said in a light tone as he took a bite of chicken.

"Good?" Alex asked with a smile.

"Actually, yeah," Robert answered in slight amazement.

"I'm glad to hear it," Alex replied. "Now try to eat all of it."

"Yes Mom," Robert teased.

"Now, since you've obviously won this battle of wits, would you mind if I step out for a moment to make a phone call?" Alex asked in a pleasant-tone.

"Not at all," Robert replied. "I didn't offend you, did I?"

Alex laughed, "Of course not. It takes a lot more than a smart aleck to offend me."

"Good to know," Robert responded more relaxed as he continued to eat his chicken.

"Okay then, I'll be right back," Alex said as he walked to the door. "I'll be right outside the door if you need me."

"I'll be fine," Robert answered.

"I know you will," Alex replied as he walked out the door and to the pay phone that was a few feet opposite Robert's room. He deposited a quarter and quickly dialed the number. When he heard a masculine voice, Alex mustered all his inner calmness and strength to reply to the voice in a civilized tone, "Hi Mitchell, it's Alex Petrovic."

"Is Robert all right?" Mitchell immediately asked.

"He's the same," Alex answered honestly.

"What do you want?" Mitchell asked shortly.

Alex took a deep breath before answering, "I had a conference with Robert's doctor a few minutes ago, and he thinks that you might have information about the past few months that could help him treat Robert more effectively."

"What type of information?" Mitchell asked in a more relaxed tone.

"I think about his moods and anything that might have happened that could have led up to his trying to commit suicide. I told him that you and my grandma are the only ones who are close to Robert, so he asked if he could possibly speak to you. Would you be willing to meet with him?" Alex asked hopefully.

"Of course I'll meet with him. When and where?" Mitchell asked.

"Can you come in tomorrow morning?" Alex inquired.

"Sure, what time?" Mitchell queried.

Alex started to relax at the progression of his conversation, "I think anytime is good. Dr. Hamilton said to just come to the information desk in the main lobby and tell the receptionist that he is expecting you. She'll call his office and then he'll come and meet you."

"I'll be there first thing in the morning," Mitchell replied.

"Thank you, Mitchell," Alex said genuinely.

"I'm not doing this for you. I'm doing it for Bobby," Mitchell replied curtly before hanging up.

Alex hung up the phone and leaned heavily against the wall a brief moment before going back in to see Robert. When he reentered Robert's room, Robert had already finished his dinner and was lying in the bed with his hands intertwined behind his head. "You look more relaxed," Alex said with a smile.

"I am," Robert replied. "Being able to freely move my arms is wonderful."

"I'm sure it is," Alex said as he sat back down beside Robert's bed. "And I'm sure it won't be long before you won't have them anymore."

"I hope so," Robert said. "Everything okay with your phone call?"

"Yes. Everything is fine. Actually better than I thought," Alex offered.

"I'm glad to hear that," Robert said. "But if you have to go somewhere, go ahead and go. Don't feel like you have to stay here with me."

"Tired of me already," Alex teased.

Robert turned serious, "Not at all. It's great having you here to talk to, and especially to be here so I don't have to have those restraints, but if you need to do something, please go and do it. I don't want to be a burden."

"Everything is fine, Robert, and you are not a burden. Don't ever think that, okay?" Alex gently reprimanded.

"Okay, if you say so," Robert said.

"I do say so," Alex said in a mock-stern voice.

*     *     *     *

Mitchell drove nervously to the hospital for his morning meeting with Dr. Hamilton. He left earlier than his normal commute to avoid the morning traffic, but an accident caused back-ups and delays in Mitchell's drive to his meeting. He had told Alex that he would come to the hospital first thing in the morning, and he did not want to be late. Robert was much too important for him to be late for a meeting with Robert's doctor. After a few eternal minutes, Mitchell pulled into the hospital parking lot. He quickly exited his candy apple red Corvette and jogged to the main entrance. He went through the revolving door and proceeded to go straight to the Information Desk.

"Good morning," the elderly lady behind the desk said with a smile.

"Good morning," Mitchell replied. "My name is Mitchell Rains. Dr. Hamilton is expecting me."

The elderly receptionist picked up the phone, "One moment please."

"Thank you," Mitchell responded.

The receptionist spoke quietly into the phone and then smiled at Mitchell, "Dr. Hamilton is with a patient, but he should be down in about ten minutes."

"Thank you," Mitchell replied and returned the smile. He went over to an available chair and sat down roughly. He read the headlines going across the bottom of the television screen that hung on the wall in the waiting area, but he could not concentrate on what he was reading. His thoughts kept taking him back to the last time he had talked to Robert. As he was absorbed in his thoughts, a tall man in khaki trousers and a white shirt with a navy blue tie came to stand in front of him.

"Mr. Rains?" the man asked.

"Yes," Mitchell responded as he stood up.

"I'm Dr. Hamilton," the doctor said as he extended his hand.

Mitchell shook the proffered hand, "Hi, how are you?"

"I'm fine, and you?" Dr. Hamilton said in a friendly voice.

Mitchell ignored the question, "How's Bobby?"

"Let's go somewhere private so we can talk," Dr. Hamilton stated as he started walking toward the elevator.

Mitchell followed closely behind him, "I apologize for being late."

Dr. Hamilton looked at Mitchell with a perplexed gaze, "What do you mean?"

"I told Alex that I would be here first thing in the morning, but there was an accident on the highway that caused some major delays," Mitchell explained.

"I didn't tell Alex to specify any certain time. I just asked him if he'd call you and ask you to come in sometime this morning," Dr. Hamilton clarified.

"I wanted to come early since it concerned Bobby," Mitchell said. As they entered a large conference room, Mitchell turned and faced Dr. Hamilton, "How is Bobby?"

Dr. Hamilton motioned for Mitchell to sit down at the large conference table, "Due to privacy laws I can't really get into his condition, but I can tell you that it's going to take some time for him to recover."

"I understand," Mitchell responded with slight apprehension. "Just tell me this—is he conscious and able to communicate?"

"Yes," Dr. Hamilton answered. "He's awake and alert and I've been able to talk to him a few times."

Relief registered on Mitchell's face, "I'm glad to hear that."

Dr. Hamilton continued, "I asked Alex to call you last night because I need to know some things about the past few months."

"What do you need to know?" Mitchell asked. "I'll tell you anything you need to know."

"What was Robert's general mood and demeanor over the past few months?" Dr. Hamilton inquired.

"The only thing that I can think of is that he was tired a lot," Mitchell answered.

"How so?"

"Well, Bobby has always been in phenomenal shape, so it was a little out of the ordinary for him to be suddenly tired all the time," Mitchell explained.

"What was his mood like?" Dr. Hamilton inquired further.

Mitchell thought momentarily, "Now that I think about it, Bobby was emotional on several occasions."

"And that was out of the ordinary?" Dr. Hamilton asked.

"Absolutely," Mitchell said with a slight laugh. "Bobby rarely showed his emotions."

"Can you explain that? Dr. Hamilton inquired with interest.

"Sure. Bobby has always been a stiff upper lip type of guy. I've only seen him cry one time in almost a decade of knowing him," Mitchell expressed.

"What for—if you don't mind telling me?" Dr. Hamilton queried.

Mitchell took a deep, calming breath, "It was right after the twins were born."

Dr. Hamilton's puzzled look stopped Mitchell, "What twins?" he asked.

"I'm sorry. Bobby's grandchildren—Alex's son and daughter," Mitchell clarified.

"Okay," Dr. Hamilton acknowledged his understanding.

"Well, to go back a little further, Alex didn't invite his father to his wedding, so it wasn't a big surprise that Alex didn't inform Bobby that he was going to be a grandfather," Mitchell continued.

"How did Robert find out?" Dr. Hamilton asked.

Mitchell sighed, "Anna." Just as Dr. Hamilton was going to ask, Mitchell clarified, "Anna is Bobby's mother—Alex's grandma."

"Please continue," Dr. Hamilton replied.

"Well, after the twins were born, Bobby sent the babies cards, with money of course, and he spent weeks prior to their birth redoing some of Alex's baby furniture, which Bobby had made before Alex was born, and he sent that all to Alex," Mitchell further explained.

"What happened?" Dr. Hamilton queried.

"The cards were returned—unopened—and the furniture was shipped back as well. The delivery driver said that nobody would sign for the packages, and the man of the house told him to send it back—that he didn't want it," Mitchell explained with latent anger.

"So Alex returned everything unopened?" Dr. Hamilton asked for clarification.

"Yes," Mitchell replied with unsuppressed anger. "I was at Bobby's when the delivery driver brought everything back."

"How did Robert take it?" Dr. Hamilton inquired.

"As usual he tried not to show his pain, but on this particular occasion, it didn't work. When he excused himself to go to the bathroom, I followed him and waited for him outside the bathroom. He had tears in his eyes, but he again tried to hide it, but I forced him to face me," Mitchell stated matter-of-factly.

"What did he do?" Dr. Hamilton asked.

"He tried to turn away, but I wouldn't let him. I forced him to acknowledge the pain that Alex was causing him," Mitchell continued.

"And did he acknowledge the pain he was feeling?" Dr. Hamilton inquired.

"He tried to keep a stiff upper lip, but he eventually broke down. He cried for a few minutes, and then he never spoke of it again."

Dr. Hamilton took a moment to digest the information that Mitchell was imparting before speaking, "You mentioned that Robert was more emotional recently. How so?"

"The last time I saw Bobby was last Thursday. He had invited me over for dinner, and we were both looking forward to a relaxing evening, but it didn't start out that way," Mitchell relayed.

"What happened?" Dr. Hamilton queried.

"As I pulled into Bobby's driveway, I passed George as he was leaving," Mitchell stated before adding, "Oh, George is Anna's boyfriend, by the way. Anyways, when I went to the door, Bobby was waiting for me, and I could tell that he was upset."

"Did Robert tell you what happened between him and his mother's boy-friend?" Dr. Hamilton asked.

"I asked, but he wouldn't say. He just asked if we could forget about everything and just enjoy our evening. I relented because I could see that he was on the verge of tears, and I didn't want to ruin our evening by talking about George."

"Was George a subject of contention?" Dr. Hamilton asked innocently.

"Not between Bobby and me. It was just that Bobby and George didn't get along—and for good reason," Mitchell added.

"What reason is that?"

Mitchell half-smiled, "Bobby had George investigated, and he found out that his suspicions were warranted. It seems George has a history of preying on lonely, wealthy, elderly ladies. Once George got in their good graces, he'd bleed their finances dry and then move on to his next unsuspecting victim."

"Did Robert share this information with his mother?"

"He didn't share the information he got from the investigator, or the fact that he had an investigator, but he did try to reason with her and point things out as delicately as possible. The bottom line is that Bobby didn't want to see his mother get hurt," Mitchell explained.

"That's understandable," Dr. Hamilton admitted. "So you didn't press Robert about the confrontation so that you could have a relaxing evening?"

"Yes," Mitchell replied defensively. "I didn't want to upset him any further."

"I'm not accusing you of anything, Mr. Rains," Dr. Hamilton said apologetically. "I'm just trying to understand."

Mitchell shook his head, "I'm sorry. I'm just a little stressed."

Dr. Hamilton nodded, "That's understandable—considering what's happened in the past few days."

"Yeah," Mitchell acknowledged with a sigh.

"How did the rest of your evening go that night?" Dr. Hamilton inquired, already sensing he knew the answer.

Mitchell smiled sadly as he remembered his last evening with Robert, "Well, our dinner was fantastic, and then we kicked back and relaxed for awhile and talked, but then things changed."

"How so?"

"I mentioned accepting an invitation for the two of us to spend the 4th at a friend's cookout, and then about going into the city with some friends to go dancing, but Bobby declined," Mitchell explained.

"Why did he decline?" Dr. Hamilton asked.

"Because of that ungrateful bastard he calls a son," Mitchell said with unsuppressed hostility.

"I don't understand," Dr. Hamilton admitted honestly.

"Bobby didn't want to jeopardize that bastard's career by being *seen* in public settings," Mitchell continued angrily.

"How could that jeopardize Alex's career?" Dr. Hamilton asked naively.

"Alex is a rising star amongst the conservatives in government. Bobby thought that if Alex's conservative colleagues found out that his old man was a homo they would blackball Alex and his career would be over," Mitchell further explained.

"What happened after Robert declined the invitation?" Dr. Hamilton asked.

"I was so frustrated that I told him that I thought it would be best if we broke up," Mitchell remembered painfully.

"How did he take it?" Dr. Hamilton asked delicately.

"He was crushed," Mitchell stated softly as he remembered the pain that was imprinted on Robert's face. "He told me he'd make things up to me and that he loved me, and he begged me not to go, but …"

Dr. Hamilton finished Mitchell's thought, "But you were frustrated and upset, and," Dr. Hamilton paused. "Most of all you were hurt. Am I right?"

Mitchell's stunned expression spoke volumes, "You understand."

"That you broke things off because you were deeply hurt?" Dr. Hamilton questioned.

"Yes," Mitchell replied. "How did you know?"

"Even from our limited conversation this morning, I can see how much you care about Robert. You were hurt that he chose to protect Alex over spending a special day with you," Dr. Hamilton espoused knowingly.

"No matter what, Bobby would always put Alex first, even though Alex didn't care whether Bobby was dead or alive. Bobby always sacrificed his own happiness for an ingrate who despised him, and that just got to me," Mitchell explained honestly.

"So how was Robert when you left?" Dr. Hamilton inquired.

"He had tears in his eyes, and he begged me not to go," Mitchell related a little guiltily. "I told him the obligatory line that we'd still be friends, kissed him on the cheek, and walked out of his life."

"Breaking up is never easy," Dr. Hamilton said to try to assuage some of Mitchell's guilt.

"I know, but I ended up lying to him," Mitchell confessed.

"How?" Dr. Hamilton asked intrigued.

"I wasn't a friend when he needed me," Mitchell said sadly.

"What do you mean?"

Mitchell hung his head, "He called me from the county jail saying he was in trouble and needed me to bring bail money, but I wouldn't even answer the phone. I had my housekeeper tell him I wasn't home."

"Why was he arrested?" Dr. Hamilton asked.

"I'm still not sure, but by my not helping him, he sat in jail from Thursday night to yesterday afternoon," Mitchell stated guiltily. "Oh my God," Mitchell said suddenly. "Am I the reason Bobby tried to kill himself?"

"Why would you think that?" the doctor questioned.

"First I break up with him, and then I reject him when he needs me," Mitchell replied as he rested his head in his hands.

"Mr. Rains," Dr. Hamilton said strongly. "You're not the reason Robert tried to commit suicide."

"How can you be so sure?" Mitchell asked dejectedly.

"Mr. Rains, listen to me. From what you've told me this morning, Robert has been showing signs of depression for months," Dr. Hamilton explained.

"Then I should have seen the signs," Mitchell said with an inward anger.

"Not unless you're a doctor or psychologist," Dr. Hamilton replied strongly, but sincerely. "The signs were subtle, Mr. Rains, so unless you were trained to look for these things, you wouldn't have seen them."

"So there wasn't anything I could have done to prevent his suicide attempt?" Mitchell asked.

"Honestly—No," Dr. Hamilton answered.

"So you think something has been going on for months with Bobby?" Mitchell asked.

"From what you've told me—yes," Dr. Hamilton responded. "Your coming here this morning has helped me a great deal."

"Why didn't Bobby tell me if something was bothering him?" Mitchell asked almost rhetorically.

"There's a lot of unanswered questions at this point, Mr. Rains, but I'm going to try to find out why all this happened," Dr. Hamilton answered sincerely.

"I'm glad I could help you this morning," Mitchell stated as he took out a business card and handed it to the doctor. "If you need anything, give me a call. Both my home and office numbers are on there."

"Thank you," Dr. Hamilton said as he took the business card. "And thank you for coming this morning."

"Take good care of him, okay?" Mitchell said sincerely.

Dr. Hamilton reached out to shake Mitchell's hand, "I'll do everything in my power to get Robert well."

"Thank you," Mitchell said as he turned to walk out the door.

# CHAPTER 12

▼

Several weeks passed without incident as Robert continued to regain his strength, but failed in regaining his memory. Emily returned home briefly to pick up the twins and the family's clothing for the long stay they anticipated at Robert's home. Alex spent each day sitting and talking with Robert, hoping that Robert would recapture his memory, but the more time that Alex spent with Robert, the more he began to like this enigmatic man.

Dr. Hamilton permitted Robert to take short walks around the second floor as long as he or Alex accompanied Robert on his journeys. Alex and Emily bought Robert several pairs of sweatpants and tee shirts, instead of pajamas, so that Robert would feel comfortable walking around the second floor.

Each day Robert would be waiting anxiously for Alex to arrive to accompany him on his walk. The walks were brief, but they provided Robert with a semblance of freedom from his lonely, isolated hospital room. As Alex arrived one morning, Robert was talking with Dr. Hamilton in his hospital room. Alex quietly pushed the door open, and Robert waved him in anxiously.

"Hi Robert. Dr. Hamilton. How's things going?"

Robert's eyes danced with excitement, "Dr. Hamilton said that we can go for a walk anywhere in the hospital."

"Did he?" Alex asked teasingly.

"Yes, I did," answered Dr. Hamilton happily, "As long as you or I go with him. He knows he's not allowed to go alone, right Robert?"

"Yeah, I promise Dr. Hamilton. I won't leave this room without you or Alex," Robert answered joyfully and truthfully.

"Good. I know I can trust you, Robert," the doctor replied honestly.

With a broad smile, Alex asked, "Well then, are you ready to go?"

"I'm all ready," Robert said with uncontained enthusiasm.

"Let's go then, if it's okay with Dr. Hamilton?"

"Fine with me. Have fun Robert," Dr. Hamilton said sincerely.

"We will," Robert answered as he was opening the door.

Alex turned back to Dr. Hamilton, "Is there any special time we should be back?"

"No. There's no curfew today," the doctor responded mischievously.

"Okay. See you later doc." laughed Alex.

Robert and Alex strolled quietly down the corridors of each floor of the hospital, except the third floor where Alex conspicuously diverted Robert's attention from the floor where Anna was staying. Alex put his arm around Robert's shoulder playfully as the two walked down the corridors, allowing Robert to revel in his freedom. Alex, instead of allowing Robert to go on the third floor, gently asked Robert if he wanted to go have lunch in the cafeteria. A joyful smile gave him his answer.

"What would you like to have, Robert?"

Robert looked suddenly perplexed, "I don't know. What am I allowed to have?"

"Anything you want," Alex laughed.

Joy radiated over his face as Robert asked, "Can I have a chocolate milkshake?"

"Absolutely! What else do you want?"

"Just a milkshake. Are you sure I can have a chocolate milkshake?" Robert asked skeptically.

Yeah, of course. Why couldn't you have a milkshake?" Alex responded with slight confusion.

"I know they're expensive. Me and mama only have milkshakes, especially chocolate milkshakes, on special occasions."

Understanding Robert's concern, Alex replied with a smile, "Well today is a special occasion. Today's our first journey off the second floor."

Robert smiled, "Yeah, I'm so glad. It gets really boring there."

"I know Robert, but let's forget about that now, okay? Don't you want anything else besides a milkshake?"

"Like what?" Robert asked anxiously.

"Well … how about some chicken or fish or a salad?"

"Yuck," Robert replied playfully. "Would a hamburger and fries be okay?"

Alex looked at Robert with surprise, realizing that he had never seen his father eat a hamburger or french fries. "Of course it's okay. Let's go order."

Alex ordered the food for himself and Robert as Robert waited patiently beside him. When the food came, Robert asked if he could take the milkshake first. Alex permitted it and Robert sucked on the chocolate milkshake as the two looked for a table nearest a window. Alex sat down and laughed, "I haven't eaten like this in years."

"Emily must keep you on a short leash," Robert mischievously replied with a grin.

Alex looked downhearted for a moment, and then a mischievous smile eclipsed his lips to mirror Robert's, "Of course she does. That's what marriage is all about."

Robert laughed heartily and Alex joined in merrily. Just to hear Robert laugh was music to Alex's ears. Never in his life did Alex ever imagine Robert having such a mischievous streak. Robert had always been stoic and humorless when Alex was growing up.

"How was everything?" Alex asked. "Better than what you've been getting, huh?"

"Yeah, that food is yucky, and I think the gelatin would stick to the walls."

"I'd agree with that, but I wouldn't try it with the gelatin. They'd probably put you back in restraints," Alex answered humorously.

"I definitely don't want that," Robert answered with a slight smile as he remembered the feeling of complete helplessness he felt in the restraints. "Having something itch was horrible."

"Well I don't think you'll ever have to deal with that again," Alex answered sincerely, but with regret for having brought up the topic.

Robert stared out the window as he slurped up the last gulp of his milkshake and set it down. Alex finished his fries and returned the food tray to the kitchen as Robert sat contently at the table. When Alex returned, the mood turned serious as Robert continued staring out the window.

"Whatcha thinking about, Robert?"

"The future," Robert answered earnestly.

"What about the future?" Alex responded with concern.

"What's going to happen to me and mama?"

"You both are going to be all right," Alex answered authoritatively.

"Are you sure?" replied Robert as he focused on Alex.

"Yes, I'm sure. I promise you that you and your mama will be all right. Now I don't want you worrying about that anymore, okay?"

"I'll try, but I can't help it."

"Why?" Alex asked with interest.

"Because I promised my father that I would always take care of mama, no matter what."

"You haven't broken your promise, Robert. Right now you need time to recover, so that when your mama comes back you'll be healthy and happy," Alex responded confidently. "You need to worry about yourself right now, okay? You need to get better."

"I know, and I promise I'll try not to think about it anymore. I feel better knowing that you took mama somewhere where she's okay"

"She's fine, Robert. Now we just have to get you better," offered a sincere Alex.

"But I feel fine, Alex. I don't feel sick," Robert said with consternation.

"I know you do, but you had a bad accident and it's going to take time for you to get better."

"Okay. I believe you, Alex."

Alex looked desperately to change the subject, "Robert, can I ask you something?"

"Sure," Robert replied with intrigue.

"What do you want to be when you grow up?"

"I just wanna be able to take care of me and mama."

"I know that, but let's just say that you and your mama had a perfect life. What would you want to be if you didn't have to work and take care of your mama?"

"I never really thought about it cause it'll never happen," Robert answered stoically.

"Well, think about it okay? What would your dreams be?"

"My father said dreams never come true," Robert answered plainly.

"They do, Robert. Trust me … dreams do come true," Alex replied painfully at the thought that Robert was never allowed to dream. The one thing that Robert always told Alex when Alex was growing up was that he should always reach for his dreams.

"I wish I was a pilot," Robert said guiltily.

"Really," Alex answered with a smile.

"Yeah. Sometimes when things are really bad, I wish I could fly away," Robert said with a distant look in his eye.

"That's wonderful, Robert."

"But it'll never come true," Robert answered matter-of-factly.
"You don't know that. Sometimes God works in mysterious ways."

# CHAPTER 13

▼

Three and a half weeks had passed since Robert and Anna were both admitted to the hospital, and both were recovering without incident. Alex visited with Robert everyday and with his grandmother every other day. Concerned about the circumstances of Anna's marriage to George, Alex went to his grandmother's doctor and asked her to notify him if there were any changes in his grandmother's condition.

Early one morning before Alex went to see Robert, Anna's doctor called Alex and asked to speak with him. Emily went along with Alex to the hospital to spend some time with Robert while Alex met with Anna's doctor. As Alex knocked on the doctor's office door, he heard George's voice from behind him. "Alex, what are you doing here?"

"I'm here to speak with my grandmother's doctor," Alex answered contemptuously.

"Oh," George replied surprised. "The doctor called me and said she wanted to see me."

"Well I guess we'll both find out what's going on with my grandmother's health. We both want the best for her, don't we?" Alex said sarcastically.

"Absolutely, I only want the best for the woman I love," George answered disingenuously.

"Good," Alex said mockingly. "Let's go talk with the doctor."

The doctor waved Alex and George into her office and asked them to take a seat. She poured herself a cup of coffee and asked the two if they wanted a cup. Both refused. Alex shifted uncomfortably in his chair and the doctor noticed his unease.

"Mr. Petrovic. Mr. Pennington. I called you both in to speak to you about Anna's progress, since you both have been part of her recovery. At this point, we have done all we can for Anna here at the hospital."

"What are you talking about?" George cut her off and replied with hostility. "She can't speak and half her body is paralyzed."

"That's correct, Mr. Pennington. What I was about to say is that Anna can either go home with options or to a rehabilitation facility."

Alex interrupted, "You mean a nursing home?"

"Not a nursing home in the way you probably think of a nursing home. What she needs is a skilled facility that offers physical therapy to get her mobile and speech therapy to help her learn to speak again."

"What did you mean when you said she could go home with options?" Alex asked.

"Well, she could go home as long as someone was there with her all the time and she could have visiting nurses come to her home, as well as physical therapists and speech therapists."

Alex nodded his head in understanding, "Doctor, what would you recommend?"

"This is totally the family's decision, but my recommendation would be a rehab facility like I mentioned," the doctor said sincerely.

"Could you recommend to us the best place?" George asked solemnly.

"The best place I know is Saint Michaels. They have an excellent facility with experienced therapists and nurses."

"Could you call them and arrange for someone to meet with us today?" Alex inquired.

"Sure, I'll call right now." The doctor looked up the number and called while George and Alex quietly spoke about the decision they were about to make. "Sister Gabrielle can meet with you at 10:30 this morning, if that is okay?" interrupted the doctor.

Alex and George looked at each other silently as Alex answered, "Yes, that's fine."

The doctor spoke a few more moments with Sister Gabrielle on the telephone about the specifics of Anna's condition before hanging up to once again speak with Alex and George. "I told Sister Gabrielle some of the specifics of Anna's condition so that she can answer any questions you may have for her. Everyone associated with Saint Michael's is very nice and helpful, so don't be afraid to ask anything, okay?

"Thank you, doctor, for arranging this for us," Alex replied gratefully.

"With the help of therapists and time, Anna should recover fully."

"So, after we meet with the nun, and if we like the place, what happens next? Will she go there today?" George asked crudely.

"If you like Saint Michael's after speaking with Sister Gabrielle, tell her that you want to admit Anna today. She'll give you some paperwork to fill out, and then she'll call us to make further arrangements."

"Then my grandmother should be moved in to Saint Michael's by this after-noon, if we like the place," stated Alex.

"Yes, but only if you feel comfortable sending her there. There are other places that you can check out if you don't like Saint Michael's."

"Good," answered George.

Alex looked down at his watch, "It's quarter after nine. Is Saint Michael's the one that's located out on Montague Drive?"

"Yes, it's on Montague Drive," replied the doctor.

"Okay George, I'll meet you there in about an hour, okay?"

"Don't you want to go together?" George asked.

"I can't. I have somewhere to go before Saint Michael's, but I'll meet you there. Wait in the parking lot if you get there before me," Alex commanded, fully knowing that he would never let George arrive there before him.

"Okay," George stammered.

Alex got up and pushed in his chair as he reached across the doctor's desk to shake her hand, "Thank you, doctor. For everything."

"Your welcome, Mr. Petrovic," she answered with a smile as she came around the desk to escort Alex and George out of the office.

*      *      *      *

Alex rushed down the hallway and into the elevator to elude George. George was unaware of Robert's hospitalization, as was almost everyone else, and he did not want George to find out about it. As Alex stepped off the elevator, he glimpsed his wife and Robert strolling down the hallway with coffee mugs in their hands. Emily and Robert laughed playfully at something as they observed a smiling Alex watching them.

"Hi guys," Alex said in greeting.

Robert took Alex buy the sleeve and pulled him aside. Alex quickly developed a look of anxiety as Robert spoke seriously, "Alex, you really need to see a doc-tor."

Alex asked grimly, "Why?"

"You need your eyes checked if you think she looks like a guy," replied Robert with a mischievous smile as he playfully put his arm around Alex's shoulder.

Emily laughed deeply at Robert's mischievousness and Alex's gullibility. "He's right you know," Emily said playfully.

Alex smirked before playfully putting Robert in a side headlock as he messed up Robert's hair. "Always the smart aleck, huh?" And what's the meaning of getting my wife involved in your wisecracking?" Alex inquired good-naturedly.

"He just wishes he was part of the team," joked Emily.

"Impossible," Robert said humorously, "He's too serious. He needs to lighten up."

Alex, Emily and Robert all enjoyed a lasting laugh before Alex broke the light-hearted mood. "Guys, uh, I mean, Robert, Emily, I have to go out for a little while, but I won't be long."

"Where you going?" inquired Emily.

"I have to go meet someone regarding the meeting I had this morning," Alex replied.

"Oh, is everything okay?" asked a concerned Emily.

"Yeah, everything is fine, and the future looks really good regarding what we talked about in the meeting," Alex answered happily.

"Will you be back later?" Robert asked hopefully.

"Of course I'll be back later. I shouldn't be that long."

"Okay, we'll be here waiting for you," Emily said sincerely.

"Robert, don't corrupt my wife. The last thing I need is a Bonnie and Clyde on my hands," Alex said teasingly.

"I'll be on my best behavior.... Scout's honor," Robert laughed as he held up the scout's salute.

Alex laughed as he kissed Emily on the cheek.

"Come on Alex, she's your wife, not your sister. Kiss her like you're supposed to," Robert teased relentlessly.

"Did they serve smart-ass cereal this morning?" Alex wryly questioned as Emily laughed uncontrollably at Robert's good-natured gibes.

"Of course not. I was born this way," Robert said with mischievous pride.

"Well then, on that note, I have to leave. Emily, watch out for this guy. He'll turn you into a smart aleck just like him."

"Hey," Robert said smirking, "Where's my kiss on the cheek?"

Alex went over and planted a big kiss on Robert's forehead, and then pulled Emily into a deep, passionate kiss. He looked back at Robert and asked jovially, "Was that better?"

"You're getting better, but you still need lots of work," Robert joked.

# CHAPTER 14

▼

Outside the main entrance to the stately Saint Michael's, Sister Gabrielle talked quietly with a resident of the facility as she waited for the arrival of her next appointment. Sitting in the parking lot, Alex jotted down a list of questions that he wanted answered before deciding to send his grandmother to this facility. After a few brief moments, George pulled into the parking lot with a look of dismay registering on his face, although he denied anything being wrong when questioned by Alex.

Sister Gabrielle, dressed in a black skirt, white button-down blouse, and a gray cardigan sweater, with a black habit that hid most of her curly, graying hair, met Alex and George with a friendly smile. She introduced herself as she led the two men into her office and offered them a cup of coffee, which they both declined. George annoyingly introduced himself as Anna's husband, and then introduced Alex to the affable nun.

"It's nice to meet you both. I got the basic information this morning regarding Anna from her doctor as you know, but I'd like to know how she's doing from the two of you."

"She can't move anything on her one side, and she can't speak," George explained.

"She's completely with it mentally, I mean she is coherent and knows what is going on around her. She can communicate with us by writing. She tries to talk, but gets very frustrated," Alex explained further.

"So you believe that she has a very strong desire to recover?" the nun asked.

"Absolutely. My grandmother is a very feisty lady, and not being able to move about or communicate is probably driving her crazy," Alex offered with a smile.

"That's good to hear. Successful therapy depends a lot on the desire of the patient to recover. Therapy isn't easy, so a strong will is necessary," the nun spelled out.

"Well, Sister, you won't find a woman with a stronger will than Anna," replied George. "My wife has an iron will," he said proudly.

"Excellent," stated the nun with a smile. "Let me take you around and show you our facility, and then I'll answer any questions you may have, okay?"

The two men nodded silently as they followed Sister Gabrielle out of her office. The Sister gave them a complete tour of the facility, including the patient residence and rehabilitation wing, which included every type of exercise machine, a whirlpool, and a swimming pool. Sister Gabrielle introduced them to several physical therapists, registered nurses, and licensed practical nurses; everybody who would be involved in patient care.

While Sister Gabrielle stepped away for a brief moment to answer a phone call, Alex and George discussed what they thought of Saint Michael's. They both agreed that Saint Michael's was the best possible place for Anna to recover.

"We'll have to discuss with the nun how we're going to pay for this," George stated matter-of-factly.

"That's not a problem. I'm sure that Anna has money in her checking account. We'll just have to get authorization to have it withdrawn," Alex stated arrogantly.

"I can do that," George answered, "I have Anna's Power of Attorney."

"How did you get her Power of Attorney?" Alex asked with irritation and concern.

"I had to pay the bills, so when Anna was able to understand, I asked her if she thought it would be a good idea so that I could pay her bills, and she thought it was," George replied unpleasantly.

"How did you get an attorney to draw up the papers with grandmother unable to communicate?" Alex asked with increasing hostility.

"The attorney came and met with Anna, and then he spoke with the doctor, and the doctor reassured him that Anna was coherent. The witnesses also swore that Anna was of sound mind," George responded conceitedly.

Alex shook his head and walked away from George as Sister Gabrielle hung up the phone. She led Alex and George back to her office to discuss any concerns that the two might have had. "Do either of you gentlemen have any questions for me?" she asked politely.

"Yes, I do," Alex replied. "What if my grandmother needs to see a doctor?"

"It can usually be arranged so that the patient's own doctor, if coming directly from Memorial, can come see her here, but if that doctor isn't available, we always have doctors on-call," she explained.

Alex nodded his head in approval, "I'm sure my grandmother would like to keep her own doctor."

"Yeah, she likes her a lot," George replied.

"Any other questions?" asked Sister Gabrielle.

"She can have visitors and stuff, just like the hospital?" Alex questioned.

"Oh yes. We encourage the family to visit as much as possible. In fact, strong family support plays a big role in how well a patient recovers," she said with a smile.

"I have a question," George interrupted. "How much will it cost for Anna to come here?"

"According to what the doctor has told me, and I'll have to get Anna's medical records from the hospital to confirm this, but I would say approximately four thousand dollars per month," responded Sister Gabrielle.

"Wow, that much?" George said crudely.

"That's fine, Sister. You have a wonderful facility here, and I'm sure my grandmother will get the best care possible," Alex interjected.

"This is a very nice place," George stated.

"No amount of money is too great if she gets better," Alex said sarcastically.

"Well, okay then, is there any other question?"

"No, I don't think so," Alex replied. "What happens now?"

"I'll have you fill out the necessary papers, and then I'll call the hospital and arrange for them to get Anna ready to be transferred here," the nun said in a business-like tone.

"How will she be transferred?" George asked.

"I'll arrange for an ambulance to go pick her up. Wait here a moment, gentlemen, and I'll get the paperwork," Sister Gabrielle responded as she left the room.

"Alex, can you tell Anna that it was your idea to send her here? I don't want her to think that I don't want to take care of her," George asked with mock sincerity.

"Yeah, I'll tell her it was my idea. I think she'll get the best care possible here, and I really think that this is the only way that she'll physically recover," Alex said truthfully.

As the two exchanged small talk, Sister Gabrielle brought in the necessary paperwork and laid it out in front of George and Alex, explaining what each page was all about. She showed George where to sign each document, and he signed without hesitation until it came to the financial document.

"How are you going to be paying for Anna's care?" the nun stated casually.

"What are the options?" asked Alex. "Can the money be taken directly out of my grandmother's checking or savings account?"

"If your grandmother's name is the only one on the account, she'll have to sign for automatic withdrawal from any of her bank accounts," Sister Gabrielle informed.

"George has my grandmother's Power of Attorney, so he can sign for that right now, can't he?" Alex said arrogantly.

"Yes, absolutely, if he's her Power of Attorney. Just sign right here on this line, Mr. Pennington, and we'll have the funds automatically withdrawn from Anna's account every month," Sister Gabrielle stated as she pointed out the correct place for George to sign.

George looked at Alex with venomous eyes as he signed the document. Alex had turned out to be more of a problem than Robert, George thought.

"Okay, everything seems to be in order," Sister Gabrielle replied with a smile. "I'll call the hospital for them to get Anna ready along with her medical records, and then I'll call the ambulance to have her transferred here."

"When do you think that will be?" Alex inquired.

"Probably this afternoon sometime," she answered. "It would be a good idea to talk with Anna and tell her about Saint Michael's before she arrives. Tell her that you have been here, and what you think of our facility. I'd also suggest to you, Mr. Pennington, that you come along with your wife in the ambulance so that she isn't frightened."

"I can do that," George grumbled, still angry over having to sign away Anna's money.

"Good. If you have any questions, either of you, please call me anytime," Sister Gabrielle said sincerely.

"Thank you Sister Gabrielle," Alex replied as he shook her hand. "I know that everyone here will take good care of my grandmother."

"Goodbye, Mr. Pennington, I'll see you this afternoon, right?" questioned the nun.

"Yeah, I'll be back when Anna comes."

"I'll see you then, and I hope to see you soon too, Mr. Petrovic."

"I'll try to stop in tonight, but if not tonight, first thing tomorrow," Alex responded truthfully.

"Take care, gentlemen, and goodbye," Sister Gabrielle said with a smile.

# CHAPTER 15

▼

Anna accepted her new accommodations without complaint and settled in nicely. With his grandmother in a place where he knew she would be taken care of, Alex focused all of his attention on Robert. Day after day, Robert continued to make progress, although he failed to regain any of his memory.

One morning before Alex went in to see Robert, the second floor head nurse stopped Alex as he got off the elevator and told him that Dr. Hamilton wished to see him. Alex went directly to Dr. Hamilton's office before going on to see Robert. As he knocked on the door, Alex heard the familiar sound of Dr. Hamilton's cheerful voice asking Alex to come in. Alex walked in anxiously as if to expect something bad had happened.

"Good morning, Alex."

"Good morning, Dr. Hamilton." Alex paused, "Did something happen?"

Noticing the apparent anxiety written on Alex's young face, Dr. Hamilton quickly alleviated Alex's fears, "No, I'm sorry I alarmed you. I've got good news."

"Really. I could use some of that," Alex said with a smile.

"I think Robert is doing exceptionally well. Well enough, in fact, to be released," the doctor said cheerfully.

"That's great," Alex said with mixed optimism. "What happens now? Does he get to come home?"

"That's up to you, but I would recommend that he go to a residential psychiatric facility."

"What do you mean, it's up to me?" Alex asked curiously.

"It's your decision, Alex. In all intents and purposes, you are Robert's guardian. He cannot be released without supervision, and he's obviously not capable of being on his own," the doctor stated matter-of-factly.

"So he could go home if I agreed to take care of him full-time?"

"Yes, but that's a lot of responsibility, Alex. I know you have a life of your own, and I commend you for your commitment so far to your father," Dr. Hamilton said appreciatively.

"What type of facility are you talking about?" Alex asked skeptically.

"It's the best psychiatric facility for your father's particular problems, and it's not far from here, so you could visit often."

"What's it called?"

"Alta Vista. It's a good place, Alex. I'm sure they could help Robert."

"I don't know, doctor. I don't feel good about this. When you say psychiatric facility, I think 'asylum.'" Alex stated anxiously.

"No, no, it's nothing like that," the doctor replied reassuringly.

"Honestly, Dr. Hamilton, if it were your father, would you send him there?" Alex questioned.

"Yes, without hesitation," came the response from Dr. Hamilton.

"But you wouldn't be his doctor any longer, would you?" asked a dejected Alex.

"I can stay on as his doctor and supervise his progress by keeping in touch with the staff at Alta Vista, and also by visiting once or twice a week."

"Would you do that?" Alex asked optimistically.

"Of course. I want to see Robert get better, and I'll stay on as his doctor until that happens," the doctor stated sincerely.

"That sounds great. As long as you think this place is the best, then I say fine, but can you wait a few days before sending him there?"

"That's no problem, but can I ask why?" asked the doctor.

"I have to go back home to tie up some loose ends, and then Emily, the kids, and I are moving back here. I don't know if it'll be permanently, but right now we need to be here."

Dr. Hamilton smiled, "You know, Robert is really lucky to have you. I never would have thought I'd be saying that after our first meeting, but I'm really glad that I'm able to."

"I never thought I'd be saying that I'm happy to be moving back here, but somewhere along the line, I realized how much I love him," Alex said truthfully.

"I'm really happy to hear that, Alex. I think I told you a long time ago that when Robert regains his memory, you both will be better off for being in each other's lives," Dr. Hamilton said sincerely.

"I didn't believe you at the time, but now I do. Each day I learn something new about his life and what he had to go through growing up. He made a lot of sacrifices."

"He's a good man, Alex."

"I know, I've always known, but it was easier to dislike him than to think otherwise," Alex said honestly.

"So do you accept his lifestyle now, or will things fall apart when he starts looking for a relationship—after he's recovered his memory, of course?" the doctor asked.

"I can accept his lifestyle. I've thought long and hard about this, and my conclusion is if he can find happiness and someone to love and have that love returned, then I'll be happy for him," replied Alex genuinely.

"I'm impressed with your change of attitude, Alex. No matter who he loves, he'll always be the same man," the doctor stated candidly.

"I know."

"What made you change your mind?"

"I thought about how much I love Emily, and how I wouldn't give her up for anyone, and that's what I was trying to do to Robert. I was trying to withhold my love and acceptance so that he would give up Mitchell. He loved Mitchell like I love Emily, and because of me Mitchell is no longer in his life."

"Why is that?" Dr. Hamilton asked, intrigued by what Alex would say.

"Mitchell told me that he broke up with Robert because Robert didn't want to jeopardize my political career by being seen in public with Mitchell. He sacrificed his happiness with Mitchell because of me," Alex said sadly.

"Do you think things could be worked out between them when Robert regains his memory? I mean, do you think Robert and Mitchell still love each other?"

"I know Robert still loves Mitchell. It was Mitchell who broke things off, but I know Mitchell still loves Robert, even if he's unwilling to admit that to me."

"Well that's good. Maybe since you were the cause of the breakup, you can also be the cause for the reconciliation," Dr. Hamilton said optimistically.

"Do you really think so?"

"Absolutely. Anything's possible," replied the doctor with a smile.

"I hope you're right."

"The doctor's always right," Dr. Hamilton said with a laugh.

"Well, so far you have a pretty good track record."

Dr. Hamilton laughed heartily, "On that note I have to go make rounds. I don't want you to think me some kind of egomaniac."

"What? A doctor an egomaniac? I never would have thought it," Alex joked.

"So, we'll set things up for Alta Vista when you get back?"

"Yeah, Today's Tuesday, right? I should be back Friday afternoon."

"Okay, we'll get things started on Friday, and Alex," he paused, "Don't worry about Robert while you're gone. He'll be fine."

"I know Robert will be fine as long as you are here."

"Have a safe trip, Alex, and don't worry about things here. Things are starting to look up, so we have ever reason to be optimistic."

"Thanks, Dr. Hamilton … for everything," Alex said sincerely.

"You're welcome. Have a good trip, and take some time to relax with your wife and kids. You deserve it."

"I will," Alex replied as he stood and shook Dr. Hamilton's hand. "Take care, doc, and I'll see you soon."

"Bye," said the doctor as Alex walked out of his office.

Alex took several moments to collect his thoughts before going in to see Robert. He knew Robert would be disappointed by Alex's impending absence, but he knew Robert would be all right as long as Dr. Hamilton was watching over him.

Alex pushed the door open, and smiled, "Hi Robert, how are you today?"

"I'm good, how are you?" Robert replied with a smile.

"I'm fine, but I have to tell you something that I hope doesn't disappoint you too much," Alex said hesitantly.

"What?" Robert asked sadly.

"I have to go out of town for a few days, but I should be back on Friday,"

"Oh, that's okay, Alex. I understand," Robert said trying to hide his disappointment.

"I hate to leave you, but I have to take care of some business. Would you like it if I bring you something back from my trip?" Alex said trying to assuage his own guilt.

"You don't have to. I'll be okay" Robert answered trying to alleviate Alex's worrying.

"Are you sure?" Alex asked concerned.

"Yeah, I'm sure. When do you have to go?"

"I can stay until after lunch, and then I have to go," Alex said sadly.

"Is Emily going with you?"

"Yeah, but I promise we'll be back on Friday."

"It's okay, Alex. Really, I understand. You and Emily have a life of your own, and you shouldn't be spending every free minute with me, even though I appreciate all you do for me," Robert replied sincerely.

"Emily and I enjoy spending time with you, Robert. We come here because we want to, not because we feel like we have to," Alex said matter-of-factly.

"I'm just saying that you two deserve to have some time to yourselves, not being stuck in some hospital," Robert replied.

"Okay, Robert, I promise that Emily and I will take some time to relax. Will that make you happy?"

"Yeah, that and maybe a million dollars and a ticket out of this place," Robert said wryly.

"That's the Robert I like—the smart aleck," Alex laughed.

# CHAPTER 16

▼

Late Tuesday afternoon, Alex, Emily and the twins packed a few things before boarding the private jet that would take them back to their lives. The twins played a game in the corner of the private jet as Emily and Alex sat back in their reclining seats for a few moments of relaxation. Alex had dealt with imminent problems over the telephone by giving directions to Danielle, but the time had come that he had to go back to his office and deal with things in person.

Emily reached out and took Alex's hand in hers as she gently squeezed, "You are going to meet with the consultant, aren't you?" she asked hopefully.

"I don't know, Em. I have so much on my mind right now."

"It won't hurt to meet with him, Alex. You need to keep your options open," she said slightly irritated.

"I know," Alex said knowing Emily was right.

"Meet with him, Alex, and just listen to what he has to say, okay? That's all I'm asking," she said sincerely.

"Okay, I'll meet with him," Alex replied with a smile.

When the family arrived at the airport, Emily's mother picked up Emily, Alex and the twins and took them to their home. The family spent Wednesday taking care of family issues and spending time with Emily's mother and father. Alex and Emily kept Robert's condition a secret from her family, but they sensed something was amiss, although they did not bring up the subject.

On Thursday, Alex took a cab to the office where Danielle was waiting in his office, typing out an important document for him to sign.

Leaning against the doorframe to his office, Alex said happily, "I'm glad that some people still work around here."

"Hey, boss. Welcome back," Danielle responded with a huge smile.

"Thanks, Danielle. How's things going?"

"Not too bad, but I'm glad to have you back," Danielle replied sincerely.

Changing the subject, Alex walked behind her to stare at the computer screen that she had been working on, "What are working on?"

"A directive that you'll have to sign. The Chairman said he wanted to see it finished by the end of the day."

"Good thing I got here when I did, but there's something I have to do before we get started and then I need to talk to you."

"Is everything okay?" Danielle asked with concern.

"There's a lot going on and I'll tell you about some of it later, but right now I have to go find the Chairman."

"He was in his office just a few minutes ago," Danielle replied.

"Thanks," Alex said quickly as he headed toward the Chairman's office. When he arrived at the Chairman's office, Alex poked his head through the open doorway, and asked, "Excuse me, sir. Do you have a minute?"

"Well, hello Alex. It's been a long time," the Chairman replied politely.

"Hi Sir. I'm sorry that I haven't been around for such a long time," Alex said genuinely.

"Come in," the Chairman said as he motioned for Alex to sit down.

"Thank you, sir."

"What can I do for you, Alex?" inquired the Chairman.

"Sir, I appreciate the time that you have given me off through family leave, but I'm afraid that I'm going to have to resign my position because I need to be with my family right now," Alex stated with surprise that he spoke without reluctance.

"Is there anything that I can do?" the Chairman asked sincerely.

"No, sir, but thank you for asking."

"I hate to see you resign, but I admire your commitment to your family. That type of commitment is the cornerstone of what our party was founded on." The Chairman rose from his seat and handed Alex a cigar. "You have a bright future ahead of you in this party, Alex, and if there is anything that I can ever do for you, please let me know."

"Thank you, sir. I appreciate everything that you have done for me," Alex replied.

"Just don't give up. Politics will be waiting for you when you're ready."

"I know, but politics is the last thing that's on my mind right now," Alex stated honestly.

"Take care of your family, Alex, and everything else will take care of its self," offered the Chairman.

"I hope you're right, Mr. Chairman," Alex said with hope.

"Always," he laughed, "It's just that nobody else sees that."

Alex laughed, "Thanks again, sir."

"Keep in touch, okay? Let us know how you're doing from time to time, and if you ever need anything, call me."

"Bye sir, and I'll try to keep in touch, and I promise I'll get the directive out before I leave today."

"Bye, Alex."

"Sir, one last thing. Danielle will keep her current position, won't she?" Alex asked.

"Yes, of course. Danielle is worth her weight in gold," the Chairman smiled.

"Good. That was my biggest concern," Alex said with obvious relief as he stood and shook his boss's hand before leaving the office.

Alex walked slowly back to his office, reliving all the happy times that he had spent in his Party office. He paused outside his office as he silently watched Danielle type on his computer. He had worked with Danielle for several years, and besides Emily, nobody knew him better. He knew that he would hurt Danielle by his decision, but he knew she would understand and want the best for him.

Danielle, sensing that someone was watching her, turned around and smiled when she realized that it was Alex who was staring. "How did your meeting go?"

"Good," Alex stated as he walked into his office and closed the door behind him. "I need to talk to you, Danielle. It's very important."

"Sure, go ahead," she said with intrigue.

"Danielle, I went to tell the Chairman that I'm resigning," Alex said as he searched for disappointment in Danielle's face.

"Why?" she asked with surprise.

"There's a lot going on at home, Danielle. Things that I haven't told you about," Alex responded softly.

"Oh," she said staggered. "Is it your grandmother?"

"Partially," Alex stated with avoidance.

"Is there anything I can do?" Danielle asked with concern.

"No, but thanks for asking. I talked to the Chairman, and your position is secure. He said you are worth your weight in gold," Alex said with a smile.

Danielle returned his smile but with sadness in her eyes, "I'll miss you, Alex."

"I'll miss you too," Alex said sadly as he pulled Danielle into a hug. "But," he paused, "I'll keep in touch."

"You better," she laughed as she returned his embrace.

The rest of the day went quickly as Alex finished up last minute business. He spent most of the time talking with Danielle about upcoming projects and the people that she would most likely be working with. Danielle caught Alex up on the recent gossip, and Alex loved hearing about every sordid detail. When the day came to an end, Alex and Danielle reluctantly said goodbye as they held each other in a friendly embrace. Danielle kissed him on the cheek and walked away.

Later that evening, Alex met with the political consultant that Emily wanted him to see. The consultant, a gray-haired, short, husky man in his mid-fifties named Berrett Anderson, spoke with Alex at great lengths over an elegant dinner at a popular political nightclub. "Alex, from the preliminary numbers that I have seen, you have an excellent chance of being elected in the next election."

"Thank you, Mr. Anderson, but I'm not sure if I want to run yet."

"Yes, of course, and I don't want to rush you, but the sooner you get started, the better your chances," Mr. Anderson explained with the zeal of a salesman.

"I understand that, but right now I have a lot on my mind," Alex said with annoyance.

"Okay, but keep what I said in mind. I'd love to run your campaign, Alex, but if you'd rather have someone else, I'll respect that."

"If I run, Mr. Anderson, I'll want you to run my campaign. It's just that I have a lot to deal with right now," Alex replied matter-of-factly.

"Okay, just don't wait too long to contact me," Berrett Anderson said as he told Alex goodbye.

"I'll keep that in mind," Alex said aloud as he finished his drink and paid the waiter who had brought the bill.

Alex sighed heavily as he waited for the valet to retrieve his car. He was relieved that he would be going home to Robert's house the next day. He worried about Robert, but he had to take care of his personal matters before he could devote all his attention to Robert's well-being.

# CHAPTER 17

▼

As the private jet landed on the small runway in Alex's hometown, Alex's car remained in the parking lot where he had left it only three days before. A cab waited next to Alex's car to take Emily and the twins back to Robert's home, as Alex prepared to go to the hospital to check up on Robert.

"I shouldn't be too long, Emily. I'm just going to drop in and say hello, and hopefully I'll be home for dinner."

"That would be nice, but I won't count on it until I see you pulling into the driveway," Emily said with a smile.

"Keep your fingers crossed," Alex replied as he started to pull away.

"Always," Emily responded as she crossed her fingers in a loving gesture.

"Bye, honey, I love you," Alex said happily. "Bye, Stevie. Bye Steffi. I love you," he said with joy as he spoke to his children before he drove away.

The drive to the hospital went by in a daydream as Alex hurriedly weaved in and out of midday school bus traffic. He pulled into the parking lot and sprinted out of the car and into the hospital with a whimsical feeling as he carried a book about pilot training that he had bought Robert as a promised gift.

As he pushed the door open to Robert's room, he froze with panic as he stared at the empty room. He looked in the closet for any signs of Robert's belongings, but he found nothing. The panic gripped his heart as he rushed down the hallway to the nurses' station. He gasped for breath as he looked for a nurse, but none were visible anywhere in the hallway. He raced down another corridor as he peered into each room, hoping to find a nurse who could tell him where Robert was, and why he had been taken out of his room.

Alex turned a corner and came face to face with a familiar nurse. He took a few deep breaths before speaking, "Nurse, where's my father?"

"He was discharged into a facility on Wednesday morning. Didn't you know about it?" The nurse asked naively.

"NO," Alex shouted. "Where's Dr. Hamilton? Damn him, he agreed we wouldn't move Robert until I got back."

"Mr. Petrovic, Dr. Hamilton was called away on a family emergency late Tuesday night and he hasn't returned yet. The doctor who was filling in for Dr. Hamilton released Robert," the nurse said informatively.

"Where did they send him?" Alex asked with barely controlled anger.

"Mar de Luz Psychiatric Facility."

"I've never heard of it. Where's it at?" Alex questioned angrily.

"It's about 35 minutes north. It used to be the old county home," the nurse answered calmly.

"DAMN," Alex shouted. "Robert was supposed to be sent to Alta Vista when I got back. He probably thinks I abandoned him," Alex said with an audible choking in his voice and sadness in his eyes before he turned and ran to catch an open elevator out of the hospital.

Alex broke all speed records on his way to Mar de Luz as heartbreaking scenarios played out in his mind. Alex fought back tears as he remembered telling Robert that Robert would be safe while Alex was gone, and now the worst thing imaginable had happened … Robert would now see Alex as a liar, and the trust between them would be compromised, resulting in compromised treatment and recovery for Robert.

Alex's stomach churned as he pulled into the parking lot of Mar de Luz. All the fears that he had expressed to Dr. Hamilton about sending Robert to an asylum were dancing in his mind and sticking in his throat. Alex ran in the front door and stopped at the desk where a young, pregnant woman typed on the computer.

"Nurse," Alex said politely, but with a note of command in his voice. The nurse did not respond. "Nurse," Alex stated louder, but still without result. Alex reached over the counter and turned off the computer monitor. "Nurse," he said angrily again.

"Why the hell did you do that?" She snapped as she looked at her monitor.

"Pay attention. Where is my father … his name is Robert Petrovic?" Alex replied as his anger threatened to overwhelm him.

The nurse turned her monitor back on and pulled up the screen that offered the room numbers of patients. "He's in room 29A," she answered unpleasantly.

"Thank you," Alex said sarcastically. He looked at the room numbers and headed in the direction of room 29. As he approached the room, he felt a tightening in his stomach that made him stop to collect his thoughts before pushing the door open.

"Oh my God," Alex cried as he covered his mouth with his hand. "Robert, oh God Robert, what have they done to you?"

Robert lay completely still in the narrow bed, being restrained at the wrists, ankles and waist and staring blankly at the ceiling. A curtain separated the room between Robert and the other patient who had the bed by the outer wall. A tray full of food sat untouched on the side of Robert's bed.

"Robert, can you hear me?" Alex asked with tears in his eyes as he leaned in close to Robert's face. Robert continued to stare blankly at the ceiling.

"Dammit," Alex cried as he went to the door and called for a nurse. A short, dark-haired nurse came running.

"What is the meaning of this shouting?" the nurse demanded.

"Why is Robert restrained to his bed?"

"Because he broke the rules and was somewhere he wasn't supposed to be," the nurse replied angrily.

"Did anyone tell him what the goddamned rules were?" Alex asked with equal hostility.

"No, but that doesn't negate the fact that he broke the rules and we can't allow the patient's to do whatever they like."

"When did this happen?"

"Wednesday"

Alex's face burned red with hatred, "You mean he has been restrained since Wednesday? What the hell is the matter with you people! Don't bother answering that because I'm taking my father out of here."

"Insult us all you want, but you can't take him out of here without a court order," the nurse replied sarcastically.

"Fine, that won't be a problem," Alex said bitterly. "In the meantime, when was the last time my father ate?"

The nurse motioned for a nurse's assistant to bring Robert's chart to her. She looked in it and replied, "He had orange juice for breakfast."

Alex shook his head in disbelief, "Why hasn't he had anything to eat this afternoon? I see a tray in the room."

"Sir, there are other patients besides your father who also need to eat. Once there is an assistant available, he'll get fed."

"Listen to me," Alex said with danger in his voice. "There better be a hot tray of food in Robert's room within the next five minutes, or I'm going to call the local television news station. Do you understand? I'll feed him, just bring me the damn tray!"

"Have it your way," the nurse said nonchalantly as she walked away.

The nurse's assistant came up to Alex and touched him on the arm, "Sir, your father hasn't really eaten since he got here. He had pudding on Wednesday, nothing yesterday except some orange juice and apple sauce, and then orange juice again today."

Alex stared at her with shock evident on his face, "Miss, can I ask you something?"

"I guess so," she replied hesitantly.

"What rule did he break, and did they do anything else to him beside restrain him?"

"The rule was that he went down a restricted hallway to a water fountain, but I don't know anything about your other question," she answered sincerely.

Alex shook his head and the nurse walked away. Alex pulled out his cell phone and dialed Antonio Daniels' office number, the attorney who had previously bailed Robert out of jail. "Antonio," Alex said into the phone.

"Yes, this is Antonio."

"This is Alex Petrovic."

"Hi Alex, what can I do for you?"

"Antonio, I need your help. It's an emergency. My father has been committed to a place called Mar de Luz."

Antonio interrupted, "What? That place is a hellhole."

"Believe me, I know. I'm here now, and they have been starving him. He was committed here without my consent when I went back home for three days to tie up some loose ends," Alex continued, "Now the nurse says he can't be released without a court order."

"I'll have one for you within the next hour. I have a meeting with a judge in fifteen minutes, and I'll ask him for a court order allowing you to get Robert out of that place."

"Thanks, Antonio," Alex replied with relief.

"Just stay close to Robert and don't allow them to do anything to him, okay? I'll drive out with the court order as soon as I get it."

"Thanks again, Antonio."

"No problem, just hang on a little while longer and this will all be over."

As Alex flipped his cell phone shut, the nurse wheeled up a hot tray of food and set it in front of Robert's door. Alex glared at the woman as he pushed the tray into Robert's room and beside his bed. Alex pulled up a chair and sat down next to Robert. Alex stroked Robert's hair gently as he spoke, "Robert, I'm going to get you out of here, I promise."

Robert continued to stare without acknowledging that Alex was sitting next to him. "This wasn't supposed to happen, Robert. I swear I never would have left," Alex said sadly. "Please forgive me, Robert. I know you probably won't trust me again, but please believe that I will never let anyone hurt you ever again."

Robert shut his eyes tightly and turned his head away from Alex. "Robert, please look at me," Alex pleaded.

Robert slowly turned his head, but his eyes would not focus. "While we're waiting for the court order so that I can take you home, I need you to try to eat, okay? I'll help you, but first we're going to take these off," Alex said as he released the restraints that held Robert motionless.

"Is that better?" Alex asked and Robert nodded slightly. "Robert, have they given you anything that's making you sleepy?"

Robert tried desperately to focus his eyes on Alex's calming voice, but to no avail. Alex took Robert's thin, cold hand in his and Robert squeezed gently. "It's all right, Robert. I know it's hard to concentrate when they give you all that medicine," Alex said apologetically.

As Robert took a bite off of the fork that Alex held for him, a male nurse and a male orderly came through the door of Robert's room. "Sir, you're going to have to step outside while we give him his medication."

Robert turned pale from panic, but Alex gently held his hand as Alex responded, "You're not giving him anything else. I'm waiting for a court order, which should be here in the next half hour. If you force the issue, I'll make sure you both are brought up on charges," Alex said maliciously as he moved his chair closer to Robert.

"Have it your way," the male nurse responded as they both left the room.

"Hey," Alex yelled, "Wait a minute."

The orderly and the nurse returned to the room, not wanting to cause a commotion.

"Why have you been doping him up? Isn't being tied down enough, or is that how you get your jollies?" Alex said bitterly as the male nurse and orderly smugly left the room.

Alex turned and looked at Robert and saw the sheer terror on Robert's face. Alex reached up and gently brushed the hair off of Robert's forehead as he smiled reassuringly at the terrified man lying in the bed. Alex picked the fork up from the food tray and held it out for Robert, but Robert closed his eyes tightly and turned his head away from Alex.

"Robert," Alex said gently with no reply. "Robert, please look at me."

Robert slowly turned his head in Alex's direction, but kept his eyes closed as if to block out the pain that he had been through.

Alex smiled as he set the fork aside and squeezed Robert's hand tightly. "Robert, I promise you that nothing bad will happen to you again. I am so sorry that this happened, but in a few minutes we'll get out of here and we'll be going home."

Robert gradually opened his eyes and looked at Alex with confusion. He tried to focus his eyes on Alex as he gently tried to squeeze Alex's hand. Alex felt Robert's grip tighten on his own hand, and Alex squeezed Robert's hand as reassurance.

"Robert, do you think you could try to eat something before we go?" Alex asked.

Robert shifted his eyes to the tray and then back at Alex. He closed his eyes wearily, but opened them in agreement. Alex stabbed the bland looking food with the fork and guided it up to Robert's mouth. Robert glanced hesitantly at the food before taking a bite. He chewed a couple of times and swallowed slowly. Alex held up the fork again, but Robert tiredly closed his eyes. Alex set the fork down on the tray and pushed it away. As Robert rested, Alex looked throughout the room for Robert's clothing. When he could not find any clothing, he opened the door and summoned a nurse coming out of an adjacent room.

"Nurse," he said firmly, "Where are my father's clothes? I know he came in here with clothes."

"Sir, your father's clothes were cut off when he was subdued and placed in his room after he broke the rules," she said strongly, but politely.

"Why did they cut his clothes off? And where are the rest of his clothes? He had plenty of clothes at the hospital and when I went there earlier today, the clothes were gone, so where did they go?" Alex asked with blatant hostility.

"The orderlies were just following protocol, and I don't know where his other clothes went. Try housekeeping," the nurse answered unemotionally.

"Thanks for your help," Alex replied with bitter sarcasm.

Going back into the room, Alex looked sadly at Robert's sleeping form lying in the narrow bed. He walked over to the side of the bed and sat down wearily. He touched Robert's shoulder without any response, so he took out his cell phone and dialed the number for Robert's house. After two rings, Emily answered amid chaos in the background.

"Em, what's going on?"

"The kids are a little wired up. What's going on? How's your dad?" Emily asked with concern.

"Terrible. That's why I called. Some new doctor shipped him off on Wednesday to an asylum-type place. Robert's in a real bad state right now, and this place has treated him like an animal," Alex said angrily.

"What? How'd that happen? Dr. Hamilton said he would wait until we got back," Emily added incredulously.

"It wasn't Dr. Hamilton. He was called away on a family emergency and hasn't been at the hospital since late Tuesday. Some new doctor sent him away."

"I can't believe this?" Emily said with disbelief.

"Neither can I. This place is a nightmare, but I have Antonio getting a court order right now so that I can take Robert out of here. That's why I called. Could you make up a room for Robert that is far enough from the kids that they won't bother him?"

"Are you bringing him home? Are you sure he wouldn't be better off back in the hospital?"

"No, absolutely not," Alex snapped. "What he's been through here has been sheer hell. I'll tell you about it when I get home."

"All right. Are you sure you want him around the kids?"

"He'll be fine and so will the kids. Make up a bedroom for him down the hall from us so that the kids won't disturb him."

"Okay, if you're sure this is the best way," Emily said with concern.

"I do, Em. He's in a really bad state right now. He thinks I abandoned him, and he's been so doped up that he can't even talk," Alex replied sadly.

"I'll make up the room as soon as I hang up. He'll be okay, Alex. He'll bounce back like he did in the hospital," Emily replied reassuringly.

"I hope so. I can't stand to see him like this," Alex said as his voice broke.

"Tell him I said hello, and that I'll see him soon, okay?"

"Yeah, I think he'll like that. Bye Em."

"Bye, Alex. We'll be waiting for you."

As Alex was turning his phone off, Antonio walked through the door holding a leather briefcase in one hand, and a piece of legal paper with a blue back on it in the other hand.

"Did you get it?" Alex asked hurriedly.

"Yes, the judge signed it, and it was filed. You can take Robert out of here whenever you want."

"Thank you, Antonio," Alex said with visible relief.

"No problem. Why don't you get Robert ready, and I'll take this legal document to the supervisor of this hellhole, and then we can go."

"Great, but can you wait here with Robert for a minute while I run out to my car to get my gym bag?"

"Sure, but why do you want your gym bag?" Antonio asked with puzzlement.

"Because Robert has no clothes. They cut his clothes off when he came in here, and the rest of his clothes are missing. I have some clothes from the gym that I always have in my car."

"Okay, go get them. I'll wait here with Robert until you get back."

"Thanks, Antonio," Alex uttered as he raced out the door.

Antonio watched Robert sleeping as he waited for Alex to come back. Alex took a few minutes before coming back with an orange gym bag. He tapped Antonio on the back and told him to take the legal papers to the supervisor.

"Robert," Alex said gently as he patted Robert on the shoulder. "Robert, come on. We're going home."

Robert opened his eyes slowly, but with the familiar unfocused gaze. He turned toward Alex's voice as Alex spoke, "You have to wake up now. We're going home."

Robert shut his eyes tightly and then reopened them as if to see if the dream was a reality. He saw Alex pulling out a navy blue tee shirt and a pair of gray gym shorts. He reached behind Robert's head and untied the loose strings that held Robert's dingy-looking hospital gown together. Robert lay motionless, unable to command his body to respond and move for Alex to help him into his new clothes. Alex awkwardly pulled the tee shirt over Robert's head, and slid the shorts up over his thin hips. Alex dug through the bag to find a pair of white athletic socks, which he pulled onto Robert's feet and midway up his shinbone. Robert sat stoically in his bed, unable to move, as Alex brushed Robert's hair with his fingers. When he was finished, Antonio came in, almost on cue.

"Everything taken care of?" Alex asked, not looking away from Robert.

"Everything is taken care of. You can go whenever you like," Antonio said happily.

"Good. Could you find us a wheelchair?" Alex asked Antonio.

"Yeah, sure. I saw one down at the end of this hallway by the supervisor's office."

"Thanks, Antonio." Alex said gratefully as he waited for Antonio to come back with a wheelchair.

Antonio returned with a wheelchair, and Alex slid it next to Robert's bed and locked the wheels. He picked Robert up under the armpits, and gently set him down in the wheelchair. Antonio walked in front of the wheelchair on the way out to the car so that Robert did not slide off the seat and onto the concrete floor. Alex quickly pushed the wheelchair to the passenger side of his car, and quickly unlocked the door and opened it.

Alex gave Antonio the car keys and asked him to open the driver's-side door and pull Robert into the passenger side of the car as Alex lifted Robert up. With the brakes locked, Alex slid his right arm under Robert's knees and the left arm behind Robert's back as he lifted him and slid him gently into the car. Antonio reached across and pulled Robert into a sitting position so that Alex could stretch the seatbelt across Robert's upper body and across his waist. Antonio reached into the backseat for a small pillow that Alex kept nearby for his children. He threw the pillow between the driver's seat and passenger seat. He would place it on the passenger side window after he was in the car, so that Robert's head could rest on the delicate pillow during the ride home. Robert closed his eyes as his body went limp from the after-affects of the drugs.

Alex shut and locked the door and jogged over to the driver's side where he gratefully shook Antonio's hand and thanked him repeatedly before getting in and turning on the ignition. Alex drove home as quickly as possible while glancing over at Robert to make sure he was all right. Robert remained sleeping with his head resting on the pillow. A small stream of drool trickled out of Robert's mouth, causing Alex to wince.

# CHAPTER 18

▼

While the twins slept comfortably in their beds, Emily lazily started to unpack the family's suitcases from their short trip home. As she was refolding the clothes that were not worn or dirty, the doorbell rang. Emily trotted down the stairs to the front door and peaked out the peephole. She opened the door wearily, "Hello."

"Hi, I hate to bother you, but is Robert here?" the man asked politely.

"No, he's not. I'm sorry, Mr. Rains," Emily answered.

"You know who I am, I'm glad. Is Alex here?" he asked with increasing desperation.

"No," she said without revealing any other information.

"I'm really sorry to bother you, Mrs. Petrovic. I know I'm not your husband's favorite person, but I'm really worried about Robert. Did something happen?"

Emily stared at Mitchell for a moment and saw the concern written on his handsome face, "Come in."

"Please tell me he's okay?" Mitchell asked desperately. "I just came from the hospital and they said that Robert wasn't there, and now you say he isn't here. Is he all right?"

"I don't know if he's okay or not, Mr. Rains. Alex just called and said that he was bringing Robert home."

"Then he's okay?" Mitchell asked, knowing that it was probably wishful thinking.

"Alex, the twins and I went home for a few days. We left late Tuesday night, and came back just a few hours ago. Before we left, Alex had a meeting with Robert's doctor, and the doctor said that Robert would be all right while we were gone, and up until we left, Robert was doing exceptionally well."

"So what happened?" Mitchell interrupted.

"Well, Robert's doctor was called away on a family emergency or something, and the doctor filling in shipped him off to what Alex called an 'asylum'."

"Oh my God," Mitchell whispered as he turned away from Emily to shield his emotions. "But you said that Alex was bringing him home, right?"

"Yes, as soon as he got the court order, he was bringing Robert home," Emily said softly.

"He needed a court order?" Mitchell asked incredulously and with a hint of anger.

"Yeah, without the court order, the damn place wouldn't release him, and they probably would have thrown Alex out. And believe me, Alex would have had to be carried out because he was not going to leave Robert in that condition," Emily said angrily.

"Would it be all right if I stayed here until Robert gets home? Maybe it will make him feel better to see me."

"You can stay, but seeing you will not help Robert at all," Emily said matter-of-factly.

Mitchell looked hurt as he spoke, "Why? Does he hate me that much?"

"No, no, not at all. He doesn't hate you, but he also doesn't know you. He has no memory, Mr. Rains. He thinks that he is fifteen years old."

"He won't know me?" Mitchell asked sadly.

"No, he doesn't know any of us. In his mind, he's fifteen years old. He remembers Anna, but we haven't told him anything about her. We just said that she went to stay with a relative while he gets well."

Mitchell looked at the floor with a stunned expression. "He doesn't even know Alex?"

"No, none of us. You can stay and see for yourself, but please don't say anything about who you are, except your name, of course. And please don't say anything about Alex being his son. Okay?"

"Yes, I promise I won't say anything," Mitchell said honestly.

"Good. Make yourself comfortable, and while you're waiting, try to brace yourself for the condition Robert is in," Emily offered sadly.

*        *        *        *

Alex pulled the car up to the front door as close as he could get without ruining the landscaping. He jumped out and ran over to the passenger side and opened the door. Robert opened his eyes momentarily, and then shut them again. Alex reached across and unfastened the seatbelt. He placed his one arm under Robert's knees, and the other arm around Robert's back and lifted him awkwardly. After he kicked the car door shut, Alex shifted Robert's weight so as to get a better grip. Alex carried Robert quickly up to the front door and kicked on it several times to get the attention of whoever was inside so that someone would open the door.

Emily opened the door. Her eyes grew large at the sight of Robert lying lifeless in Alex's arms. "Is he all right?" she asked in a whisper.

"No, but he will be just by getting out of that hellhole," answered Alex. Alex carried Robert into the living room and gently laid him on the sofa. Out of the corner of his eye, Alex saw the devastated look on Mitchell's face. "Hi Mitchell," Alex said politely and without anger.

"Hi," Mitchell muttered while his eyes never left Robert. "Is he okay?"

"He's drugged right now, and I don't know how much they gave him, so I don't know when he may wake up. He was up for a few minutes while we were waiting for the court order, but not since then," Alex stated. "He hasn't said anything yet." Alex sat down on the coffee table and gently rubbed Robert's forearm, "Robert. Come on Robert, open your eyes. You're safe now."

"Is there anything I can do?" asked a stunned Mitchell.

"No, but thanks for asking," Alex said genuinely.

"What happened there, Alex?" Emily asked quietly.

"Look at him. He has a few days growth on a beard, he hasn't been bathed, and he hasn't been fed since Wednesday morning in the hospital," Alex responded.

"You mean they didn't feed him for all those days?" Emily asked mortified.

"Yeah, that's exactly what I mean. He drank a glass of orange juice today, some orange juice and apple sauce yesterday, and pudding on Wednesday, at least that's what the nurse told me."

"Didn't they bring him a tray to eat?" Mitchell asked innocently.

Alex shot a quick glare at him, "Yeah, but it's a little hard to eat when your hands are tied down."

"How long was he restrained?" Emily asked horrified.

"Since Wednesday, shortly after his arrival. Apparently he broke some kind of rule by going to a water fountain that was in a restricted area. Some of his medications make him thirsty. Of course nobody told him it was a restricted area, but that didn't matter. They tied him down—both wrists, both ankles and at his waist, and then they drugged him up to keep him quiet," Alex replied angrily as he flashed back to the image of Robert lying in that bed, staring blankly at the ceiling.

"Oh my God," Mitchell said sadly. "How could they do that to him?" he muttered more to himself than to Alex or Emily.

"I called and left messages for Dr. Hamilton, so as soon as he gets his messages, he should call me back. I'm just hoping that what they did to him in that hellhole won't be permanent," Alex said sorrowfully.

"Everything will be fine. Robert is tough," Mitchell said meekly.

"He's tough, but one can only handle so much," Alex said simply as he rubbed Robert's shoulder and gently touched his unshaven face. "Come on, Robert. Open your eyes. Your partner in crime is here," Alex said as he smiled at Emily.

Robert slowly opened his heavy eyes, half afraid of where he would be. He blinked a few times as he tried to focus. The drugs coursed heavily throughout his body and distorted his thoughts, but he was inwardly happy when his eyes focused on a friendly face.

"Hi Clyde," Emily said smiling.

Robert tried to coordinate his mind with his mouth. After a few moments of trying to form the words, Robert slowly spoke, "Hi Bonnie."

Alex's gloomy attitude perked up, "Oh no, now I'll have to deal with both of you—two smart asses in one house." He tousled Robert's hair playfully, "Please Lord, give me strength to survive the wisecracking that these two will subject me to."

Robert looked around before asking sleepily, "Where am I?"

Alex answered, "We're at my dad's house."

Robert became agitated as he tried desperately to sit up, "I can't stay here."

Alex placed his hand reassuringly on Robert's shoulder, "Of course you can. My dad doesn't care if you stay with me. In fact, he would welcome you. Now, relax, okay?"

Robert shrugged Alex's hand off his shoulder, "I don't want to stay here."

"Would you rather go back to the hospital?" Alex asked innocently.

"NO," Robert practically shouted, half angry, half panicked.

"Okay, okay," Alex said in an effort to calm Robert. "You don't have to go back to the hospital, but you're going to have to stay here with Emily and me."

Robert laid back down on the sofa, despondent. He looked off absently in the distance as he whispered, "I want to go home."

Emily looked at the sad look on Alex's face, and then to the emotional, pained look on Mitchell's face before moving closer to Robert and taking his hand gently in hers, "Robert, Alex told me on the phone that you haven't had much to eat. Would you like something?"

Robert smiled tiredly at Emily, "No thanks, Emily."

"How about a chocolate milkshake?" Emily asked enthusiastically.

Robert's eyes lit up slightly, "Really?"

"Of course," Emily replied happily. "I'll do anything to help make my Clyde feel better."

"Thanks, Em. I'd really like a chocolate milkshake," Robert said sincerely.

Emily patted Robert lovingly on the shoulder, "I'll be back in a few minutes."

"Thanks, Em," Robert reiterated.

As Emily walked out of the room, Robert closed his eyes and turned away from everyone still in the room. Alex moved closer and tapped Robert on the shoulder to get his attention, "Robert, I've called and left messages for Dr. Hamilton, and as soon as he calls back, I'm going to ask him to come out to see you."

Robert grumbled irritably, "I don't want to see any doctors."

"I know you don't, but I want to make sure that you're all right. That place gave you a lot of drugs," Alex said gently.

"I'll be fine,' Robert grumbled.

"I know you will, but I want to make sure. It won't take long for Dr. Hamilton to check you out," Alex explained.

"Whatever," Robert said with further irritation.

Alex glanced over and noticed Mitchell sitting quietly. Alex again tapped Robert on the shoulder, "Robert, there's someone here I want you to meet." Alex motioned Mitchell to come closer so that Robert could see him.

"Who?" Robert said with annoyance.

"Robert, this is Mitchell Rains," Alex replied as he indicated who Mitchell was.

"Hi Robert," Mitchell said as enthusiastically as he could.

Robert focused his eyes on the stranger sitting across from him, "Hi." Robert paused a moment, "Are you another lawyer?"

Mitchell stared dumbfounded, "No, I'm a ..."

Alex interrupted, "Mitchell is a friend of the family."

"Nice to meet you," Robert said politely.

"It's nice meeting you as well," Mitchell said as he tried desperately to hide his disappointment. As he searched for something to say to Robert, Emily reentered the room.

Emily smiled at Robert, "Here you go, Clyde."

Robert rolled over and tried to sit up, but the exertion left him panting. Alex took hold of Robert's upper arms and helped him to a sitting position. "Thank you, Alex," Robert said appreciatively before reaching for the milkshake. "Thank you, Bonnie."

"You're welcome," Emily said tenderly. "I hope it's okay."

Robert took a long sip on the red, white and blue straw before nodding his head in the affirmative, "It's delicious."

"I'm glad you like it," she said with genuine caring.

The awkward silence in the living room was shattered by the loud ringing of Alex's cell phone. Alex got up quickly from his seat, reached into his pocket to retrieve the phone, and quickly walked out of the living room. Emily excused herself and followed Alex into the foyer, leaving Mitchell alone with Robert.

Mitchell watched Robert closely for a few moments while he tried to decide what to say to him. He smiled as he asked, "How's your milkshake?"

Robert replied stoically, "It's good."

Mitchell felt the awkwardness increase as he sat there opposite the man he loved. Mitchell tried again, "How are you feeling?"

Robert glanced over at Mitchell, "Fine."

"Really?" Mitchell asked with gentle skepticism.

"Yeah," Robert replied unemotionally. "A little sleepy, but I'm okay."

"I'm glad to hear that," Mitchell said sincerely.

"Thanks," Robert replied in a monotone before taking another drink from his milkshake.

"I know you don't want Dr. Hamilton to come out to see you, but honestly Robert, it's for the best," Mitchell explained tenderly.

"I don't trust him," Robert said coldly.

"Why?" Mitchell asked concerned.

"Dr. Hamilton and Alex sent me to that place," Robert again replied stoically.

"I know you feel betrayed, Robert, by both of them, and believe me I'd feel the same way if I were in your place, but I can tell you truthfully that neither of them had anything to do with sending you there," Mitchell explained sensitively.

"How do I know I can believe what you're saying?" Robert asked with skepticism.

Mitchell could not stifle his laugh, "You can't, but let me explain something. I'm a friend of Alex's dad—not Alex. Alex and I have never gotten along, so you can believe I'd never lie for him."

"What about Dr. Hamilton?" Robert questioned.

"Honestly, I can't give a definitive answer, but I believe he's a good man. I truly don't think he would have sent you there. If he had, I don't think he'd call Alex back," Mitchell explained.

Robert closed his eyes tightly and leaned his head back before lamenting, "I don't know who I can trust."

Mitchell moved closer to Robert as he spoke, "Robert, I know I'm a stranger to you, but I swear you can believe what I've told you. Alex and Emily have your best interest at heart, and," Mitchell paused and smiled widely, "You couldn't find a more beautiful place to stay."

"I'll take your word on that," Robert replied totally devoid of emotion.

"You'll see tomorrow when you're feeling better what a beautiful place this is. There's a huge swimming pool, a basketball court, a tennis court, and," Mitchell paused. "There are several horses here."

Robert, still feeling the affects of the drugs, remained stoic, "It sounds nice."

Mitchell, trying to be as enthusiastic as possible, reiterated, "You'll see tomorrow. You're going to enjoy being here."

Robert just nodded, only semi-interested in what Mitchell was saying, "It can't be any worse than where I've been."

Mitchell smiled sadly at Robert as he tried to think of something to say. Mitchell was saved from further conversation when Alex and Emily walked into the living room.

"That was Dr. Hamilton on the phone. He has to stop at the hospital and then he's going to come out here," Alex explained.

"Great," Robert said sarcastically.

"It won't be bad, Robert," Alex said reassuringly. "I promise."

"How long before he gets here?" Robert asked.

"Probably about twenty minutes," Alex replied.

Robert took a final sip of his milkshake, "Fine."

"If you're ready, I'll help you upstairs to your bedroom," Alex said before turning to address Mitchell. "Would you mind helping us out?"

Mitchell was slightly taken aback by Alex's generosity, "Yeah, I'll do whatever you need me to do."

"For now you can help me help Robert upstairs," Alex said as he turned to Robert. "I know the drugs are still in your system, so we'll give you a hand."

"Fine," Robert said with annoyance. He leaned forward and tried to stand on his own. After being upright for only a few seconds, an intense wave of dizziness hit Robert hard, causing him to fall backwards onto the sofa. Alex and Mitchell both instinctively reached for Robert as he was falling, but their efforts came up short. Alex smiled sadly as he reached for Robert's hand and Mitchell reached for his other hand.

Robert laughed as he was pulled upright, "I haven't been this out of it since me and Jake got soused on his grandfather's moonshine."

Alex, Mitchell and Emily all stopped in their tracks with mouths agape. Alex asked with bewilderment, "What did you say?"

Robert replied proudly, "I said I got soused on moonshine."

Alex continued, "When did this all happen?"

"I think we were about twelve. We had the best time, but the hangover the next day was horrible," Robert explained with a wry smile adorning his face. "The funniest thing was when Jake fell off his horse face-first into a cow patty."

Alex, Mitchell and Emily stared at each other in bewilderment, causing Robert to suddenly feel uncomfortable, "I probably shouldn't have said anything."

"No, no," Alex said quickly, hoping to keep Robert's mood more upbeat. "It's just that we didn't expect such a story from you. You're always on your best behavior."

Robert's devilish smile spoke volumes, "Not always."

"Didn't your parents have something to say about you coming home drunk?" Alex inquired.

"Give me some credit, Alex. We stayed in the barn that night, and I didn't go home until I was done being sick," Robert answered, astonished that anyone would think him that stupid.

"I see," Alex responded.

"I'm not that dumb. My parents would have beaten me senseless if they knew," Robert explained matter-of-factly.

"What about now?" Mitchell asked innocently.

"What? If they knew about the moonshine?" Robert repeated for clarification.

"Yeah," Mitchell responded softly.

"Well," Robert started, "My father wouldn't have anything to say since he's dead, and my mama," Robert paused momentarily. "Well, she'd probably still beat me senseless." Robert suddenly felt his legs weaken and then buckle beneath him. Mitchell and Alex's strong, yet gentle grips on Robert's arms kept him from collapsing onto the floor. Alex and Mitchell moved to stand on each side of Robert and put their arms firmly around Robert's back.

"I think we better go upstairs now," Alex said simply. "Are you okay, Robert?"

Robert felt weak and lightheaded, but he answered as usual, albeit very weakly, "I'll be okay."

Alex glanced over at Emily, "Can you show Dr. Hamilton to Robert's room when he gets here?"

"Yeah," Emily answered before stepping in front of Robert. "I'll see you tomorrow, okay?"

"Okay," Robert said in a voice slightly louder than a whisper.

"Feel better," Emily said softly before stretching to place a kiss tenderly on Robert's cheek.

"I will," Robert responded softly.

Alex and Mitchell slowly and gently supported Robert in the long walk from the living room to the second floor of the stately mansion. Panting heavily from the long walk and the drugs still in his system, Robert hesitated as they approached the bedroom door.

Mitchell offered his support, "It's okay, Robert. Alex and I are right here."

Robert nodded silently his acknowledgment of Mitchell's support.

"Remember what I told you," Mitchell said tenderly as Alex opened the bedroom door.

Robert took a deep breath and exhaled slowly before entering the room. The anxiety was steadily building within him as his eyes darted around the room. The large room, complete with a king-size bed and a spacious bathroom, looked comfortable enough, but Robert felt an eeriness about the place and he did not want to stay.

The cloud of anxiety filled the room, as Alex tried to ease Robert's fear, "It's okay, Robert. Everything's going to be okay. Emily's and my room is right across the hall if you need anything."

"Thanks," Robert said solemnly. As his legs threatened to give out beneath him, Robert said simply, "I need to lie down."

"Okay," Alex replied with concern as he and Mitchell quickly ushered Robert to the bed. "Rest awhile. We'll let you know when Dr. Hamilton arrives."

"Thanks," Robert muttered sarcastically.

Mitchell helped Robert situate the many pillows on the bed to make Robert more comfortable. Mitchell pulled the blanket up to Robert's waist as he leaned closer, "Everything's going to be okay."

"I hope so," Robert whispered as he fought to keep his eyes open.

"It will be, I promise you," Mitchell reassured. "Now close your eyes and rest. You're safe here."

Robert nodded and closed his weary eyes. Within moments, he was sleeping soundly and peacefully, as Alex and Mitchell kept watch by the door. Alex noticed Mitchell staring sadly at Robert.

"It's hard, isn't it?" Alex said softly as he diverted his eyes toward Robert.

"What?" Mitchell asked.

"Seeing him like this," Alex answered compassionately.

Mitchell closed his eyes and sighed, "Part of me is dying inside."

"He's going to get better," Alex said confidently.

"I know," Mitchell said hesitantly, unsure of whether he believed it or not.

Alex saw Mitchell start to become emotional, so he changed the subject, "I want to thank you, Mitchell."

Mitchell's face showed his surprise, "For what?"

"For helping me get Robert up here, and ..." Alex said before getting interrupted.

"No, Alex, I want to thank you for allowing me to be here," Mitchell said with his eyes full of gratitude.

"I'm truly glad you're here," Alex said appreciatively. "I also want to thank you for what you said to me in the hospital a few weeks ago."

"Alex, I ..." Mitchell fumbled with his words before Alex interrupted.

"I'm serious, Mitchell. I'm glad you said to me what you did. You made me face responsibility," Alex stated honestly.

"I don't know what to say," Mitchell replied.

"You don't have to say anything," Alex said smiling. "Just know that I'm glad you did what you did."

"Thank you, Alex. I'm truly at a loss for words," Mitchell replied.

As Alex was about to speak, they heard a faint knock on the door. Alex quietly opened the door, "Hi Doc. I'm glad you're here."

"Hi Alex," Dr. Hamilton said as he entered the room. Dr. Hamilton looked at Mitchell and took a moment to process who he was, "Hi. Mr. Rains, right?"

Mitchell reached to shake Dr. Hamilton's hand, "You remembered."

Dr. Hamilton looked at Robert sleeping on the bed before turning to face both Alex and Mitchell, "How is he?"

"Exhausted," Alex answered. "I think the drugs they gave him are still affecting him. Mitchell and I both had to help him up here, and then he practically collapsed on the bed."

"That doesn't surprise me," Dr. Hamilton said matter-of-factly. "That place needs to be shut down."

"Don't worry. I'm going to look into it," Alex said forcefully.

Dr. Hamilton approached the bed and tapped Robert softly on the shoulder, but Robert did not awaken. Dr. Hamilton gently shook Robert's shoulder until Robert opened his eyes. "Hi Robert."

Robert blinked a few times until he adjusted to the light and comprehended what was going on around him. When he recognized Dr. Hamilton, Robert rolled over on his side away from the doctor without saying anything.

Dr. Hamilton said softly, "Come on, Robert. I need you to stay awake for a few minutes." When Robert did not move or answer, Dr. Hamilton walked around the bed and knelt down. He gently shook Robert's shoulder again, "Robert, I need you to wake up."

Robert reopened his eyes slowly. "Sorry," he said apologetically.

Dr. Hamilton smiled, "It's okay. No need to apologize. I just need for you to stay awake for a few minutes, okay?"

"Okay," Robert said softly as he rolled onto his back.

"How are you feeling?" Dr. Hamilton asked as he sat down on the edge of the bed.

"Tired," Robert answered wearily.

"Once all the drugs that they gave you are out of your system, you'll feel a lot better," Dr. Hamilton explained.

"When will that be?" Robert questioned.

"Honestly, I don't really know because I don't know what they gave you or how much," Dr. Hamilton answered.

"Okay," Robert nodded slowly as he fought the urge to close his eyes.

"Are you ready to go?" Dr. Hamilton asked.

"Go where?" Robert asked, half-asleep.

"Back to the hospital," Dr. Hamilton stated innocently.

"NO," Robert practically shouted as he instantly became fully awake at the mention of the word 'hospital.'

Alex interjected softly, "Doctor, Robert's not going anywhere."

Dr. Hamilton stared perplexed at Alex, "What do you mean?"

"Robert's not going anywhere. He's going to stay here with Emily, the kids and me," Alex explained matter-of-factly.

Dr. Hamilton stood up to face Alex, "Are you sure about that?"

"Yes," Alex said simply.

"Do you understand what that's going to entail?" Dr. Hamilton questioned with concern evident on his face.

"Yes, we do," Alex said as he walked over and sat down next to Robert. "We'll be fine."

"Okay," Dr. Hamilton said reluctantly. "If you think you're up for it."

"We are," Alex replied firmly.

"And what about you, Robert?" Dr. Hamilton asked.

Robert, still filled with anxiety about going back to the hospital and totally oblivious to Alex's comments, muttered sadly, "I want to go home."

"Robert," Dr. Hamilton said gently. "How do you feel about staying here with Alex and his family?"

Robert repeated more forcefully, "I want to go home."

Dr. Hamilton glanced at Mitchell and then to Alex before responding to Robert firmly, "Where is home, Robert? If you can tell me where you live, I'll let you go home."

Robert rolled back on his side, dejected, "I don't remember."

Dr. Hamilton sat back down next to Robert and spoke to him more tenderly, "Robert, when you remember, then you can go home. Until then, where would you rather stay—with Alex or at the hospital?"

Robert whispered despondently, "With Alex."

"Okay," Dr. Hamilton replied. "I'll consent to that, but you're going to have to continue coming for your appointments."

"Of course," Alex interjected. "Robert will be at any appointment you schedule."

"Will you agree to that, Robert?" Dr. Hamilton asked.

Robert replied stoically, "Yeah."

"Good," Dr. Hamilton responded before turning to Alex and Mitchell. "Can you guys excuse us for a few minutes?"

"Sure," Mitchell replied as he and Alex headed for the door.

After Alex and Mitchell were out the door and the door closed behind them, Dr. Hamilton turned to Robert, "First, Robert, I want to apologize for the past few days." Dr. Hamilton's voice was full of compassion as he continued, "I know you went through hell these past few days, and I know you probably feel betrayed by both Alex and myself, and that's understandable, but I assure you that neither of us had anything to do with what happened these past few days."

"I just want to forget everything that happened," Robert said solemnly.

"That's understandable," Dr. Hamilton replied. "But I need to check you out to make sure you're okay, and I need for you to try to remember a few things."

"Like what?" Robert asked softly.

"Did they give you any pills, like the ones you were taking in the hospital?" Dr. Hamilton inquired.

"All the different colored pills?" Robert asked for clarification.

"Yes," Dr. Hamilton answered. "You took them several times a day."

"No," Robert said confidently. "They didn't give me any pills."

"Just shots," Dr. Hamilton stated knowingly.

"Yeah," Robert nodded sadly.

"I'm sorry about that Robert," Dr. Hamilton said sympathetically.

"I just want to forget that place," Robert said sadly.

Dr. Hamilton answered compassionately, "I know you do. I'm just going to do a quick exam to make sure you're okay."

"Okay," Robert replied subdued.

Dr. Hamilton took Robert's pulse and then checked his blood pressure. He looked in Robert's eyes with a flashlight and in Robert's mouth. Dr. Hamilton put his stethoscope back on, "Robert, can you lift your shirt up so that I can listen to your heart and lungs?"

Robert obeyed without question and lifted his shirt up to his shoulders. Dr. Hamilton's eyes grew wide, "How did you get these bruises?"

Robert did not respond. Instead he closed his eyes and turned his head away from the doctor.

Dr. Hamilton examined the bruises more carefully, "Robert, could you sit up for a moment?"

"Sure," Robert said softly as he sat up gingerly.

Dr. Hamilton lifted Robert's tee shirt up in the back and raised it to his shoulders to expose even more bruises on Robert's back and sides. Dr. Hamilton did not mention the bruising as he gently placed the stethoscope on Robert's bruised upper back, "Take a deep breath."

Robert complied without question.

Dr. Hamilton listened to Robert's lungs and was satisfied with the results. "Okay, Robert, you can lie back. I just need to listen to your heart."

Robert leaned back until he was lying down. Dr. Hamilton placed the stethoscope gently on Robert's heart and listened intently. When the results were satisfactory, Dr. Hamilton took off his stethoscope and placed it back in his bag before sitting down on the bed beside Robert, "I'm going to talk to Alex about getting you some dinner, and I'm going to call the pharmacy so that you can start taking your medication again tomorrow." Dr. Hamilton started to walk to the door before he stopped and addressed his patient, "Just lie back and relax for a little while, and I'll be back."

"Okay," Robert replied softly as he once again closed his eyes.

Dr. Hamilton opened the bedroom door and quietly closed it behind him so that Robert would not hear his conversation. Alex and Mitchell waited anxiously for word about Robert's condition. Alex broached the subject, "How is he?"

"He's covered with bruises," Dr. Hamilton replied. "Didn't you notice the bruising when you were helping him get dressed?

"No," Alex replied. "I was in a hurry to get him out of there, and I just quickly helped him into the shorts and tee shirt that I brought in from my car."

"What did they do to him?" Mitchell asked with a mixture of anger and sadness.

"Robert's chest, abdomen, back and upper arms are covered with bruises. I asked him how he got them, but he turned away from me and wouldn't talk about it," Dr. Hamilton explained.

"That's not good, is it?" Alex asked.

"No, it's not," Dr. Hamilton explained. "He's probably a little dehydrated, but nothing life-threatening."

"I'll make sure he gets plenty to eat and drink tonight," Alex stated.

"Good," Dr. Hamilton replied. "I'm going to stop out tomorrow morning to see how he's doing, if that's okay with you?"

"Of course," Alex said. "I'll do anything to get Robert well again."

"I know you will," Dr. Hamilton said sincerely. "I'll call before I come out."

"That's fine," Alex replied.

"Now I need to know which pharmacy that you use so that I can call in Robert's medication," Dr. Hamilton stated.

"Percy's," Alex answered. "When should he begin taking them?"

"I'll write out an instruction sheet for you," Dr. Hamilton explained. "There are a lot of pills, and he needs to take them every day."

"I'll make sure he takes them whenever he needs to," Alex replied sincerely.

"I know you will," Dr. Hamilton responded with a smile. "Now," he paused to take a deep breath and to collect his thoughts. "Do you think you can get Robert something to eat?"

"Sure," Alex replied. "I'll go find Emily and see what she can whip up."

"Good," Dr. Hamilton stated as he looked from Alex to Mitchell. "Mr. Rains, I need for you to do something if you don't mind."

"Anything," Mitchell replied sincerely.

"To keep Robert awake until he eats, I'm going to have him take a bath or a shower, and I need for you to stay with him in the bathroom in case he gets dizzy or lightheaded," Dr. Hamilton explained.

"Sure," Mitchell responded. "No problem."

"How did Robert respond to you earlier?" Dr. Hamilton inquired.

"He talked to me for a few minutes," Mitchell answered.

"He responded positively to Mitchell," Alex interjected.

"Good," Dr. Hamilton said with obvious relief. "Robert feels that Alex and I betrayed him, so I'm glad that you're here. I think he'll be more agreeable to you staying with him in the shower than Alex or me."

"I'll do anything you ask," Mitchell replied truthfully.

"Okay, then let's go talk to Robert," Dr. Hamilton stated as he opened the door to Robert's room.

"Tell Robert I'll be bringing him up something to eat soon," Alex offered.

"Okay," Dr. Hamilton stated as he walked in the bedroom and over to the bed where Robert was sleeping peacefully. He sat down on the edge of the bed and gently tapped Robert on the shoulder until Robert opened his eyes. "Robert, Alex is going to bring you up something to eat in a few minutes. In the meantime, I want you to take a shower or a bath to keep you awake, okay?"

"Yeah, I guess so," Robert said groggily.

"Since you're still having the side affects of the drugs, Mitchell is going to stay in the bathroom with you while you shower to make sure you don't pass out," Dr. Hamilton explained.

"I'll be fine," Robert muttered softly.

"I know you will, but to be on the safe side, Mitchell is going to stay with you," Dr. Hamilton reiterated.

"I'll just be there in case you need anything, okay?" Mitchell said softly.

"Okay," Robert acquiesced.

"Okay then, I'm going to call the pharmacy, and I'll be back in a few minutes," Dr. Hamilton offered.

"We'll be fine," Mitchell added as Dr. Hamilton walked out the door.

"I know you will," Dr. Hamilton replied from the hallway.

Mitchell went over to the side of the bed and sat down, "I know you don't need any help, Robert, but the drugs that they gave you are still affecting you, so I'm just going to sit outside the shower and wait for you, okay? You can have all the privacy you want," Mitchell added with a smile.

"Thanks," Robert said with relief.

"Do you need any help to the bathroom?" Mitchell asked.

"I'm not sure," Robert answered honestly.

"Okay," Mitchell said as he extended his hand to Robert. "Let's get you into the shower."

Robert took Mitchell's hand and let Mitchell pull him into a standing position. Robert stood still for a few moments to let the waves of dizziness pass, and then he took a few steps to the bathroom. Mitchell followed behind closely to catch him if he fell, but Robert shakily made it to the bathroom. As he entered the bathroom, he turned to look at Mitchell. "I'll get you a towel and washcloth, and then I'll give you your privacy, okay?"

"Okay," Robert replied.

Mitchell went to the linen closet and pulled out a large, fluffy navy blue towel and matching washcloth and handed them to Robert, "Here you go."

"Thanks," Robert replied as he took the towel and washcloth.

"Go ahead and get in the shower, and I'll come back in once you're undressed so that you can have your privacy," Mitchell said tenderly.

"Thank you," Robert reiterated as Mitchell stepped outside the bathroom door. Robert clumsily pulled the tee shirt over his head and pushed the shorts to his ankles. He leaned heavily against the wall as he kicked the shorts off and yanked off his socks. Robert let the towel sit on the counter, but took the washcloth into the large, spacious marble shower. He basked in the warmth of several shower jets that rained water down upon him. Robert lazily soaped up the washcloth and began to wash himself free of the smell of that dreadful asylum, but he quickly tired out. He struggled to finish washing himself as he leaned heavily against the marble wall to prevent himself from falling.

Robert called out weakly, "Mr. Rains?"

Mitchell immediately replied, "Yes."

"Can you get me a towel, please?" Robert asked feebly.

Mitchell heard the weakness in Robert's voice, "Are you okay?"

Robert inhaled deeply several times before answering, "I'm not sure."

Mitchell opened the shower door and quickly handed Robert the towel, "Here, wrap this around your waist and I'll help you out of there."

"Thanks," Robert replied weakly as he took the towel and did as Mitchell instructed.

"Can I come in?" Mitchell asked.

"Yeah," Robert managed to utter between his deep breathing.

Mitchell pushed the shower door completely open and stepped inside to find Robert leaning heavily against the wall with his eyes tightly closed and his hands holding onto the wall, "Robert, I'm going to put my arm around your back and I want you to put your arm over my shoulder, okay?"

Robert opened his eyes and nodded, "Okay."

As Mitchell slowly guided Robert out to the toilet, he noticed Robert's erratic breathing, "Are you all right?"

Robert nodded slowly, "I think so."

"Here, sit down here for a moment and I'll help you dry off," Mitchell said tenderly as he helped Robert gingerly sit down on the toilet.

"Thank you," Robert said appreciatively.

"Do you feel lightheaded?" Mitchell asked as he looked down sympathetically at Robert.

"A little," Robert replied honestly.

Mitchell placed his hand on Robert's shoulder, "Lean forward with your head bent down and that should help."

Robert did what Mitchell suggested and within moments Mitchell noticed that Robert's breathing was back to normal and his body appeared more relaxed. Mitchell retrieved another towel and went back to stand in front of Robert. "Are you feeling any better?"

Robert looked up slowly and forced a smile, "Yeah."

"I'm going to help you dry off, okay?" Mitchell asked.

"Okay," Robert replied as he tried to sit back up straight.

"It's okay to stay like you are. You don't have to sit up," Mitchell explained.

Robert smiled gratefully, "Thanks."

"You're welcome," Mitchell said with a genuine smile as he ran the towel gently down Robert's back. His smile quickly turned to a frown when he saw the deep yellow bruises covering Robert's back. After completely drying Robert off, Mitchell stepped back and forced a smile, "All done."

"Thank you," Robert replied more strongly.

"Do you think you can make it to your bed if I help?" Mitchell asked.

Robert slowly lifted his head, "I think so."

"Wanna give it a try?" Mitchell asked encouragingly.

"Sure," Robert replied confidently.

Mitchell walked over beside Robert and knelt down, "Put you arm around my shoulder." Robert followed Mitchell's orders without question. "Okay Robert, just take your time and lean on me for support."

"Okay," Robert responded gratefully.

After several eternal minutes and a hellishly short distance to walk, Robert arrived at the side of his bed, exhausted and panting from the exertion. He plopped down on the bed and let out a loud sigh.

"You okay?" Mitchell asked once again.

Robert smiled through his exhaustion, "Yeah, thanks."

Mitchell smiled genuinely, "No problem." He looked in the closet and in the dresser drawers as he explained, "I'm looking for something comfortable for you to put on."

Robert looked down at the towel wrapped tightly around him and then back at Mitchell, "You don't like my towel?"

Mitchell could hear the teasing in Robert's voice, "Of course I like your towel, but I think you'd be more comfortable in something a little drier."

"You're right," Robert said with a smile. "I was just teasing."

Mitchell laughed, "I know." He continued to look throughout the bedroom for something for Robert to put on, but when he found nothing, he turned back to Robert, "Will you be okay here by yourself for just a minute or two?"

Robert looked at Mitchell questioningly, "Yeah, I'll be fine. Why?"

"I'll be right back with something dry for you to put on," Mitchell explained.

"Okay," Robert replied.

"Just lie back and relax, and I'll be right back," Mitchell stated caringly as he walked out the door.

"All right," Robert said to an empty room. While briefly alone, Robert decided to take a mental inventory of the large bedroom, but his eyes started to get heavy, and before he realized that he had fallen asleep, Mitchell was back and sitting beside him on the bed.

"Are you okay?" Mitchell asked concerned.

Robert blinked a few times before answering, "Yeah, I'm okay. I just drifted off for a moment."

"I'm sure you're exhausted, especially after the day you've had," Mitchell said compassionately.

"I'd rather forget this day," Robert said sadly.

Mitchell commiserated, "I know you would." He lifted up the tee shirt and boxers that he found in the other room, "I found some clean, dry clothes for you."

Robert smiled tiredly as he tried to sit up, "Thanks."

"Need some help?" Mitchell asked as he saw Robert struggling to get up.

"I think I can manage," Robert replied as he took the tee shirt and pulled it awkwardly over his head. As Robert reached for the boxers, Mitchell caught a brief glimpse of uneasiness in Robert's eyes.

"I'm going to straighten up the bathroom while you finish getting dressed," Mitchell explained matter-of-factly to ease Robert's anxiety.

Robert nodded appreciatively, "Thank you."

"No problem," Mitchell called out from the bathroom. "I'll get that wet towel when you're finished."

Robert kept the towel firmly around his waist as he slowly inched the blue cotton boxers up over his hips. Exhausted, Robert laid back in the bed, "I'm finished with the towel."

Mitchell reappeared from the bathroom, but before stooping down to retrieve the wet towel from the plush carpeting, he noticed Robert breathing uneasily again, "Are you okay?" Mitchell asked with a soft voice filled with compassion.

"I'm okay," Robert said tiredly.

Mitchell gathered up the sheet and blanket and pulled it up to Robert's waist without saying a word. As Mitchell picked up the wet towel, the bedroom door opened. Dr. Hamilton held the door open as Alex carried a large tray overflowing with various foods and drink over to the bed.

"Here you go, Robert," Alex stated affectionately as he sat down on the edge of the bed.

Dr. Hamilton gathered the various pillows and stacked them up at the top of the bed, "Come on, Robert. Emily prepared you a healthy meal, and I expect you to eat it all."

Robert closed his eyes briefly, took a deep breath and struggled to push himself into a seated position with the pillows at his back.

"Need help?" Alex asked.

Robert shook his head strongly and answered forcefully, "No, I can do it myself."

After watching silently from the bathroom door, Mitchell turned out the bathroom light and started for the door to leave. When Robert spotted Mitchell about to leave, he called out softly, "Mr. Rains?"

Mitchell stopped suddenly and glanced briefly in Robert's direction, "Bye Robert. Take care of yourself."

Robert nodded and with deep appreciation he said softly, "Thank you, Mr. Rains."

Mitchell turned away quickly to hide the tears in his eyes and exited the room quietly. Outside in the hallway, with the door securely shut and a semblance of privacy, the tears that Mitchell had fought back from the moment he saw Alex carrying Robert through the front door fell in waves over his soft, shaven cheeks.

Mitchell took several deep, cleansing breaths before searching frantically in his pockets for a tissue. He wiped his eyes and nose and leaned against the wall while fruitlessly trying to regain his composure. At last he decided that he was composed enough to walk through the long hallways of the mansion to escape from the nightmare that was encompassing him, but out of nowhere he heard a feminine voice call his name. He tried to ignore the voice and quickened his pace, but the figure behind the feminine voice stepped in front of him.

"Mr. Rains? Are you okay?" Emily asked with concern.

Mitchell gave a quick, "Yes," as he turned his face and tried to continue his exodus.

Emily gently touched Mitchell's elbow and looked him straight in the eye, "I don't think you are." She lead him slowly to the sofa and they both sat down, "Here, sit down and catch your breath."

"I'm okay, Mrs. Petrovic," Mitchell uttered unconvincingly.

Emily took Mitchell's hand in hers and squeezed it tenderly, "It's okay to be sad. I can only imagine how devastating it is for you to see him like that. He's going to be all right, Mr. Rains," Emily stated as she stared into his crystal blue eyes.

"Promise me that's true," Mitchell whispered. He stared briefly at Emily as her kind words seeped in, and the tears began to flow again freely, "I'm dying inside, Mrs. Petrovic."

Emily instinctively put her arms around Mitchell and pulled him into a tender, sympathetic embrace, "He's going to be okay."

Mitchell cried softly into Emily's shoulder as he whispered, "I hope you're right."

Emily gently rubbed Mitchell's back and shoulders as she continued to hold him. After a few moments, she pulled back slowly and wiped a tear from Mitchell's cheek, "You're still in love with him."

Mitchell's eyes softened as he spoke with absolute sincerity, "Yes. I've never stopped."

Emily smiled broadly, "When Robert regains his memory, you can tell him what you've just told me."

Mitchell frowned, "He probably won't want to hear it, Mrs. Petrovic."

Emily squeezed Mitchell's hand softly, "Please, call me Emily, and don't sell yourself short, Mr. Rains."

Mitchell wiped his eyes with the back of his hand, "I'll call you Emily if you call me Mitchell. Deal?"

Emily took Mitchell's hand and shook it playfully, "Deal. Mitchell, why don't you go home and relax? You look exhausted," Emily said sympathetically.

"I'll never be able to relax not knowing how Robert is," Mitchell said sadly.

"How about I call you later this evening after Dr. Hamilton leaves?" Emily asked.

"I would really appreciate that, although I don't deserve any of your kindness, especially after I abandoned Robert when this all happened," he stated despondently.

"You didn't abandon Robert. Just between you and me, I think you did the right thing by stepping back and forcing Alex to take responsibility," Emily stated matter-of-factly.

"I hope you're right. I can't stand to see him like this," Mitchell said as the tears once again threatened to run down his cheeks. "I wish I could make this all go away, back to when we were happy."

"I know you do, Mitchell. We all do, but what's done is done. We just have to deal with what's at hand, and that is helping Robert find his way back to us," Emily said calmly.

"Do you think he will find his way back?" Mitchell asked with hope ringing in his question.

"Honestly," she paused. "Yes I do, but I think it's going to take a while for that to happen."

"My greatest comfort in all of this is that I know Robert is in the best hands possible. You and Robert have a great repartee, and I can see in his eyes that he adores you," Mitchell said as he smiled at Emily.

"And I adore him also. He's a special man, and you are very lucky, because I'm guessing he adores you too," Emily said as she patted Mitchell on the knee as she was rising from the sofa.

"I would give anything if that were true," Mitchell said sadly.

"You'll see when he regains his memory."

"I just wish there was something I could do for him now," Mitchell replied with frustration. "If only I could change places with him and spare him all the pain that has built up over all of these years."

"Keep the faith, Mitchell. Robert will recover, and then the two of you can work things out. If that's what you want?" Emily asked.

"Yes, more than anything," Mitchell answered defensively.

"Good. Now go home and rest. I'll call you later this evening."

"Okay, I'll go, as long as you promise," Mitchell answered.

"I promise," Emily stated as she crossed her heart playfully.

"Can I ask you something before I go?"

"Sure, go ahead," Emily replied.

"Have you changed your mind about Robert's sexuality? I mean, you just said that when Robert gets better that we can work things out. Don't you despise and hate our 'type' of people anymore?"

"I think I can speak for Alex as well when I say that all that we want for Robert is for him to be happy, and we're for any means that may take. I know from what Alex has told me, that you broke things off with Robert, and that Robert still loves you, or at least he did before all this happened," Emily stated honestly.

"I'm stunned. I never would have thought that we'd get your blessing."

"Do you still love Robert?" Emily quizzed.

"With all my heart," Mitchell responded emotionally.

"Then I think I can speak for my husband when I say that you are welcome in this house anytime you want. I know it's hard for you to see Robert like this, so why don't you stay in touch by phone, and we'll do the same if anything changes with Robert's condition. What do you say?" Emily inquired.

"I'd say that that is a great idea. Thank you Emily. You don't know how much this means to me," Mitchell responded gratefully.

"Oh, I think I do," she said affectionately. "After all, I do know what it's like to love a Petrovic."

Mitchell winked at Emily and hugged her gently, "Thank you so much."

"You're welcome, now go home and get some rest," Emily instructed with mock sternness.

"Yes ma'am," Mitchell replied as he headed for the door.

# CHAPTER 19

▼

The following morning Robert awakened around nine a.m. to find Alex slumped over and snoring in a chair at the foot of the bed. As Robert slowly threw the blanket off and started to rise, Alex awakened with a fright and quickly jumped to his feet.

Robert laughed, "Are you okay?"

Embarrassed, Alex responded, "Sorry about that. I was in the middle of a dream."

"Must have been some dream," Robert teased.

Alex sat down and took a long cleansing breath, "How are you feeling?"

Robert stretched and yawned, "Better than yesterday."

"Glad to hear it," Alex said sincerely. "Let's go down and get some breakfast."

"Sounds good to me," Robert replied as he looked down at his present state of dress. "But don't you think I need some clothes?"

Alex chuckled, "That might be a good idea. Wait here and I'll be right back."

Robert absentmindedly walked to the window and stared out at the beautiful flower garden that lined the outer perimeter of the swimming pool. Deep in his own thoughts, Robert did not hear Alex return to the bedroom.

Alex, noticing Robert's introspective mood, inquired, "What's up?"

"Nothing," Robert replied. "I was just admiring the flower garden by the swimming pool. I don't think I've ever seen such a beautiful array of flowers."

Alex gazed out the window, noticing the flower garden for the first time. "They are magnificent." Alex paused as he remembered, "My dad always grows flowers—ever since I can remember."

After Robert glided a pair of grey sweatpants on and quickly pulled on a pair of socks that Alex had retrieved, the men walked side-by-side out of the bedroom. When Robert was in the hallway, he stopped momentarily and mused, "This place is huge."

"Yeah," Alex laughed. "I guess my dad likes a lot of space."

As the two walked through the long hallways in comfortable silence, Robert admired what he saw and rubbernecked to see into some of the rooms. "I think this place is bigger than my entire town."

Alex smiled to himself as they finally made their way to the kitchen. When Alex saw Emily sitting at the counter sipping her coffee, he called out from the kitchen entrance in a relaxed voice, "Hey Em, look who has come to see you!"

Emily smiled warmly as she came over to hug Robert, "Hi Clyde."

Robert smiled broadly as he warmly embraced her, "Hi Bonnie."

Emily pulled gently out of the their embrace and took Robert's hand in hers, "Have a seat and I'll get you something for breakfast."

"Thanks Bonnie," Robert said appreciatively as he took a seat at the kitchen counter.

Emily kissed Alex on the cheek and whispered in his ear, "Can I talk to him for a moment?"

Alex nodded, "Yeah, that's fine." He walked over and put his hand on Robert's shoulder, "I'll be back in a few minutes, okay?"

Robert smiled, "Yep."

"I have a few business calls to make, so you're going to have to keep Emily company, okay?" Alex said good-naturedly.

"Yep," Robert answered.

"We'll try not to get into any trouble," Emily teased.

Alex shook his head in mock defeat, "How am I ever going to survive you two being in cahoots?"

"We'll play fair, right Em?" Robert joked.

Emily winked at Robert, "Of course we will."

"Scout's honor," Robert said as he made a salute.

"Me too," Emily chimed in.

Alex hung his head as he jokingly asked, "What did I do to deserve the shenanigans these two will put me through?"

"I don't know, but if we come up with an answer, we'll let you know," Emily teased.

"Good one, Bonnie," Robert offered as he patted Emily on the back.

"Thanks Clyde," Emily replied with a laughing smile.

Alex threw up his hands, "I'm going while my sanity is still in check."

"Bye Honey," Emily continued teasing.

"Bye," Alex replied as he exited the door.

Emily faced Robert and smiled, "What do you want for breakfast?"

Robert pondered the question, "What would you like?"

"Hmm," Emily mused. "Pancakes and strawberries sound good."

"Yeah," Robert agreed. "Pancakes and strawberries definitely sound good."

"Then pancakes and strawberries it will be!" Emily replied.

As Emily prepared the breakfast, Robert looked absently out the window. When Emily noticed Robert's solemn look, she asked, "So, my dear Clyde, how are you feeling?"

"A lot better than yesterday," Robert replied thankfully.

"I'm glad to hear that," Emily said sincerely. "We were all worried about you."

"I know that *you* were worried," Robert replied.

Emily, knowing what Robert was hinting at, stated, "I wasn't the only one. Alex, Dr. Hamilton and Mitchell were all worried about you as well."

"Really," Robert said skeptically.

"Yes," Emily said as she put the pancakes on Robert's plate.

"How can you be sure?" Robert asked a bit shyly.

"Women's intuition," Emily said with a wry smile. "Seriously, Robert, Alex and Dr. Hamilton both feel terrible about what happened to you."

"I'm not so sure about that," Robert replied.

"Alex still feels guilty about what happened," Emily explained.

"Innocent people don't feel guilty," Robert added.

"He feels guilty about leaving you," Emily explained tenderly.

"Really?" Robert asked skeptically.

"Yeah," Emily replied. "Do you honestly think that I would have left Alex send you to such a place? Alex would not leave until he had assurances from Dr. Hamilton that you would be okay while we were gone."

Robert reached for Emily's hand, "I'm sorry Em. I never really thought of it that way."

"It's okay," Emily said sincerely.

"No, it's not," Robert replied as he stood and started pacing slowly from the window back to the table. "I don't blame Alex," Robert paused to collect his thoughts. "And I don't really blame Dr. Hamilton either."

Emily, noticing that something was bothering him, motioned for Robert to sit back down, "If you don't blame them, then what's bothering you Clyde?"

Robert sat back down tiredly, "I can't shake that place, or the feelings of being left there."

Emily came around the table and hugged Robert firmly. "It's okay now, Clyde. You're safe here. I know you went through hell at that place, but I swear to you that you'll never feel abandoned ever again."

Robert squeezed Emily tenderly, "Thank you, Bonnie."

Emily kissed Robert on the forehead before she started teasing, "You may not want to thank me after spending time with Alex, the kids and me."

Robert looked at Emily seriously, "Are you sure you want me around your kids? I'll totally understand if you don't want me near them."

Emily smiled sincerely, "I'd be lying if I said I wasn't initially concerned."

The look of melancholy crept onto Robert's handsome face as he listened to Emily, but Emily continued, "But my concern was for you, Robert."

"What do you mean?" Robert asked.

"I was concerned that you would not get the time to rest and relax with the two whirling dervishes around. Those two have an overabundance of energy."

Robert's melancholy melted away, "I can't wait to meet them."

Emily smiled, "You'll get you chance later this afternoon."

"Are you sure it's okay for me to be around them?" Robert asked optimistically.

"Of course. Why wouldn't it be?" Emily inquired.

Robert closed his eyes tightly, "Dr. Hamilton and Alex both said before that I was badly injured, but I didn't feel injured. It wasn't until I was sent to that place that I began to think that I have some type of mental problem."

"What makes you think that?" Emily inquired with concern.

"Well," Robert started as he held his head with his eyes tightly shut. "I don't have any injuries and that place I was at is an asylum."

"How do you know that?" Emily questioned.

"Is it?" Robert questioned softly. "And please tell me the truth."

"Yes, that place is an asylum," Emily answered honestly.

"Then I do have mental problems," Robert stated rhetorically.

"The only problem that I'm aware of is that you lost your memory in an accident," Emily explained tenderly.

"But I don't remember an accident," Robert said with frustration.

"That's what I'm saying, Robert. You lost your memory. That's why you're working with Dr. Hamilton," Emily explained in a calming tone.

"Will I ever get my memory back?" Robert asked optimistically.

"I believe that with all my heart," Emily said sincerely.

Robert smiled and winked at Emily, "Then I believe it too."

"So you're not angry with Alex or Dr. Hamilton?"

"No," Robert answered. "I don't blame either of them."

"I think you should tell both of them that because they both care about you and want to see you get better," Emily explained maternally.

"I will," Robert promised.

"Maybe you can get Alex to give you the grand tour of the grounds when he's done with his business calls."

"That would be nice," Robert responded. "And it will give me the opportunity to tell him that I don't blame him."

"Sounds like a good idea to me," Emily offered. "Alex feels terrible about what happened to you, Robert. You telling him that you don't blame him will be just the right medicine for him."

Robert smiled sadly at Emily, "I just want to forget that place."

"I know you do. Hopefully we can all put the past few days behind us and move on," Emily stated.

"I hope we can too," Robert said.

"What can we hope to do?" Alex questioned as he sauntered into the kitchen and overheard the remnants of Robert's and Emily's conversation.

"Forget bad memories," Emily said to her husband.

"Oh," Alex said a little surprised at the seriousness of the conversation between Emily and Robert. As Alex was going to respond, Robert interrupted.

"Are you busy?" Robert inquired of Alex.

Taken a little off guard, Alex answered, "No. Why?"

"Emily mentioned that you might show me around this place. That is if you're not too busy?" Robert stated a little timidly.

Alex smiled as he looked from Robert to Emily and then back to Robert, "No, I'm not too busy. I'd love to give you the grand tour."

"Would you like some breakfast before your long walk?" Emily asked lovingly of her husband.

Alex kissed Emily on the cheek as he walked to the refrigerator to get a bottle of orange juice, "No, juice is fine for now." Alex smiled at Robert, "Are you ready for the grand tour?"

Robert looked down at his feet, "I think I need a pair of shoes first."

Alex and Emily laughed as Alex headed for the door, "I'll be right back with your shoes."

"Thanks," Robert said as Alex disappeared.

Emily put her hand on Robert's shoulder, "I think you made his day."

"All I did was ask him to show me around," Robert responded seriously.

"It was a lot more than that, Robert. Alex was worried that you'd never want to have anything to do with him ever again," Emily explained.

"That's crazy," Robert replied. After uttering the words he laughed, "Maybe I shouldn't be saying that something is crazy—especially since I was in a place for crazy people."

Regardless of the seriousness of Robert's institutionalization, Emily laughed at Robert's response. "You're not crazy, Clyde."

"I hope not," Robert replied as Alex reappeared in the doorway holding a new pair of running shoes.

"What don't you hope?" Alex inquired after overhearing the last few words of the conversation.

"It's not important," Emily answered.

Alex handed the running shoes to Robert as he inquired skeptically, "Really?"

"Yes, really," Robert answered as he pulled the shoe laces tight.

Alex stared questioningly at Emily before dropping the subject. As Robert tied the last shoe, Alex feigned a smile, "Ready to go?"

Robert stood up slowly and a little unsteadily, "Yep, I'm ready."

Alex and Emily both looked at Robert with deep concern, "Are you okay?" Alex asked.

Robert nodded, "I'm okay."

"Are you sure you feel okay, Clyde?" Emily inquired tenderly. "If you're not feeling up to it, you and Alex can do the grand tour later."

Robert embraced Emily softly, "I'm okay. Really."

"Let's go then," Alex stated with feigned enthusiasm as he put his hand on Robert's shoulder and ushered him to the door. Alex looked back over his shoulder at Emily, "We'll be back later."

"Have a good time," Emily said as the two disappeared through the doorway.

Alex guided Robert slowly to the large French doors and opened them to reveal the lush carpet of grass before them. Robert slowly walked alongside Alex as he took in all the sights, stopping momentarily here and there to let the beauty of the estate sink in. After walking around a small portion of the estate, Robert's pace slowed and the exhaustion overtook him.

"Are you okay?" Alex asked with deep concern.

Robert stopped walking and sat down clumsily alongside a row of trees. "I just need a moment."

"Okay," Alex replied as he sat down next to Robert.

Robert inhaled deeply several times as the two sat beside each other in silence. Robert took a long cleansing breath and exhaled deeply before addressing Alex. "Alex?"

"Yeah," Alex replied.

"I don't blame you for what happened to me," Robert explained matter-of-factly.

"Really?" Alex responded off guard.

"Yeah," Robert answered. "I don't blame you or Dr. Hamilton, and I want to say I'm sorry for how I acted last night."

"You don't have to apologize, Robert. You were under the influence of a lot of drugs," Alex explained gently as the emotional roller coaster of the past few days threatened to overcome him. "I'm glad you don't blame me or Dr. Hamilton. We both want you to get well."

"Do you think I'll get well soon—like in the next three or four weeks or sooner?" Robert asked hopefully.

"I honestly don't know, Robert," Alex answered as he saw the veil of melancholy mixed with frustration cloud Robert's countenance. "Why are you in such a hurry?"

"I just want to get better so I can go home and go back to school," Robert explained.

A wry smile crept onto Alex's lips, "You're the only guy I think in history that actually wants to go back to school."

Robert shrugged, "Could be."

The two sat a few more minutes in silence as Robert regained his strength. Alex stood and dusted the freshly mowed grass from his trousers. He extended his hand to assist Robert, and as Robert stood, he reached behind and dusted his pants. As the two commenced their leisurely stroll around the grounds, Alex stopped abruptly.

"Wait a minute," Alex said as a knowing smile grew wide. "You don't want to go back to school for homework and all that stuff. You want to go back because there's someone there you want to see."

Robert turned away to hide his huge grin, "Why would you think that?"

Alex took Robert's arm and turned him so that they were facing each other. Robert could not conceal his smile as Alex asked, "Am I right?"

"Maybe," Robert teased.

"No maybes. I'm right, aren't I?" Alex said.

Robert's eyes sparkled as he replied, "Yeah, you're right."

"Does this person have a name?" Alex inquired genially.

"Of course she has a name. It's Gina," Robert responded as his eyes lit up as he spoke her name.

Alex, at the mentioning of the name, turned slightly away from Robert to conceal his emotions. He could hear the thump of his heart beating in his chest. After a long cleansing breath, Alex asked, "Who's Gina?"

Robert's smile grew as his eyes sparkled, "She's the prettiest girl in school."

"It sounds as though you have a crush on this girl," Alex surmised as he listened to Robert talk about his mother.

"I do," Robert replied.

"And does she know how you feel about her?"

"Of course she does. I love her and she loves me," Robert answered confidently.

"Really?" Alex said.

"Yes, Really. That's why I'm anxious to get back to school," Robert explained.

Alex took a moment to collect his thoughts, "Why can you only see her at school?"

Robert started kicking small pebbles on the walking trail, "Her parents won't let her see me."

"Why?" Alex questioned.

Robert frowned, "They said I'm not good enough for her and that I'll never amount to anything."

Alex fought to keep his anger concealed, "They said you'd never amount to anything?"

"Yep," Robert answered. "But Gina and I love each other and we're going to make it work. For now we can only see each other in school, but I'm working hard so that we can be together when we're both eighteen."

"You're going to get married?" Alex asked with weary disbelief.

"Yes," Robert answered self-assured. "I asked her if she wanted to get married when we're both eighteen, and she said yes. Nobody knows—so please don't tell anyone, okay?"

Dumbfounded, Alex replied, "Okay."

"We have almost everything planned, so that is why I'm in a hurry to get back. I miss her," Robert explained with a touch of longing in his voice.

"You really have thought this through," Alex said more to himself than to Robert.

"We both have," Robert replied.

"What about children? Have you thought about that?" Alex questioned.

"Yes, we have. We both want children," Robert answered confidently.

"How many?" Alex inquired further.

"It doesn't matter to me as long as they are healthy. I just want to be able to give my children what I didn't have," Robert explained.

"And what is that?" Alex questioned.

"A father who loves them unconditionally and who would do anything for them," Robert explained with sincerity.

Alex turned away to hide his emotions. He took a moment to stop the quivering of his lips before stating, "You'll be an excellent father, Robert. Any child would be lucky to have you as a dad."

"I just want my children to know that I love them and would do anything for them. I never had that in my life, so I'm going to make sure my children grow up in a peaceful, loving atmosphere." Robert explained.

"I'm sure you will," Alex responded emotionally.

"But first I have to get well so that I can go back home," Robert stated impatiently.

"You're going to get better, Robert," Alex offered. "And in the meantime, you can rest and relax here at my dad's place."

"Are you sure he won't mind?" Robert inquired.

Alex laughed, "No Robert, he won't mind. I promise."

"Okay," Robert said. "Someone said last night that your dad has horses. Can we go see them?"

Alex smiled as he pushed his emotions back inside, "Sure. The barns are this way."

# CHAPTER 20

▼

A few weeks elapsed and Robert continued to grow stronger every day, although his brain did not surrender it's bitter hold on his most cherished and haunting memories. Each day of Robert's life was spent outdoors with Alex playing tennis or riding the thoroughbreds that Robert had once so eagerly and joyfully purchased, or swimming with his beautiful twin grandchildren that he did not even recognize. At least once a day, Robert would meet Emily for breakfast and joke about the previous days events or the misadventures that Robert had had with Alex or the twins. Two days a week without fail, Alex would drive Robert to the hospital for his appointments with Dr. Hamilton.

On a gloriously bright morning as Robert was drinking his orange juice and Emily was sipping her coffee and laughing over their mutual admiration and teasing of Alex, Alex came into the spacious kitchen that overlooked the enticing blue waters of the oval-shaped swimming pool with a grim look upon his face.

"Honey, what's wrong?" Emily asked.

"Business," Alex said too quickly, which caused the suspicious eyebrows of his wife to raise. "It's nothing really," he continued, "But there is someone I have to meet this morning regarding the business."

Emily slowly nodded her understanding that the business he referred to was probably Robert's construction business, and she dropped the subject so as not to concern Robert.

"Will you be back for lunch," Robert asked nonchalantly.

"Not if you're cooking," Alex teased.

"Hmm, Robert. I think Alex is catching on, but he's still not up to our smart ass caliber," Emily smirked as she took a bite of a croissant.

"Nope, he's got a long way to go before he's in our league, Bonnie," Robert said as he playfully slapped Alex on the back as Alex sat down next to him at the kitchen table.

"I'm with you on that, Clyde," Emily said as she imitated the slap to Alex's back.

Alex playfully got up from his chair that was positioned between Robert and Emily, "Well if that's the way you want to be, I'll take my ball and bat and go home."

Robert and Emily looked at Alex and then at each other before letting out a hilarious roar. Robert tried to take a drink of his orange juice, but his attempt was made in vain as the orange juice spurted out as his self-control wavered causing the uproar to continue. Seeing the orange juice fly out of Robert's mouth, Emily nearly choked on her croissant as the hysterics continued over Alex's banal, but authentic attempt at humor.

Alex tried his best pseudo-wounded act, but Emily and Robert continued their unabated laughter until Alex joined in with the gregarious pair who had grown especially close during Robert's recovery. "Okay, I give up. You two are the masters," Alex offered.

"There you go again," Robert said in his harmless sarcastic tone.

"What? What did I do again?" Alex asked with a smile, knowing he was about to be once again playfully insulted.

"Take a good look at Emily. She's a woman, therefore she wouldn't be a master, but a mistress," Robert explained as he took advantage of Alex's gullible nature.

Alex pretended to be irate, "My wife better not be someone's mistress."

"Oh God, he's hopeless," Robert laughed as he through his arms in the air.

"I only have eyes for you, my love. You may be gullible, but you're really cute," Emily teased as she hooked her arm around Alex's neck and pulled him into a passionate kiss.

"You're a damn lucky man, Alex. Lucky, that is, that you have a wife to take care of you," Robert kidded as he contorted his body around the couple as they continued their kiss.

Emily ended the passionate kiss as Alex's face turned a brilliant shade of crimson. Alex looked at Robert and smiled, "I'm not lucky, I'm skillful. I hunted Emily down like a fox in a henhouse, and then I charmed her with my world class charm and wit. Even the likes of James Bond, Mr. Double O Seven himself, would be in awe of my suave sophistication when it comes to the opposite sex."

Robert looked at Alex with the most mischievous of grins, "Mr. Double O Seven? That's pretty pathetic. You never told anyone that story before have you? I mean, I'm the one who gets tied to the bed and locked up in the rubber room, but if you tell people that one, Mr. Double O Seven, I'm afraid me and you will be sharing the same room in the loony bin."

Alex looked startled for a moment until Emily started to howl with laughter at Robert's joking description of his treatment, and Alex joined in on the laughter as he playfully put Robert in a side-headlock. "I don't want to share a rubber room in the loony bin with you," Alex teased. "You'd get me into trouble, and probably put in a straight-jacket."

Robert quizzically looked at Alex for a moment as he pondered Alex's statement. "Hmm, I think you would look good in a straight-jacket. I mean, it really couldn't look much worse than most of the outfits that you put together when Emily isn't around to do it for you," Robert laughed, as Emily doubled over in tears from all the hilarity.

"That's true, sweetie. You couldn't put together an outfit if your life depended on it," Emily playfully tormented after she regained a minute portion of her composure.

Alex walked over and put his coffee mug in the dishwasher. He feigned a frown as he continued, "Okay, I'm leaving now for my business meeting. You two behave!"

"You're not wearing that are you?" Emily continued teasing in the same vein as before.

"Yeah, you better let Emily take you back upstairs and pick out another outfit," Robert playfully joked. "On second thought, you better not. Mr. Double O Seven might turn on his charm and sophistication and end up missing the meeting," Robert continued mercilessly.

Alex stomped playfully out of the kitchen with one hand tugging Emily along with him, "Goodbye, Robert. I'll make sure Bonnie rejoins you in a few minutes."

"And you said you were Double O Seven," Robert said mockingly. "It'd take him a lot longer than a few minutes."

Emily stopped dead in her track as she laughed at Robert's playful sarcasm and uncanny ability to tease Alex about every word he said. Alex shook his head in mock disapproval at the duo who stood laughing uncontrollably in front of him, "Aw, where did I go wrong?"

Robert regained his composure as he put his arm lovingly around Alex's shoulders. "You know we love you. We would never tease anyone who we didn't know and love, right Bonnie?"

"Right Clyde," Emily replied as she put her arm lovingly around Alex's shoulders, making the three of them join in a group hug.

"You two are too much!" Alex exclaimed, playfully defeated and resigned to do battle another day. "I'll see you later, Robert."

"Bye Alex. Good luck with the business meeting, and remember, Double O Seven knows exactly when to use the charm and wit. Don't come on too strong in the meeting. You don't want them to think that you're loopy," Robert said with a wry twinkle in his eye.

"I'll try to remember that, Moneypenny," Alex replied with a fake tip of his imaginary hat. "Em, can I see you for a second before I go?"

"That's not fair!" Robert exclaimed jovially. "Why does she get to be 'M'?"

"Because the lady is always the boss," Alex replied diplomatically.

"At least in this house," Robert teased as he winked at Alex on his way out of the kitchen.

"And don't you forget it," Emily said with mock authority.

Alex pulled Emily close as he waited for Robert to get safely out of distance so as not to overhear the conversation that he was about to have with his wife. After checking to see that Robert had exited the area, Alex's face turned serious as he looked into Emily's eyes.

"What's happened, Alex?" Emily asked.

"I got a call this morning from a woman who claims to be a reporter for the county newspaper," Alex explained.

"What did she want?"

"She said that she had the 911 tape from the time of Robert's incident, and she was hypothesizing about what had happened," Alex continued in a serious tone.

"Did she know what happened?"

"I don't know what she knows about Robert, but she knows who I am," Alex replied..

"What do you mean … she knows who you are?" Emily asked with a hint of terror coloring her tone.

"She knows I am, or was, a high ranking political consultant and Party official, and that I am thinking of running for Congress in the next election," Alex answered stoically.

Emily sat down as if she had been hit in the stomach. "What did she want?"

"I don't know, that's why I'm going to meet her. I don't have a good feeling about this, Em," Alex answered softly as he sat down next to his wife and pulled her close.

"What are you going to do if she knows about Robert?" Emily asked as she snuggled close in Alex's arms.

"I don't know," Alex said plainly. "I don't know what's the right thing to do," Alex said at the perplexity of the situation.

"You may be faced with the choice of Robert, or your future in politics," Emily replied sadly.

"Maybe we're reading too much into this. How could she possibly know what happened?" Alex asked rhetorically.

"How did she know the 911 tape referred to you and Robert?" Emily asked.

"Because the damn 911 operator asked me my name. I thought she was delaying the ambulance with her damn questions, so I just answered her. I told her who I was, and of course she had to ask the address," Alex replied angrily as he mentally replayed the conversation.

"Did she ask anything else? Like what happened?" Emily quizzed.

"Yeah, she asked what happened and I told her my father had an accident and was badly hurt. She pressed me about the type of accident, but by that time I heard the ambulance sirens in the distance, so I hung up on her," Alex related as he mentally remembered looking at the crimson ligature marks that had cut into Robert's neck.

Alex shook his head to clear away the memories, but they came flooding back to him in a deluge of images and sounds. "Can you believe that one of the paramedics told the other one to be careful around Robert … because he was one of them?" Alex relayed angrily.

"Because he was one of whom, a homosexual?" Emily asked perplexed.

"Yeah, he didn't want to touch him because he was gay. It didn't matter that Robert was barely breathing and unconscious. That bastard treated him like he had the plague," Alex replied with hatred dripping from his every word.

"The main thing is that Robert is okay, and he's okay because you saved his life," Emily said in an attempt to make her husband feel better.

"Yeah, he's relatively okay, but how do I know that I wasn't part of the reason he tried to kill himself?" Alex asked guiltily.

"You can't think like that, Alex," Emily reprimanded.

"How can I not? Up until that day, I basically felt the same way as that paramedic," Alex said with a mixture of sadness and anger at himself.

"You don't feel that way now, do you?" Emily asked, already knowing the answer.

"No, of course not. Somewhere along the way I realized that Robert is a really good guy. And he has always been a good guy, but I was too damn busy worried about how my career would be affected by him. He gave me anything I wanted growing up, and he loved me no matter what. His unconditional love for me killed his relationship with Mitchell."

"What? You never did tell me why they broke up, but I can't imagine it being over you. Hell, up until that day, you hadn't talked to your father in years," Emily replied.

"I hadn't talked to him in years, but he never stopped loving me, and he never stopped putting my well-being ahead of his own. The split between those two wasn't mutual. Mitchell ended it because Robert forever put me ahead of himself, and Mitchell was tired of seeing Robert sacrifice his own happiness for an ungrateful ass like me. And you know what, I don't blame Mitchell for doing so. I have been an ungrateful ass, but Robert shouldn't suffer because of me," Alex said painfully.

"I think there still is a chance for those two to get back together, once Robert regains his memory. I mean, I can see it in Mitchell's eyes that he still loves Robert," Emily explained optimistically. "And he told me he has never stopped loving Robert."

"I know he still loves Robert too, and since I was the reason for their split, I'm also going to be the reason for their reconciliation," Alex said confidently.

"What made you change your mind?" Emily asked eagerly.

"Well, for one thing, Dr. Hamilton and Mitchell tag-teamed me into seeing the light. My homophobia didn't go over well with the good doctor, and Mitchell rightfully made me take responsibility," Alex replied.

"That's the reason you changed.... because you were browbeaten into it?" Emily answered in disbelief.

"No, let me finish. I realized after you came to be with me after this all happened that you loved me completely. To be loved like that is rare, wouldn't you say? Well, I figured that if you can be loved like that by somebody, and you can reciprocate that love, then nobody should stand in your way. I withheld my love and acceptance of Robert, hoping that he would give up the love of his life. Well he lost that love, and look what happened. I would never let anyone tear us apart, Em, and yet that is what I tried to do with Robert and Mitchell," Alex answered sincerely.

"Well, the important thing is that you don't feel like that anymore, right?"

"Absolutely. I'm not going to interfere in Robert's love life ever again, that is if he ever remembers who he is," Alex replied honestly.

"With the exception of trying to get Robert and Mitchell back together?" Emily questioned.

"Yes, I owe him that, and then after that, I won't get involved."

"I love you, Alex Petrovic," Emily whispered as she planted a small kiss on Alex's cheek. "You've changed a lot since we got here, and it's definitely for the better. It really warms my heart to see you and Robert joking around and spending time together," Emily answered sincerely.

"You know what? I really enjoy spending time with him. And seeing the two of you together conspiring every morning makes me appreciate both of you even more," Alex said with a sincere and heartfelt smile that lit up the room.

"You better go," Emily said as she took Alex's hand in hers and pulled him up.

"Yeah, it's time to deal with the devil," Alex said gloomily.

"Give 'em hell, Double O Seven," Emily replied with a wry smile.

"I think I've created two monsters," Alex joked as he headed for the front door.

# CHAPTER 21

▼

Alex knew in his mind, while he drove to the meeting place, that he was going to come face to face with someone who wanted something from him. "But what could anyone know about Robert?" Alex asked himself. As he played every possible scenario over in his mind, the familiar, but irritating ring of his cell phone slapped Alex out of making guesses and assumptions. "Hello," Alex answered.

"Hi Alex, it's Antonio."

"Hey Antonio, what's up?" Alex asked in a friendly tone.

"Can you meet me this afternoon?" Antonio asked.

"What's wrong?" Alex replied pessimistically.

"Nothing's wrong. It's good news, actually. But, I don't want to go over it on the phone," Antonio explained.

"All right. I can meet you anytime this afternoon."

"How about you meet me at my office at one o'clock?" Antonio inquired.

"That sounds good, as long as nothing's wrong."

"Nothing's wrong. You need to relax, Alex," Antonio teased.

"Yeah, I know. You're not the only one to tell me that," Alex responded playfully.

"Okay, then I'll see you at one o'clock in my office."

"I'll be there," Alex replied as he flipped his cell phone shut.

As he was waiting at the stoplight that led into the parking lot where he was supposed to meet the mystery woman, the butterflies in Alex's stomach danced frenetically as he suddenly felt weak. Alex's adult life had been spent in politics, so he knew the angles of blackmailers. His mind raced as he wondered whether the woman knew about Robert's suicide attempt or his homosexuality, or both.

Would she try to blackmail Alex into paying large sums of money to keep quiet about Robert's condition? As he sat in his car waiting for the woman to show herself, he turned on the radio. An instant smile appeared on his handsome face. The song was one that Robert would sing when he did not think anyone was around to hear him. Suddenly, Alex regained his strength and purpose, and was ready to take on anyone who got in his way.

The loud rumble of a rusty muffler shook Alex out of his daydream. Pulling next to him, a short-haired blonde woman driving an old, rusty, loud relic of an automobile rolled down her window and motioned for Alex to do the same. Alex and the mystery woman were now face to face, and the anxiety began to build in Alex's gut.

"Hello, Mr. Petrovic," announced the young, blonde woman.

"I'm at a disadvantage. You know who I am, but I don't have the privilege of knowing who you are," Alex said cavalierly.

"I'm sorry. My name is Trudy Frazier."

"Okay, Trudy, what do you want?"

"You're to the point. I like that," Trudy complimented.

"How about an answer then?" Alex said authoritatively.

"Fine. I want you to help me land a reporter's job in the capital," Trudy said seriously.

Alex stared at the young woman before bursting out into laughter. "Now why would I do that?"

"Because you're such a nice guy, and besides, if you don't, the world will know what has been going on in the Petrovic family," she continued sternly.

"And whose interest would that pique? Why would people care about what goes on in my family?" Alex said nonchalantly, trying to deflect any concern.

"Well, I have found that people are quite interested in the lives of politicians. You having such an important position, and then resigning from it, would pique a few peoples interest for sure. And then, of course, is the matter of you running for Congress. I'm sure your constituents would be interested in the personal lives of their future Congressman and his family," she said sarcastically.

"You don't know anything about my family," Alex answered defensively.

"Are you sure about that?" Trudy teased.

"My family is nobody's business but mine, understand?" Alex snapped.

"Well, it could be just your business, if you give me what I want. If not, I'm sure my readers would thoroughly enjoy the story of the Petrovic's."

"Go to hell," Alex replied.

"Fine, I'll just go back to the newspaper and write the feature story of how former Party official and big-time political consultant, Alex Petrovic, frantically called 911 regarding an accident involving his father," she said arrogantly.

"So … my father had an accident. That's hardly concern for your readers," Alex said disdainfully.

"That's probably true, but it would be of concern if they knew the accident resulted in the elder Petrovic landing on the second floor of Memorial Hospital," she paused. "Correct me if I'm wrong, but the second floor is the psychiatric ward, right?" she questioned conceitedly.

Alex glared at the reporter with venomous eyes, "What do you want?"

"I told you. I want your help landing a job in the capital," she said with an evil smile.

"Why? Can't you get a job on your own?" Alex replied arrogantly.

"Yes I can, but it is so much more fun this way," she hissed.

"I'll have to think about it," Alex said honestly.

"Fine, but don't think too long, or my feature on your family will go to print."

"I'll get back to you in a few days. If this story comes out before I give you my answer, you will regret the day you ever heard the name Petrovic. Understand?" Alex stated angrily.

"Oh yes, I understand," Trudy responded before pulling out of the parking lot.

Alex remained in his car listening to the radio while he watched his black-mailer leave the parking lot. "What am I going to do?" he thought to himself. Whilst he was sitting in the parking lot, images of Robert hanging by the rafter, staring blankly into space at the hellhole asylum where he was completely restrained, and being forcibly held down while he was being injected with anti-psychotic drugs came flooding into Alex's weary mind. The hell that Robert had already endured was enough. The last thing Alex wanted was for Robert to have to go through any more pain or humiliation.

Alex pulled the gearshift into drive and threw gravel all over the parking lot as he pulled out angrily onto the main road. He spent the next few minutes of the ride back to Robert's house remembering haunting images that Robert had suffered, and in turn, he had suffered along with Robert. When he briefly closed his eyes, he would see Robert's lifeless body twisting in the barn, or he would hear Robert's screams as Robert was being forcibly restrained and injected with medication. "I won't let that woman hurt him," Alex said aloud. As he was pulling into Robert's private driveway, a song came on the radio that caused Alex to tear up. He sat there and listened until the song ended, and then he walked with pride up to the ornate front door.

As Alex walked inside, he was greeted by the hyperactivity of his twins as they ran full speed through the foyer and into the living room. "What are you doing?" questioned a befuddled Alex.

"Playing tag with Robert," came the jubilant screams of his precious children.

"Oh," Alex muttered as he saw Robert come through the study door and into the living room where he masterfully tagged little Stevie.

Emily came into the living room after hearing her husband's voice. She quickly went over to Alex and led him off to the quiet of the study. The twins knew that the study was off limits, so Alex and Emily could have a private conversation.

"What happened?" Emily inquired.

"She's blackmailing me," Alex said sadly.

"What did she want?"

"She wants me to help her land a reporting job in the capital in exchange for her not printing a story about Robert," Alex explained.

"What does she know about Robert?" Emily questioned.

"Thankfully, not everything, but enough to hurt him. She knows that I called 911 regarding an accident, and that Robert ended up in the psychiatric ward of the hospital," Alex continued sadly.

"What are you going to do?" Emily queried.

"I don't know," replied Alex.

"You know that if you help her, your political career will always be haunted by this," Emily offered as a reality check.

"Yeah I know, but if I let her print that article, Robert will be forever haunted by it, as will I," Alex explained.

"When do you have to tell her your answer?" quizzed Emily.

"In a couple of weeks. Hopefully I'll be struck by some godly wisdom by then."

"I don't know what to tell you, honey," Emily replied solemnly.

"I don't know what I'll do," Alex said as he looked at his watch. "Damn, I have to go. I told Antonio I would meet him after lunch."

"What did he want?"

"I don't know, but he said it wasn't bad news or anything to worry about," Alex explained.

"That's good to hear," Emily said with a smile. "Maybe you should ask Antonio about this woman."

"I think I will," Alex stated as he kissed his wife on the cheek. "I see everyone is in high spirits."

"Yeah, Robert and the kids have been running around since you left. I truly don't know how he does it. He may think he's fifteen, but his body is still fifty," Emily said smiling.

"I hope I have his energy when I'm fifty so that I can chase you around like that," Alex teased.

"In your dreams, Mr. Petrovic," Emily laughed as she took Alex's hand and led him out to the front door.

"Do you think you can hold down the fort?" Alex jested.

"Absolutely. Robert is my buddy, and we can double team the little people," Emily laughed.

"See you later," Alex said as he headed out the front door.

"Bye, Alex. Good luck."

# CHAPTER 22

▼

Alex arrived at Antonio's traditionally styled law office at 12:50p.m. He checked in with the receptionist and sat down in a large black leather chair while he waited for Antonio to return from lunch. As he flipped inattentively through a men's magazine left lying on a cherry-wood coffee table, Antonio walked into the reception area and asked Alex to follow him. The two young men walked through several large wooden doors until they came to a large corner office that overlooked the river. Antonio took off his suit coat and motioned for Alex to have a seat.

"What's up?" asked a relatively nervous Alex.

Noticing the anxiety written plainly on his friend's face, Antonio smiled as he spoke, "Don't worry, Alex. I told you when I called that it was nothing to worry about."

"Then what's going on?" Alex replied.

"I have some good news regarding your father's assault case," Antonio stated before he was interrupted by Alex.

"Hold on. Before I forget," he paused as he reached into his back pocket and pulled out his wallet. "Here's the check for the money that I owe you for bailing out my father."

"I had forgotten all about that," Antonio said honestly before taking the check and continuing with his information about Robert. "Since I haven't dealt with a criminal case in a long time, I took out all the stops and investigated every detail about the night that your father was arrested."

"Did you find something out?" Alex questioned.

"I went to the bar where all this occurred and asked a few of the patrons some questions. Most of those present were also there the night Robert was arrested. I simply asked them what happened."

"And?" Alex asked anxiously.

"Well, most of them said that as soon as Robert walked in the door that they started letting him know he wasn't welcome there. Most came out and shouted that 'his' type wasn't welcome at their bar."

"Go on. That doesn't sound like anything new," Alex said despondently.

Antonio continued, "Robert didn't bother with anyone—he just ordered his drinks and sat there quietly until the bartender, yielding to his redneck patrons, no doubt, refused to serve him anymore."

"That's when they called the police?" Alex questioned.

"Yes, and two officers came and escorted Robert out of the bar. According to most of the people in the bar, Robert was intoxicated at this point."

"So what happened?" Alex asked curiously.

"Well, at this point, most of the patrons stayed in the bar and couldn't give me any further information," Antonio explained.

"So we still have nothing?" Alex asked sadly and dejectedly.

"No, a couple who was only in the bar a few minutes before Robert was refused service, decided to leave when the officers arrived. They were outside and witnessed everything that happened," Antonio said proudly.

"So, tell me. What did they see?" Alex asked optimistically.

"More importantly, it was what they heard. As the officers were leading Robert out, the couple overheard the one officer say that he knew this man. The other officer asked how he knew him, and the officer said that his sister knew Robert and that she made his nephew quit going to the same place where Robert frequented because she didn't want her son anywhere near a queer," Antonio stated indignantly.

"What happened then," Alex asked.

"Well, according to the couple, Robert staggered toward the parking lot, apparently for his car, but one of the officers grabbed him and reprimanded him."

"What the hell did they have to reprimand Robert for?" Alex asked angrily.

"Apparently, again based on the couple's assessment, they told Robert not to come back to this bar, and then they arrogantly asked why he wasn't at a fairy bar, or something along that line," Antonio related.

"Those bastards," Alex erupted.

"Well, Robert must have felt the same way because he swore at the officers. After that, they tried to frisk him, but Robert resisted and back-handed one of the officers," Antonio continued. "The other officer pepper-sprayed Robert, cuffed him, and threw him in the back of the patrol car."

"I don't blame him, Antonio. Look at the way they treated him," Alex responded indignantly.

"I know," he smiled, "And that is why I got the charges dropped against Robert," Antonio said with unabated delight.

"What? How?" Alex asked stunned.

"I had the couple sign affidavits of what happened, and then I took the affidavits to the District Attorney. Oh, and I also took the affidavits of several other people who had been harassed by these two officers in the past," Antonio said proudly.

"I can't believe this! Well, yes I can. You're the best, Antonio. How can I ever thank you?" Alex asked jovially.

"I was just doing my job. Besides, it was fun doing a little investigating. I actually got to get out of the office for a little while," Antonio said with a wide grin.

"You're the best, Antonio."

"Well, occasionally, maybe," Antonio said humbly. "Why don't you go home and celebrate this chapter being over. I know there is still a lot more to go, right?"

"Unfortunately, yes, but this is the best news I could have heard today," Alex replied relieved.

"Everything all right?" Antonio asked.

"There is something I want to ask you. I had a call this morning from a reporter who turns out to be blackmailing me. Is there anything I can do?"

"What did she want?" Antonio asked with intrigue.

"She wants me to help her get a job in the capital, or she is going to print a story about my family, especially about Robert being in a psychiatric ward following some sort of 'accident,'" Alex explained.

"You can call the police. Blackmail is a crime," Antonio stated.

"Yeah, I know, but I can't subject Robert to anything like that right now. If something came out in the papers and he read it, I think it would destroy him," Alex said simply.

"Yeah, but if you help her, it could destroy your political career," Antonio replied seriously.

"I know. I don't know what I'm going to do. I have a couple of weeks before I give her my answer. Maybe a miracle will happen in that time," Alex said tongue-in-cheek.

"Maybe," Antonio joked. "Start working those rosary beads, my friend," Antonio said as he good-naturedly slapped Alex on the back.

"If only …" Alex said as he rose and walked to the door.

"Hey," Antonio said, "If you need anything, let me know, okay?"

"I will. Thanks Antonio. I owe you so much," Alex said sincerely.

"Yeah. Don't forget, one day I may cash in my chips," Antonio joked.

"Whatever and whenever. You know where to find me," Alex said amiably as he walked out the door and into the long hallway.

Out of curiosity, Alex drove out to the bar where Robert was harassed and later arrested. In his anonymity, Alex walked up to the bar and sat down.

"What'll be?" came the low voice from behind the bar.

"Whiskey," Alex replied as he mentally inventoried the patrons in the bar. Two men in dirty tee shirts and work boots sat at the end of the bar and sipped on bottled beer. Two middle-aged woman sat at a table and ate wings and drank cheap beer from a can. The women both wore short shorts and revealing tank tops. As one of the women went to the jukebox, the two men at the bar watched her as she leaned over to play a country song. Both whistled as she turned to them and grinned.

"Here you go," said the bartender as he handed the whiskey to Alex. "Are you new around here?" asked the bartender.

"Yeah, I was hesitant to come here because I heard that this place was for queers," Alex said in a deep voice as he drained the whiskey shot.

"No!" exclaimed the bartender. "We had a fairy come in here a few months ago, but we made sure he wouldn't come back," he said proudly.

"Really? How'd you do that?" questioned Alex.

"I called my brother-in-law. He's a local cop and he can't stand queers," the bartender replied with a satisfied grin. "They took him outside, slapped him around and then took him to jail."

Feeling suddenly sickened, Alex threw down a few dollars and walked out of the bar.

# CHAPTER 23

▼

Two weeks passed from the time that Alex received the welcome news that Antonio had gotten the assault charges dropped against Robert. Alex breathed easier knowing that when Robert regained his memory, he would not have to worry about a criminal charge hanging over him. Knowing the humiliation that Robert had suffered that night, Alex felt greater sympathy for Robert and showered him with kind words daily causing some confused stares from Robert.

Shortly after midnight on a cool fall evening, Alex and Emily were stirred from their slumber by a muffled cry that came through the monitor that was placed in Robert's room. Alex leapt out of bed and ran down the hallway and threw open the door. Robert, sitting upright in his bed, raggedly rubbed his head.

"What's wrong?" asked Alex quickly, with sincere concern.

Robert continued to rub his head and wipe the tears from his eyes without looking up or responding to Alex's question.

"Robert, you're scaring me. What's wrong?" Alex sat down on the bed next to Robert and gently rubbed his leg. "What happened?"

Robert fell back onto his pillow and covered his eyes. Alex reached down gently and pulled Robert's hands away from his eyes. "What happened?" Alex asked emotionally.

Robert turned his head to the side, away from Alex's stare. "I don't know. I don't remember," Robert answered in a soft tone that was barely audible.

"What don't you remember, Robert? It's okay to tell me," Alex said as he gently turned Robert's cheek so that Robert was now facing him.

"I had a bad dream," Robert answered.

"You had a bad dream? Like a nightmare?" Alex questioned.

"Yeah," Robert said as he closed his eyes tightly.

"What's wrong, Robert? Does your head hurt?" Alex asked with deep concern in his voice.

"Yeah, it hurts really bad, and it won't stop," Robert answered on the verge of tears.

"When did it start hurting?" Alex asked.

"When I was having the nightmare," Robert responded in a voice no louder than a whisper.

Alex gently turned Robert on his side, and massaged the muscles in the back of Robert's neck. The muscles were taut with spasms, and Robert groaned when Alex massaged a sore spot. "Relax for a few minutes while I go call Dr. Hamilton," Alex softly commanded.

"No, please Alex, don't call Dr. Hamilton. I just need a couple of aspirins," Robert pleaded.

"Are you sure? I'd feel better if we called Dr. Hamilton," Alex explained.

"No, I'll be fine with a couple of aspirins," Robert continued.

"All right. I'll be right back with some aspirins. Try to relax, okay?" Alex replied.

"I'm not going anywhere," Robert tried to joke, but the sound that emanated from his lips was a whimper of pain.

Alex returned quickly with a bottle of aspirins and a glass of water to find Robert lying on his side, with his arm pressed tightly against his eyes. Alex opened the bottle and poured out two aspirins and tapped Robert lightly on the leg. Robert rolled over and opened his mouth as Alex placed the aspirins in his mouth and handed Robert the glass of water. Robert took a gulp of water, handed the glass back to Alex, and rolled back over on his side with his arm shielding his eyes.

"Did the neck massage make you feel any better?" Alex asked helplessly.

Without rolling over or looking up, Robert spoke quietly, "I'll be okay, Alex. Go back to bed."

"No, I'm going to stay here for awhile," Alex instructed.

"Okay," Robert paused for a moment as he collected his thoughts through the pain. "I'm sorry I woke you up."

"Don't apologize, Robert. If you don't feel well, I want to know," Alex said sincerely.

"Okay," responded Robert.

"Try to get some sleep now. I'll be here for awhile, but if you wake up and need me and I'm not here, just yell for me, okay" Alex gently instructed.

"Okay," Robert said softly as he covered his eyes.

Alex searched quietly through a dresser to find a blanket. He curled up in a large chair that sat near the window in Robert's surrogate bedroom. Alex pulled the blanket up over him and looked at Robert lying uncomfortably in the bed. His mind immediately went back to the first night that Robert spent in the hospital. The night that Robert was manhandled by the orderly and the resident. The night that Robert awakened to a world that he was unfamiliar with, and unfamiliar with most of the people in that world. Alex tried to shut his eyes, but the images and sounds of Robert's pain and misery came flooding back, haunting his conscience.

Robert tossed and turned in pain until the early hours of the morning. Alex remained in the chair throughout the night, worrying about Robert's abrupt headache. Robert groaned throughout the night, never achieving the blissful slumber that he so desperately needed. When the sun was rising, Alex tapped Robert gently on the shoulder. Robert grumbled something incoherent, causing Alex to worry even more. He gently rubbed Robert's back, and with this Robert rolled over and looked through pain-filled eyes at Alex.

"Robert, I want you to come downstairs and get in the Jacuzzi," Alex commanded softly.

"My head hurts too bad to get up," Robert mumbled in pain.

"I know it does, but the hot water in the Jacuzzi may relax you enough to make your head stop hurting," Alex explained.

"All right," Robert replied as he threw the blankets off of him. "My swim trunks are out in the pool house," Robert explained as he stood up slowly, but unsteadily.

"That's okay, just go in in your boxers," Alex replied.

"Are you sure that's okay?" Robert questioned as he tried to get his balance.

"Absolutely," Alex said confidently. "I hope this helps. I know you haven't slept all night," Alex said sympathetically.

"I hope it helps too," Robert mumbled as he staggered toward the door, rubbing his temples in a futile attempt to relieve the pain.

"I'm going to call the hospital and see when Dr. Hamilton gets in," Alex said as he followed Robert out the hallway. "If you're still in pain, I'm taking you to his office as soon as he gets in."

"I think that's a good idea," Robert said sadly.

Alex worried at Robert's tone and his unusual acceptance of going to the hospital when he was not scheduled for an appointment. Alex walked beside Robert and put his arm around Robert's shoulder. Robert flinched from the weight across his neck, and Alex pulled his arm away and apologized.

"Don't apologize, Alex. I'm just really hurtin' right now," Robert replied.

"I know you are, and we're going to find out why. If the hot tub doesn't work and you still hurt so bad, I'm going to just take you into the emergency room and have them contact Dr. Hamilton," Alex explained softly, but with authority.

After lying in the hot, bubbly waters of the Jacuzzi for only a few minutes, Robert climbed out and wrapped a towel over his head.

"What's wrong, Robert?"

"That hot water is making me feel worse," Robert explained with pain emanating from his sad, mahogany eyes.

"I'm going to help you upstairs to change your clothes, and then we're going to the emergency room," Alex commanded gently as he led Robert by the arm up the stairs and into Robert's bedroom. After he helped Robert dry off, Alex helped him put on a pair of sweatpants and a long sleeve tee shirt. Alex led Robert over to the bed to lie down as he went to change.

Alex rushed down the hallway to his bedroom and swung the door open, startling Emily out of her restless sleep. "What's wrong, Alex?" Emily asked groggily.

"I'm taking Robert to the emergency room," he replied quickly as he pulled on a pair of jeans and a polo shirt.

"What's wrong?" Emily asked in a scared tone.

"He has a terrible headache, and his neck is all knotted up. He's been up all night, tossing and turning in agony," Alex explained as he tied his shoes. "I had him get in the hot tub just a few minutes ago, thinking maybe it would make him feel better, but it only made him feel worse."

"Alex, is he all right?"

"No Em, I'm really worried about him. I've never seen him this sick or in this much pain. When I look in his eyes, all I see is pain, and that scares me," Alex said as his voice cracked.

Emily reached out to stop Alex. "He'll be all right, Alex. The ER will give him something to feel better."

Alex leaned down and kissed Emily on the cheek. "I'm going to have them call Dr. Hamilton when we get to the ER. He knows Robert's history and all the drugs that he's taking," Alex stated as he walked toward the door.

"Be careful, and don't worry about things here," Emily commanded gently. "Tell Robert I hope he feels better."

"I will. I love you, Em," Alex said as he rushed out the door.

"I love you too," Emily softly yelled.

\*          \*          \*          \*

Alex drove as fast as he could to the hospital while Robert laid down in the back seat and rested on the way. Pulling into the parking lot of Memorial Hospital's Emergency Room, Alex pulled as close as he could to the front door, even though parking there was restricted for longer than fifteen minutes. Alex reached back and unlocked the door before getting out, and as he opened the back door, Robert lifted his head awkwardly.

"Come on, Robert. We're here," Alex said softly as he extended his hand to help Robert out of the SUV. Alex held onto Robert's arm as they entered the hospital and came upon the emergency room triage nurse.

"Nurse, can you help us?" Alex asked politely.

"Come on in," the friendly, middle-aged nurse replied as she pointed to the door. "What's the problem, gentlemen."

"Robert," Alex indicated by directing his eyes on Robert, "Is a patient of Dr. Hamilton's. He woke up in extreme pain around midnight."

"What sort of pain?" the nurse questioned as she motioned for Robert to sit down.

"My neck hurts really bad and my head is killing me," Robert said wearily.

"Did you fall or hit your head yesterday or last night?" asked the nurse.

"No, I woke up from a bad dream, and my neck and head hurt really bad," Robert explained.

"And is the pain as bad as last night, or has it gotten worse?" the nurse continued.

"Worse," Robert muttered as he covered his eyes with his hands.

"Nurse, can you have someone call Dr. Hamilton?" Alex asked.

"I'll tell the attending the problem and have him call him right away," the nurse answered. "Wait here one moment," she instructed. The nurse walked out into the hallway and returned with a wheelchair. She pulled the wheelchair beside the chair where Robert was seated. "Sir, you can come with me," she said as she helped Robert into the wheelchair.

"Can I go with him?" Alex asked.

"You need to get him registered, and then you can go back to be with him," the nurse explained politely.

Alex kneeled down to look at Robert as he spoke to him, "I'll be back as soon as I get you registered, okay? I shouldn't be long," Alex explained gently as he held Robert's hand.

"I'll be all right," Robert said wearily, causing Alex anxiety. Alex knew how much Robert hated hospitals, and especially being there alone, and from Robert's statement, he indicated that he did not mind being there alone.

The nurse pushed Robert quickly back to the emergency room. She stopped at the desk to address a young doctor, "I need you to call Dr. Hamilton right away."

"What's the patient's name that I'm calling for," the young doctor inquired.

"Robert, uh," she paused. "Sir, what is your last name?" she asked Robert.

"Petrovic," Robert said softly.

"How do you spell that?" the doctor asked as he looked up Dr. Hamilton's telephone number.

"I've always spelled it P . e. t. r. o. v. I c," Robert answered in a pained tone as he spelled out his last name.

"Okay, you can take him into room 4," the doctor said as he dialed the telephone.

"Thank you," the nurse answered as she took Robert across the hall from the ER desk. She locked the breaks on the wheelchair and helped him onto the bed. "Someone will be in to talk with you shortly," the nurse said gently.

"Thanks," Robert muttered as he laid down awkwardly on the narrow bed, turning from the light.

"Would you like me to turn the light off?" the nurse asked sympathetically.

"Yeah, that would be great," Robert replied.

As the nurse was leaving Robert's room, Alex stopped her in the hallway outside Robert's room. "Did someone call Dr. Hamilton?" Alex questioned.

The nurse pointed to the doctor, "He's talking to him now."

"Thank you," Alex said gratefully.

As Alex was about to go into Robert's room, the doctor motioned for him to come to the desk. "Are you Alex?" the doctor asked, holding the phone to his ear.

"Yes," Alex answered.

"Okay," the doctor said to Alex before turning his attention back to the telephone call. "I'll get that started, and we'll see you shortly," the doctor said into the telephone receiver before hanging up to face Alex. "That was Dr. Hamilton. He wanted to know if you were here with Robert," the doctor explained.

"Did he tell you anything about Robert?" Alex questioned.

"He gave me some temporary orders for Robert's care until he gets here. That should be in about 30 minutes. He also said that you are Robert's son, but Robert doesn't know that, so we'll keep that a secret from him," the doctor continued.

"Thank you," Alex responded gratefully.

"You can go in with Robert. A nurse will be in shortly to take his vitals," the doctor explained.

"Okay," Alex replied as he pushed open Robert's door to find Robert lying on his side in the darkness with his arm over his eyes. "How are you feeling?" Alex asked gently as he touched Robert's knee to let him know that he was there.

"Not good," replied a pained Robert.

"Dr. Hamilton will be here in about a half an hour, but he gave the ER doctor some orders. That doctor said a nurse will be in shortly," Alex said as a petite nurse adorned in purple scrubs pushed Robert's door open. "And here she is," Alex said with a smile.

"Hi Robert, how are you feeling?" she asked as she went over to stand beside Robert.

"Awful," Robert responded honestly.

"Well, we're going to try to do something about that, so you feel better," the nurse said gently as she went over to a drawer and pulled out a hospital gown. "Robert, I need you to put this gown on, okay? Do you need any help?" she asked.

Alex reached for the gown, "I'll help him." Alex went over to Robert and took his hand to pull him up into a sitting position. "What can he leave on?" Alex asked politely.

"Uh, his underwear, shoes and socks should be okay to leave on," she answered.

Alex pulled the long sleeve tee shirt over Robert's head and put the gown on him, tying it loosely in the back. "Lie back so I can pull your sweatpants off," Alex instructed softly, with Robert complying.

"Dr. Hamilton gave us some orders to do before he gets here, so just lie back and relax, okay?" the nurse explained tenderly.

"Okay," Robert replied.

The nurse took Robert's blood pressure, his pulse, his temperature, and observed his breathing rate. "You told the triage nurse that you woke up with this headache and neck pain?" the nurse asked.

"Yeah," Robert whispered.

"Did you hit your head on anything or fall?" the nurse continued questioning.

"No, I just woke up with it like this. I had a bad dream, and I woke up in terrible pain," Robert explained as he tossed about on the narrow bed.

The nurse put up the safety railings on both sides as she continued, "Do you remember what you were dreaming?"

"No," Robert said shortly.

"Okay, I have to check with Dr. Mueller to see if Dr. Hamilton ordered an IV," the nurse explained.

"Is that the doctor who called Dr. Hamilton," Alex asked.

"Yes, he'll be checking in with Robert until Dr. Hamilton arrives," the nurse replied as she was walking out the door.

Alex stood beside Robert's bed and took Robert's hand in his, causing Alex to flinch, "Your hand is really cold," Alex said as he reached for Robert's other hand. "So is this one," Alex said with concern. "Are you cold, Robert?"

"No, just my hands. They've been like that all night," Robert said without alarm.

Alex rubbed Robert's left hand gently between his own, and then repeated the task with Robert's right hand. Neither hand warmed, causing Alex some concern.

A few minutes elapsed before the young doctor entered the room. "How are ya feeling, Robert?" Dr. Mueller questioned.

"The same," Robert replied without moving, an act which caused the greatest pain.

"Dr. Hamilton should be here shortly, but the nurse is going to come in to start an IV and draw some blood," the doctor explained in a gentle tone.

Robert nodded and closed his eyes. As the doctor was leaving, the petite nurse entered the room carrying a small basket. She set the basket down on the tray beside Robert's bed and lowered the safety railing on his right side. "Robert, I need you to roll over on your back," the nurse instructed.

Robert complied slowly, but as he turned over, he reached out to hold Alex's hand with his left hand.

The nurse applied the tourniquet tightly around Robert's bicep as she felt for a vein on the back of Robert's hand. Wiping the best vein she could find with alcohol, she pushed the needle in firmly, causing Robert to flinch. The nurse pulled the needle back out as she explained, "That wasn't a good vein, so we're going to have to try this again."

Robert sighed sadly as Alex watched the nurse's inexperience with horror. She tried a different vein, and it went in without any problems. She next tapped on the inner part of Robert's forearm looking for a vein as Dr. Hamilton walked in without saying anything to the nurse. He looked at Robert, who had his eyes tightly shut, and he smiled at Alex as he stepped beside the nurse to stop her.

"Nurse, why are you going to stick him again?" Dr. Hamilton asked, causing Robert's eyes to pop open.

"Your order was to draw blood and start an IV, right?" the nurse asked annoyed.

"Yes, that was my order, but that doesn't answer my question," Dr. Hamilton responded in equal annoyance. "Draw the blood from the IV needle," he commanded. "Why would you subject him to three needle sticks?" he asked in a dark tone.

"Two needle sticks," the nurse corrected.

"Three," he answered with his voice slightly rising. "I can see where you missed the vein the first time," he responded.

The nurse turned away and picked up the first tube and filled it with blood from the sight Dr. Hamilton ordered. As she finished filling all the tubes, Dr. Hamilton watched her closely, as he stood next to Alex. She picked up her basket and snapped her gloves off angrily as she left the room. "Nurse, please take those blood samples to the lab, personally," he instructed to the nurse as she was leaving, in an obvious reprimand to her mistakes.

"So what happened, Robert?" Dr. Hamilton asked as he stepped to the other side of Robert's bed.

"I woke up with an awful headache and a pain in my neck that won't go away," Robert explained.

"When did you first feel the pain?" Dr. Hamilton questioned gently.

"When I woke up. I don't know what time it was," Robert replied.

Dr. Hamilton looked over to Alex, knowing that he would know the answer. "Midnight," Alex said simply.

"Does it feel about the same as last night when it first started, or has it gotten worse?" the doctor asked.

"Worse," Robert replied.

"And you didn't fall or hit your head on anything?" Dr. Hamilton continued as he opened Robert's chart.

"No, I had a bad dream and I woke up in pain," Robert answered painfully.

"That must have been one heck of a dream," Dr. Hamilton joked. "Do you remember what it was about?"

"No, I don't remember anything about it," Robert replied honestly.

"Where is the pain in your head?" the doctor asked.

"Right here," Robert answered as he pointed to the area above his left eye and temple area.

"It doesn't hurt anywhere else? Just right there above your left eye and extending back toward your temple?" the doctor asked.

"No, it doesn't hurt anywhere else, just where I said," Robert answered softly as he shifted his position in the narrow bed.

Dr. Hamilton took a moment to look over Robert's chart from the time Robert arrived. "Your vital signs are all good," he explained. "Did you take anything to try to ease the pain?"

"Two aspirins," Robert replied.

"And that didn't help at all?" the doctor asked, more as a statement than a question.

"No," Robert muttered.

"Okay, Robert, I need you to roll over on your side, toward Alex," the doctor instructed and Robert obeyed. Dr. Hamilton felt Robert's neck and down between Robert's shoulders. "You're really knotted up. Did the neck pain start at the same time as the headache?"

"No," Robert replied, causing Alex and Dr. Hamilton's eyebrows to raise. "It has been hurting on and off for a while now," Robert explained.

"Why didn't you say anything?" asked Alex.

"I don't know. It wasn't that bad and I was sorta afraid to say anything," Robert said shyly.

"Robert," Dr. Hamilton interrupted. "You need to tell me everything and anything that is hurting you."

"I just did," Robert tried to joke.

"Will you tell me if anything is hurting you from now on?" Dr. Hamilton said in a tender tone.

"I promise," Robert said softly.

"Good. I know you'll keep your promise," Dr. Hamilton responded. "You can roll back over on your back now," the doctor instructed, and Robert complied. Dr. Hamilton sat down on the small stool by Robert's bed. He pulled an instrument off the wall and slid his stool next to Robert's bed before standing. He looked in both of Robert's ears before returning the instrument to it's place on the wall. Next he pulled out a small penlight and asked Robert to sit up on the bed. "I know this light is going to bother you, Robert, but I need to look in your eyes."

"That's okay," Robert replied sadly.

Dr. Hamilton shined the light into Robert's eyes, and instructed Robert to move his eyes in all directions. "Okay, that wasn't so bad, was it?" Dr. Hamilton stated.

"No, not too bad," replied Robert.

Dr. Hamilton leaned over the top of Robert's bed and pulled the head of the bed upright so that Robert could lean back, but still remain seated. Robert leaned back and smiled, "Thanks."

"I want you to watch my finger and follow it with your eyes without moving your head, okay?" Robert nodded in the affirmative and obeyed the doctor's orders. "Good. Now I want you to grab hold of my two fingers and squeeze as hard as you can."

Alex interrupted teasingly, "You better be careful, Doctor. He may break your fingers."

Dr. Hamilton laughed, "Yeah, you're probably right, but since Robert isn't feeling well, I'll take my chances."

Robert complied and did what he was asked. "Good. Now I want you to hold out both of your arms to the side, like this," Dr. Hamilton said as he demonstrated. "Now close your eyes." Robert held out his arms and closed his eyes. "Take both of your arms and fold them in until you touch the tip of your nose," the doctor further instructed and Robert obeyed. "Good. Alex, can you help me get Robert up on his feet?"

"Sure," Alex said without hesitation. Alex and Dr. Hamilton each gently held one arm as Robert stood up slowly. When he had his balance, Alex and Dr. Hamilton let go.

"Okay, now I need you to stand on your tip toes and walk in place," the doctor continued.

"This seems really silly," Robert replied.

"I know it seems that way, but it does have a purpose. Okay, now I want you to stand on your heels, with your toes pointing in the air, and walk in place."

"Is this right?" Robert asked as he complied with the doctor's wishes.

"Yes, that's good. You can lie back down now," Dr. Hamilton said as he and Alex gently helped Robert back into bed.

"Doctor, a little while ago I noticed that both of Robert's hands are ice cold," Alex offered.

Dr. Hamilton felt both of Robert's hands. "I noticed that when he squeezed my fingers," he answered without noticeable concern.

"That's not something to be concerned with?" Alex asked sincerely.

"It could be," the doctor answered. "Now I know this is going to sound really silly, but could you tell me what you had to eat yesterday?"

"Sure," Robert said. "I had bananas and milk for breakfast, a bologna sandwich for lunch, and pizza for supper," Robert replied.

"Pizza, with pepperoni?" the doctor asked.

"Yeah," Robert answered.

Dr. Hamilton shook his head slightly as he smiled, "Do you remember what else you ate the last couple of days?"

"I had ham and eggs for breakfast the other morning, pepperoni rolls for lunch, and a hotdog for supper," Robert reported.

"Doctor, what's wrong with him? You seem to have an idea," Alex asked.

"Yeah, I do. Robert's neurological exam is normal, as are his vital signs. I'm going to send him for a CT scan of the head and neck to make sure there isn't anything happening there, but from the location of the headache, the food that he ate over the past couple of days, the cold hands, the intolerance to bright lights, I'd say that Robert has a really bad migraine. Let me ask you this, Robert. Did you see any funny zigzags or anything in front of your eyes before your head started hurting?"

"What do you mean?" Robert asked confused.

"Like when you look at the sun or a bright light. The little spots you see," the doctor explained.

"No, I didn't have anything like that," Robert answered.

"Were you nauseated since your headache started?" Dr. Hamilton asked.

Robert looked at him with confusion. "Did you feel like you had to throw up, but couldn't?" the doctor explained.

"Yeah, when I move around, I feel like that," Robert replied. Dr. Hamilton shook his head knowingly.

"If the CT scan doesn't show anything, and it is a migraine, he's going to be all right then?" Alex questioned.

"If the CT is normal, then I would diagnose a migraine, and yes, he'll be all right," the doctor answered with a smile.

"I'm not going to die?" Robert asked wryly as he closed his eyes.

"No, you're not going to die," Dr. Hamilton reassured. "You have to stick around to keep Alex on his toes," Dr. Hamilton teased as he tried to ease the fears.

"That's right, Robert. I couldn't survive without your daily sarcasm and constant ribbing."

Robert laughed softly, causing him to wince from the pain. "When is this going to stop hurting?" Robert asked.

"Well, I'm going to give you something through your IV now, so that the CT scan doesn't bother you, and then, if the CT is okay, I'll give you something that will take away the pain. Sound good?" the doctor asked.

"Yeah. Is this CT thing going to hurt?" Robert asked shyly.

"No, not at all. All you have to do is lie there and be still. It'll take only a few minutes or so," Dr. Hamilton explained.

"Okay," Robert replied.

"Good," Dr. Hamilton said as he made notes in Robert's file. "I'm going to go see if a Radiologist is available for the CT scan, and then I'll be back in a moment with the medication to help you relax."

"Thanks, Doc," Robert said sincerely with Alex repeating his sentiments.

Alex took hold of Robert's cold hand and rubbed it gently. "You're going to be all right," Alex said with a grateful smile. Robert nodded his head and closed his eyes until Dr. Hamilton came back.

"We're in luck. The radiologist and the technicians just started their shifts, so Robert will be the first one," Dr. Hamilton explained as he administered the medication through the IV line. When he finished, an orderly gently pushed open the door and Dr. Hamilton motioned for him to come in. "Are you ready to go for a ride, Robert?"

"Yeah," Robert said groggily as Dr. Hamilton and the orderly pushed Robert's bed out into the hallway and toward the elevators.

Alex walked beside Dr. Hamilton as they made their way toward the radiology lab. "Looks like someone got dressed in a hurry," Alex teased as he gently pulled on Dr. Hamilton's crooked tie.

Dr. Hamilton looked down at his disheveled appearance and smiled, "Yeah, I got a call, so I had to dress in a hurry."

"Undoubtedly without the aid of your wife," Alex joked.

Dr. Hamilton laughed out loud as he looked around the side of the bed and spoke to Robert, "Hey Robert, Alex is trying his hand at sarcasm."

"Without success, right?" Robert jibed.

"I'd say that's a safe bet," Dr. Hamilton teased as he saw the tension start to ease in Alex's face. The orderly pushed a button and the doors to the radiology lab swung open. Dr. Hamilton waited for the technician to come over to introduce himself. "Robert, these guys are going to get everything started. There's nothing to worry about, okay?"

"Okay," Robert responded as the orderly and the technician lifted Robert off his bed and onto the table. As they were sliding Robert into the CT, Robert lifted his head slightly and smiled a reassuring smile at Alex.

Alex waited with Dr. Hamilton and the radiologist in the office as the CT was being performed. Alex watched in amazement as he saw the different images of Robert's brain and cervical spine. Robert lay still with the help of the medication. Dr. Hamilton asked through the intercom several times if Robert was all right, and from a soft, weary voice came a simple "Yeah."

"Okay," Dr. Hamilton said to Alex, "You can go out and greet him if you want."

"Is it done?" Alex asked astonished at the technology.

"Yeah. The orderly and the tech will take Robert back to the ER, and I will be down shortly after we review the results," Dr. Hamilton explained.

"Okay," Alex said as he pushed the door open and walked over to stand beside Robert. "How was it?" Alex asked.

"Okay," Robert replied as he tightly closed his eyes.

The orderly and the technician transferred Robert back onto the bed and started to push him out of the lab, as Alex explained, "These guys are going to take you back to the ER, and then Dr. Hamilton will be down to talk with us as soon as he reviews your results with the radiologist."

Robert nodded without saying anything and without opening his pained eyes. Alex walked beside Robert's bed as he was pushed back to the ER, and as soon as Robert was safely back in his room, Alex softly pushed the dark hair back from Robert's forehead. Robert stirred, but never opened his eyes. With Alex standing vigil at his bedside, Robert muttered softly, "Why did this happen, mama?"

Alex leaned in closer and spoke gently, "Why did what happen?"

Robert did not reply as he again stirred, causing Alex to realize that Robert was dreaming. Alex continued to softly stroke Robert's hair, hoping that he would say something else.

"… said not to put your neck out for no one," Robert whispered aloud as he continued the dream. "Only for you, mama."

Alex continued to listen intently as Dr. Hamilton pushed the door open. Alex put his index finger to his lips to quiet Dr. Hamilton's approach. Alex leaned in closer, but Robert turned to his side without muttering another word. Dr. Hamilton, looking confused, tapped Alex on the shoulder, and Alex indicated to Dr. Hamilton he wanted to speak to him outside.

"What's wrong?" Dr. Hamilton asked.

"I was brushing the hair off his forehead when he started mumbling something. I thought he was awake, but he must have been dreaming," Alex explained.

"What did he say?" Dr. Hamilton inquired.

"He asked 'why did this happen, mama?' And then he went on to say something that made my hair stand on end," Alex said a bit frightened.

"What?" Dr. Hamilton asked.

"He whispered as if he was repeating something that someone had told him, to 'not put his neck out for no one,' and then he said, as if talking to his mother, 'only for you, mama.'" Alex took a deep breath before continuing, "What's going on here?"

"I thought there might be a possibility that Robert's conscience is starting to remember, but his body still isn't ready to accept it," Dr. Hamilton explained. "Of course, that's just a guess. There's no way to tell, definitively."

"So that could also be a cause of the headache? His body's way of resisting remembering?" Alex asked.

"There's no way to tell," Dr. Hamilton replied as Alex leaned heavily against the wall outside Robert's room. "I have good news. The CT scan was negative."

"It's just a migraine then?" Alex quizzed.

"Yes. Let's go in so I can tell Robert," Dr. Hamilton said as he pushed the door open. He went over to stand beside Robert, who never opened his eyes or acknowledged their presence. "Robert," Dr. Hamilton said softly as he tapped Robert on the shoulder.

Robert slowly opened his eyes to see Alex smiling, "I must not be going to die."

"Of course you're not going to die," Alex said with a grateful smile.

"Robert, the CT scan was negative, so we can go ahead and give you some medicine," the doctor explained. "How are you feeling?"

"My head still hurts really bad," Robert replied.

"Well, once you get the medication, you'll start to feel really good," Dr. Hamilton said good-naturedly.

"Great," Robert responded painfully as the purple-clad nurse entered the room. "It's going to hurt though, isn't it?"

"Not at all," Dr. Hamilton said as he looked at the nurse who he instructed to come to the room. "Do you have the results?" he asked her.

"Yes," she said as she gave them to him. "Is it a migraine?" the nurse asked in a sincere manner, as if she had done her penance.

"Yes," Dr. Hamilton said shortly as he read over the report before addressing Robert and Alex. "Your blood tests were all fine," he said.

"That's good to hear," Alex said.

"You can go, nurse. I'll administer the medication to this patient," Dr. Hamilton said shortly, still obviously upset by the nurse's previous actions. "I'll be right back."

"We'll be waiting," Alex said as he rubbed his eyes.

Dr. Hamilton returned shortly and injected a drug into Robert's IV line. "You're going to start feeling better in a few minutes," Dr. Hamilton addressed Robert.

Robert nodded his head and closed his eyes, "I sure hope so."

"Is he going to get any more of these headaches?" Alex asked, causing Robert to open his eyes to hear the answer.

"It is a possibility, but there are a few things we can do to try to prevent that from happening," Dr. Hamilton explained. "We'll go into this more in depth at Robert's next appointment, but the first things we have to do is make dietary changes."

"Like what?" Alex inquired, as Robert listened intently.

"Certain foods can trigger migraines. Foods like processed lunch meats, cheeses, the preservative MSG, certain fruits and vegetables, chocolate, and milk products to name a few," the doctor explained.

"So that means no more chocolate milkshakes every night," Alex said as he looked at Robert sadly.

"Probably not every night, but there is a possibility that you can still have them. I don't want you to worry about that for now, okay? We'll go over 'safe' foods at the next appointment. In the meantime, try to eat a healthy diet, okay, Robert?" the doctor continued.

"What can I eat?" Robert asked.

"Until you come in again, try to eat fish or chicken or pork, and maybe a salad or two, and try to avoid caffeine if you can. And stop nipping at the red wine when Alex isn't around," Dr. Hamilton teased.

"So that's where all the wine has gone?" Alex laughed.

"Yeah, I hit the bottle after you go to bed," Robert joked.

"Okay, on that note, I have to go. I'm going to start making rounds, so I'll be back in a little while," Dr. Hamilton responded.

"Okay," Robert said.

"The nurse will be in to check on you a couple of times," the doctor explained.

"She won't have any sharp instruments, will she?" Alex wryly inquired.

Dr. Hamilton shook his head as he smiled, "Absolutely not."

"Can I go home soon?" Robert asked as the drugs started to take affect.

"If you're feeling better when I come back down, and if you don't have any type of reaction to the medicine, then you can go," the doctor explained happily.

Robert nestled his head into his pillow as his body began to relax. He rested quietly for several minutes before the purple-clad nurse returned. She took Robert's pulse and spoke to him softly, "How are you feeling, Robert?"

Without opening his eyes, he replied, "Good." He immediately returned to his dream-like state for fifteen more minutes until the nurse returned again. Alex was sitting on the stool, resting his chin in his hands. The nurse applied the blood pressure cuff and took Robert's blood pressure without alerting him or even causing him to stir. The nurse looked at Alex as she wrote the information in Robert's chart, "Dr. Hamilton should be down in a few minutes."

"Thank you," Alex replied politely.

Within five minutes, Dr. Hamilton pushed the door open gently to find Robert sleeping comfortably and Alex leaning sleepily against the wall. Dr. Hamilton tapped Alex gently on the shoulder. "How's he been?"

"Good. He's been sleeping," Alex answered.

Dr. Hamilton looked inside Robert's chart before awakening Robert from his slumber, "How are you feeling?"

"Great," Robert said with glassy eyes.

"That's what I wanted to hear," the doctor answered. Dr. Hamilton checked Robert's pulse one last time and pulled off the stethoscope that he was now wearing around his neck and listened to Robert's heart. "Well, since you're feeling better, I think I'm going to kick you out of here and make room for someone who's sick," the doctor teased.

"That's fine with me," Robert said with a smile.

Dr. Hamilton gently removed the IV from Robert's wrist. "You can go ahead and put your clothes on," Dr. Hamilton said as he looked at Robert's glassy eyes. "Better yet, Alex better help you get dressed and I'll get your paperwork ready," Dr. Hamilton said as he smiled at Alex.

"That sounds good, doc," Alex stated as Dr. Hamilton left the room.

Alex slipped Robert's sweatpants up over his running shoes, untied the hospital gown, and pulled the long sleeve tee shirt over Robert's head. Robert sat there with a stoned look as Alex helped him get dressed. As Alex finished his task, Dr. Hamilton returned with the paperwork and handed it to Alex to sign. Alex signed without reading over it, as Dr. Hamilton pushed a wheelchair into Robert's room.

"Your chariot awaits," Dr. Hamilton said impishly to Robert.

Robert stood up unsteadily as Dr. Hamilton helped him into the wheelchair, "Do you guys have any questions?"

"I don't think so. Robert, do you have anything you want to ask?" Alex asked.

"No," Robert answered groggily.

"Alex, I want you to call my office this afternoon and let me know how Robert is doing, okay? I'll be here until five o'clock."

"Sure, that's no problem," Alex responded.

"Now I want you to call me right away if the pain comes back, okay? That way we can get you something phoned in so that you don't have to be in pain for so long," the doctor explained.

"Okay," Robert replied.

"Where did you park, Alex?" Dr. Hamilton asked.

Alex smiled, "In a fifteen minute parking space."

"Bring your car over to the ambulance entrance. There wasn't any ambulances there, but still try to pull to the side. It was raining when I came in this morning, and it's still drizzling," the doctor instructed.

"Okay," Alex answered.

"We'll meet you at the ambulance entrance," Dr. Hamilton said as he pushed Robert down the hallway.

"I've always wanted a chauffeur," Robert laughed.

"Now I definitely know that you're feeling better," Dr. Hamilton laughed.

As Dr. Hamilton and Robert waited at the double doors of the ambulance entrance, Dr. Hamilton kneeled down to speak to Robert, "Will you promise me that if you have any more pain, you'll tell me, or have Alex tell me?"

"I promise," Robert said seriously.

"Good," Dr. Hamilton said with a smile.

As Alex pulled the SUV to the ambulance entrance, Dr. Hamilton pushed the button on the wall and the doors swung open. He pushed Robert to the passenger door of the SUV and locked the wheels of the wheelchair. Robert reached for the handle on the side of the SUV and stepped onto the running board before sliding clumsily into the front seat.

"Don't forget your seatbelt," Dr. Hamilton reminded.

"I won't," Robert mumbled as he reached around and clicked the seatbelt. "Thanks doc," Robert said gratefully.

"You're welcome, and remember what I said. Now go home and get some rest, you and Alex," the doctor instructed.

"I won't give you an argument on that one," Alex said as he yawned.

"Drive safely," Dr. Hamilton said sincerely.

"I will. Thanks Doctor," Alex said.

"You're very welcome," the doctor said as he shut the door of the SUV.

Robert held up his hand and waved, as Alex leaned over to look out the window as he waved at Dr. Hamilton. The SUV pulled out and they were on their way home.

# CHAPTER 24

▼

A busy week passed quietly for Robert after his sudden headache landed him in the emergency room. During one of his routine twice a week visits, Dr. Hamilton explained about the dietary changes that needed to be instituted to ward off potential reoccurrence, and Robert followed the guidelines without complaint.

With the twins happily adjusted in their kindergarten class after just six weeks, Alex began focusing heavily on Robert's construction business. He had no problems fulfilling contracts that had already been signed, but Alex could not enter into a contract without the legal paperwork, and for that to be carried out, Robert would have to be declared incompetent. Alex would not subject Robert to a legal hearing for any reason, so he started spending more and more time at the construction offices. During the first few months of Robert's recovery, Alex felt comfortable handling Robert's business affairs from home via the computer and phone calls, but now that Robert was doing better, and the business cycle was in a downswing, Alex spent as much time as he could learning the business and working all the contacts that he knew. His work started to pay off when one of his former political colleagues, now in private life, wanted to expand his company. Every day Alex learned more and more about Robert's life, not only his personal life, but his business savvy as well.

Robert spent time chatting with Emily every morning while Alex drove the twins to school. When Alex came home, he and Robert would take a walk or go horseback riding before Alex would leave in the afternoon to go to the office. After lunch and Alex had gone, Emily and Robert would secretly watch their favorite daytime dramas, or as Robert would correct Emily, soap operas. After the shows ended, Emily would tend to the household business of running a family, and Robert would usually go outside to shoot hoops or into the den where he would sit on the stool to the baby grand piano and gently tap the keys. He would look out and daydream as he admired the landscaping of the back yard. Alex would return in the afternoon with the twins. After dinner, in which they would all sit down together to eat, Alex would disappear into Robert's study, and Robert and the twins would play boisterously in the living room as Emily tended to what she called "Mom Business."

On a chilly Friday morning in October, Alex returned from dropping the twins off at school. He paced about the kitchen, causing Robert to inquire, "What's wrong?"

"It's just business. I'm sorry Robert, but I won't be able to spend time with you this morning like we usually do," Alex said pensively.

"That's okay I'll find something to do," Robert answered nonchalantly as he walked out of the room.

Emily greeted Robert warmly in the hallway outside the kitchen. "There's something bothering him, Bonnie," Robert said.

"It's probably just business," she said trying to alleviate any suspicion.

"Yep, that's what he said," Robert replied.

"Nothing to worry about then," Emily said as she kissed Robert tenderly on the cheek. Robert smiled and went on his way.

Emily entered the kitchen and found Alex pacing. "What's up?" she asked.

"Today's the day," he said stoically.

"Oh, that dreadful woman wants an answer. Do you know what you're going to tell her? You haven't said much about it for weeks now," Emily said non-accusatorily.

"I know I haven't said much, but I do know what I'm going to tell her," he replied.

"What?" Emily inquired.

"I'm going to do what she wants. I can't put him through any more pain, Em. He's stuck up for everyone else his entire life, and now I think it's time someone sticks up for him," Alex explained.

"When did you decide this?" Emily said non-judgmentally.

"In the emergency room that morning when he had that headache. He said something that day while he was sleeping that gave me chills," Alex answered anxiously.

"What did he say?" Emily asked with concern.

"During the dream, he was talking to his mom, and then he said, as if someone had told him this, 'to never stick your neck out for anyone,' and then he said 'only for you mama.'"

Emily looked at Alex with shock, "That's a little eerie."

"Yeah, I thought so too," Alex said as he sat down heavily. "That's why I can't put him through anything else."

"I understand, honey," Emily said as she leaned over and kissed Alex on the lips.

"Thank you, Em. I don't know what I would do without you," Alex said sincerely.

"Well, handsome, you're never going to have to find out," Emily answered with a smile.

Alex stood up with new found confidence. "Thank you," he said as he walked out the door.

Driving to the designated meeting place, Alex knew in his heart that he had done the right thing. He pulled in to find the blackmailer waiting for him. He told her his answer without explanation, and gave her the specifics about when she would hear from him again. She nodded her head in satisfaction at the outcome. As she was about to pull out, Alex spoke loudly, with a threatening quality to his words, "Remember, if I find out that you are behind anything getting out about, not only my father, but my family as a whole, I'll destroy you. Remember, that's my town, and I have very loyal friends."

✳      ✳      ✳      ✳

Alex returned home in a lighter mood and enjoyed laughing with Emily and Robert as they ate lunch. The mood was broken when the phone rang. Alex walked over to the telephone and answered it with a lighthearted tone in his voice, "Hello," he paused, "This is Alex. Oh hi," he said as he walked out of the kitchen so that no one could hear him. "Did something happen to my grandmother, Sister?" The response allowed Alex to smile. "What can I do for you then?" After listening intently for a few seconds, Alex's face turned red. "What? There should have been enough money in her account to pay for at least five months." Alex nodded as he listened. "I'll take care of it. I'm on my way to the bank, and I'll bring you a check over this afternoon. How much is due?" Alex took out his pen and prepared to write down the number. "Fifty-one hundred?" he asked and then smiled. "Okay, Sister. I'll see you this afternoon. By the way, has my grandmother's husband been in to visit her lately?" Alex shook his head in anger. "Thanks Sister Gabrielle. I'll see you later," Alex said as he hung up the phone.

"Who was that?" Emily asked as Alex re-entered the kitchen.

"The Sister from Saint Michaels," Alex answered without trying to give away any information that would cause Robert to question him.

"Oh," Emily replied. "Everything okay?"

"No, there's a problem with the checking account—insufficient funds," Alex said as anger tinted his words.

"You're kidding?" Emily asked disbelieving.

"No," Alex said in a controlled tone, "All the money's gone, or at least what is needed for the invoice."

"I'll be in the living room if you want me," Robert said as he picked up his plate and put it in the sink.

"You don't have to go," Alex and Emily both said too quickly.

"All this business stuff is boring," Robert said, flashing a smile as he exited the room.

"What are you going to do?" Emily inquired.

"I'm going to the bank to see what's going on," Alex said as he took a last sip of iced tea. "And then I'm going to pay Saint Michaels."

"Robert was right about him all along," Emily said knowingly.

"Yeah, he knew George was a goddamn gold digger from the moment he met him," Alex said angrily. "I asked Sister Gabrielle if he had been in lately to see my grandmother."

"And?" Emily asked.

"He hasn't been in to see her for weeks," Alex said as he gathered his things together.

"Your grandmother is lucky to have you," Emily said sincerely.

"Yeah," Alex sighed wearily. "I'll see you later."

"Bye," Emily said as she kissed Alex on the cheek. "Be careful."

"I will. I love you," Alex said tenderly.

"I love you too," Emily replied.

\*     \*     \*     \*

Alex bypassed the young teller at the bank and asked to speak directly to the manager, but was told that the manager was not back from lunch. In the manager's stead, Alex agreed to speak to the senior customer service representative.

"How may I help you, Sir?" the middle-aged, neatly dressed lady asked as she led Alex into her office.

"My name is Alex Petrovic," Alex said before being interrupted.

"Are you related to the man who has the construction business?" she asked politely.

Alex paused for a moment before answering, "Yes, he's my father."

"Oh, how nice to meet you. Mr. Petrovic is such a gentleman. He usually comes in about once a month," she paused as her words enlightened her. "But I haven't seen him for several months now. I hope everything is okay," she said sincerely.

"He's been really busy," Alex answered evasively.

"How can I help you today, Mr. Petrovic?" the lady asked.

"I've been told that there is a problem with my grandmother's account," Alex replied.

"What type of problem? And I guess I should ask, is this about Anna Petrovic's account?"

"Yes, it's about my grandmother Anna's account. A few months ago my grandmother had a stroke, which left her in need of a nursing rehabilitation center. She's been in Saint Michael's since she left the hospital," Alex explained.

"Okay," the senior customer service representative said as she listened intently.

"Well, it was arranged that the bill for Saint Michael's would be directly taken out of my grandmother's account every month," Alex continued.

"Okay, did your grandmother authorize this?" she asked.

"No. At the time my grandmother was in no condition to be handling such things. Just days prior to her stroke, she got married, and when we were looking at Saint Michael's, I found out that her new husband had her power of attorney," Alex continued.

"Did he have it prior to her stroke?" she asked.

"No, which makes me think that she wasn't competent to sign any papers, but regardless, he had her power of attorney and he signed the papers authorizing the Saint Michael's bill to be directly withdrawn from my grandmother's account. At that time there was approximately twenty thousand dollars in my grandmother's account, which you can verify, I'm sure," Alex said intelligently.

"What's the problem with the account?" the lady asked.

"Well, I got a call today from Saint Michael's to tell me that my grandmother's bill wasn't paid because of insufficient funds. Can you look at her account and tell me if that is true?" Alex asked.

"I'm sorry Mr. Petrovic, but I can't give any of that information to you without authorization from your grandmother," the lady explained respectfully.

"You can't give me that information, but you can let her husband drain her account without a second thought," Alex said irritably.

"I'm really sorry, Mr. Petrovic," she repeated.

"Not as sorry as you will be when my family withdraws all of our accounts from this bank," Alex said heatedly as he stood up to leave.

Overhearing the last part of the conversation, the bank manager intervened. "Sir, I'm the manager. Can I help you?"

"Apparently not, according to your senior customer service rep," Alex said sarcastically.

"Please, come into my office," the manager said as he opened the door for Alex. "What is the problem?"

"My name is Alex Petrovic. My father owns Petrovic Construction," Alex said proudly.

"Yes," the manager smiled, "Mr. Petrovic is one of our best customers."

"Not for long, once I tell him how I've been treated," Alex said coyly.

"What can I do to help make the situation better?" the manager asked nervously.

"I need to know what my grandmother's bank balance was when she entered Saint Michael's, and what has happened with her account. I know she had at least twenty thousand dollars in her account, and now her account is empty and Saint Michael's hasn't been paid," Alex explained. "She should have at least ten thousand dollars in her account."

"Do you have her power of attorney?" the manager asked.

"No. Her new husband has it. He had her sign it while she was in the hospital, and believe me, she wasn't competent to sign any legal document," Alex further explained.

"Is your grandmother competent now?" the manager asked.

"Yes, she's doing very well, and her mind is perfect," Alex replied.

"Okay, what you need to do is have your grandmother revoke her husband's power of attorney and give it to you, and then we can access her accounts," the manager explained. "Legally, we can't give out that information without your grandmother's permission."

"Fine, I can do that, but can you do something for me?" Alex asked. "I know you value my family's business," Alex said deviously.

"Yes, and I'll do what I can," the manager said eagerly.

"Can you freeze my grandmother's account until I return? Who knows what other kind of withdrawals her husband may try to make, and I don't want her to have to be responsible for penalties on her account," Alex explained.

The manager smiled nervously before answering, "I don't see why we couldn't do that until you return this afternoon with the power of attorney."

"Good. Now I need a cashier's check for fifty-one hundred dollars for Saint Michael's," Alex said.

"That's no problem. Are you withdrawing that from your personal account?" the manager asked as he motioned for a teller to come to his office.

"Yes," Alex replied as he handed the manager an endorsed personal check.

"One moment, Mr. Petrovic," the manager said with a smile.

# CHAPTER 25

▼

After the altercation at the bank, and the subsequent resolution to the problem, Alex drove home wearily. It was well past five o'clock when he walked through the front doors, and he was instantly greeted by two little angels who ran to the door to hug him.

"Hi daddy," Stevie and Steffi said in unison.

"Hello, little people. How are my babies today?" Alex asked tenderly as he sat down on the sofa in the living room.

"DAAAADDDDD," the twins said, "We're not babies."

"You'll always be my babies," Alex teased as Robert and Emily entered the room.

"Hi Robert, Hi Em," Alex said lovingly.

"Hi Alex," Robert said.

"How'd things go?" Emily asked.

"Can we talk about that later?" Alex asked as the twins still sat on his lap.

"Go ahead," Robert said. "I'll take these little ones outside while you two discuss business."

Alex looked at Robert and smiled, "Thanks Robert."

Robert picked up Steffi in his arms and Stevie climbed on his back for a piggyback ride. When they were out of sight, Alex motioned for Emily to follow him into the study.

"So what happened?" Emily quizzed.

"At first I got the run-around at the bank, but then I got that straightened out. I had to have my grandmother sign over her power of attorney to me, and thankfully she didn't mind. She knew in her heart what George had done," Alex replied.

"Did you pay Saint Michael's?" Emily asked.

"Yeah, and I told Sister Gabrielle to send my grandmother's invoice to me every month," Alex explained. "I also had Sister Gabrielle and one of the priests witness grandmother signing the power of attorney so that it would hold up to any type of scrutiny, unlike the one George had her sign when she was obviously incompetent," Alex said.

"That was a good idea," Emily said as she took Alex's hand.

"I just feel so damn dumb, Em. I should have had the power of attorney grandmother signed for George nullified as soon as I found out about it," Alex said with anger directed at himself.

"Come on, Alex. You had a lot on your mind then. You can't expect yourself to do everything. You did the best you could, and I'd say that you did a hell of a good job with what you were confronted with," Emily said sternly but caringly.

"I don't know. I feel responsible for a lot of this," Alex said with the same anger.

"You just had a bad day today," Emily replied.

"You can say that again. First that bitch, and then that … that," Alex paused as his face turned crimson. "That bastard George stealing all her money. Why didn't grandmother listen to her son?" Alex said with latent anger directed at his grandmother.

As Alex and Emily continued their conversation, and Alex continued his ranting and raving about the day, Robert and the twins entered the study smiling. "Hey Alex, we just heard the ice cream truck. Do you have some change we can borrow?" Robert asked joyfully.

"NO!" Alex yelled.

Robert stared dumbfounded at Alex for a moment before he quickly left the room. Realizing what he had done, Alex jumped up and followed him out of the study. "Em, you and the kids can start supper," Alex said as he left the room in pursuit of Robert.

Robert was across the living room and almost to the double doors that led out onto the patio when Alex reached for him and grabbed him by the arm, "Robert."

Robert twisted around with his arms up over his head and face in a protective posture as he lost his balance and fell backwards onto the floor. He quickly sat up and pushed himself as far against the wall as possible.

Seeing what he had done, Alex rushed over to Robert and knelt down in front of him, "Please Robert, I'm not going to hurt you."

Robert slowly lowered his arms from over his head and gazed at Alex with a mixture of fear and sorrow, "I'm sorry Alex. I know better than to ask for money."

Alex sadly sighed, "No, Robert, that's not why I said no. I didn't want anyone to ruin their supper."

"I'm sorry," Robert repeated.

"Please don't apologize. I'm the one that's sorry. I was having a bad day, and I never meant to take it out on you," Alex explained.

"It's okay, Alex," Robert said sadly. "I understand."

"Robert, please believe that I would never hurt you," Alex pleaded.

Robert nodded his head as he rubbed his wrist from the fall.

"Are you hurt?" Alex asked fearfully.

"No, I'm all right," Robert answered.

"Good," Alex said as he looked sorrowfully at Robert. "Robert, can I ask you something?"

"I guess so," Robert responded.

"Does someone hit you?" Alex asked tenderly.

Robert rubbed his wrist as he looked at Alex uneasily.

"It's okay to tell me," Alex replied.

"My dad when he was drunk," Robert said uncomfortably.

"Can you tell me about it?" Alex asked.

At first reluctant, Robert explained, "Every Saturday dad would get drunk, and when he'd come home, he'd fight with mama. I'd try to protect her, but he was stronger than me," Robert answered sadly.

"So he would hit you?" Alex asked.

"Yeah. He always told me to take care of mama, and when I would try to, he'd say that obeying him was the most important rule of the house. He'd say get out of the way, but I'd always come between them," Robert said as he closed his eyes.

"He'd tell you the most important thing was to look after your mom, until he'd get drunk, and then he'd expect you to stand by and let him beat on her," Alex surmised.

"Yeah," Robert replied.

"Did he ever hurt you?" Alex asked fearfully.

"A couple of times," Robert answered.

"How did he hurt you, Robert?" Alex questioned.

"One night I got between him and mama, and he grabbed me by the collar and threw me into the kitchen. I hit my head on the edge of the table," Robert explained as he pointed to the scar near his eyebrow. "It was bleeding so bad and wouldn't stop. Mama kept holding towels on it trying to make it stop, but it wouldn't, so me and her walked to the doctor's office so that I could get stitches."

"Didn't you have a car?" Alex asked.

"Yeah, but mama didn't know how to drive, and dad wouldn't drive me to the doctor. He said to be a man and shut up," Robert recalled.

"So what happened?" Alex continued.

"The doctor stitched me up and we walked back home," Robert replied.

Alex nodded his head in disgust, "So that's how you got that scar."

"Yeah," Robert said sadly.

"You said he hurt you a couple of times. What else did he do?" Alex questioned.

"One Saturday night he came home and was screaming at mama about something. I stepped in front of mama to prevent him from punching her. He hit me instead and I fell backwards across the coffee table, dislocating my shoulder. He was crazy that night, and he ran over and kicked me. I thought he was going to kill me until mama hit him over the head and knocked him out," Robert remembered painfully.

"What happened next?" Alex asked, frightened of the answer that he would hear.

"Mama helped me up and I went to lie down in my room while mama got our coats. I couldn't even straighten my arm out. While she was helping me, dad woke up and came to my bedroom door and started screaming at us both. Mama hurried up and locked the door, but he wouldn't let us out all night," Robert recollected.

"You mean you spent the night in your bedroom with a dislocated shoulder because he wouldn't let you out?" Alex asked angrily.

"Yeah. He fell asleep just before sunrise, and me and mama left. On the walk to the doctor's office, Father Josef passed us on his way to the church to have mass. He picked us up and took me to the doctor's office. Before the doctor put my shoulder back into place, I heard Father Josef talking to mama and the doctor. When I woke up a few hours later, Father Josef was back and talking to mama."

"Did he take you home then?" Alex inquired.

"Yeah, but he made me and mama stay in the car while he went and talked to dad. He was gone for a long time, and when he came out, dad was with him carrying a suitcase," Robert related.

"Did your dad move out?" Alex asked.

"For a little while. Father Josef talked him into going to a place to dry out," Robert remembered.

"Did he dry out?" Alex questioned.

"Yeah," Robert replied.

"Did he ever hit you again?" Alex asked.

"No. He got sick a few weeks after he came home, and then he died," Robert answered without emotion.

"Well, at least he didn't hit you again," Alex said as he smiled at Robert.

"Yeah," Robert said.

"Robert, please know that I would never hurt you, and I'd rather cut off my own arm than hit you," Alex said emotionally. "Do you believe me?"

"Yeah, I believe you," Robert answered quietly.

"Will you forgive me for yelling at you?" Alex pleaded.

"Of course I forgive you. You're the best friend I've ever had," Robert said as he smiled at Alex.

Alex turned his head to hide the tears that threatened to fall. "The same here," Alex managed to utter. The two sat on the floor for a few moments more before Alex extended his hand to Robert to help him up. As Alex was pulling Robert up, Alex pulled him into an awkward hug. "I have to go out for a little while. Emily and the kids are eating supper. Would you wait till I get back and have supper with me?" Alex asked hopefully.

"Sure, I'll go out and shoot some hoops until you get back," Robert answered happily.

"Great, I'll let Emily know where you'll be, and I'll be back shortly," Alex replied.

"Take your time. I'm not going anywhere," Robert said with a smile.

Alex returned his smile and walked out of the room.

# CHAPTER 26

▼

Driving to Saint Michael's allowed Alex's overwhelmed brain to take a few minutes to reevaluate what had happened earlier in the day. As days went, this was one of the worst. As Alex pulled into the parking space at the back entrance to Saint Michael's, he remembered the look in Robert's eyes as Robert told him that he was his best friend, causing Alex to smile.

Alex strolled by the front desk and waved at the nurses that he had come to know over the weeks that his grandmother had been living there. He stopped outside her private room and looked in through the open door to see his grandmother relaxing in bed watching an old movie on television. Alex knocked gently on the door, "Hi Grandma, can I come in?

"Alex," she said excitedly. "Please come in."

"How are you doing today?" Alex asked as he kissed her on the cheek.

"I'd be doing a lot better if I knew what was going on here today," Anna said knowingly.

"What do you mean?" Alex asked craftily.

"I know something is going on. I overheard the nurses talking about my bill not being paid," Anna replied. "And then you come and have me sign those legal papers."

"Don't worry about that, Grandma. I've taken care of everything," Alex said sincerely.

Anna looked dejectedly at Alex, "He stole all my money, didn't he?"

"Who?" Alex asked.

"George," Anna replied. "He waited until I was in here, and then he took my money and left."

Alex looked at his grandmother and knew that she deserved to hear the truth, "Yes, Grandma. He took all your money from your checking account, but I don't want you to worry about that, okay? The last thing you ever need to worry about is money."

"He was right," Anna said sorrowfully.

"Who was right?" Alex asked intrigued.

"Bobby. He told me that George was just using me to get to my money, but I wouldn't listen to him. I thought he was trying to control my life, but he was just trying to protect me like he had always done," Anna explained. "And then I go and hurt him when all he was trying to do was save me from getting my heart broken."

Alex interest piqued immediately, "What do you mean you went and hurt him?"

"I told him that he was no longer my son," Anna paused as a tear slipped down her cheek. "I disowned my only child."

Alex's mouth dropped open at his grandmother's revelation. As if a light bulb had been lit, all the pieces finally fit. "What did you say?" Alex asked disbelieving.

"I told your father that if he didn't back down on George, I would disown him. He told me he was just looking out for me and that he always would, no matter what. And then I told him that I no longer had a son," Anna recalled painfully. "But Alex, I didn't mean it. I swear I didn't mean it. I was just so damn mad at him, and then I didn't get a chance to apologize because of this stroke."

"Oh, Grandma," Alex said as the full impact of the situation hit him.

"Is your father okay, Alex? I know I hurt him, and I haven't seen him to tell him how sorry I am for saying that," Anna replied.

Alex took a deep breath before speaking, "No Grandma, he's not okay."

"What happened, is he sick?" she asked in a slight panic.

"Grandma," Alex said as he held her hand gently. "What I'm about to tell you is going to be very difficult to hear, but you have to believe me when I say that things are getting better every day, okay?

"Please tell me, Alex. You're frightening me," Anna said as she squeezed Alex's hand.

"The day you had your stroke, I was on my way here to bail out Dad. On the plane I got a call saying that you had had a stroke, so I came to the hospital instead. I called an attorney friend to bail out Dad, while I went to the hospital. After Dad was released from jail, he immediately came to the hospital to see you, but George intervened and had Dad escorted out of your room and banned from seeing you," Alex related.

"What?" Anna said dumbfounded.

"Yeah, I wasn't there to witness what happened, but apparently George told Dad that Dad caused your stroke when he called you for help while he was in jail," Alex continued.

"No," Anna insisted.

"The guards escorted Dad out of the hospital and he went home. I couldn't believe that Dad would let George have him thrown out, so I went to Dad's house to talk to him. When I got there, I couldn't find him. One of the ladies who works there, I think her name was Mrs. Butler, said that Dad had come in and was acting strange," Alex continued.

"How was he acting?" Anna asked.

"I don't know, but she was worried, so I told her to stay there while I went looking for him. I searched all over the grounds, and then I heard a loud noise from the barn, so I ran in," Alex paused to compose himself.

"Was he there?" Anna asked.

"Yeah Grandma, he was. I found him hanging by a rope from the rafters," Alex related painfully.

"Oh my God," Anna cried. "Oh my God. Is he okay? Please tell me he's okay!" Anna cried hysterically.

"I got him down and called the ambulance, but Grandma, he's not okay. Not yet, at least. The doctor said he suffered some type of mental breakdown, and he was in the psychiatric ward in the hospital the same time you were in the hospital. He was in the hospital for many weeks, longer than you were there, actually," Alex explained.

"Is he going to be okay? All this time he's thought that I didn't love him," Anna said as the tears continued to flow.

"He's going to be okay, eventually, but he never thought you didn't love him," Alex said.

"How could he not have, after what I said?" Anna replied sadly.

"Because he lost his memory, Grandma. From the time he woke up in the hospital, he thinks that he is fifteen years old. He doesn't know who I am, or Emily, or the twins," Alex explained.

"What? He thinks he's fifteen?" Anna asked.

"Yes. He has no memory in between fifteen and fifty. He knows you, and asks about you all the time. I told him that you were staying with your sister while he recovered. I had to tell him that he was in an accident, and that is why he was in the hospital for all those weeks," Alex continued.

"He doesn't remember what I did then?" Anna asked.

"No," Alex said simply.

"Where is he now?" Anna worried.

"He's at home. Emily, the twins and I moved back to take care of him. He doesn't even know the house that he's living in is his, and that he built it. He asked one time where he was, and I told him my Dad's house, and he said that he couldn't stay there," Alex recounted sadly.

"Oh Alex, I have to go to him. I have to see my Bobby," Anna said desperately.

Alex paused a moment to think about the situation, and remembering the conversation he had just had with Robert regarding Stefan, he agreed with Anna. "I think that would be a good idea, Grandma, but you can't push him into remembering anything, okay? You can't apologize to him because he wouldn't know what you were apologizing for, and then he'd get suspicious," Alex instructed.

"I'll do whatever you say," Anna said honestly.

"Good, because the doctor said that his memory has to come back on its own," Alex replied.

"I just want to see him, to tell him that I love him," Anna said as she started to get out of bed.

"Okay," Alex said as he pulled a wheelchair in from the hallway. "Are you sure that it's all right if you leave for awhile?" Alex asked.

"I don't care if it's okay or not. My Bobby needs me," she said as she sat down in the wheelchair.

\*     \*     \*     \*

As Alex pushed his grandmother through the ornate front doors of Robert's home, Emily came into the foyer to greet her husband, and was pleasantly surprised to see Anna. "Hi grandma Anna," Emily said warmly.

"Hi Emily," Anna said as she looked around frantically for Robert.

Hearing the dribbling of a basketball coming closer, Alex tapped his grandmother on the shoulder, "I think he's coming."

Anna smiled as she saw Robert open the double doors of the living room carrying a basketball. Robert whistled jovially without being aware of who was watching. Alex pushed his grandmother's wheelchair into the entrance to the living room and caught Robert's attention.

Robert turned around slowly, knowing that Alex had returned and was now ready to have supper. As he glimpsed Anna sitting in the wheelchair, his youthful smile faded into terror as he dropped the basketball and stammered, "Oh my God! What have I done?" Robert's face turned pale as he continued, "I did this," he cried. "I am so sorry. Oh God, what have I done?" He turned around and ran out the double doors before Anna or anyone else could say anything.

"Stay with Grandma," Alex instructed to Emily as he ran after Robert. "I'll call Dr. Hamilton when I find him," Alex said as he ran out the double doors.

Emily bent down in front of Anna to face her, "Grandma Anna, it's going to be okay?"

Anna was inconsolable, "I did this to him, Emily. He almost died because of me."

Emily pulled Anna into a gentle embrace and held her while she cried. "Alex knows what to do, and if necessary, Dr. Hamilton will tell us what to do," Emily said reassuringly.

Robert darted out the double doors of the living room and nimbly weaved through the patio furniture that adorned the large back patio without slowing down or missing a stride. After passing through the patio, Robert hit a full paced sprint as he ran directionless from the house. Alex called out after him, but nothing or no one would stop, or even slow down, Robert's retreat.

Several hundred yards behind Robert, Alex continued to call out for Robert, but to no avail. As Robert approached a particularly steep hillside, his shoes slipped on the evening dew blanketing the grass, and he tumbled down the hillside. With a jolt of adrenaline surging through his veins from witnessing Robert's fall, Alex ran faster than he ever thought possible to the top of the hillside. As he peered down the deep slope of the hillside, he witnessed Robert lying on his side, with his knees pulled up toward his chest and his hands covering his face. Alex listened carefully and heard soft whimpers coming from the bottom of the hill.

Alex cautiously slid down the hillside to where Robert was lying. Alex touched him gently, "Robert, are you okay?"

Robert continued to cry, but did not respond to Alex's question. Alex positioned himself in front of Robert and spoke again, "Are you hurt?" When Robert failed to respond, Alex tried to gently pull Robert's arms away from his face, but Robert fiercely resisted. Alex stepped back, and as he listened to Robert cry, he searched for any visible signs of injury from the fall. When Alex could find no apparent injuries, but continued to hear Robert's cries, he pulled out his cell phone and walked a few feet away so that his conversation would not be overheard.

"Dr. Hamilton, please," Alex said to the lady who answered the phone.

"Who's calling?" the lady asked.

"Alex Petrovic. Tell him it's an emergency," Alex said in a panic.

Within a brief moment, Dr. Hamilton's voice came on the phone, to Alex's great relief, "Alex, what's wrong?"

"It's Robert. My grandmother wanted to see him, so I brought her here, and when he saw her, he snapped and took off running," Alex related frantically as he continued to watch and listen to Robert lying on the ground crying.

"Where is he now?" the doctor asked.

"I followed him and when he got to the hillside on the far end of the property, he slipped on the wet grass and fell down the hillside. When I got to him, he was lying on his side, like in a fetal position, and was crying. I asked him if he was hurt, but he didn't answer. When I tried to gently pull his arms away from his face, he fiercely pulled his arms back," Alex continued.

"I'm on my way. Stay with him, okay? Don't let him out of your sight," Dr. Hamilton instructed.

"I won't. When you get here, drive around to the tennis court. When you get out of your car, look to your left and you'll see a hillside with a lot of trees. That's where we are," Alex explained.

"I'll be there in a few minutes," the doctor said.

"Should I try to talk to him?" Alex asked.

"No. Just let him cry if that's what he's doing. Let him cry himself out, okay?" Dr. Hamilton said. "Alex," he continued in a reassuring voice, "Your father may have just gotten his memory back."

Alex flipped his cell phone shut and sat down on the wet grass a few feet away from where Robert was still lying. He was still in the same position, and was still crying. Alex looked at Robert and then, with a tear in his eye, he looked up to the sky, "Please God. Let him be okay"

Within a matter of minutes, Alex heard a car driving toward the tennis courts. He glanced down at Robert, who still lay crying and motionless, and then climbed up the hillside to flag down Dr. Hamilton. As soon as he made it to the top of the hillside, Alex saw Dr. Hamilton jogging toward him carrying a medical bag.

"How is he?" Dr. Hamilton asked as he stopped at the top of the hillside.

"The same. He hasn't moved, but he's still crying," Alex said. "Come on," Alex instructed, "But be careful. The grass is really slippery."

"You said this all happened when Robert saw his mother?" Dr. Hamilton questioned.

"Yes," Alex said. "He turned pale when he saw her, and then he kept saying something like 'look what I've done.'"

"Is your grandmother better?" the doctor asked as they carefully descended the slope.

"Pretty much, but she still needs a wheelchair," Alex answered.

"Seeing your grandmother in the wheelchair may have caused his memory to snap back. Seeing her was like a cue to remember," Dr. Hamilton said as he made his way safely to the bottom. He quickly ran over to Robert and kneeled down beside him. "Robert, can you hear me?"

Robert whimpered quietly as he shielded his eyes and face with his arms. In his own world, he did not hear the men around him.

"Come on Robert, talk to me," Dr. Hamilton said in a deep, caring voice while he visually looked for injuries. When Robert failed to respond, Dr. Hamilton gently took Robert's wrist and tried to pull it away from Robert's face. Robert angrily, but instinctively, pulled his arm back and away from Dr. Hamilton's grasp.

"Robert," Alex said soothingly. "Come on. We're just trying to see if you're hurt."

Dr. Hamilton shook his head at Alex, "Talking isn't going to help right now." Alex instinctively knew what he meant and nodded his head in agreement. Dr. Hamilton turned away from Robert and pulled out a syringe and a drug vial. He filled the syringe and addressed Alex, "When I get into position, I want you to grab both his arms quickly and hold them tight while I inject him in the thigh. Do you have any questions?"

"No," Alex said as he positioned himself behind Robert.

When Dr. Hamilton gave the word, Alex grabbed Robert tightly around both wrists and held them to the ground while Dr. Hamilton injected him in the thigh with the medication. Within moments, Robert was sedated.

"Good job," Dr. Hamilton said to Alex.

"I'm just glad you're here," Alex said in a worried tone.

"Come on, let's carry him up to the house," the doctor said as they both lifted Robert and carried him across the vast expanse of land that made up Robert's home. When they got to the living room double doors, Alex took Robert fully in his arms as Dr. Hamilton opened the doors. Inside, Emily and Anna waited anxiously. When Anna saw Alex carrying a lifeless Robert in his arms, she cried out, but Dr. Hamilton stopped her by putting his index finger to his lips. Emily went to Anna and explained that Robert was in good hands now that Dr. Hamilton had arrived.

Alex carried Robert up the stairs and to the end of the hall where Robert had been staying in the surrogate bedroom. He gently laid Robert down on the bed and sat down wearily beside him. Dr. Hamilton came over and checked Robert's pulse and observed his breathing.

"What am I going to do if he wakes up and this happens again?" Alex said anxiously.

"Is there a back way that I can go out to my car without the other's seeing me?" the doctor asked.

"Yeah, make a left outside this room, and there is a door at the end of the hallway that leads out that way, but it's always kept locked. That's why we couldn't come in that way," Alex explained.

"I'll unlock it until I get back from my car," the doctor said.

"What do you need in your car?" Alex asked as Dr. Hamilton was already out of the room.

Alex gently brushed Robert's hair back off his forehead and touched his cheek. Deep black circles had appeared under Robert's eyes, and Alex wiped the tear-stained dirt off Robert's pale face while he waited for Dr. Hamilton to reappear. Dr. Hamilton re-entered carrying a canvas bag. He came over to stand in front of Alex as he pulled out the items in the bag. He took the white cloth restraints and applied them to Robert's wrists and around the bed frame. Alex watched as Dr. Hamilton applied the restraints carefully and gently, "Thank you."

"I think it's for the best tonight since we don't know what kind of mental state he's in right now. I didn't think you'd mind this time," the doctor said sincerely.

"No, I don't," Alex said gratefully.

Dr. Hamilton opened his medical bag and filled another syringe. "I'm really not supposed to do this, but I'm going to leave this here for you to give to him if he wakes up and is overly agitated. If that happens, give this to him and then call me immediately, okay?" the doctor instructed.

"Yeah," Alex said dumbfounded. "But I don't know how to give him that."

"It's easy. Just tap it a couple of times, and then push the plunger a little bit to expel the air. After that, stick it in his thigh like I did out there tonight. Push it in as far as it will go, push the plunger to release the medication, and then pull it back out. It's simple," Dr. Hamilton explained.

"Okay, thanks," Alex said as the situation started to catch up with him causing his knees to buckle.

"You need to get some rest," the doctor ordered.

"I'll be okay," Alex said wearily.

"Get some rest, Alex. Robert should sleep through the night without any problems, and you need to be ready for a long day tomorrow if he's gotten his memory back," the doctor said sympathetically.

"What'll happen if his memory did come back?" Alex asked.

"We'll just have to wait and see if that happens," Dr. Hamilton explained.

"I better get some sleep then," Alex said with a stressful smile.

"Yeah, and let me know how he is first thing in the morning, okay?" the doctor asked.

"I will," Alex answered.

"Call me if you need me. You have my home phone and my cell phone, right?" Dr. Hamilton asked.

"Yeah, and don't worry—I'll call if I need you," Alex said.

"Good. I'll talk to you tomorrow, and I'll probably see you early tomorrow afternoon. Earlier if you need me."

"Bye, Doc. Thanks so much for coming tonight," Alex replied gratefully.

"Just doing my job," Dr. Hamilton smiled as he stopped at the door. "I'm going to go out the back door, but I'll make sure it's locked, okay?"

"Yeah, that's fine. Thanks again," Alex said as Dr. Hamilton disappeared.

Alex wearily picked up the telephone and called down to the living room on the intercom. Emily picked up and Alex explained what had happened and that he was going to spend the night in Robert's room. When Alex hung up the phone, he pulled out a blanket from the dresser and climbed into the chair by the window and fell almost instantly asleep.

# CHAPTER 27

▼

A steady stream of sunlight filtered in through the crack in the curtains, causing Alex to turn his head sleepily away from the unwelcome light. After an unsuccessful try to avoid the sunlight, Alex groggily realized where he was, and instantly glanced over to the bed. Robert had his head turned slightly toward the window, looking out at the landscape below. Seeing that Robert was awake, Alex jumped out of his chair and raced over to the side of Robert's bed.

"How are you feeling?" Alex asked tenderly.

Robert paused a moment, and without looking at Alex, he responded, "Like a failure."

"What?" Alex said. "Why do you say that? You're not a failure," Alex gently reprimanded as he sat down next to Robert on the bed.

Robert tugged on the restraints as he spoke matter-of-factly, "Being tied to your own bed isn't exactly a picture of success."

"Well," Alex smiled shyly, "You just had a bad night last night."

Robert closed his eyes and shook his head. He briefly glanced at Alex before speaking, "Come on, Alexander. If I hadn't been a failure, you wouldn't have had to babysit me for the past several months."

Emotionally and fully realizing what was happening, Alex answered, "No, I would have spent the past several months mourning your death and never knowing why you killed yourself."

Robert turned his head away from Alex as Alex continued, "All these months I've been trying to figure out why, Dad, but I was always missing the most important piece of the puzzle. I knew about your fight with George, and about Mitchell breaking up with you. I knew about your being arrested and put in jail, but even all those things put together wouldn't have pushed you that far. It wasn't until last night when I saw Grandma that I found out the answer. You did this, Dad, because Grandma said she disowned you," Alex explained sternly.

Robert pulled on the restraints and continued to stay turned away from Alex. "That's why, isn't it? But Dad, Grandma didn't mean it," Alex said in a gentle tone. "She said those words in anger, and then she had a stroke and couldn't tell you that she didn't mean what she said. Dad ... Grandma loves you. That's why she came last night, to see you. I hadn't told her anything about what had happened to you, and I didn't tell you anything that had happened to her because I wanted you both to get better without having to worry about each other."

Robert sighed sadly, "She meant what she said."

"No, Dad, she didn't. She loves you. And you know what, Emily loves you, the twins love you, and when they find out that you're their grandpa, they're gonna love you even more. Mitchell loves you, and Dad," Alex paused as he touched Robert gently on the cheek. "I love you, too."

Robert looked at Alex with disbelieving eyes, "You loved me when I thought I was fifteen years old. I'm a grown man, Alexander. What's going to happen when I start dating? How are you going to feel when you see me holding hands with a man, or kissing a man?" Robert said matter-of-factly.

"If it's with Mitchell, I'll be a very happy man," Alex said.

Completely caught off guard by Alex's answer, Robert continued, "Mitchell left me. He doesn't love me anymore."

"That's where you're wrong, Dad. Mitchell loves you completely."

"What brought about all the support for Mitchell? You despised our relationship, and now that he's no longer in my life, you tell me he still loves me. Is this some kind of game you're playing with me?" Robert asked suspiciously.

"No," Alex said with a hint of anger. "I'm not playing games with you. I told you he still loves you because I know for a fact that he does. He told me so, and Emily too."

"Why all the support for Mitchell?" Robert asked, disbelieving his son's change of attitude.

"When this all happened, I tried my damnedest to shrug responsibility. I knew Grandma couldn't take care of you because of her stroke, but I thought for sure Mitchell would step up and take over. After all, you two were a couple, but when I tried to pawn off responsibility, Mitchell really let me have it. He verbally beat the hell out of me. But you know what, Dad? After I got over being pissed, I realized that everything that he said was true. He made me take responsibility, and I'll forever be grateful to him for that."

"So you changed your mind because Mitchell told you the truth," Robert said skeptically.

"Not completely. After Mitchell chewed me out, Dr. Hamilton had a go at me. He made it clear that my attitude was not welcome. And you know what, where I first dread coming to the hospital, I soon looked forward to it. I enjoyed spending time with you. Everyday I learned something different about you, and the more I learned, the more I realized and remembered what a good guy you really are."

"There's a big difference between fifteen and fifty," Robert said sarcastically.

"Yeah, maybe so, but I saw you for who you really are, without any walls built up. I know your heart and soul, Dad. That doesn't change no matter if you're fifteen or fifty." Alex smiled at Robert, "You know something? Yesterday you gave me the best compliment that I could ever get. You told me I was your best friend, Dad. That means more to me than you'll ever know."

"But will it last?" Robert asked sadly and skeptically.

"I hope forever. When I ran into that barn and saw you hanging there, my heart stopped. It literally stopped. I tried to move, but I was paralyzed. I have never been so scared in all my life. After I got the rope off the rafter, I laid you on the floor and begged you not to die. I begged you, Dad, and you didn't let me down." Alex turned his head away and spoke in a whisper, "You've never let me down."

Robert stared intrigued at Alex for a moment before he tried to roll over on his side but was prevented by the restraints. Alex looked sadly at Robert as he reached to undue the restraints. As Alex released the last restraint, Robert rubbed at his wrists gently. Alex sat on the bed a moment before speaking, "Will you promise me something, Dad?"

"If I can," Robert said honestly.

Alex broke down in tears from all the pent up stress that had accumulated and sobbed as he spoke, "Promise me you'll never try to leave me again."

Robert sat up in the bed and pulled Alex into an embrace. He held Alex for a few moments while Alex cried. "I love you, Alexander," Robert said tenderly as he continued to hold Alex. "And I promise I'll never try to leave you again."

Alex pulled slightly out of the embrace to look into Robert's face. The man looking back at him was not the man who Alex had taken care of the past months. The man looking back at him was his Dad. Robert smiled genuinely at Alex as Alex smiled back with tears running down the sides of his face. "I love you too, Dad."

After retrieving a few tissues from the bathroom to wipe away the remaining tears, Alex returned to find Robert still sitting up in bed examining the grass stained shorts that he still wore. Robert gently rubbed his thigh as Alex came back to sit on the bed. Robert looked at him wearily, "What happens now?"

Alex pretended to study Robert's appearance, "Well, I think that maybe you should take a bath."

Robert laughed, "You're learning."

"Let's go down to your bedroom so that you can take a bath or shower, and then get dressed in your 'real' clothes," Alex suggested.

Robert nodded in agreement. As the two quietly made their way down the hallway, past the other bedrooms, and into Robert's master bedroom, Robert stopped and peered into a full length mirror. Staring at his image, he grimaced at what he saw looking back at him.

"Trust me Dad. You look great compared to some other times over the past few months," Alex said jokingly.

"Great," Robert exclaimed sarcastically.

"While you're in the shower, I'm going to go see if Grandma is awake yet. She told Emily last night that she wants to see you first thing, if that's okay with you? Remember Dad, you don't have to do anything that you don't feel comfortable doing. So if that means that Grandma has to wait a few hours or even a few days to talk to you, then she's just going to have to accept that," Alex explained.

"I'll see her," Robert said without emotion.

"Okay, and while you're in the shower, I'm going to call Dr. Hamilton to let him know that you're doing all right. He was worried about you last night," Alex said.

"That's fine," Robert said as he walked into the bathroom. He stared at the door briefly, and decided to let it open.

Alex came up behind him and started to pull it shut, "You can shut the door, Dad. I trust you."

When Robert stepped into the marble shower, a flash of memory jolted his brain. Suddenly he felt sick and his knees trembled. He leaned heavily against the wall and let the hot water cascade over his head as he tried to focus on the flash of memory. He hung his head, causing an intense spasm to grip his neck. As the muscle knotted painfully, the memory came into full focus. This was the place, the shower, that he had made the fateful decision to end his own life. If only he had known that his family loved him then. Temporarily relaxing as he replayed the conversation with Alex, Robert smiled at the possibility that his son, daughter-in-law, grandchildren, mother and ex-lover still loved him. "Oh, Mitchell," he sighed contentedly as he imagined what Mitchell had said to Alex. "I hope it's true. If only ..." he said before he heard the sound of the bedroom door opening.

Alex walked in his father's bedroom and sat down. In previous times such an action would have been completely alien to him. He waited patiently for Robert to exit the shower. When Robert came out, Alex frowned, "Why didn't you shave?"

"I couldn't find a razor," Robert answered, knowing fully why he could not find one.

"Hold on," Alex said as he got up to leave the room.

"It's okay, Alexander. I understand. I haven't exactly given you reason to trust me," Robert said sincerely.

"You've given me a good reason. The only reason I need, and that's your promise you made about never leaving me," Alex said confidently as he left and quickly returned with a razor. "Here," he said as he handed it to Robert.

When Robert returned from the bathroom, Alex smiled, "Feel better?"

"Yes, I do," Robert replied as he pulled out black-pleated gabardine pants and a slate gray tee shirt. He dressed quickly, combed his hair, and snapped his platinum Rolex onto his wrist. "How's my mother?"

"She's doing fine," Alex said honestly. "Emily is helping her get bathed and dressed, and then they should be down for breakfast. What do you say we go down for some breakfast? There's a lot I have to tell you," Alex said.

"That's fine," Robert said as they both left Robert's master bedroom. When they got to the kitchen, Robert inquired, "Did you speak to Dr. Hamilton?"

"Yeah," Alex paused as he poured a glass of milk. "He's going to stop out later this morning to see you."

"Great," Robert said reluctantly.

"Come on, Dad. He's been great. I don't know what I would have done without his help," Alex explained.

"I know. I appreciate all that he's done, but I'm not exactly thrilled to see any more doctors, including him," Robert said of his experiences.

"I know, but if it wasn't for him, I wouldn't be talking to you like this right now. I owe him everything," Alex said as Robert nodded his understanding. "So, what can I make you for breakfast?" Alex asked.

Robert laughed, "A little bit of salmonella to start off the day?"

"That's what I like to hear," Alex said. "Who would have thought you were such a smart ass?"

Robert smiled mischievously, but with a hint of melancholy. "I just want some orange juice for right now," Robert said as Alex poured him a glass and handed it to him.

"A lot of things happened over the past several months, but I don't want to overwhelm you with everything right now," Alex said sincerely.

"How about the basics then?" Robert replied.

"Well, first of all, I made sure Grandma had the best care and rehabilitation. She has been at Saint Michael's for the past couple of months, but if it's okay with you, she could move in here for awhile," Alex said.

"I guess that will depend on how well things go this morning," Robert replied. "How did you keep him from keeping her locked up as a prisoner in her own home?"

"Who? George? You were right about him. He's an asshole, but he overestimated his abilities," Alex said proudly.

"How so?" Robert asked.

"He thought he could screw a Petrovic and get away with it," Alex said with a wry smile.

"What happened?" Robert asked as he smiled at Alex's statements concerning George.

"We'll get to that later. I was lucky along the way because I had my friend Antonio helping me. Do you remember him? He's the attorney I sent to the jail to bail you out," Alex said.

Robert put his head in his hands, "Damn. I guess I don't have to worry about what's been going on around here because I'll be going to jail. I've had to have missed court dates," Robert said disappointedly.

"The last place you're going is to jail, Dad. I hired Antonio, and he did an incredible amount of investigating, and guess what?" Alex asked.

"What?" Robert replied.

"He got the charges dropped. Antonio found witnesses who saw and heard everything that night, so you don't have to worry about that anymore," Alex continued proudly.

"Thank you," Robert said sincerely, "But there are other things I have to worry about. My company is probably in shambles," Robert said sadly.

"Oh contrare," Alex said goofily. "Your business is doing well. I kept things going the best I could. All the contracts that you had signed were fulfilled or are presently being fulfilled. I couldn't sign any new contracts, but I do have some people interested in having construction done when you are feeling better. I could have had papers drawn up so that I could enter into contracts on your behalf, but I wasn't going to take you to court and have you declared incompetent. Your business was in fine shape, so there was no immediate need to have new contracts in place," Alex explained.

"I don't know what to say," Robert said dumbfounded. "I owe you so much."

"There is something that I'd like from you, Dad," Alex responded.

"Anything," Robert said before adding, "within reason."

"I'd like to come work for you at your company," Alex answered.

"No," Robert said plainly. "I don't want you to work for me." Disappointment clouded Alex's face before Robert could continue, "I would really enjoy it if you would come work *with* me."

Alex smiled, "Are you sure?"

"I have always wanted to work side by side with my son," Robert explained sincerely.

"Thank you, Dad," Alex replied at his father's comments.

"I'm the one who should be thanking you, Alexander. You saved my life, and not only that, you allowed me to get to know my grandchildren and you stayed and took care of me. For that I will always be grateful," Robert offered honestly.

Alex came over and stood next to his dad as the two looked absently out of the window and into the crystal blue swimming pool. Emily came through the doorway of the kitchen and smiled. It was the first time that she had seen Robert dressed in designer clothes. She coughed lightly to get their attention, "Hi guys."

Alex walked over to Emily and kissed her tenderly on the lips, "Hi Em."

"Hi," Robert replied shyly.

"Alex, could you go check on your grandma? She was trying to pick out something to wear, and I think she could use your help deciding," Emily instructed her husband. In a whisper, she continued so that Robert would not hear, "I'd like to talk to him alone if that's okay?"

"That's fine," Alex replied. "Hey Dad, I'll be back in a few minutes. Grandma needs my expertise," Alex explained to Robert as he walked out the door.

Emily poured a glass of orange juice and came over to stand next to Robert, who had continued to peer out the window at the still water of the pool. "Hi Robert," she said tenderly.

"Hi Emily," Robert said without making eye contact.

"How are you feeling? I was really worried about you last night," Emily said genuinely.

"I'm fine. A bit overwhelmed, but fine," Robert answered shyly.

Emily sat her orange juice down on the table and took Robert's hand in hers and held it lovingly, "The thing that I feared most about this day was that I would lose my 'Clyde.' I don't think that I could handle that," Emily said sadly.

"I don't know if he still exists," Robert answered softly.

"No matter what has happened, I want my 'Clyde' to know that I love him," Emily said as she took her other hand and gently turned Robert's face toward hers. "And that I love my father-in-law too."

Through piercing mahogany eyes, Robert looked at Emily with disbelief and hope, "I only wish that were true."

"It is, Robert. I love you, and I don't want anything to ever come between us," Emily said candidly.

"I really hope you mean that, Emily. I love you too, but one of my greatest fears is that you'll go back to hating me once you see me for who I really am. I couldn't bear that," Robert said emotionally.

"Nothing is going to change how I feel about you. Over these past several months, you and I bonded in a way that I never thought possible. For the first time in my life, I'd actually look forward to the mornings because I knew I'd get to see you, and undoubtedly get to laugh with you," Emily explained.

"I enjoyed our time together as well," Robert replied.

Emily teared up as she pulled Robert over to the table to sit down. "I'm so sorry for the way that I've treated you all these years, Robert. I was so unfair. I didn't make up my mind about you. I judged you by what Alex said about you, and that wasn't fair. You're a great guy, regardless of who you go out with or have a relationship with," Emily explained.

"Why the change?" Robert asked.

"Well, I've gotten to know Mitchell over the past several weeks, and you know what?" Emily asked.

"What?" Robert asked hesitantly.

"I really like him," Emily said as she smiled at Robert. "And besides," she paused, "He's really cute."

Robert laughed out loud, "Yeah, he is, isn't he?"

"Oh yeah," Emily smirked before she became serious. "Mitchell has had a really tough time over the past several weeks."

Robert became alarmed, "Is he okay?"

"He will be when he finds out you regained your memory," Emily said happily.

Disappointment weighed heavily on Robert's handsome face as he took a drink of his orange juice. "He can get on with his life then," Robert said sadly.

"The only way he'll be happy is if that life is with you," Emily replied.

Robert looked at Emily with a perplexed stare, "Why do you say that? He made it clear to me that he didn't want to be part of my life."

"Did Alex tell you about how Mitchell chewed him out?" Emily asked.

"Yes, but what does that have to do with wanting me back?" Robert inquired.

"When Alex called Mitchell the day after all this happened, Mitchell went to the hospital and chewed Alex out good. Mitchell left, and we didn't hear from him again until the night we came back from our trip home to find you in that asylum. Apparently Mitchell had been secretly checking in from time to time to see that you were all right in the hospital. When he went to the hospital and you weren't there, he came here. He said, 'I know I'm not your favorite person, but I'm really worried about Robert.' He just wanted to know that you were okay, even if it meant coming out here to see Alex."

"Being concerned doesn't mean he still loves me. Hell, he'd be concerned about a dog hit by a car and go check on it every once in a while," Robert said sorrowfully.

"I could see he was really worried that night, so I asked him in. I told him that you had been transferred and that Alex was bringing you home once he got the court order. He asked if he could stay, hoping that if you saw him it would make you feel better. Without thinking, I told him that you seeing him wouldn't make you feel better," Emily paused. "Robert, it was as if I tore a hole in his soul. I then explained about your memory, but it didn't help matters much."

"He was here that night," Robert said as he closed his eyes to try to remember.

"Yes, and when Alex carried you in and laid you on the couch, I could unmistakably see Mitchell's heart breaking. It killed him to see you like that. And believe me, you didn't look too good that night after the hell those people put you through," Emily continued.

"I didn't feel all that great either," Robert said forlornly.

"When Alex was taking you upstairs to wait for Dr. Hamilton, he asked Mitchell to help him get you upstairs. When Mitchell was leaving, I could see how emotional he was, so I got him to sit down to talk to me. After we started talking, I realized how much he loved you. I asked him point blank, 'do you still love him?' and he said unequivocally 'yes.' We talked about this day, when you'd regained your memory, and I asked him if he would come back and want to start over in a relationship, and he said 'yes.'"

"I think having Mitchell come back is beyond my control," Robert replied.

"Well, that night I could see how much it hurt him to see you like that and not be able to do anything about it. I could see it in his eyes that all he wanted to do was hold you in his arms until you were better. We made a pact that night, he and I. I promised I would keep him informed on how you were doing, especially that night after Dr. Hamilton left, and he promised to keep in touch. Out of that mutual pact of caring about you, Mitchell and I became good friends. We talk on the phone every day. Who would have thought that I would become friends with the man that Alex claimed to be a degenerate only a few months before?"

"Alexander claimed that I was a degenerate as well," Robert replied sadly.

"Well, my dear Robert, he's seen the light, so to speak," Emily joked. "And don't worry about him ever changing. If he does, I'll beat the living daylights out of him. I won't let anyone ever slander my 'Clyde' or my buddy Mitchell ever again, and you have my word on that," Emily said sternly.

Robert laughed softly, "Thank you, Bonnie."

Emily grinned and pulled Robert into a tender embrace. As he was pulling away, Emily took his hand and continued, "I better go check on Alex and Grandma."

"Why?" Robert asked.

"I left Alex in charge of helping Grandma find something to wear," Emily laughed.

"Oh no! God only knows what she'll have on with the two of them brainstorming about fashion," Robert joked.

"It's clear to see that the two of them are related," Emily said merrily.

"Yeah, bad taste in clothes is definitely hereditary," Robert replied.

"How did it skip you? You look like you just stepped out of the pages of a men's fashion magazine," Emily inquired.

"I'm gay, it's in our bylaws," Robert joked as he smiled genuinely at Emily.

"I love you Robert. Please don't ever change," Emily laughed.

"I'll try not too, but are you sure you like me as a grown-up?" Robert said impishly.

"Absolutely. What is it about you Petrovic men?"

"I don't know, but if you find out, could you let me know?" Robert teased.

Emily laughed jovially as she heard Alex's voice coming from the other room. "I think Double O Seven is bellowing."

"We won't keep him waiting then," Robert said as he offered his arm to Emily as they walked out the door.

Standing at the edge of the living room, Alex and Anna waited patiently for Emily and Robert to appear from the kitchen. As Emily and Robert approached, arm in arm, Anna called out to her son, "Please stay there ... I'll walk to you."

Before Robert could open his mouth to say anything, Anna started walking slowly toward him with a considerable limp. When she was in arms reach, Anna said to her son, "See Bobby, I'm okay. You didn't do anything to me." Anna started to wobble and Robert reached out to steady her, but instead Anna threw herself forward and into his arms. "I'm so sorry, Bobby," she cried as she buried her head in the front of his shirt.

Robert looked stoically at Alex and Emily. Alex could see the discomfort on Robert's face, but he excused himself regardless, "Dad ... Emily and I are going to check on the kids and then make some breakfast. We'll be in the kitchen if you need us."

Before Robert could protest Alex and Emily's abandonment, the pair had left him to deal with the woman who still clung to the front of his shirt, crying and apologizing frantically.

"I'm so sorry. Please forgive me, Bobby. I never meant to hurt you," Anna kept repeating.

Robert gently pushed her away as he addressed her politely, "I think you should sit down."

"Bobby? You do believe me, don't you?" she asked.

"Please mother, sit down. I don't want you to fall and hurt yourself," Robert said as he avoided her question.

"You're still looking out for me, even after all I've done," Anna said sadly. "I never meant for this to happen."

"I'm responsible for my own actions. It was my decision to do what I did, and now I have to face the consequences of that decision," Robert said matter-of-factly.

"But I drove you to this," Anna said sorrowfully. "I am so sorry, Bobby."

"Please," Robert snapped. "Please quit apologizing already."

"I'm sorry," Anna said stunned. "I just don't know what else to say. When I saw Alex carrying you through those doors last night, I thought that I had lost you forever. I couldn't bear to think of my baby being in so much pain."

"I'm not a baby," Robert snapped angrily. "I'm a grown man, and I can take care of myself."

"I know you can, Bobby. You've always been able to take care of yourself. I think that's what I resented so much," Anna revealed.

"You resented me," Robert said astonished. "What the hell for?"

"Because I had to rely on you for everything. That night I told you those hurtful words ...," Anna said before she was interrupted.

"You can say them, mother. 'You're no longer my son.'" Robert replied.

"Yes, that's what I said, and I wish I never had. I thought you were trying to control my life," Anna explained honestly.

"Control your life?" Robert repeated. "I gave you anything that you have ever wanted. No, mother," he exclaimed angrily, "You got me confused with another Petrovic. My father controlled you. Not me. I worked my ass off to give you a better life. What did he ever do for you except beat the hell out of you every Saturday night?"

"He gave me you," she said lovingly.

"Maybe we both would have been better off if he hadn't," Robert replied.

"Don't say that, Bobby. I love you," Anna said as she reached out for Robert's hand.

Robert pulled his hand away, "I can't do this right now."

"Please, Bobby," she pleaded. "You have no idea how I felt before I met George. I was so lonely, and then he came along and made me feel alive again."

"And where is George right now, mother?" Robert asked sarcastically.

"Somewhere living off my money," Anna responded sorrowfully.

"Really?" Robert replied mockingly.

"Yes. You were right about him, and if it wasn't for Alex, I would probably be out in the street right now," Anna explained.

"Why do you say that?" Robert asked suspiciously.

"Didn't Alex tell you what happened?" Anna asked.

"No. He didn't want to overwhelm me," Robert said sarcastically.

"I'm sorry. I thought you knew all about it."

Robert stood up and walked over to the double doors and looked out before speaking, "I never would've thought that you'd let anyone come between us. After all we had been through together, you let some hustler come in and turn you against me."

"Bobby ...," Anna said before being interrupted.

Robert closed his eyes as he remembered back, "You know, it broke my heart when I called from the jail and got your answering machine. I knew you were there, but you wouldn't pick up the phone. You didn't know what had happened to me, but that didn't matter, did it? I pleaded with you to bring the money to the jail, money that I would have paid you back, but you couldn't be bothered. Mitchell wouldn't come, and you wouldn't answer the phone. Do you have any idea what it's like to be thrown into a jail cell and not know when you may get out? Do you have any idea what it's like to spend a couple of hours, let alone a couple of days, with those redneck cops? They had a grand old time at my expense."

"I'm sorry," Anna muttered.

Robert held up his hand angrily to halt her words, "And then I find out that you had a stroke, so I race over to the hospital looking like something that just crawled out of the gutter, and I go in and plead with you not to leave me, and to forgive me, and if you'd do that, I would accept George. But then the door flew open and George called me out into the hallway and called security. He said that I couldn't go back in to see you, and that I was banned from your room. I told him to go to hell, but apparently he had every right to do so," Robert paused as he took a deep breath, "since he was your husband."

"Bobby. Please let me explain," Anna pleaded.

"Oh, I bet you had a good laugh at me while you listened to your answering machine. So much so that you ran out and got married. But you know what mother," Robert turned around and looked at her, "I still wasn't going to let him keep me from seeing you until he told me that I was the cause of your stroke."

"What? How could you have been the cause?" Anna asked perplexed.

"How? I don't know—maybe being stigmatized over having a queer son who was locked up in jail while you celebrated the happiest day of your life," Robert said bitterly.

"Don't you talk like that!" Anna commanded.

"Sorry, mother. Nobody controls my life. Oh, wait a minute. That's your life that nobody controls. You feared that I was trying to control your life, but yet you left two of the worst men in your life control you without a thought. I gave you everything that you ever wanted, and what did they give you? Huh? A weekly beating from one, and an empty bank account from the other," Robert said without remorse.

"You don't know what it's like, not having anyone to share your life with," Anna said emotionally.

"You had great friends, and you had family. You didn't only have me. In the other room is your grandson and his wife, and your great-grandchildren," Robert replied angrily.

"That's different. You don't know what it's like to be lonely and not have someone to love," Anna tried to explain.

"No," Robert said sarcastically. "I wouldn't know anything about that. I just lived for twenty years in a loveless marriage to Alexander's mother, denying who I was. No, I wouldn't have any idea what it's like not to be fulfilled and happy."

"Please Bobby. You have to believe that I never meant what I said that night," Anna said through tears.

"And how do I know you mean what you say right now?" Robert said sarcastically. "I'm sorry, I can't do this."

"Bobby, please don't walk away," Anna pleaded.

Robert walked to the door and let her pleas fall on deaf ears. He walked out the front door and started for the pond. Anna limped quickly to the kitchen and interrupted Alex and Emily's breakfast with the twins.

"What's wrong, Grandma?" Alex asked.

"He's so angry with me, Alex. He walked out," Anna explained.

Alex got up and walked toward the door, "Where did he go?"

"I don't know. He went out the front door," Anna said.

"He just needs some time, Grandma," Alex said as he walked out.

# CHAPTER 28

▼

Alex strolled outside trying not to look suspicious of Robert leaving his own house. He found Robert skipping stones angrily across the pond at the edge of the grounds. Alex walked over quietly and picked up a stone and skimmed it across the water, creating several ripples.

"Are you okay?" Alex asked tenderly.

"I'm fine," Robert replied shortly.

"What happened?" Alex asked.

"I just couldn't sit there and hear her say she was sorry over and over again," Robert explained.

"Maybe it was too soon to see her," Alex pondered out loud.

With his eyes full of rage, Robert looked at Alex as he continued, "She accused me of trying to control her life. I gave up my own life to take care of her because of some fucking promise that I made to a man that I hated. I was fifteen, Alexander. She should have taken care of me, but instead I gave up everything that I ever wanted for myself to make a life for us."

"I don't know what to say, Dad," Alex said sincerely, but stunned at his father's choice of words.

"That night that bastard George came here, I even let him get away with punching me. I should have broken his fucking neck instead of trying to break my own," Robert continued furiously.

"Come on, Dad. Let's go for a walk," Alex said as he reached for Robert's hand.

"I didn't bring my sunglasses," Robert explained. "It's too sunny out here, and I don't want to get a headache."

"Stay here and I'll go get them, and then we'll go for a walk," Alex said sincerely.

Robert continued to skim stones furiously across the pond as Alex returned carrying Robert's black Raybans. He looked up and saw the concern written on Alex's face. As he reached out to take the sunglasses from Alex, Robert patted him on the shoulder as he spoke reassuringly, "I'm okay, Alexander."

"I know you are," Alex replied. "I just feel bad that I made you see Grandma this morning."

"You didn't make me see her, Alexander. It was my decision," Robert explained.

"I feel like I pushed you into it, though," Alex said.

"Can we get something straight right now?" Robert asked as he stood face to face with his son.

"What?" Alex asked with alarm.

"From the time that I woke up this morning and from now on, the decisions that I make are my own. I appreciate everything that you've done for me over the past several months, but when I woke up this morning I had my senses back, so I'm quite capable of making up my own mind," Robert paused. "And I'm also capable of facing the consequences for those decisions."

Alex nodded his understanding. "I just want you to be happy, Dad."

"I know you do, and I love you for it," Robert smiled at his son. "But I'm all right. I promised you that I would never try anything like this again, and seeing as I keep every promise, like the ridiculous one I made to my father all those years ago, you can pretty much bank on me keeping it," Robert said lightheartedly.

"Dad," Alex said sadly. "I do trust you. I just couldn't deal with losing you."

"You're not going to lose me," Robert said tenderly.

"Okay," Alex said semi-enthusiastically. "Let's go for a walk then."

"Lead the way," Robert replied.

The two walked along the horse path and continued out to the edge of the hillside where Robert had fallen the night before. Alex stopped a moment and looked down over the edge, remembering what had happened to his father the night before. Alex nodded to his father to look over the edge, "Do you remember?"

"Remember what?" Robert asked.

"Last night," Alex replied.

Robert looked over the edge and responded, "I don't remember much about last night."

"What do you remember?" Alex asked.

Robert shook his head in an attempt to remember, "I remember talking to you on the floor in the living room, and then going outside to shoot some hoops. When I came in I saw my mother sitting in a wheelchair in my living room."

"You don't remember anything else?" Alex inquired.

"No," Robert responded honestly.

"You ran out the back door and ran out here. I followed you, even though you ran too damn fast for me to keep up, but I saw from a distance you slip on the wet grass and fall down over this hillside," Alex explained as he motioned toward the hillside.

Robert rubbed his sore shoulders and joked, "I guess that explains why I'm so sore."

"Yeah," Alex laughed, "That would probably explain it."

"So what happened next?" Robert inquired.

"I climbed down to make sure you weren't hurt, but you wouldn't talk to me. You were laying on your side crying," Alex explained.

Robert cringed, but Alex interrupted, "Don't be embarrassed. There's no shame in crying. Isn't that what you always told me?" Alex asked.

"You remembered?" Robert said disbelieving.

"Yeah, I remembered," Alex responded with a smile.

"What happened next?" Robert asked.

"Well, I called Dr. Hamilton and he told me to keep an eye on you until he got here. When he got here, we slid down so that Dr. Hamilton could check you out, but you wouldn't respond."

"I don't remember any of this," Robert responded.

"I hope you're not going to hate me for this, but I held you down while he sedated you. That's why your thigh is sore," Alex explained gently.

"Why would I hate you for trying to help me?" Robert asked.

"Well," Alex paused. "You didn't exactly have an affinity for needles."

Robert sighed, "So then what happened? Or don't I want to know?"

"We carried you up to the house and put you to bed," Alex replied.

"Oh," Robert said. "I guess it could have been worse."

"Yeah, it could have been, but thank God you woke up this morning and you're all right," Alex said gratefully.

"Amen to that," Robert replied half-jokingly.

Alex and Robert turned around and started walking back toward the house. They were silent for several minutes before Alex slowed down, "Can I ask you something Dad?"

"Anything you want," Robert replied.

"Would it be okay if Emily, the kids and I stay here with you for a while?" Alex asked hesitantly.

"Oh God. My mother, you, Emily and the kids all under one roof. I'm definitely going to need a shrink," Robert joked.

Alex laughed loudly, "What a smart ass!"

"Seriously," Robert said. "You can stay as long as you want."

"Does that mean that Grandma can stay as well?" Alex asked.

"It's a big house. Besides, you and Emily went to visit her quite often didn't you? This way you can save some time," Robert replied.

"You don't have to see Grandma if you don't want to," Alex offered.

"I know. Like I said, it's a big house," Robert said.

"We won't stay forever, I promise," Alex said lightheartedly.

"You can stay as long as you want," Robert reiterated.

"Just until our new home is built," Alex replied.

Before Robert could respond to his son's comments, Dr. Hamilton pulled into the driveway. Dr. Hamilton got out of his car and leaned against the hood as he waited for Alex and Robert to walk to the house. He studied Robert's attire and was pleasantly shocked at how well Robert looked in his normal clothes. Alex walked up to the car, "Hi Doc."

"Hi Alex," the doctor responded with a smile. As Robert stepped into direct sight, Dr. Hamilton smiled as he greeted him, "Hi Robert."

"Hi Doctor," Robert said as he reached to shake the doctor's hand. "I guess I should say that I'm glad to meet you."

"The same here," the doctor said sincerely.

"Come on, let's go inside," Robert said.

As the three were walking to the front door, Emily appeared, "Hi Doctor. I wasn't sure where these guys were," she explained.

"Hey Em, you don't have to worry about losing your Clyde," Alex said jovially.

"Why?" she inquired.

"I asked Dad if it'd be okay if we stayed here for awhile, and you know what he said?"

"What?" Emily asked with a smile.

"How did you say that, Dad?" Alex asked as he looked to Robert who was acting serious. "He said about having Grandma, me, you and the kids under one roof, that he would need a shrink," Alex explained with a mischievous grin.

Dr. Hamilton and Emily laughed out loud. Dr. Hamilton regained his composure and asked Alex, "Are you staying?"

"Yeah, that's what we were just talking about," Alex said as he put his arm around Robert's shoulder. "Like I was saying Dad, we're just going to stay until our new house is built."

"Where are you building?" Robert asked.

"Emily and I bought the property across the street," Alex replied.

"The Stanley place?" Robert asked.

"Yeah," Alex answered. "There was about twenty acres, so we bought it."

"I thought about buying that property when it first went on the market, but I really didn't have a need for it. This place is big enough," Robert explained.

"You think?" Alex teased. "Anyways, I asked all around the county and everybody recommends that I hire this guy. His name is something like Peterosky, Pertivovic, or something like that. It's an immigrant sounding name," Alex smiled.

"*Petrovic*, as spoken in the old country. Or thankfully Americanized to Petrovic," Robert said as he correctly enunciated the differences in the name.

"Yep, that was it," Alex teased. "Seriously Dad, you came highly recommended, but of course we're going to have to see a sample of your work before we hire you," Alex continued teasing.

Robert stopped and looked at Alex before continuing sarcastically, "You've been living in one for the past several months."

Emily started to giggle as Alex said in joking defeat, "I guess you have a point there."

As they walked into the living room, the doctor asked Robert if there was someplace quiet where they could talk.

"Alexander, is there somewhere we can talk privately?" Robert asked.

"Yeah, your study. The kids know they aren't allowed in there. I didn't want them to be around your computer," Alex explained.

"Thank you," Robert replied before he addressed the doctor, "Please Doctor, this way."

Dr. Hamilton followed Robert through the hallway and into the beautifully decorated study. "Please sit down," Robert instructed politely before he went to open the small refrigerator that he kept in the corner of the study. "Can I get you anything? Some orange juice, ice tea, bottled water?" Robert asked.

"No thank you. I'm fine," the doctor replied.

"Do you mind if I ..." Robert asked as he pulled out a bottle of water.

"No, go ahead," Dr. Hamilton replied. As Robert sat down on the opposite end of the sofa, Dr. Hamilton continued, "How are you feeling?"

"A bit overwhelmed," Robert answered. "And embarrassed."

"Why do feel embarrassed?" the doctor asked.

"For what I did, for what I put everyone through, including you. I'm sorry that you've had to come out here on those occasions," Robert replied genuinely.

"Please don't feel embarrassed about that. I was just doing my job," the doctor responded amiably. "And about what happened and what you did, believe me Robert, I can understand why you chose to do what you did."

Robert looked at him with disbelief, "Really?"

"With everything that had happened to you in the course of those few days, I can understand why you did it. Anybody, if faced with similar circumstances, could have chosen to do the same thing, and many have," Dr. Hamilton explained.

"That still doesn't make me feel less embarrassed," Robert replied.

"How are you feeling otherwise?" Dr. Hamilton asked.

Robert took a long drink from his bottled water before replying, "I'm having difficulty concentrating, and when I go to say something, it seems like I have to search for the words."

"That's probably from the medication that I gave you last night," the doctor answered. "How do you feel physically?"

"My muscles are sore, especially in my upper body, but after Alexander showed me the hillside that I fell over, I feel surprisingly well," Robert replied lightheartedly.

"Yeah, that was quite a fall. I didn't get to check you over last night, so before I go I want to make sure you don't have any injuries, okay?"

"Sure," Robert replied.

"How's your neck?" the doctor asked.

"I had an intense spasm this morning in the shower," Robert answered. He took another drink and continued stoically, "Doctor?"

"Yes," Dr. Hamilton answered.

"Did I do permanent damage to my neck with the rope?"

Dr. Hamilton frowned slightly, "It's a possibility. Before you couldn't remember when it had started hurting. Do you remember now?" the doctor questioned.

"I first noticed it when I woke up in the hospital," Robert answered.

The doctor nodded his head, "It's a possibility that there's some soft tissue damage, but there are several different treatments that are available to try, such as physical therapy and different anti-inflammatory drugs." Dr. Hamilton smiled at Robert, "We'll make sure we find something that helps, okay?"

"When can I start working out?" Robert questioned.

Caught slightly off guard, Dr. Hamilton replied, "What's the hurry?"

"I feel better when I work out. Right now I feel like I have no stamina," Robert replied.

"You have a gym here in the house, right?" the doctor asked.

"Yes," Robert answered.

"I don't see any problems with you starting out slow, but try to avoid anything that has to do with your neck muscles or your upper back muscles. You can work on any type of lower body exercises, but for right now, try to avoid putting any type of stress on your neck area until we know how bad an injury we're dealing with, okay?" the doctor instructed.

"That's fine. I'm looking forward to getting back to running," Robert replied.

"You're a runner?" the doctor asked intrigued.

"Yes, up until the past several months, I would run five or six miles a day, and then usually about ten miles on Saturdays," Robert explained.

"Wow," Dr. Hamilton said. "Now I know why you were in such good shape."

"I'd be lucky if I could run a mile right now," Robert said pessimistically.

"Does Alex run too?" the doctor asked.

Robert smirked, "I don't think so. Alexander was never much into staying in shape."

Dr. Hamilton laughed before saying seriously, "It seems like you and Alex are getting along quite well."

"For now," Robert answered as he turned away to look out the window.

"You don't think it's going to last?" the doctor asked.

"Unfortunately, no," Robert answered sadly.

"Why?"

"Because my son is a politician—a conservative who tows the party line no matter what. He goes along to get along. How do you think his colleagues are going to react when they find out that he has a fag father who tried to kill himself?" Robert explained.

"I don't think Alex sees it that way," Dr. Hamilton replied.

"Maybe not right now, after being away from them for these past months. And then him getting to know me when I thought I was a teenager. But I'm not an innocent teenager; I'm a man. I'm afraid that when he sees me with a man, all the old feeling will come back and he'll leave again," Robert clarified.

"When I first met Alex, I would have agreed with you, but seeing how he's changed over these past months, I think he's accepted you for who you really are," the doctor responded.

"He told me how you made it clear to him that his attitude wasn't welcome," Robert said.

"I was just telling him the truth. I don't tolerate prejudice in any form, especially when it's directed at one of my patients." Dr. Hamilton explained.

"Thank you," Robert replied.

A light knock on the study door interrupted the conversation, "Who's there?" Robert called out.

"It's me," said a soft child's voice.

Robert got up off the sofa and went over to open the door. On the other side of the door stood an innocent little angel. Robert smiled softly, "Hi Stef. What's wrong?"

Steffi reached up for Robert to pick her up. As he held her, she answered shyly, "I can't find anyone. Me and Stevie was playing hide and seek, and he left me and didn't come back. I looked for Mommy, but I couldn't find her or Daddy."

Robert looked down at Dr. Hamilton still sitting on the sofa, "I'm sorry about this."

"It's fine," Dr. Hamilton said with a friendly grin as he addressed Steffi, "And who is this little princess?"

"Steffi," she said shyly as she buried her head in Robert's shirtfront.

"Is this guy your buddy?" Dr. Hamilton asked her as he pointed to Robert.

Steffi shook her head in the affirmative as she clung to Robert. Robert carried her over and sat down with her behind his desk. "Let's see if we can find your Mommy and Daddy. Would you like to help me?" Robert asked tenderly.

"Yeah," Steffi said eagerly.

"Okay," he said as he pulled the phone over in front of them. "Push this button here," Robert instructed as she pushed the intercom button for the living room. "Alexander," Robert said. Robert showed Steffi the next button to push and she happily pushed it, clearly fascinated by the magic of the intercom. "Alexander," Robert said with the message going into the foyer. With no answer, Robert instructed Steffi to push two of the buttons simultaneously as he spoke, "Alexander."

"Yeah, Dad," came the reply.

"Steffi is here with me in the study. She couldn't find you or Emily," Robert explained good-naturedly.

"I'm sorry, Dad. I'll be right down to get her," Alex said annoyed.

"No hurry. She's fine," Robert replied.

"Okay, I'll be down," Alex answered.

"Daddy's mad at me, isn't he?" Steffi said slightly afraid.

"No Stef. Why would he be mad at you?" Robert asked tenderly as he hugged her.

"He told me and Stevie we weren't allowed in here," Steffi answered anxiously.

"It's okay since I'm in here with you," Robert said alleviating her fears. "What are you going to do today?" Robert asked his granddaughter.

"I wanted to go swimming, but Daddy felt the water and said that it's too cold," she answered disappointed.

Robert shook his head and laughed, "That's because your Daddy doesn't know that the swimming pool has a heater on it."

"It does?" Emily asked with fascination.

"Yeah. I'll tell you what. Later this morning I'll go out and turn the heater on, and then in the afternoon if it's okay with your Mommy and Daddy, maybe you and Stevie can go swimming," Robert explained happily.

Steffi's eyes shined brightly, "Will you come with us?"

"I'm not sure, sweetie. Maybe," Robert answered as the door of the study opened.

"Dad, I am so sorry," Alex apologized.

"It's okay, Alexander. We were just talking about Steffi's plans for this afternoon," Robert answered jovially.

"Steffi, let's go," Alex said half-upset.

"Alex, really, she was no problem. She's quite a lovely young lady," Dr. Hamilton commented.

Alex smiled proudly, "Thank you, Doctor." He took Steffi by the hand, and as he led her out of the study, she turned around and waved at Robert. Robert smiled and waved back.

Dr. Hamilton broke the silence, "You have a lovely granddaughter, Robert."

"Yes, she is lovely. I'm a lucky man," Robert said plainly.

"If I were a betting man, I'd say that lovely child and her brother are going to be spoiled by their grandfather," Dr. Hamilton joked.

"Absolutely. I missed the first five years of their lives, and I hope to make up for every minute that I missed," Robert answered.

"Is it okay if we continue?" Dr. Hamilton asked.

"Sure, go ahead," Robert replied.

"How did things go this morning with your mother?" Dr. Hamilton asked as he saw Robert's mood visibly change.

"Not well. I walked out on her," Robert answered.

"Why?" the doctor asked intrigued.

"Because I couldn't listen to her apologize over and over again," Robert answered angrily.

"Why was she apologizing?" Dr. Hamilton asked.

"For telling me that I was no longer her son," Robert said shortly.

Dr. Hamilton's eyebrows shot up, "What?"

"The night that Mitchell broke up with me, my mother came over and told me to stay out of her relationship with George. When I refused, she told me that if I didn't change my mind that she would disown me—that I would no longer be her son," Robert explained.

Dr. Hamilton looked at Robert with astonishment written on his face. "She told you that you were no longer her son?" the doctor asked disbelieving.

"Yes. She accused me of trying to control her life, but this morning she told me I was right all along. George drained her bank account and took off," Robert answered. "She was apologizing for pushing me to do what I did," Robert added.

"Did what she say push you to do what you did?" the doctor asked.

"You can say it, Doctor. I tried to kill myself," Robert corrected.

"Okay, did what she say push you to try to kill yourself?" Dr. Hamilton repeated.

"Not completely. It may have been the catalyst, but I think it was a combination of everything that happened over those few days," Robert answered honestly.

Dr. Hamilton smiled at Robert. "Getting your memory back was a big step, Robert, but you still have a lot to work through. The road ahead is going to be long, and at times bumpy, but I know that you're going to be okay"

"I hope so," Robert answered.

"You have to remember, this problem didn't come about overnight. This has been building since you were a teenager, so it's going to take time to work through it. But now you have your family to lean on, and from what I've already seen today, they have you to lean on as well. That's what family is all about, supporting each other through the good times and the bad," Dr. Hamilton explained.

"I just hope it lasts," Robert said pragmatically.

"I think it will. Is there anything you'd like to talk about that's concerning you or bothering you?" the doctor asked sincerely.

"No, I just wish I had some privacy. Like today, when I walked out on my mother. I needed to be by myself to think and sort things out, but Alexander came right out. I know he's just concerned about me, but I need to be alone from time to time to think," Robert answered.

"I can talk to Alex and explain that you need time alone. Actually, I think it would be a good idea," the doctor responded.

"Really?" Robert asked disbelieving.

"Yes. If you could have some private time this afternoon, what would you do?" Dr. Hamilton questioned.

"I'd take my horse, Sebastian, on a slow, lazy walk around the grounds," Robert replied.

"Do you have a cell phone?" Dr. Hamilton asked.

"Of course," Robert answered slightly confused at the question.

"I'll talk to Alex and tell him that you need some private time, but that you'll take your cell phone with you, and you'll check in, say every hour or so. How does that sound?" Dr. Hamilton asked.

"That sounds great," Robert answered honestly.

"Good, I'll talk to Alex and tell him what's going on, but first I want to check you over to make sure that you weren't hurt last night," Dr. Hamilton instructed.

"That's fine. I have to change my clothes to go riding, so why don't you just come up to check me over before you talk to Alexander," Robert offered.

"That's fine. Lead the way," the doctor replied.

Robert led Dr. Hamilton out of the study and took the back way up to the upstairs. As Robert turned the door handle to his bedroom, Dr. Hamilton looked perplexed, "I thought your bedroom was down the hall further?"

"No, this is my bedroom. Alexander put me in that room down the hall when I came home so that the kids wouldn't disturb me. Not like that would ever happen, since I insulated the walls so heavily that they're practically soundproof," Robert said merrily.

Dr. Hamilton walked in and marveled at the beauty of Robert's master bedroom. As Robert searched through his closet for appropriate riding attire, Dr. Hamilton studied the artwork and decorations that adorned the classically decorated master bedroom. As Robert laid the clothing over a chair, Dr. Hamilton asked, "Are you ready?"

"Yeah," Robert answered plainly.

Dr. Hamilton examined Robert's upper body, especially the areas that Robert described as being sore. He moved Robert's limbs slowly to ascertain his range of motion, and when he was satisfied that Robert wasn't injured, he gave Robert the go ahead to get dressed. As Robert dressed, Dr. Hamilton went downstairs to find Alex.

As Dr. Hamilton explained Robert's need for privacy to Alex, Anna entered the room walking slowly with a cane. She stepped from behind Alex to look at Dr. Hamilton, "Are you my son's doctor?" she asked.

"I'm Dr. Hamilton, and yes I'm treating Robert," Dr. Hamilton replied.

"Please Doctor, is my Bobby going to be okay?" Anna asked seriously.

"Dr. Hamilton," Alex interrupted, "This is my grandmother, Anna."

"Mrs. Petrovic, as I was just telling Alex, Robert needs some privacy. He needs some time to process what has happened, and the last thing that he needs is to be pressured," Dr. Hamilton instructed firmly.

"I just want him to be okay," Anna said as tears started to form.

As Alex reached to comfort her, Robert walked into the room to witness what was happening. Robert saw his mother, and turned around to address Dr. Hamilton, "Thank you again, Doctor."

"Bobby," Anna called out as Robert started to leave.

"Grandma," Alex reprimanded softly. "Remember what the doctor just said."

"I'm sorry," she said quietly.

"Wait up, Dad," Alex called out after him as Dr. Hamilton followed.

Robert stopped and waited at the door leading out to the grounds. When Alex met him at the door, he asked, "What's your cell phone number?"

Robert told it to him as Alex wrote it down on his forearm. "Anything else?" Robert asked.

"No," Alex said, "Just be careful."

"I will be. I appreciate everything that you've done for me Alexander, but ...," Robert replied before he was interrupted.

"I know, Dad. I understand," Alex said sincerely.

"Take it easy out there, Robert," Dr. Hamilton said. "I'll call you later to see how you're doing."

"Fine," Robert said with growing impatience.

"Do you need help saddling your horse?" Alex asked.

"No, I can handle it," Robert said as he opened the door and walked out. "I'll see you later."

"Be careful," Alex yelled back.

"He'll be fine, Alex. Isn't he an experienced rider?" Dr. Hamilton questioned.

"Yeah, but that's not what I'm worried about," Alex said anxiously.

"What are you worried about then?" the doctor asked.

"He'll be in the barn alone for the first time since it happened," Alex replied.

# CHAPTER 29

▼

Robert walked happily to the barn to saddle his favorite horse, Sebastian, for the long, lazy walk across his estate that he had planned to clear his head. As he made his way to the stable that housed Sebastian, Robert stopped and stared at the barn at the farthest end of buildings. It was a surreal moment, the picture perfect barn against the bright autumn hues that dangled from the lush line of trees that bordered the property. It was the first time that he had thought about what had happened that day all those months ago. Robert stood and stared, unable to break the gaze of the barn or the heavy feeling in his legs. He finally managed to take a few steps, and they subconsciously were toward the barn. Unable to break the gaze even to look to see if anyone was watching, Robert reached out anxiously and pushed open the door.

He took a deep breath and walked in, but froze immediately. Lying on the floor of the barn, under the heavy wooden rafter, laid a broken chair in a heap. Robert's eyes darted to the side of the chair and felt a wave of nausea pass over him that brought him to his knees when he witnessed the thick, knotted rope lying mockingly on the ground. He instinctively reached for the course rope, and when his hand made contact, he wretched violently. Wave after wave of nausea enveloped him as he knelt helplessly on the ground with the rope staring contemptuously at his every action.

After managing to pull himself into a sitting position, Robert reached up and felt his knotted neck muscles, causing him to frighteningly flashback to the events of that day. He remembered lying in the shower on the marble floor as the water poured down over his head. He heard his mother's voice over and over again saying that he was no longer her son. He heard Mitchell saying goodbye. Robert snapped back to reality for a brief moment, but the intensity of the memories flooded back and he recalled whilst he sobbed relentlessly in the shower what he had to do. An eerie calm transcended his soul and slowed his heartbeat to a steady beat as he dressed and walked out of the house.

Robert tried to shake his head violently to purge the memories, but they kept gnawing at him as he closed his eyes and surrendered to their visions. He remembered the smell of the freshly cut lawn as he walked purposefully to the farthest barn, knowing that it had a high rafter and a thick piece of rope that he had once thought about making into a swing out over the pond. As if in a trance after hearing his mother and Mitchell simultaneously, Robert folded the rope into a noose and tied it tightly. He pulled the dusty, cobwebbed chair over to the middle of the barn and sat down dejectedly with rope in hand. He flashed back to his promise to his father that he would always look after his mother. He had failed. He had failed his mother and his father. He remembered his father telling him to never stick his neck out for anyone. Well, he thought, he would stick it out for himself and end the miserably failed life that he had led. Alexander hated him, his grandchildren were barred from knowing him, Mitchell left him, and his mother disowned him. "What a dismal failure you are, Robert Petrovic," he heard himself say aloud.

He stared at the thick noose and slowly slipped it over his head. The rope was plenty long enough, all he had to do was tie it over the rafter and then all his pain and failures would be over forever. With a single tear leaking out of his eye, Robert stood up on the chair and threw the rope over the rafter in a half-hitch knot. He knew the rope was strong and that the half-hitch would hold for his intended purpose. Standing there, he pictured Alexander when he was a little boy, and then his mother smiling in his living room, and then finally Mitchell smiling and putting his arms around Robert to give him a hug. He closed his eyes tightly and whispered, "I'm sorry."

Robert's head snapped back as he violently came back to reality. He gasped for breath as he sat there with his head between his knees. When he realized how the scene had ended, with Alexander finding him dangling from the rope, Robert fell on his side and cried uncontrollably at the thought that he had made his son witness such an event. Robert pounded his fist angrily against the floor until his hand hurt, and then he just lay there, completely exhausted both physically and emotionally. As the tears started to subside, Robert remembered what had happened when he had awakened in the morning. He recalled the look in Alexander's eyes as he released the restraints and burst into tears as he told his dad that he loved him. Robert smiled through his tears. After all, Alexander had told him that he loved him, and his new best friend, Emily, had told him the same thing. The bonds that he had formed with his son and daughter-in-law were genuine. He wasn't imagining anything. Even Dr. Hamilton commented on their relationship as, of all things, a family. Out of the darkness that had descended, a new light had formed and was burning brightly.

Robert slowly pulled himself up and dusted himself off before once again picking up the rope. He stared at it for a moment and then threw it down as he walked out of the barn with a smile. As he strolled to the stable to saddle Sebastian, a heavy burden felt as if it had been lifted. He smiled as he rubbed Sebastian gently on the nose causing his black thoroughbred to whinny happily. Robert saddled him gently and then took him out for a long overdue walk around the estate.

After several hours of uninterrupted joy of slowly strolling and galloping around the estate, Robert decided, after checking in only twice that it was time to stop and go back to the house. The time alone had provided Robert with the peace he needed to come somewhat to terms with what he had witnessed in the barn. Closing his eyes would still produce some of the haunting images, but they were not as bad as when he was lying on the barn floor with the noose in his hands.

When Robert walked into his house, it appeared to be deserted. There were no sounds of people talking or children playing, and no one was to be found. Capitalizing on a few more minutes solitude, Robert started for his bedroom to change his clothes. As he was about to open the door to his bedroom, Emily came out of the shadows and startled him.

"Hi Clyde, how was your ride?" she asked enthusiastically.

"Wonderful," Robert replied happily.

"I'm glad to hear it," Emily said with a smile.

"Emily, I don't want to sound ungrateful, but it's just that I'm so used to being by myself …" he said before being interrupted.

"Robert, you don't have to explain. I understand. Everybody needs time to himself or herself from time to time," Emily said sincerely.

"It's just that I don't want to hurt Alexander's feelings by wanting to be alone. He literally saved my life, and I don't want him to think that I don't still need him now that I have my memory back," Robert explained.

"He knows that," Emily replied. "But we all need to be alone from time to time, and this is your house, so you can do whatever you want in it, and we'll all respect that."

"Thank you Emily," Robert said gratefully.

"You're welcome," Emily responded.

"Emily, can I talk to you for a minute while we're alone?" Robert asked.

"Sure," she replied.

"While I was out riding I did a lot of thinking, and I just wanted to let you know that when I start going out socially again that I won't bring anyone here while the kids are here," Robert explained.

Emily shook her head in disagreement, "Robert, this is your house. We're guests here, and we're not going to tell you who you can bring to your home."

"I know it's my house, but I'm not going to put you or Alexander in a position to answer questions that the kids would inevitably have if they saw me with someone. They're too young to understand, and I wouldn't put either you or Alexander in such an awkward position," Robert explained sincerely.

"Okay, if that's what you want, that's fine with me," Emily smiled mischievously. "Frankly, I wish I could put off having any type of sex talk, hetero—or homosexual, until they are at least twenty."

Robert laughed, "I don't think that'll work. Anyways, by the time you give them 'the talk,' you'll probably have to ask them questions, not the other way around."

Laughing heartily, Emily replied, "You're probably right."

"Where's everyone at? It's so quiet around here," Robert asked.

"The kids went to one of their friend's house for the afternoon, Grandma is taking a nap, and Alex is down at the pool house," Emily answered.

"What's he doing down there? Is he going swimming?" Robert questioned.

"No, he was looking over something from your business. He wanted me to ask you to come down when you had some free time," Emily replied.

"Hey, by the way, Steffi told me earlier that she wanted to go swimming today, but Alexander told her it was too cold. I guess he doesn't know that the pool has a heater, does he?" Robert joked.

"Probably not," Emily laughed. "Would the heater warm it enough when it's this chilly outside?"

"Absolutely. It's just like going into a hot tub on a cold day. I've actually gone swimming when it was about fifty degrees outside, and I wasn't cold at all. The water gets nice and hot," Robert explained.

"I'll have to tell him that," Emily joked. "You know, Alex is more into reading a book than spending time doing anything strenuous like swimming."

Robert laughed, "I guess we'll have to work on that then, what do you think?"

"I think that would be a great idea," Emily replied playfully.

"Operation Alexander, Double O Seven," Robert said roguishly.

"I like that," Emily laughed. "Now, can I ask you a favor?"

"Sure, you can ask me anything you want," Robert replied seriously.

"When things start to calm down for you and you're not so overwhelmed, could you please take Alex shopping and make sure he buys some stylish clothes?" Emily asked lightheartedly.

"Absolutely, if that's what you want, but I have to confess the last time I took Alexander shopping, it was a total nightmare. He has a style all of his own!" Robert laughed.

"Yeah, I know. That's the problem," Emily laughed. "But, if he's going to be working with you side by side, he can't be looking like some out of style slob."

"You know, that request is like a mission—impossible," Robert teased.

"If anyone can do it, Robert, you can. Besides, do you really want to see him dressed in khakis, white shirt, red tie, blue blazer, and penny loafers every single day? That, to me, would be like slow torture," Emily replied impishly.

"You've definitely got a point there. I'll see what I can do," Robert smiled.

"Thanks, Robert," Emily said as she returned his smile. "I'm really glad that you're part of my family, and not only that, but also one of my dearest friends."

"The same here," Robert replied. "Well, I better get changed and go down to see what Alexander is cooking up with the business."

"I'll see you at dinner?" Emily asked.

"Definitely. Talk to you later, Bonnie," Robert said as he pushed the door to his bedroom open and gently closed it behind him.

Robert quickly undressed and climbed back into the shower. He stood there with the water cascading down his back, but the images that haunted him earlier in the shower were nowhere to be found. He dried off and dressed himself again in the same clothes that he had on earlier in the day, the black dress pants with the slate gray tee shirt.

# CHAPTER 30

▼

Robert sauntered to the side door of the pool house and walked in. He looked around, and having not seen Alexander, he called out, "Alexander?"

"Yeah Dad, I'll be right out," came Alexander's response.

Robert walked over to the large picture window and stared out at the crystal blue water of the elegant swimming pool. When he heard the sound of footsteps, he turned around slowly to acknowledge his son, but hesitated when he saw the scene before him. He stood there, dumbfounded, but managed to utter, "Mitch."

Mitchell walked slowly out of the back room with Alex and stopped at the corner of the room. Alex continued to walk past his father and toward the side door to exit, before he spoke, "I'll be up at the house if you need me, and I'll make sure you aren't interrupted."

"Alexander ...," Robert muttered anxiously.

"See you later," Alex replied with a smile as he walked out the door and pulled it shut tightly behind him.

Mitchell slowly walked toward Robert as he said softly, "Hi Robert."

Robert nodded his head as affirmation of the greeting, and then quickly went back to the window to look out, as if for some type of rescue from the present situation. Mitchell walked up to stand directly in front of Robert, and as he spoke, he smiled tenderly, "I am so sorry, Robert."

Robert held up his hand to halt his apology, "Please. I can't bear to hear any more apologies."

"Okay, then, how do you feel?" Mitchell asked.

"I'm fine, Mitchell. I woke up this morning with my memory back," Robert replied before pausing to emphasize his next words. "So you can go ahead and get on with your life now."

Mitchell, looking perplexed, asked, "What do you mean?"

"I mean exactly what I said. The last time we spoke, you said that you wanted to get on with your life … that you were still a young man and wanted to do so many things, so now you can go and do that. I'm still not sure why you waited," Robert explained in a matter-of-fact tone.

"The only way I want to get on with my life is if you're in it," Mitchell answered tenderly.

Robert shook his head in semi-angry disbelief, "Why are you doing this? You made it perfectly clear to me the last time we saw each other that you didn't want to have anything to do with me."

"Well, I was wrong, and I'm not doing anything except trying to tell you how I feel about you," Mitchell responded.

"And," Robert replied shortly. "How do you feel about me?"

"I love you," Mitchell said affectionately.

Robert shook his head in disbelief and walked over to sit on the arm of the sofa. "No you don't," Robert replied.

"Yes, I do. When I saw Alex carry you into the house that night he brought you from that asylum, I thought I would die right on the spot. You looked so bad, so much in pain, but there wasn't anything I could do," Mitchell replied.

"And how do you think I felt having lived through that place? Hmmm? You want to know what they did to me?" Robert asked as his angry voice started to rise. "They took me to a place that was totally strange to me. I was scared, but there wasn't anything I could do about it. They left me in a room by myself.... Well, that isn't true. There was another man, but he was unconscious in the other bed. Well, I looked around for a cup for some water. You see, the medication that I take makes me thirsty, so I really needed a drink of water. I looked around but couldn't find a cup, so I walked out into the hallway to see if I could find a nurse to ask for some water. I didn't find any, so I waited by my room. After a few minutes, I started walking down the hallway, and to my great luck I saw a water fountain, so I ran over to it and took a nice, long drink," Robert explained.

"What happened?" Mitchell asked.

Robert glared into Mitchell's blue eyes, "I heard people yelling. When I went to turn around, four men grabbed me and threw me face down onto the concrete floor."

Mitchell looked horrified, "Why?"

Robert did not bother to answer Mitchell's question, but instead continued his story, "They then picked me up and carried me to a room far down a hallway. They took me inside, and once again, threw me face down, but this time it was softer. You see, I was in the proverbial "rubber room" where everything was padded. The floor was covered with padding, and the walls were also padded with thick padding. As I was lying on the floor, I saw one of the men pull out a pair of scissors and systematically cut off all of my clothing. I was now lying on the floor face down, completely naked. But it wasn't over yet, you see. They brought out a belt with thick padded leather cuffs attached to each side. The put the belt around my waist and attached both of my wrists in the cuffs. I was then left to lie there, face down in a cold, dark room, completely naked and completely helpless."

"How long did they keep you there like that?" Mitchell asked aghast.

"About an hour I think, and then they came back, took out a long hypodermic needle, and stuck it in my ass to sedate me. When I was completely out of it and couldn't talk, they wrapped a sheet around me and carried me back to my room where they put me in my bed, tossed a hospital gown over me, and proceeded to restrain my wrists and ankles to the bed. Every few hours, two men would come in, roll me over, give me a shot, and then leave. This went on from the time I got there until the time Alexander came and got me out," Robert said in a strong voice.

Mitchell started to cry, "I'm so sorry Robert."

"Enough," Robert yelled.

Mitchell sobbed as he reached for Robert's hand, but Robert pulled it away, "I just don't know what to say, except that I'm sorry."

"You don't have to say anything. I was there because of what I did. Nobody forced me to do anything, and that place was one of the consequences of my actions," Robert answered very stoically.

"Robert, I know I should have been with you by your side when you were admitted to the hospital, but I just couldn't stand to see you like that. It broke my heart," Mitchell said sincerely.

"And it broke my heart when I called you from the jail and you wouldn't even acknowledge that you were there. I knew you were standing there when I was talking to your housekeeper. My mother wouldn't answer her phone, and you wouldn't talk to me. How do you think that made me feel, knowing that the two most important people in my life had abandoned me?" Robert asked in a controlled tone of anger.

"I don't know what to say," Mitchell answered dejectedly.

"Well, I'll tell you Mitch, jail is quite an experience," Robert said sarcastically. "I already had a hangover from trying to escape from the words of my mother and you that were haunting me," Robert said before being interrupted.

"What words?" Mitchell asked innocently.

"Well," Robert paused, "My mother told me I was no longer her son, and that she was disowning me, and," Robert paused again as he stared at Mitchell. "You said that you no longer wanted to be a part of my life, that it was best that you break up with me, that you were a young man who wanted to enjoy life ... apparently without me," Robert said with sarcasm dripping from his every word.

"I was wrong," Mitchell said meekly.

"I guess that's best left up to interpretation. Back to the jail experience ... like I already have said, I had a hangover, but then mix that with a direct shot of pepper spray into your face, and the feeling that you get from that, well, can't be expressed properly in words. But, that agony went away after about a day, but the humiliation was on the grandest scale possible. You always told me that when people are harassing you, or calling you names, that the best thing to do is walk away. Well Mitch, you can't do that in a jail cell. I just had to sit there and take it, and believe me, those redneck cops kept up an unending barrage of derogatory remarks and hurtful comments. But that still wasn't the worst part.... No, the worst was having to use the toilet in front of them all. The combination of the pain from the hangover and pepper spray, the unending comments and commentary about what I freak I am, and the humiliation of having to use the toilet in front of my tormentors made for quite an experience, don't you think?" Robert asked nonchalantly, trying to hide his pain from the incident.

"Robert, please, you have to believe that I never would have left you there if I knew what would happen," Mitchell pleaded.

"Really? Wasn't it your point to teach me a lesson? Like I was some little recalcitrant child who needed to learn the hard way?" Robert asked, his voice rising again. "The best part was that you didn't have any idea what had happened to me. You just assumed that I deserved what I was getting by being thrown in jail. That, or you thought that it was some pathetic attempt on my part to get you to come back to me."

"Oh God, you hate me," Mitchell cried. "And I don't blame you, I hate me too."

"Hate you?" Robert said incredulously. "Hate you? I could never hate you."

A glint of hope danced in Mitchell's eyes, "You don't hate me?"

"No," Robert replied shortly.

"Robert, please come and sit down and talk to me," Mitchell pleaded.

"What do you want from me?" Robert snapped.

"I want you back. I want us to be together again. I want our lives to be like they used to be," Mitchell answered.

"Our lives will never be like they were. The Robert you knew died. He put a rope around his neck and killed himself," Robert replied matter-of-factly.

"Don't say that," Mitchell responded with a frown.

"Don't say what? That the Robert you knew died, or that he wrapped a rope around his neck?" Robert asked.

"Both," Mitchell replied sadly.

"Why? It's the truth. Don't you want to hear the truth? Look at me, Mitchell," Robert commanded. "I tied a noose in a rope and put it around my neck and tried to end my life. I had no reason to live, so why should I have gone on? Hmm? Nobody loved me," Robert explained before he was interrupted.

"Stop it," Mitchell cried. "I love you, Robert. I always have, but I made a mistake," Mitchell sobbed as he reached once again for Robert's hand.

Robert pulled his hand away and got up to walk out, "I can't do this right now."

"Please Robert," cried Mitchell. Robert continued walking toward the door when Mitchell jumped off of the sofa and grabbed Robert tightly at the spot where the neck and the shoulder meet.

"Owwwww," Robert cried loudly as he fell painfully on the floor. Under Mitchell's hand, the muscle knotted and shot searing pain through Robert's arm and up his neck and into the back of his head. "Uummmppph," Robert mumbled as he writhed on the floor in agony.

"Oh God, Robert. I'm sorry. What have I done?" Mitchell cried hysterically as he saw Robert writhing in misery. "Wait here, I'll call Alex," he uttered in complete hysterics.

"No," Robert muttered meekly. "I'll be all right."

"I didn't mean to hurt you Robert," Mitchell continued sobbing as tears flowed freely down his face and landed in a puddle on the floor.

Robert gingerly reached over and touched Mitchell's hand, "I know you didn't."

"Can I help you up?" Mitchell asked shyly as the tears continued.

"Give me a second, and the spasms should ease up a little," Robert said softly through the pain. "Just don't touch anyplace on my upper back or neck, okay?"

"Okay," Mitchell answered sincerely between sobs as he very gently helped Robert stand. With a hand around Robert's waist, Mitchell led him to the sofa and very gently helped him sit down. "I'm sorry," Mitchell said sadly.

Robert closed his eyes tightly before he spoke, "Please stop saying that."

"Is there anything I can do to ease the pain?" Mitchell asked sincerely.

"I'll be okay," Robert said slightly smiling through the pain.

"Please be honest with me, Robert. Do you hate me?" Mitchell asked.

"Hate you? No, I could never hate you," Robert paused. "I love you, Mitchell. You were the love of my life. How could I ever hate you?"

Mitchell could not contain his excitement, "Did you just say that you love me? Please tell me I didn't imagine that."

"You didn't imagine that," Robert replied. "I do love you."

"Then everything will be okay," Mitchell stated with total joy.

"Wait," Robert said. "I did say that I love you, and I do, but that doesn't mean everything is going to be okay"

"Bobby," Mitchell started but then looked away. "I love you. When Alex told me that you were in the hospital and that you almost died, I almost died as well. If your attempt had been successful, they would have had to dig two holes because I couldn't, and can't, live without you," Mitchell said sincerely and honestly.

"Mitch," Robert said matter-of-factly. "I love you, but things have changed." He emphasized his next words, "I've changed."

"But change can be good," Mitchell added. "Right?"

"In some instances … yes, but I can't say for this instance," Robert explained. "I don't know what the future holds, but for right now—I need to be on my own."

"I love you, Bobby," Mitchell said with tears glistening in his eyes. "And I'm so sorry I hurt you." Mitchell went to embrace Robert, but Robert pulled back. The countenance of pain etched on Mitchell's face echoed the pain he felt in his heart. "I hope someday you can forgive me."

"It's been an overwhelming day," Robert replied stoically. "If you don't mind, I need to go lie down."

"Sure," Mitchell managed to utter softly. He paused, "Bobby?"

"Yes?" Robert replied.

With a cracking voice and a profoundly sad smile, Mitchell responded, "Take care of yourself, okay.?"

Robert returned Mitchell's sad smile, "You too." Robert turned and walked determinedly out the front door of the pool house, leaving Mitchell alone and heartbroken, and unable to do anything to change Robert's mind.

A few eternal moments later as Mitchell was about to leave, Emily walked through the front door of the pool house. She went straight to Mitchell and pulled him into a loving embrace. As Emily pulled Mitchell silently closer, Mitchell fell apart and wept unabashedly in her arms.

"What am I going to do without him?" Mitchell cried.

"He just needs time—that's all," Emily consoled as she continued to hold her friend.

"Do you really think so?" Mitchell asked with hope-filled eyes as he pulled away to search Emily's eyes.

"Mitchell," Emily smiled reassuringly. "Robert loves you. I know that to be a fact."

"How can you be so sure?" Mitchell asked half-despondently, half optimistically.

"I looked into his eyes as we talked about you earlier," Emily answered honestly. "I could see how deeply he loves you just be watching his expressions."

"He told me he loves me," Mitchell admitted sadly. "But I hurt him so deeply. How could he ever forgive me?"

Emily laughed, "Are we talking about the same person?" She took Mitchell by the hand and led him to the sofa. "Seriously, Mitchell, I've only known Robert for a short amount of time, but what I've learned in that short time is that that man has the most understanding, compassionate nature of anyone I've ever known."

"But he's so angry with me," Mitchell interjected.

"Yes, but you have to put yourself in his shoes. Think about it ... the last time you talked to him, his world was beginning to crash around him, and now he regains his memory and everything is almost perfect. He's confused, and he's hurt and he's scared. Think about it—wouldn't you be?"

"You have a point," Mitchell conceded. "But do you think I really have a chance of making things right between us?"

Emily smiled, "Of course I do. In fact, I'd bank on it."

"I hope you're right," Mitchell said with a sigh.

"Just give him some time. He needs to process things in his own way and time."

# CHAPTER 31

▼

The invitation said black tie and to bring a guest to the exclusive dinner party and fundraiser held annually at the country club. Robert flip flopped about whether he should go or not. He did not have a date, but Emily insisted that he go solo, just to get back into the social scene. She pointed out that he had not gone to any social events since his hospitalization, and it was important for a businessman to mingle occasionally.

Robert acquiesced and found himself standing inside the spacious walk-in closet trying to find his tuxedo. After several moments of moving hangers back and forth in an almost futile attempt to find his tuxedo, Emily startled him from behind.

"You scared me," Robert said as he exhaled.

Emily took Robert's hand and led him out of the closet to where he found his tuxedo spread out on the king-size bed. "Here you go, Clyde."

"Where did you find it?" Robert inquired.

Emily smiled, "In the walk-in closet. I took it out a few days ago to have it dry cleaned."

"No wonder I couldn't find it," Robert stated as he stared down at the black tuxedo lying on the bed. "I'm still not sure this is a good idea. Maybe I should stay home."

"Absolutely not," Emily responded strongly. "You need to get out and mingle a little. Plus, it's good for your business."

"Then you and Alexander should be going as well," Robert suggested.

"We weren't invited," Emily reminded. "Besides, you don't need us tagging along on a social occasion."

"Okay, okay, I give up. I'll go," Robert said in defeat. "But I'm not staying long."

Emily stood on her tiptoes to kiss Robert tenderly on the cheek, "Go and try to have a good time, okay?"

Robert pulled Emily into a warm, friendly embrace, "I'll try."

A few hours later, Robert sauntered into the living room wearing his custom-fit black tuxedo with a black vest and black bow tie. Emily voiced her thoughts, "Hubba hubba, Clyde."

Robert blushed from the compliment, "Thank you, Em."

"You look great, Dad," Alex offered.

"Thanks," Robert replied. "You're just glad that you don't have to go."

Alex laughed, "You got that right."

"Will you two stop?" Emily stated with a bit of sternness in her voice.

Feeling a bit chastised, both men relented. Robert stepped in front of Emily and asked, "Is my tie okay?"

Emily straightened the tie around the arrow collar of the crisp white shirt, "Everything is fine. You look great, Robert."

"Thanks Em," Robert replied sincerely. "I guess I should be going."

"Have a good time, Dad," Alex said.

Emily kissed Robert on the cheek, "Have a great night."

Robert took his car keys out of his trouser pocket and started for the door. "Don't wait up," he said jokingly as he walked out the front door.

*       *       *       *

The clear twinkling lights entwined between the tree lined parking lot gave off an essence of warmth at the country club. Robert pulled his new black Jaguar up to the valet parking post and waited for a well-dressed attendant to come and park his car.

Robert engaged in small talk with the young attendant who was fawning over Robert's new Jag. As the attendant pulled away to park Robert's car amongst the full array of luxury vehicles, Robert saw a small group of people standing outside the main entrance. As he walked closer, he noticed a familiar face—the lady who was his accountant for many years. Rebecca was an elegant lady of middle-age, with short strawberry blonde hair, pale skin and a gregarious smile. Robert casually walked up to Rebecca and greeted her with a kiss on the cheek.

"Hello handsome," Rebecca said amiably as Robert kissed her cheek.

"Hello beautiful," Robert replied. "It's been a long time."

"Too long," Rebecca offered. "You get more handsome every time I see you."

"Stop," Robert replied. "You make me blush."

Rebecca laughed mischievously, "I can make you do more than blush, I assure you if I had the opportunity."

"I'm sure you could," Robert replied blushing. "Maybe someday I'll take you up on that."

"Anytime, handsome," Rebecca responded sincerely.

As Robert made his way up the sidewalk to the front entrance of the country club, he suddenly stopped in his tracks as his breath caught in his throat as he gazed upon the person standing next to the front door. Mitchell Rains stood alone by the front door waiting for the host to direct him to his seat. He was adorned in a black tuxedo with a pewter-colored vest and bow tie—with a matching handkerchief in his coat pocket. Mitchell looked out into the small crowd of people and almost immediately his blue eyes locked onto Robert. When they saw each other, they both genuinely smiled. Robert made a quick path to the front door and found himself standing in front of Mitchell for the first time in months.

"Hi," Robert said smiling.

"Hi," Mitchell replied warmly. "I didn't think you'd come tonight."

"I didn't want to, but I was bullied into it," Robert said with a comical sigh.

"It's good to see you," Mitchell said sincerely.

"You too," Robert added.

As Mitchell searched for something to say, the hostess appeared and called Mitchell's name. "I have to go," Mitchell said with a touch of sadness in his voice.

"I'll talk to you later," Robert answered as Mitchell disappeared into the country club.

Robert socialized as best he could until it was time to be seated. He laughed to himself at the choice of tablemates—on his left was Candice Marley, a beautiful recent divorcee with money to burn, and on his right, elegant Kitty Donaldson, a spoiled widow with an insatiable appetite for both money and men. Robert took a long drink of water as Candice went on about sailing with offers to teach Robert everything he ever wanted to know. Robert kept up the conversation with both Candice and Kitty as he discreetly stole glances of Mitchell from across the room.

As dinner ended, the orchestra started playing popular tunes and the guests started to fill the dance floor. Before Robert had a chance to protest, he was being pulled onto the dance floor by Kitty Donaldson. After the song was over, Candice Marley cut in and Robert danced her around the floor. When the song ended, Robert excused himself to catch his breath.

Robert ordered a ginger ale and sat down at the bar. Within a moment, a feminine hand touched his shoulder and lingered in his graying hair. "Rebecca?"

"Dance with me, handsome," Rebecca commanded softly.

Robert reached for Rebecca's hand and kissed it softly, "I'd love too."

The two walked to the dance floor holding hands and seeing only each other in their gaze. As they moved in sync with the music, the heat of attraction between them caused the other dancers to leave the floor. It was only Robert and Rebecca on the floor, with all eyes from the country club crowd upon them. Robert pulled Rebecca close as the music faded and kissed her tenderly on the lips. She licked her lips seductively as she kissed Robert on the cheek.

As Robert was leading Rebecca off the dance floor, he suddenly realized that Mitchell was witness to his and Rebecca's seductive little dance. "Will you excuse me?" Robert asked Rebecca.

"Of course," Rebecca replied. "Just don't leave me waiting too long."

Robert went to the bar and ordered another ginger ale as his eyes searched the ballroom for any signs of Mitchell. After looking throughout the ballroom and dining room with no signs of him, Robert headed outside. Standing uneasily near the valet parking post was Mitchell. Robert quickened his pace to get to Mitchell before his car was ready.

"Mitch?' Robert called out as he came up to Mitchell.

"Yeah," Mitchell replied with the hurt apparent in his voice.

"You're not leaving, are you?" Robert asked, but already sensing the answer.

Mitchell remained standing with his back to Robert, "Yes, I am."

Robert came to stand in front of Mitchell, "I was hoping we'd have a chance to talk."

"You've been a little busy since dinner," Mitchell said with sarcasm, but the hurt he was feeling made his statement sound sad and painful.

"I'm sorry," Robert offered sincerely.

"For what?" Mitchell asked. "You didn't do anything wrong."

"Yes I did," Robert said sadly as he faced Mitchell squarely. "I hurt you by dancing with those women."

"You don't owe me an explanation, Robert," Mitchell advised strongly.

"I didn't mean to hurt you," Robert explained. "Please come back inside and stay awhile."

"I can't Robert," Mitchell explained. "It's too hard for me."

Robert gazed at Mitchell sympathetically, "It's hard for me too."

"What?" Mitchell replied sadly.

Robert smiled genuinely as he put his hand on Mitchell's shoulder, "You look so incredibly sexy in that tuxedo."

Mitchell blushed before turning serious, "Please stop."

"Stop what? You know I've always found you irresistible in a tuxedo," Robert reminded.

"Please," Mitchell paused. "Stop."

Robert reached for Mitchell's left hand and held it lovingly, "What's wrong?"

Robert's sudden onset of public affection and the soft, loving tone of his voice threatened to overwhelm Mitchell. Mitchell gently pulled his hand away and turned away from Robert. "I can't do this Robert."

"Do what?" Robert asked softly.

"I can't let my guard down," Mitchell explained. "I couldn't survive getting my heart broken again."

"What makes you think you'd get your heart broken?" Robert asked.

"Just seeing you dance with those women put a dagger through my heart. If I let my guard down, I'd never recover," Mitchell explained sadly.

Robert once again took Mitchell's hand in his and pulled him closer, "You're not going to get your heart broken," Robert explained as his lips gently brushed Mitchell's lips.

"Please Robert," Mitchell pleaded sadly.

Robert gently took Mitchell's face in his hands and kissed him softly at first, and then more intensely as the kiss deepened. As Robert pulled back to look into Mitchell's eyes, he saw a longing hope that he himself had felt. "I'm sorry that I hurt you in the past, Mitch. I know how much I hurt you that day in the pool house after I got my memory back, but I had to do things that way. My world was upside down then and I didn't know how to handle things."

"What about now?" Mitchell inquired softly.

"I've learned how to handle things better, and I know who and what I need in my life," Robert explained. "And what I need and want in my life is you."

"What?" Mitchell uttered completely off guard.

"That is if you want to give us a second try?" Robert asked.

"You mean you don't want a one night stand with me?" Mitchell asked befuddled.

"I want us to have a second chance," Robert explained. "I was afraid before because of all the mental problems I was dealing with, and I didn't want you to get stuck in the middle, but now I'm ready to start living again—and the only person I want to do that with is you."

Mitchell threw his arms around Robert's neck and hugged him, "I love you."

Robert pulled out of the embrace to look Mitchell in the eyes, "I love you too."

The valet of the country club pulled Mitchell's candy apple red Corvette to the curb, "Here you go, sir."

Mitchell reached into his trouser pocket and pulled out a ten dollar bill and handed it to the car attendant, "Thank you." Mitchell faced Robert with pleading eyes, "Come to my place?"

Robert nodded, "I thought you'd never ask."

The car attendant interrupted briefly, "Sir, can I get your car?"

"Yes, thank you."

"I have to move—I'm blocking traffic. Do you want me to wait?" Mitchell asked.

"No, go on home and I'll be there in a few minutes."

"I love you, Robert. Please drive carefully."

"I will," Robert replied. "And I love you too."

$$*\qquad*\qquad*\qquad*$$

The warm rays of the early morning sun streamed through the large bay window in Mitchell's living room. Clothes were strewn about throughout the living room to the master bedroom as if the person or persons wearing the clothing was in a hurry to shuck the articles as quickly as possible.

Robert was soundly sleeping with Mitchell's head resting on Robert's muscular chest. Mitchell's body almost naturally melded to Robert's body, and they both slept peacefully until the alarm clock next to the bed went off and scared them into a state of awakeness.

Mitchell jumped up and quickly shut off the loud, annoying alarm clock. He leaned against Robert and smiled, "Good morning."

"Good morning," Robert reiterated.

"This isn't a dream, is it?" Mitchell asked.

Robert reached up and pulled Mitchell into a long, fulfilling kiss, "It's not a dream."

"What changed your mind, Bobby?" Mitchell inquired as he rested his head on Robert's chest.

"It wasn't a matter of changing my mind. I missed you, Mitch, and you've always known that I love you. I just needed some time to work things out—that's all," Robert explained.

"Well, I'm glad we're back on track, and nothing is going to derail us ever again," Mitchell insisted.

"I'll second that," Robert offered.

After a few moments of silence, Mitchell started to laugh, causing Robert to sit up to find out what was going on, "What is it, Mitch?"

Mitchell continued laughing, "To the uninformed country club guest last night, the money would have been on you waking up in Rebecca's bed—or Kitty or Candice's bed."

The warmth that emanated from Robert's smile surrounded Mitchell and gently embraced him. Robert took Mitchell's hand in his, "I woke up in the only bed I wanted to wake up in."

"Last night was the first time in months that I was able to sleep," Mitchell confessed.

"We're going to make it work this time, Mitch," Robert assured.

"I'll do whatever I have to," Mitchell said. "I love you Bobby."

Robert pulled Mitchell to him and held him against his body, "I love you too."

Mitchell savored those words for a brief moment before leaning on his elbow and looking into Robert's handsome face, "What can I make you for breakfast?"

"What time is it?" Robert inquired a bit sleepily.

Mitchell stretched to see the digital clock on his dresser, "It's twenty-five after eight."

Robert sighed, "I have to go. I have meetings scheduled throughout the day."

"Cup of coffee?" Mitchell offered.

Robert nodded, "A cup of coffee would be great."

As Mitchell tended to making a pot of coffee, Robert got dressed as he walked throughout the condo looking for various articles of clothing. By the time the coffee was ready, Robert had found all of his clothing. He smiled seductively at Mitchell, "Last night was quite a night, and that was just the beginning."

"I'm already looking forward to our next encounter," Mitchell said as he winked at Robert.

*        *        *        *

Robert gently closed the side door off the garage as he made his way to the kitchen. He walked in with his white shirt wrinkled, the black bow tie wrapped around the collar and his coat lazily thrown over his shoulder. Emily and Alex sat at the counter finishing their breakfasts.

"Good morning," Robert said in an upbeat tone.

"Good morning," Emily replied as she smiled at Robert's appearance. "Looks as though you had a good night."

"Yes I did. I'm glad you talked me into going."

"You have meetings this afternoon with those new suppliers," Alex said matter-of-factly.

"I remember," Robert replied.

"See you later, Em," Alex stated abruptly as he got up and left.

Robert stared dumbfounded at Emily, "Did I do something?"

Emily put her hand on Robert's shoulder and lead him to the counter to sit down. "You stayed out late on a school night without calling," Emily explained with a chuckle.

"I'm sorry," Robert said sincerely. "I had no idea that my staying out would cause a problem."

"It's okay, Robert."

"It must not be okay if Alexander is upset. I must have worried him," Robert stated a bit guiltily.

"You didn't worry him, Robert. He didn't know until a little while ago that you didn't come home last night," Emily explained.

"Why's he so upset then?" Robert inquired.

"I don't think he's upset," Emily explained. "It's just the sudden realization that his Dad has sexual needs."

"Oh," Robert muttered. "I'll patch things up with him later."

"So," Emily said enthusiastically. "Was this person someone special? Come on Clyde—dish!"

Robert laughed at Emily's exuberance, "Okay, I'll dish." He paused a moment before continuing, "Yes the person I spent the night with is special."

"What's he like?" Emily inquired eagerly.

Robert's eyes sparkled, "You already know him."

"Who?" Emily asked, almost drowning in anticipation.

"I spent the night with Mitch," Robert announced proudly.

Emily threw her arms around Robert's neck and squeezed him tight, "Oh Robert, I'm so happy for you. Does this mean you two are back together?"

Robert smiled involuntarily, "Yes, we're officially back together. We're going to take things slowly."

Emily could not contain her giggle, "You started taking things slowly this morning, right?"

A wry smile danced on Robert's lips, "Yes, that's right. First thing this morning."

"I'm so happy for you, Robert."

"Thanks Em," Robert replied. "I hate to cut this short, but I have several meeting today."

"No problem," Emily said. "Just one last thing before you go."

"What's that?"

"Aren't you glad that I bullied you into going last night?" Emily asked.

Robert kissed Emily on the cheek, "I'm forever grateful."

*      *      *      *

Robert stopped outside his son's closed office door and gathered his errant thoughts. He knocked gently three times and waited, "Come in," came the voice from inside.

"Hi," Robert said.

"Hi," Alex replied.

"I want to talk to you about last night, Alexander," Robert said firmly.

"You don't owe me any explanations. It's your house and you can come and go as you please," Alex explained with the hurt apparent in his voice.

"That's true—everything you said, but I should have called and let you know I wasn't coming home last night. I'm not used to anyone caring what I do," Robert explained.

"I care, Dad. And so does Emily. I was worried something happened to you," Alex stated honestly.

"On the upside, I don't stay over someone's place often," Robert said to try to lighten the mood.

"I'm glad everything's okay," Alex said truthfully.

"It's more than okay," Robert stated as he headed for the door. "My one night stand wasn't a one night stand."

"You spent the night with someone you know?" Alex inquired.

"Yes," Robert replied. "And it's someone you know as well."

"Who?" Alex asked intrigued.

"I spent the night with Mitch," Robert answered.

Alex smiled genuinely at his dad, "I'm glad to hear that."

"You really mean that, don't you?" Robert questioned.

"Yes I do," Alex answered sincerely. "I just want you to be happy."

"Thank you, Alexander," Robert said with heartfelt gratitude as he walked out of Alex's office.

# CHAPTER 32

▼

Over the next several months, Robert's mental health improved, as did the relationships he had with everyone in his life. The twins absolutely adored their grandpa, and Robert allowed them both to wrap him around their little fingers. Robert and Alex's relationship grew deeper as they both learned about each other, and father and son soon fell into a pattern of learning to work together, although there was no doubt in anyone's mind who the boss really was, and that was Robert. Mitchell and Robert grew closer than either of them thought possible, although they had always dreamed their relationship would work out this way. Mitchell even talked Robert into going on a weeklong adventure over the New Year's holiday, to the delight of Alex, Emily and Dr. Hamilton. Robert continued to see Dr. Hamilton on a regular basis, which allowed him to deal with his past and the stresses of the present.

In the spring, as business was picking up for the summer construction period, Robert and Alexander both threw themselves into their work, with the agreement that they both would take time off to relax and enjoy life when either of them started to feel stressed. They both were also involved in designing Alex and Emily's new home. Alex also received a telephone call in the spring that surprised and delighted him. He could not wait to share the information with his dad, and when his dad came into the kitchen one weekday morning, dressed in his expensive, tailor-made navy blue suit, Alex could not contain his excitement. As Emily helped the twins with their breakfasts, Alex addressed Robert, "Good morning, Dad."

"Good morning, son," Robert said jovially as he poured a glass of orange juice. "Good morning, Emily," he said as he walked over to where the twins were seated. "Hello, how's my wonderful grandkids today?" he asked as he kissed them both on top of the head.

"Good," Steffi and Stevie chimed in grinning.

"Hey Dad, I got some news. Good news, I think," Alex said tentatively.

"Really? What kind of news?" Robert inquired with his full attention.

"One of my former political colleagues with the Party called me last night," Alex answered.

Robert forced himself not to frown, "No doubt they want you back."

"They mentioned it, but I turned them down. There is no way I'm leaving your company. I love working for you," Alex explained trying to break the tension that he could see in Robert's eyes.

"Alexander … how many times do I have to tell you? You work with me, not for me," Robert corrected.

"Whatever you say, Pops," Alex teased. "But we all know who the boss is."

"Yeah, your boss is definitely Emily," Robert teased back.

"Thank you, Robert," Emily laughed.

"You're quite welcome," Robert said as he lifted his glass to Emily. "Now son. What did your colleague want?"

"Well, it seems that some of the Party officials would like me to sort of act like a consultant to new candidates in this area. You know—give advice, help with speeches, etc.," Alex explained.

"That sounds very interesting. Did you accept?" Robert inquired.

"Not yet," Alex answered.

"Why in heavens not?" Robert asked slightly taken aback.

"I'm not sure I'm ready to go back to that type of environment. Besides, it would take time away from my family, and I'm not sure I'm ready to give that up," Alex explained.

"Son, if this is something you really want to do … go and do it. I love having you work with me at the office, but if this is something that will make you happy, please do it. I never want you to sacrifice your dreams for me," Robert replied seriously.

"No Dad, I love working with you, and I don't want to give that up," Alex answered.

"What about part-time?" Robert asked.

"You'd be willing to let me work part-time during the busiest time of the year?" Alex asked, overwhelmed at his father's generosity.

"Of course. I love you, Alexander, and I know that you love politics, so if you want to work with me and work as a consultant, then that's fine. Just having you and your family in my life is the greatest blessing that I could have ever gotten," Robert answered gratefully.

"Thank you, Dad. I love you too," Alex replied sincerely as he patted his dad on the back. "Now I have a lot to think about."

As everyone was seated and eating breakfast, the telephone rang loudly and Robert got up to answer it. He smiled when he heard the voice on the other end of the line. "Hi Mom. What's up?" he listened as Anna explained her situation and then he replied, "I'll stop by on my way to the office. No Mom, it's no problem." Robert stood silently with the receiver to his ear as he listened to his mother and then he responded, "Mom, I'll fix it. There's no need for me to ask one of my employees to come out. I'll fix it for you. Just relax. Now, is there anything you or Dorothy need?" Robert asked sincerely. "Okay Mom, I'll be there in a few minutes. Bye."

"What's wrong?" Alex asked.

"I think your grandmother is neurotic," Robert joked. "She says that the light switch won't work and that several of the appliances aren't working right," Robert explained.

"What'd she want you to do, send one of your employees over to find the problem?" Emily asked merrily.

"Yes, she doesn't want to bother me with such trivial matters," Robert replied. "It sounds like a fuse, so it shouldn't take me long to find out what's wrong."

"Do you want me to come with you?" Alex asked.

"No, I can handle it, plus I think it's your grandma's way of getting me to come over," Robert said with a wink.

"I'm so happy that things worked out the way they did for Grandma," Alex replied.

"Yeah, I am too. My Mom needs her independence, and luckily her friend Dorothy needed a place to stay after her husband died," Robert answered.

"It's great that they can stay independent by relying on each other," Emily said smiling. "And it doesn't hurt to have a loyal son who can check in on them, and fix their electrical problems when they need it," Emily said as she winked at Robert.

"Yeah, well, just call me Saint Robert," Robert joked as he got up to leave. "Bye Emily," he said, and as he walked over to each child, he leaned down to give each one a hug and kiss on the cheek, "Bye kiddos. Have a good day at school."

"Bye, grandpa. I love you," Steffi said with a smile.

"I love you too, grandpa," Stevie replied.

"I love you too, kiddos," Robert said as he walked out of the room. As he was at the door, he turned to Alex, "I'll see you at the office."

"Bye, Dad. Tell Grandma I said hello," Alex instructed.

"I will," Robert replied as he walked out.

Alex sat restlessly in his office at his Dad's company as he pondered the implications of taking on the role of advisor for up and coming new stars in his political party. He stared at his computer monitor, but looked past the information on the screen. All he could think about was his father's generous offer of allowing him to work part-time so that he could remain involved with his former first love—politics. Alex was torn between being loyal to his father, and pursuing a role in politics that he had always wanted. He rested his head in his hands and took several deep breaths before he heard a noise outside his office. He walked over and opened his large office door to see Robert carrying an arm full of blueprints into his office.

"Hey Dad. How's things at Grandma's?" Alex asked teasingly.

"Just great," Robert answered as he opened his office door and dropped the blueprints onto the large black leather sofa that sat in his office.

"Did her saintly son fix her electrical problems?" Alex continued teasing.

"Of course. I think she just wanted to see me," Robert replied with a smile.

"Everything's okay then?" Alex asked more seriously.

"Yeah, it was just a fuse," Robert answered as he sank down in his swivel chair. "What are you up to?" Robert inquired.

"Nothing yet," Alex answered with a shy smile. "I can't seem to concentrate," Alex admitted.

"Alexander," Robert paused briefly. "I meant what I said this morning."

"I know you did, Dad, and I love you for understanding, but I'm still not sure I want to get sucked back in," Alex explained.

"Are you worried about what your colleagues will think if, or when, they find out about me?" Robert asked tenderly, but seriously.

"No," Alex answered too quickly, betraying his answer. "That's not it, really."

"It's okay, Alexander. I understand, and I'm sorry that I can't be someone who you can be proud of and talk about to your colleagues," Robert answered in a heartfelt tone.

"Don't talk like that," Alex reprimanded. "I am proud of you, Dad. Don't you know that?" Alex answered half-upset.

"But I'm not someone you can tell your colleagues about," Robert replied. "And that's fine with me. Really, it is."

"Dad … I am proud of you," Alex said sadly.

"I know, but you can't let who I am hold you back from accomplishing your dreams. Do you hear me? That would kill me, Alexander," Robert said emotionally.

"I promise that I'll do what's best for me and my family," Alex responded honestly.

"Good, now what do you say we try to get some work done?" Robert replied as he picked up a blueprint to look over.

"Oh yeah, that," Alex teased. "I guess that would be a good idea ..." Alex's comments were interrupted by the intercom in Robert's office.

"Mr. Petrovic," came the lady's voice through the telephone intercom.

"Yes Helen," Robert replied.

"There is a woman on line two who says it's an emergency, a Katherine. She says she is Mr. Rains' secretary," Robert's secretary related.

"Thanks Helen, I'll take it," Robert replied.

Robert reached for the receiver and pushed the button for line two. "Hello, this is Robert Petrovic."

"Oh good ... you're there ... I'm sorry ... Mr. Petrovic ...," Katherine spoke unsteadily.

"What's wrong, Katherine?" Robert asked with alarm ringing in his voice.

"It's Mr. Rains ... he's been ... hurt ... really bad," she said before being interrupted.

"What? What happened?" Robert almost shouted.

"Some men jumped him from behind ... when he got out of his car ... I found him when I got here lying in the parking lot," Katherine said through tears.

"Is he all right?" Robert asked in a panic as Alex stood in the doorway and listened.

"The paramedics are working on him now ... but he's hurt really bad, Mr. Petrovic. He asked me to call you," Katherine explained slowly through tears.

"Will you ride with him in the ambulance to the hospital?" Robert asked with trepidation ringing in his deep voice.

"Yes," Katherine replied.

"Ask one of the paramedics which hospital they are taking him to," Robert commanded and Katherine obeyed.

"They said Mercy," Katherine answered.

"I'll meet you there. Tell Mitchell I'm on my way, and to hold on, okay?" Robert instructed.

"What happened?" Alex asked with alarm as Robert hung up and started for the door.

"Mitchell was attacked outside his office this morning … he's hurt really bad," Robert said fearfully.

"Do you want me to come with you?" Alex asked sympathetically.

"No, just take care of things here," Robert replied as he was already down the hallway and pushing open the front door of his office building.

"Call and let me know how he is," Alex shouted from the door into the parking lot. Robert nodded his head that he would, and with that Robert was racing out of the parking lot in his Jaguar convertible.

*     *     *     *

Robert raced to Mercy Hospital in record time, breaking all the speed limits, and running a few stop signs where he knew that he would be safe to do such a thing. He parked his car in the emergency entrance and ran in, stopping briefly at the nurse's desk, before seeing Katherine standing near a room that was labeled "trauma." He ran over to her and she threw her arms around him, "How is he?" Robert asked as he returned her embrace.

"Not good," she replied sadly. "I had to step out to talk to the police, and they said they'd be right back, but I haven't seen an officer yet."

"I need to see him," Robert frantically replied as he looked for a nurse.

"There's one of the doctors that first went in with him," Katherine said as she pointed out the doctor to Robert.

"Excuse me," Robert said as he approached the doctor, with Katherine in tow.

"Yes, can I help you?" the doctor asked politely.

"Yes, I need to see Mitchell Rains," Robert replied with anxiety wearing on his handsome face.

"Are you a family member?" the doctor asked.

"Yes," Robert answered shortly.

The doctor looked skeptically at Robert for a moment before Katherine interrupted, "He's a family member, doctor. Mr. Rains asked me to call him when we were waiting for the ambulance."

"Okay, you can go in then, but you'll have to step out when you're asked," the doctor instructed.

"Fine," Robert replied as he hurriedly ran to the door marked "trauma." As he pushed it open, Robert caught his breath when he saw Mitchell lying immobilized on a backboard. Robert grimaced at the sight of the neck brace, … the tape that held Mitchell's head immobilized, … the backboard, … the full-mask oxygen, … the IV's, … the large splint on Mitchell's right arm. Gathering his courage, Robert walked over to the side of Mitchell's bed and took his left hand and held it tenderly. "Mitch," Robert said softly.

"Robert? Is that you?" Mitchell asked frightened.

"Yeah, I'm here," Robert replied gently.

"Come closer so that I can see you," Mitchell asked frantically through his clenched jaw.

"I'm right here," Robert soothed as he stepped closer and saw the damage that was done to Mitchell's face. Both of Mitchell's eyes were black and slightly swollen. His nose was crooked and bleeding under the oxygen mask, and his jaw looked like it was misaligned. "How are you feeling?" Robert asked, knowing it was a stupid question as soon as he spoke it.

"Terrible," Mitchell muttered through the pain.

Robert stroked Mitchell's hair affectionately as he continued to hold his left hand, "What happened, sweetie?"

At the sound of Robert's loving words, Mitchell broke down and cried as he explained, "I got jumped from behind when I got out of my car."

"How many were there?" Robert asked sympathetically.

"I think three," Mitchell answered between sobs.

"Okay, shhhh. I'm here. You're safe now," Robert said as he tenderly kissed the top of Mitchell's head. "I promise I won't let anyone hurt you ever again."

"I'm sorry, Bobby," Mitchell continued to cry.

"You have nothing to apologize for," Robert replied warmly. "You did nothing wrong."

"I should have fought back," Mitchell replied.

"Mitch," Robert paused. "You were attacked from behind. Blindsided. There's really not much you could have done," Robert reassured.

"I felt so helpless," Mitchell confessed.

"I know," Robert paused. "Your going to be okay, Mitch. I promise."

"Did the police come?" Mitchell asked as he started to regain his composure.

"They're talking to Katherine right now," Robert replied.

"They won't do anything about it," Mitchell replied stoically.

"Did they attack you because …" Robert was interrupted.

"Yeah," Mitchell replied as the tears started to flow again.

"Shhhh, it's going to be all right Mitch. I'll take care of you," Robert responded as he gently lifted Mitchell's hand and kissed it lightly.

Mitchell clung to Robert's hand as he heard people suddenly arguing in the hallway. With the look of fright and trepidation imprinted on his face, he continued his fierce hold on Robert's hand. Robert leaned in close so that Mitchell could see him, and Robert noticed the shear terror in Mitchell's eyes. "You're safe now," Robert said soothingly.

Mitchell shut his eyes tightly for a brief moment before he opened them as tears once again cascaded down his face. "I'm so sorry, Bobby," Mitchell uttered through the tears.

"Shhhh," Robert said. "There's nothing to apologize for. You did nothing wrong," Robert emphasized caringly.

Mitchell continued to sob when Robert realized, as if a light had been turned on, that something else might have happened. Robert asked compassionately as he tenderly stroked Mitchell's hair, "Did they hurt you another way?"

Mitchell stared at Robert for a moment and then fell apart emotionally as he said, almost inaudibly through the tears, "Yeah."

"Did they …," Robert started to ask when his question was interrupted by a moan of agony and terror, fully answering Robert's question without it even having to be asked. Robert turned away briefly to blink away the tears that had formed in his eyes. When he regained his composure, he leaned in close to Mitchell's ear and whispered, "It's going to be okay. I'm here now, and I love you."

Mitchell grasped Robert's hand as the tears continued to fall. Robert kissed him lovingly on the temple, slightly below where the orange strap held his head immobilized on the backboard. Robert waited for Mitchell to regain his composure before he continued asking him questions about what happened, "Did you tell the doctor what they did to you?"

"I didn't have to. When the nurse was taking my clothes off, she found blood on my pants, and the doctor guessed what had happened, and then he asked me and I told him," Mitchell replied unsteadily.

"Okay," Robert said softly. "Just rest now, and try not to talk. I'm here, and I'm going to take care of you."

Mitchell shut his eyes and tried to breathe deeply, but the pain in his body prevented him. Robert noticed that with almost every breath that Mitchell took, his face contorted in pain, causing Robert to worry.

After a few moments, a tall, slightly overweight male doctor in his mid-thirties entered the room and spoke softly to both Mitchell and Robert. "Hi, I'm Dr. McManus," he said as he reached to shake Robert's hand and Robert responded by introducing himself. "Mr. Rains, do you remember me?" the doctor questioned as he stepped beside Mitchell and leaned in so that Mitchell could see him.

"Yeah," Mitchell muttered.

"Good. The technicians are here to take some x-rays, so I'm going to have to ask you to step outside, Mr. Petrovic," Dr. McManus said politely.

"No," Mitchell protested.

Robert took Mitchell's hand and held it lovingly as he spoke reassuringly, "It's okay. I'll be right outside, and when they're done, I'll come back in." Robert leaned in and smiled, "The sooner they take the x-rays, the sooner they'll get you off that backboard."

"Really?" Mitchell asked. "It hurts like hell."

"That's right, Mr. Rains. If the x-rays show that there are no injuries to your neck or back, then we'll take you off that backboard and remove the neck brace and the straps holding your head still," the doctor explained.

Mitchell indicated his understanding and approval. "Doctor?" Mitchell muttered.

"Yes," the doctor replied.

"If I'm not able to make decisions for myself, Robert is to make them concerning my treatment," Mitchell said authoritatively.

"Does he mean you?" Dr. McManus asked Robert.

"Yes," Robert replied.

"That's fine. I'll have someone from the legal department come down and make up a power of attorney for medical treatment for you, okay?" the doctor said politely.

"Thank you," Mitchell said as he shut his eyes, obviously relieved that he would have something to indicate that Robert would make any important decisions for him if something happened.

The doctor opened the door and motioned for the x-ray technicians with their portable x-ray machine to come into the room. Robert leaned in and kissed Mitchell affectionately on the top of the head as he whispered, "I'll be right outside."

Outside the room, Robert stopped Dr. McManus, "Is he going to be all right?"

"His injuries appear to be somewhat extensive, but we won't know anything until we get the x-rays back, and then I'm going to send him for a CT scan to rule out any head injuries," the doctor explained.

Robert looked at the doctor uncomfortably, "Do you think he has a head injury?"

"We need to rule it out, especially with the type of facial injuries that he appears to have," Dr. McManus answered cordially.

"Do you know what they did to him?" Robert asked emotionally.

"Yes," the doctor answered compassionately. "He told me when he was first brought in."

"How badly did they hurt him … that way, I mean?" Robert asked in a soft voice.

"I haven't been able to examine him yet. If the x-rays clear his spine, then we'll be able to take him off the spinal board and examine him," the doctor paused. "By law we have to follow certain procedures, and an officer will ask him questions about what happened and photograph his injuries," Dr. McManus explained.

"Is the officer trained in this sort of thing?" Robert inquired.

"Yes, absolutely. Officer Charbonneau is very good at dealing with victims of violent crimes. She is very compassionate and easy to talk to," Dr. McManus said reassuringly.

"It's a lady officer?" Robert asked.

"Yes," the doctor replied.

"Good," Robert said with obvious relief.

"Mr. Petrovic, are you a family member of Mr. Rains?" the doctor inquired.

"Yes," Robert said defensively.

"I didn't mean to accuse you of anything," the doctor explained. "Can I ask you what your relationship is to him?"

Robert stared straight into Dr. McManus' eyes and replied proudly, "I'm his boyfriend."

The doctor nodded and Robert continued, "Do you have a problem with that?"

"No, not at all," Dr. McManus replied sincerely. "Why don't you go get a cup of coffee or something? It's going to be a long day."

"I'm fine. I don't want to leave him," Robert explained.

The doctor nodded his understanding, "You can go back in as soon as the tech's leave. Now, I'm going to call the legal department to have them send someone down."

"What happens next for Mitchell?" Robert questioned suddenly.

"I'm going to have a surgeon come down to examine him with me regarding the assault," the doctor responded.

"Why?" Robert asked shocked.

"By the amount of blood on Mr. Rains' pants, it's possible that he suffered some internal injury," the doctor explained. "I'm also going to call an ENT specialist, an oral surgeon, and an orthopedic surgeon to consult on Mr. Rains' other injuries. It's apparent to me that he has a broken nose, broken jaw and some damage to his right hand, so I'm going to call them to review Mr. Rains' x-rays, and then they'll continue treating him for those injuries," the doctor replied softly.

"Thank you, Doctor.," Robert said as he turned to walk back over to stand outside Mitchell's room. After a few minutes, Katherine returned and rubbed Robert gently on the back to get his attention. "Did you meet with the police?" Robert asked.

"Yes. One of the officers took me to the police station so that I could look at some mug shots," Katherine answered.

"Any luck?" Robert inquired cynically.

"Yes," Katherine said as Robert turned to look at her. "I was able to identify one of the men, but unfortunately I wasn't able to identify the others."

"How were you able to identify one of them if you weren't there?" Robert asked.

"I passed their car speeding out of the complex on my way into the office," Katherine explained.

"Were you able to identify the make of the car?" Robert asked with hope.

"Not the kind of car, but I described to them what it looked like," Katherine said.

Robert hugged her warmly, "Thank you."

"I just wish I could've done more," Katherine said emotionally.

"Why don't you go home and rest. You've had a rough day," Robert said with concern.

"Is there anything I can do for you before I leave?" she asked.

"Actually, there is. I want you to have one of the police officers take you back to get your car, and I want you to have him or her wait for you while you go in the office to get Mitchell's appointment book. I don't want you to be there alone while those animals are still free," Robert explained.

"Should I call and cancel all of Mr. Rains' appointments for the week?" Katherine inquired.

"I would really appreciate it," Robert answered.

"Will you keep me informed about Mr. Rains' condition?" Katherine asked.

"Of course," Robert answered with a slight smile. "Thank you for everything."

"You're welcome. I'll call and cancel all of Mr. Rains' appointments as soon as I get home," Katherine explained. "Tell Mr. Rains' I hope he feels better, and I'm thinking about him."

Robert hugged Katherine gently, "I will, and I'll call you as soon as I find out anything."

Katherine pulled away gently and looked directly into Robert's eyes and smiled, "He'll be okay now since you're here."

"Thank you," Robert said appreciatively. "Make sure you have a police officer go with you, okay?"

"Okay," Katherine answered. "I'll go find the officer who I spoke with earlier," she said as she turned and left.

Robert leaned back against the wall outside Mitchell's room and shut his eyes as the reality of the situation set in. While he was taking a few moments to collect his thoughts, he heard a small commotion and noticed that the x-ray technicians had finished with Mitchell's x-rays. He waited for the techs to remove their equipment and then he went in see how Mitchell was doing.

"Hi," Robert said as he took Mitchell's hand. "How are you feeling?"

"I hurt like hell," Mitchell answered through his clenched jaw. "When are they going to give me something for the pain?"

"I don't know, honey, but I'll go find out," Robert replied softly.

"No, please don't leave me," Mitchell pleaded frantically.

"Okay, shhhh, I'm not going anywhere. I'm right here," Robert said as he leaned in and kissed Mitchell on the top of the head.

"Were you waiting long? I've lost track of the time," Mitchell asked.

"It wasn't that long. I talked to the doctor and then I talked to Katherine," Robert explained.

"Did she talk to the police?" Mitchell inquired.

"Yeah, and she had some good news," Robert answered.

Perplexed, Mitchell asked, "What?"

"She was able to identify one of the men who attacked you, and," Robert paused. "She was able to give them information about the car."

"She doesn't know everything that happened to me, does she?" Mitchell asked in a slight panic.

"No," Robert said softly. "I didn't tell her anything."

Mitchell shut his eyes in relief. "We don't have to tell anyone, do we?" Mitchell asked anxiously.

"No, Sweetie, we don't have to tell anyone," Robert said reassuringly. "But an officer is going to come in and ask you some questions, and take some pictures of your injuries."

"Ugh," Mitchell groaned. "Why?"

"They have to according to the law," Robert explained.

"To hell with the law," Mitchell said angrily. "What has the law ever done for me," he paused, "Or for you?"

"I know, Sweetie," Robert answered sympathetically before being interrupted by the door opening.

"How're you doing, Mr. Rains?" Dr. McManus asked.

"Terrible," Mitchell replied. "When are you going to give me something for the pain?"

"Very soon, just hold on for a little longer," Dr. McManus answered. "We're going to take you for a CT scan now."

"Can Robert come?" Mitchell asked.

Dr. McManus looked at Robert as he spoke, "He can walk with you to the lab, and wait for you there."

"Will you come with me?" Mitchell asked Robert with silent pleading in his voice.

"Of course," Robert said as he squeezed Mitchell's hand.

"When you get back, we should have the results of your x-rays, and then we'll start treating your injuries and alleviating your pain, okay?" Dr. McManus explained.

"How long will this take?" Mitchell asked.

"It won't take that long," the doctor answered.

"Robert told me a police officer is going to be there when you examine me," Mitchell said with embarrassment.

"Yes, that true, but it's nothing to be embarrassed about," Dr. McManus said as he moved closer to Mitchell. "Mr. Rains," the doctor said tenderly, "You were the victim of a violent crime. The officer who will talk to you is very good and she is very easy to talk to, so you can relax. It's really nothing to worry about," Dr. McManus explained.

"That's easy for you to say," Mitchell said sarcastically as two orderlies came in to take him to the lab.

# CHAPTER 33

▼

Dr. Hamilton drove to his favorite little diner on the edge of town to relax and enjoy his lunch after a rough morning in the hospital. He sat down at the counter and ordered his usual—a roast beef sandwich and a cup of coffee. As he waited for his sandwich to be made, he watched and read the closed-captioning of the local news that ran across the bottom of the small television screen that hung from the far corner of the lunch counter. When he saw the name "Mitchell Rains" appear across the screen, Dr. Hamilton loudly asked the waitress to turn off the mute button and turn up the volume, which she did without question. After only hearing part of the news report, Dr. Hamilton pulled out his cell phone and started dialing as he walked outside.

He waited anxiously for someone to answer, and when he heard the woman's voice answer, he spoke quickly, "Hi, is Robert there?"

"No, he's out of the office," Helen said politely.

"Is Alex there?" Dr. Hamilton asked.

"I can check. Who may I say is calling?" Helen queried.

"Erik Hamilton," he replied before adding, "Dr. Erik Hamilton."

"One moment, Doctor," Helen replied as she rang Alex's office. "Alex?"

"Yes Helen," Alex replied.

"There is a Dr. Erik Hamilton on line one. He asked for your father first, and then he asked to speak with you," Helen explained.

"Thanks Helen," Alex said politely as he pushed line one on his phone. "Alex Petrovic," he said.

"Hi Alex, it's Erik Hamilton," the doctor replied.

"Hi Doc. How are you?" Alex inquired graciously.

"I'm fine, thanks. I'm sorry to bother you," the doctor said before Alex interrupted him.

"You're not bothering me," Alex said genuinely. "What can I do for you?"

"Well, I was just watching the news, and I pray that what I heard isn't true," Dr. Hamilton said before Alex interjected.

"I'm afraid it is," Alex said sadly.

"What happened?" Dr. Hamilton asked sincerely.

"Mitchell was attacked outside his office this morning," Alex related.

"Is he okay?" the doctor asked optimistically.

"No," Alex said sadly. "Far from it."

"How badly is he hurt?" Dr. Hamilton questioned gently.

"Well, Dad just called a little while ago, and he said that they broke Mitchell's nose, his jaw, seven ribs, and several bones in his right hand, including his thumb," Alex paused. "He also has a bruised lung and a badly bruised kidney."

"Oh God, Alex," the doctor replied at the list of Mitchell's injuries. "How's Robert?"

"You know Dad. He's a tower of strength for the one's he loves," Alex answered sorrowfully.

"When did he find out? About Mitchell, I mean?" the doctor asked.

"Mitchell's secretary found him in the parking lot and called 911, and while the paramedics attended to Mitchell, she called Dad, and Dad asked her to ride with Mitchell to the hospital and he would meet her there. He's been there since right after Mitchell was taken to the ER," Alex explained.

"Did he seem to be all right when you talked to him?" Dr. Hamilton questioned.

"Yeah, he sounded all right. Upset, but other than that, he sounded okay," Alex answered.

"Well, at least they caught the men who did this," Dr. Hamilton said as a sort of consolation.

"Yeah," Alex replied. "From what I heard, there were three of them."

"That's what the news said," the doctor related.

"I hope them getting arrested helps make Mitchell feel better," Alex replied.

"I hope so too," Dr. Hamilton responded sympathetically. "Hey, when you talk to your Dad, tell him if there is anything I can do for him or Mitchell, to call, okay? Anytime—day or night."

"I will," Alex said truthfully. "Thanks Doc, for calling. And for caring."

"If you talk to Mitchell, tell him that I hope he feels better," the doctor instructed politely.

"I will. Emily and I are going to see him after dinner. Dad asked me to stay here and take care of business, but we're going this evening to check up on him as well," Alex explained.

"If he needs to talk, Alex, have him call me. Like I said, he can call anytime—day or night. I know this has to be very stressful on him, so try to keep an eye on him, okay?" Dr. Hamilton instructed.

"I'll definitely keep an eye on him, and thanks Doc for calling," Alex replied graciously.

"Take care, Alex. I'll talk to you soon," Dr. Hamilton said as he flipped his cell phone shut and returned to the lunch counter to await his roast beef sandwich.

# C H A P T E R   34

▼

Outside Mitchell's private hospital room stood an intimidating, tall, muscular man with a security uniform, a nine millimeter handgun, and an intense gaze who monitored everyone who approached the corridor leading to Mitchell's room. The security officer, hired by Robert to guard Mitchell's room, checked identifications and questioned anyone who came near, or tried to enter, the private room where Mitchell was resting and Robert was absentmindedly trying to read the newspaper.

Around lunchtime the security officer opened the door to Mitchell's room quietly and asked Robert to step outside for a moment. As Robert walked out of the room, he smiled tiredly at the man who was waiting patiently outside in the hallway.

"Hi Doc," Robert said wearily.

"Hi Robert," Dr. Hamilton said with a friendly smile. "How's Mitchell?"

"He had surgery this morning on his hand, and right now he's still a little groggy," Robert explained.

"How did the surgery go?" Dr. Hamilton asked.

"The doctor said it went well, but that Mitch is going to need several more to repair all the damage," Robert explained matter-of-factly.

"I'm sure he's in good hands," Dr. Hamilton said optimistically.

"I hope so," Robert said.

"Does Mitchell know the police caught the men who did this to him?" Dr. Hamilton asked.

"Yeah, I told him last night," Robert replied unemotionally.

"Hopefully that made him feel better, knowing that those thugs are off the streets," Dr. Hamilton offered.

"Yeah, but for how long are they going to be off the streets? Probably not very long," Robert responded.

"I can't understand why they had to beat him like they did just to rob him," the doctor said sadly.

Robert looked at Dr. Hamilton with disbelief, "You've got to be kidding me."

"Why?"

"Rob him? You think this was a robbery?" Robert questioned harshly.

"That's what they said on the news," Dr. Hamilton replied.

"Don't believe everything you hear, Doctor," Robert said sternly. "Mitchell had over four hundred dollars in his wallet, several credit cards, a Rolex watch, a gold ring, and his new Corvette was parked not even ten feet away and those bastards didn't take anything. How can that be a robbery?" Robert replied caustically.

"Why then would they do this to him?" the doctor asked naively.

Robert shook his head in disbelief, "Why do you think?"

Suddenly a look of understanding swept over Dr. Hamilton's face, "Because he's ..."

"That's right," Robert said interrupting.

"... gay." the doctor finished. "Oh, Robert. I'm so sorry."

Robert absently ran his fingers through his hair, "He was just going to work, not bothering anyone, and this is what happens."

Dr. Hamilton stared softly at Robert before asking, "How are you doing?"

"I'm fine," Robert replied unemotionally.

"Did Alex tell you I called yesterday?" the doctor asked.

"Yes, he did. Thank you," Robert answered. "It means a lot to me and to Mitchell that you called, and that you've taken time out of your busy schedule to come by to visit."

"We may have come to know each other by you being my patient, but as I've gotten to know you and your family—Alex and Emily and Mitchell, the more I've realized that I look at you all as my friends. I know doctors are supposed to keep a professional relationship just that, but I've come to regard you all as friends," Dr. Hamilton explained sincerely.

Robert smiled, "Thank you Doc. I'm honored that you consider us friends."

As Robert and Dr. Hamilton were talking, Dr. Santiago, Mitchell's cocky hand surgeon, walked up behind them and interrupted, "Erik?"

"Pete!" Dr. Hamilton said with surprise. "How are you?"

"I'm fine. What are you doing here?" Dr. Pete Santiago asked amiably.

"I came by to check up on my friends," Dr. Hamilton answered.

"Do you know Mr. Rains?" Dr. Santiago inquired curiously.

"Yes I do, and Robert too," Dr. Hamilton explained.

"Interesting," Dr. Santiago mumbled. "Mr. Petrovic, I'd like to talk to you about Mr. Rains."

"You can say whatever you have to say in front of Dr. Hamilton," Robert offered.

"Okay," Dr. Santiago replied. "As I told you earlier, the surgery went well, but that he'd probably need several more surgeries to repair all the damage."

"Yes, that's what you said earlier," Robert said slightly annoyed.

"Okay, well, if things go well, and Mr. Rains doesn't have any complications, he should be able to be discharged tomorrow," Dr. Santiago explained.

"That's great," Robert said with relief.

"But," Dr. Santiago continued. "He can't be left alone. He'll need around the clock supervision." Dr. Santiago paused before asking, "Does Mr. Rains live alone?"

"Yes he does, but he's going to be staying with me," Robert explained.

"Can you give him around the clock supervision? I mean, it's not an easy task," Dr. Santiago stated.

"Yes, I assure you, Mitchell will be well taken care of," Robert said defensively.

"Pete, trust me, Mitchell will get the best treatment available," Dr. Hamilton interjected.

"Okay, if you're sure you can do it, that's fine with me, but I'm going to have a social worker talk to you later this afternoon about having nurses come in to check on Mr. Rains on a regular basis," Dr. Santiago replied.

"I'll hire as many nurses as he needs," Robert said with growing annoyance.

"Okay, then I'll check back on Mr. Rains later in the day," Dr. Santiago said. "Erik, it was nice seeing you."

"Same here," Dr. Hamilton replied as Dr. Santiago turned and walked quickly away.

"Are you friends with him?" Robert questioned.

"Absolutely not!" Dr. Hamilton replied. "I was just being polite. He and I went to medical school together, and I can see that he never lost his cockiness."

Robert laughed, "Let's go in to see if Mitchell's awake so I can give him the good news."

Dr. Hamilton followed Robert into the room and stood at the foot of the bed as Robert went to the side of Mitchell's bed and gently lifted Mitchell's left hand and held it tenderly, "Mitch."

Mitchell mumbled briefly before opening his eyes as far as the swelling would allow, "Robert," he said.

Robert stepped closer and smiled at Mitchell, "You have a visitor."

Mitchell opened his eyes as wide as he could and tried to focus them as he looked around the room. When he saw a figure standing at the bottom of the bed, he looked up at Robert and then back down to the bottom of the bed. "Who's there?" Mitchell asked as he continued to try to focus his swollen eyes.

"Dr. Hamilton," Robert replied softly. "He came by to see how you were doing."

"Hi Mitchell," Dr. Hamilton said amiably. "How are you feeling?"

"I've been better," Mitchell answered lightheartedly.

"Well, I just wanted to stop by to see how you were doing, so I'm going to leave you to rest now," Dr. Hamilton said softly.

"Thanks Doc, for coming. It means a lot," Mitchell replied sincerely.

"Feel better, okay?" Dr. Hamilton instructed. "I'll see you again soon."

"Bye Doc," Mitchell replied.

"Thanks Doc," Robert offered sincerely as Dr. Hamilton opened the door and exited. Robert turned his attention back to Mitchell, "How are you feeling?"

"I don't know," Mitchell responded tiredly.

"I have some good news," Robert said as he smiled at Mitchell.

"I could use some of that," Mitchell joked.

"I just talked to Dr. Santiago, and he said that if there aren't any complications, that you could go home tomorrow," Robert explained optimistically.

"Oh," Mitchell said dejectedly.

"What's wrong? I thought you'd be happy to be getting out of here," Robert questioned.

"I am," Mitchell paused. "But," he took a deep breath and looked away before continuing, "I'm afraid to go home."

"Mitch," Robert said tenderly as he stroked Mitchell's hair. "You don't have to be afraid because you're coming home with me."

"What?" Mitchell asked slightly confused. "To your house?"

"Yeah," Robert replied softly as he sat down on the corner of the bed and looked directly into Mitchell's swollen eyes. "Honey," Robert started, "It may be my house, but it's our home—yours and mine, and it will always be your home, no matter what."

Mitchell smiled painfully, "I love you, Bobby."

"I love you too," Robert said as he leaned forward and tenderly kissed Mitchell on the lips. "Now I think you better get some rest," Robert instructed as Mitchell complied and shut his eyes.

"Will you be here when I wake up?" Mitchell suddenly asked as his eyes opened once again to look at Robert.

"Of course," Robert smiled. "I told you I wouldn't leave you alone."

Mitchell nodded as his eyes closed heavily and within minutes he was sleeping peacefully.

# CHAPTER 35

▼

Several weeks passed as Mitchell slowly recovered from his multiple injuries at Robert's house and in Robert's bed. When Mitchell's assailants were set free on a technicality and legal loophole, Robert hired extra security for his home and had new security systems put in place. If one of the assailants wanted to orchestrate a revenge attack on Mitchell at Robert's house, he would be met with a show of force that would rival the National Guard.

On a warm, breezy spring day, Robert helped Mitchell walk outside onto the terrace that provided a view of the blooming flowers that snaked around a trellis on the side of the house. After a few minutes of soaking up the warm sun and scenery, Mitchell indicated to Robert that he wanted to go back inside, and Robert obliged.

Robert led Mitchell over to the bed and helped him to lie down. "Can I get you anything?"

"No, I'm fine," Mitchell replied.

"I have to go downstairs to my study to get the figures off the computer, so I'm just going to call Katherine from there, okay?"

"Yeah, that's fine. Just tell her to keep up with the emails and the phone calls, and please thank her for me," Mitchell instructed.

"I will," Robert replied as he started to walk out the door. "Just say something loudly if you need me, and the receiver will pick it up," Robert explained as he walked out the door.

As Robert pulled the data from the spreadsheet onto the monitor, he picked up the phone and dialed the number for Mitchell's office. "Katherine," he said as the feminine voice answered.

"Hello Mr. Petrovic," Katherine said with a slightly shaky voice.

"What's wrong?" Robert questioned.

"I didn't want to worry you the other day, especially after Mr. Rains had just had another surgery, but …," Katherine explained before being interrupted.

"What?" Robert demanded apprehensively.

"The men who attacked Mr. Rains were hanging around outside the day before yesterday," Katherine explained.

"Did they bother you in any way?" Robert asked.

"No, but I called the police anyways, and they came and told the men to leave, but afterwards the police officer told me that he couldn't do anything to them because this is a public place and they are allowed to walk through it. He could only arrest them if they are bothering someone," Katherine explained.

"Damn," Robert responded angrily. "Have they been back since then?"

Katherine paused before answering, "Yes, Mr. Petrovic. They are out in the parking lot right now."

"Dammit," Robert repeated. "Okay, Katherine, I want you to lock all the doors and don't open them until I get there, understand?"

"Yes, I understand, but what are you going to do, Mr. Petrovic? There are three of them and only one of you," Katherine offered.

"Don't worry about that. Just lock all the doors and don't answer the phone. Let voice mail pick up," Robert instructed.

"Okay," Katherine replied.

"Those sons of bitches," Robert yelled angrily. "I'll be there in a few minutes."

\*       \*       \*       \*

As Emily was walking toward the living room, her attention was diverted to the loud voice emanating from Robert's study. Quietly she crept over to eavesdrop outside the closed door. As she heard the receiver of the phone being slammed down onto the base, she quickly jogged back to the kitchen and acted busy.

Within a few seconds of Emily's impromptu eavesdropping, Robert stalked into the kitchen and confronted Emily, "Emily, can you do me a favor?"

"Sure," Emily replied. "Anything."

Robert handed her the receiver to the monitor in his room, "Can you stay with Mitchell for a little while?"

"Sure, I'd be happy to," Emily responded honestly.

"You don't have to sit with him or anything, just keep this receiver with you, and if he needs something, he'll let you know through the receiver," Robert explained.

"That's no problem," Emily replied as she walked over and looked into Robert's eyes. "Is everything all right?"

Robert turned away and started for the door, "Just keep an eye on him. I shouldn't be long."

Emily casually walked over to the window and watched Robert fly down the driveway in his sports car. As she replayed the conversation over in her head, she became more frightened. She knew that Robert was probably talking to Mitchell's secretary. After all, he called her every day at the same time to go over pertinent business that needed to be dealt with as Mitchell recovered. "Why was Robert swearing during their conversation?" Emily asked herself.

As she was about to pick up the phone to call Alex, Alex opened the front door and greeted her with a smile. When Alex saw the look on his wife's face, his smile quickly faded.

"What's wrong?" Alex asked quickly.

"I'm not sure," Emily answered. "I overheard Robert talking to Mitchell's secretary, and Robert sounded irate. He was even swearing, saying something like— those sons of bitches."

"Where's Dad now?" Alex questioned.

"He left," she replied. "He asked me if I would keep an eye on Mitchell, and when I said I would, he left in a hurry."

"What was his mood?" Alex quizzed.

"Dark," she replied. "But he tried not to let me see it."

"Damn," Alex said as he ran his fingers through his hair. "I have to find him."

As Alex and Emily were about to start making telephone calls to try to locate Robert, the doorbell rang loudly, causing them both to jump. Alex sprinted over to the door and opened it. "Hi Doc," Alex said surprised.

"Hello," Dr. Hamilton said as he studied Alex carefully. "What's wrong? Did I come at a bad time?"

"I'm worried about Dad," Alex replied as he motioned the doctor into the house.

"Why? Did something happen?" the doctor questioned.

"We don't know," Alex replied.

Emily came over to Alex, "I've tried several times to reach Mitchell's secretary, but she won't answer."

"She's probably letting voice mail handle the calls," Alex explained. "Did you try Dad's cell phone?"

"No, but I will," Emily answered as she quickly dialed Robert's number. She waited, and then a message came on asking her to leave a message. "He's not answering," Emily explained.

"Dammit," Alex said in frustration. "I'm going to look for him."

"I'll go with you," Dr. Hamilton said. "My car is right outside, plus you can fill me in on what has happened."

"Fine," Alex replied. "Let's go."

"Be careful," Emily instructed.

"We will," Alex responded. "If you hear from Dad, call me on my cell phone."

"I will," Emily said as she waved goodbye to them.

# CHAPTER 36

▼

Robert pulled into the parking lot and parked his Jaguar in Mitchell's reserved parking space. He slammed the car door loudly and sprinted into Mitchell's office building where he encountered a very frightened Katherine.

"I am so glad you're here," Katherine stated wearily.

"Has anything happened since I called?" Robert asked.

"No," Katherine responded, "But they're still outside, or at least they were a few minutes ago when I looked out the window."

"Okay," Robert said purposefully. "I want you to stay here and lock the door when I leave, and not open it for anyone but me. Understand?"

"Yes sir," Katherine said with a shaky voice. "Should I call the police?"

"No. Absolutely not. They wouldn't do anything anyways. Just stay here and don't answer the phone. I'll be back in a few minutes," Robert instructed.

"Please be careful, Mr. Petrovic," Katherine quietly pleaded.

"I'll be fine," Robert replied as he opened the door and stepped outside. "Lock this door and don't open it for anyone except me."

Katherine quickly obeyed and locked the door and took up a position out of sight from the parking lot, but still allowing a view of most of the front of the building. She watched as Robert walked outside and stopped near his car. As she watched Robert, her heart started beating rapidly as she saw three figures approach him from the side.

Robert stood tall as the three men, all in their late twenties or early thirties, approached him. The apparent leader of the group, an average sized man with long hair and a short beard, addressed Robert mockingly.

"Well, well, well," the leader repeated nastily. "What do we have here?"

The youngest of the attackers, a lanky, muscular man, asked naively, "Who is it?"

"It seems we have been graced with the appearance of the fag's boyfriend," the leader said contemptuously.

Still uncomprehending the situation, the youngest man asked, "Who is he?"

The third attacker, a clean-shaven, average height, athletically built man chimed in, "He's the boyfriend of the fag that we sent to the hospital a few weeks ago."

Robert stared all three of them down before speaking, "You think you're so tough jumping someone from behind. You're just a bunch of pathetic cowards."

"Haven't we declared this a 'fairy-free zone'?" the youngest of the attackers asked sarcastically.

"You think you're so tough jumping him from behind. Well let's see how tough you are when you're facing someone head on," Robert said defiantly.

"Keep it up and we'll send you to the hospital as well," the leader said before adding, "Or maybe you came to get satisfied like your boyfriend did."

Robert felt his hands clench before he spoke, "Why don't you give it your best shot? Or maybe you're just afraid to fight someone who is facing you. Only cowards blindside their victims."

"That's it," said the leader. "Get him."

The youngest of the attackers ran haphazardly toward Robert in an attempt to knock him to the ground. Robert sidestepped him, but grabbed the attacker's collar and pulled him closer to him. In a lightning fast move, Robert turned the man sideways and brutally kicked him directly on the side of his knee, causing the man to scream in pain as the bones in his leg poked out of the skin and out through the light fabric of the man's pants.

As the two other attackers were planning their attacks, Alex and Dr. Hamilton pulled into the parking lot to witness everything that was happening.

The second attacker, who had pulled out a survival knife from his boot, grasped the knife tightly as he moved deliberately toward Robert. The attacker swung the knife wildly at Robert, who ducked out of the way. Alex looked on in horror as the man continued to try to stab Robert with the serrated blade of the survival knife. Robert, with a stealth type move, grabbed the arm of the attacker and twisted the arm holding the knife behind the attacker's back, causing the attacker to drop the knife. Having the attacker in a vulnerable position, Robert punched him brutally in the kidneys and applied pressure to his arm, causing the man's arm to dislocate at the shoulder. Before Robert could continue the attack, the leader came up behind Robert with the intent to grab him around the neck, but Robert sensed the attack and quickly turned and kicked the leader in the abdomen. Robert diverted his attack to the leader who was now lying on the ground, gasping for breath. Robert moved closer to him, and as he approached the leader, Robert kicked him again in the abdomen.

"Get up!" Robert yelled at the leader. As Robert allowed the leader to stand up, he quickly assessed the scene and knew that he was in command of the situation. When the leader stood up shakily, Robert spun and kicked the leader, landing a resounding blow to the face from a lightning fast spinning roundhouse kick. The leader hit the ground with a thud.

Robert looked over at the man who had tried to attack him with the knife. Moving to stand over him, Robert grabbed the man by the hair and pulled him to a standing position. As the man cried and pleaded for mercy, Robert punched him directly in the nose, causing blood to spurt everywhere. Robert continued to hold the man by the hair, although the man had crumpled to one knee after being hit square on the nose. As the man was kneeling, Robert backhanded him across the side of his face, opening up a large cut above the man's eye. As the man pleaded and begged, Robert stood him up and punched him repeatedly in the ribs, ignoring the screams that could be heard at least a mile away. As Robert was about to strike the man again, he caught movement from the leader out of the corner of his eye.

Robert launched a new offensive against the leader, with a merciless barrage of precision strikes and kicks that landed on the intended targets. Robert twisted the leader's arm behind his back and shoved him roughly against the building. Taking the leader's hair in his hand, Robert slammed the leader's head brutally against the wall of the building, causing blood to splatter on the wall. With his hand still holding the leader's head, Robert leaned in from behind to whisper in the leader's ear, "Do you feel like a tough guy now?"

Watching in horror from the parking lot, Alex and Dr. Hamilton gathered their nerves and started to walk toward Robert. Robert saw them, but continued his mission of destroying the men who had attacked Mitchell.

After whispering in the leader's ear, Robert kicked him in the back of the knee and threw him roughly onto the pavement. Setting his sights on the man who had tried to attack him with a knife, Robert went over to the man and bent down with his knee on the man's back. Robert grabbed the man's arm and jerked him roughly to his knees. As the man pleaded and begged, Robert took the man's right thumb and twisted it painfully as he stared down at the man. As Robert pondered his next barrage of attacks, Alex yelled out to him.

"DAD," Alex yelled. "Stop! Please stop."

Robert ignored his son's pleas as he continued to twist the man's thumb. Robert leaned down and grabbed the man's chin, forcing the man to look at him. "Put your hand flat on the pavement," Robert instructed fiercely.

"Please," the man cried.

"DO IT," Robert raised his voice.

The man slowly placed his hand flat on the pavement, visibly trembling, while Robert stood over him.

"DAD," Alex yelled out again. "Stop!"

Robert, once again ignoring his son and concentrating on the task at hand, stomped and crushed the man's hand as he held it on the pavement. The man screamed and begged for Robert to stop.

Glancing over at the youngest man who Robert incapacitated first with a blow that broke the man's leg, Robert focused once again on the leader. Pulling the leader to his knees roughly, as he had done just a moment before with the other attacker, Robert spoke calmly as he grabbed the man by the hair, "Put you hand flat on the pavement."

"No, please," the leader screamed, fully knowing what was going to happen. "I'm sorry, please don't, PLEASE."

"NOW," Robert yelled, as Alex and Dr. Hamilton yelled out to Robert to stop his attack.

The man slowly placed his hand flat on the pavement as he continued to beg and plead for mercy. When his hand was flat, Robert crushed the leader's thumb and hand with a quick strike. Still holding the leader by the hair, Robert spoke to him again calmly, "Look at me."

As the tears and blood flowed freely from the leader's face, he looked up at Robert with pleading in his eyes. Robert stared at him for a brief moment before he spun around with a spinning backhand, and caught the man flush on the jaw, causing blood to fly out of the leader's mouth.

"Dammit Dad," Alex yelled, "STOP IT."

Robert knelt down beside the leader and spoke, "See how you like eating through a straw." As the leader blubbered with tears and pleas, Robert looked over to the youngest attacker, who locked eyes with Robert. As Robert stood up slowly, the youngest attacker trembled and cried out loudly, "PLEASE NO. I'm sorry. PLEASE."

Robert looked over at the man who had tried to attack him with a knife, and then back to the leader who was prostrate on the ground in front of him. He leaned down and grabbed the man by the hair once again. As Alex and Dr. Hamilton approached, Robert said calmly but dangerously, "If I ever see you, or hear that you are within a mile of my boyfriend, I'll make sure that what you got right now is a picnic compared to what I'll do to you next time. Do you understand?"

The leader nodded.

"I said, do you understand?" Robert said raising his voice.

"Yes," mumbled the leader through his broken jaw.

"Good," Robert replied. Still holding onto the leader's hair, Robert spoke again calmly but dangerously, "You think you're so tough. Look at me,"

The leader looked up at Robert painfully as Robert continued, "This fag just kicked all of your asses." With a powerful shove, Robert pushed the leader back onto the pavement as he added, "Don't ever forget that!"

Alex stared at Robert as Robert stood and straightened his clothing. Dr. Hamilton called 911, but did not offer any assistance to the men who lay bleeding on the pavement. Robert turned away from his son and Dr. Hamilton without saying a word, as he started toward Mitchell's office.

"Wait," Alex called out angrily.

"What?" Robert said abruptly.

"What?" Alex repeated incredulously. "What the hell is all of this?"

"It doesn't concern you Alexander," Robert replied as he knocked on the door of Mitchell's office. "It's safe now," Robert explained as Katherine opened the door and hugged him gratefully. After pulling out of the embrace, Robert walked past a stunned Dr. Hamilton and Alex to get into his sports car.

# CHAPTER 37

▼

As Robert walked through the front door of his home, Emily came running to him from the living room. Robert frowned tiredly at Emily as he asked, "What's wrong? Is Mitch okay?"

"He's fine," Emily answered before asking, "Are you okay?"

"I'm fine, why?" Robert asked.

"We were worried about you," Emily explained. "Alex and Dr. Hamilton came looking for you."

"I saw them," Robert answered simply. "Was Mitch all right while I was gone?"

"Yeah, he's fine," Emily answered.

"Thank you Emily, for keeping an eye on him while I was out," Robert said gratefully.

"Anytime. You know I would do anything for you and Mitchell," Emily replied sincerely.

"I know," Robert replied. "You don't know how much that means to me."

"I hope you also know that you can talk to me about anything, at any time," Emily explained.

"Thanks Emily," Robert said tiredly. "I'm going upstairs now, so I'll take the receiver."

Emily handed Robert the receiver and noticed the abrasions on Robert's knuckles, "Are you sure you're okay?"

"Yeah, I'm fine," Robert replied. "When Alexander comes home, tell him that Mitch and I don't want to be disturbed."

"I'll tell him," Emily responded as Robert walked toward the stairs and out of sight.

\*     \*     \*     \*

As Robert slowly turned the doorknob to his bedroom, he took a deep breath and momentarily closed his eyes before opening the door and entering. Mitchell was lying on the bed with his upper body propped up on a stack of pillows so that he could watch television. As Robert entered the room quietly, Mitchell turned the television off and turned to face Robert.

"Robert, what's going on?" Mitchell asked with concern.

"Nothing to be concerned about," Robert answered, hoping that Mitchell would drop the questioning.

"Please don't keep me in the dark, Robert. I know something is going on," Mitch replied.

"I'm not keeping you in the dark," Robert responded.

"The hell you aren't! You go downstairs to call Katherine, and then I hear your car racing out of the driveway, and you don't reappear for over an hour. What the hell is going on?" Mitchell demanded.

"Okay, I'll tell you. When I called Katherine, she said that the men who attacked you were hanging around outside your office two days ago. She called the police, but they told her those animals weren't doing anything wrong by walking in a public place. When I called her earlier, she said those animals were once again outside your office and she was frightened, so I told her that I would come out there," Robert explained.

"You went out there to confront them," Mitchell stated in disbelief.

"Yes, I did," Robert confessed.

"Why?" Mitchell asked somewhat angrily.

"Because they were lying in wait for you to return, and they were scaring the hell out of Katherine," Robert explained sternly.

"I could move my office, Robert, so that Katherine wouldn't be afraid and I wouldn't be harassed," Mitchell answered defiantly.

Robert sat down on the bed and stared into Mitchell's eyes before continuing angrily, "Why the hell should you have to do anything to accommodate those animals? You did nothing wrong, but you're willing to make all the sacrifices. Can't you see how wrong that is?"

Mitchell started to fall apart emotionally as Robert spoke angrily. Mitchell looked away, and with tears in his eyes, he spoke unsteadily, "It's just that I don't want you to get hurt protecting me."

Robert melted as he turned Mitchell's face to look directly into his own. Robert sat down next to Mitchell on the bed and pulled Mitchell into his arms as they both reclined back against the stack of pillows. "Mitch," Robert spoke tenderly, "I never would have went if I knew I couldn't handle the situation."

Mitchell broke down and cried against Robert's chest as Robert held him tenderly. "I love you, Bobby."

"I love you too, Mitch," Robert said sincerely. "I love you more than anyone or anything in this world."

Mitchell looked up at Robert with his eyes full of hope, "Even more than Alex?"

"Yes, even more than Alexander," Robert said as he kissed Mitchell on the forehead tenderly. "I love my mother and Alexander and Emily and the kids, but I love them because we share the same family bond—the same blood, so to speak, but I love you for you. Out of seven billion people in this world, I chose you to love, and thank God you chose me as well. You are my life, Mitchell Rains."

"I couldn't live without you. You know that, don't you?" Mitchell asked as his tears started to subside.

"I know honey, and I couldn't live without you either. Is that why you're upset? You think that I was reckless going out there, and possibly getting killed and never coming back?" Robert asked gently.

"I couldn't handle that, Bobby," Mitchell answered.

"Honey, I knew what I was doing, and I never would have went if I knew there was a chance of me not coming home. I would never leave you like that," Robert explained tenderly as he held Mitchell close in his arms.

"Promise me that you'll never leave me," Mitchell asked as he held Robert tight.

"I promise," Robert replied as he kissed Mitchell on top of the head.

Mitchell looked up at Robert questioningly, "What did you do to them?"

"I made sure that they'll never hurt you again," Robert answered.

"How did you do that?" Mitchell asked curiously.

"Let's just say that they'll be having a nice long vacation in the hospital, and when they get out, they know what will happen to them if they ever come near you," Robert explained matter-of-factly.

"You messed them up?" Mitchell asked with a curious smile.

"Totally," Robert replied devilishly. "Let's just say that the surgeons at the hospital will have a busy night putting them all back together again."

"Thank you Bobby," Mitchell said lovingly.

"For what?" Robert inquired.

"For loving me, and for protecting me," Mitchell answered sincerely as he snuggled closer to Robert. "You're my hero."

"I wouldn't say I'm a hero, but I'll always love and protect you, Sweetie," Robert replied as he kissed Mitchell on the forehead.

As Robert and Mitchell held each other lovingly on the bed, the door to the bedroom suddenly flew open and in came a disillusioned Alex. Alex looked at Robert holding Mitchell closely and tenderly in his arms. "I need to speak to you," Alex said angrily to Robert.

"In a few minutes," Robert replied unemotionally. "Can you please excuse us for a few moments?"

"I'll be waiting," Alex said as he hurriedly left the room to stand outside in the hallway with Dr. Hamilton.

Mitchell turned slightly to look at Robert, "What was that about?"

"I'm sure Alexander is going to read me the riot act," Robert replied.

"Why?" Mitchell questioned.

"Because he and Dr. Hamilton witnessed me dealing with the animals that attacked you," Robert explained.

"How did Dr. Hamilton get into the mix?" Mitchell asked.

"I don't know. The only thing I can figure is that he was coming here to visit you, and when he arrived, Alexander asked him to help find me," Robert replied as he kissed Mitchell on the forehead. "Don't worry about them."

"Don't let them condemn you for what you did," Mitchell stated before continuing. "You did what you did for me, and I'm grateful, so don't let them talk down to you. They have no right."

"I know, Honey, and I won't. The only person I have to answer to is you," Robert said as he smiled at Mitchell.

As Mitchell snuggled closer to Robert, the door opened once again. "I need to talk to you," Alex said angrily.

Robert slid over to the side of the bed before leaning back and kissing Mitchell tenderly on the lips. "I love you," Robert said softly, but loudly enough to be heard throughout the bedroom.

"I love you too, Bobby. Remember what I said," Mitchell replied as Robert winked at him and walked out the bedroom door.

As Robert exited the bedroom, he shut the door gently before being hit with an angry question, "What the hell did you do?"

Robert glared at Alexander before speaking, "Not here. I don't want him upset."

"Fine, we'll go to your study," Alex added irritably.

When Alex and Dr. Hamilton were already in the study, Robert closed the door and turned to face them. "Okay, what do you want?" Robert asked annoyed.

"What do we want?" Alex repeated. "What the hell just went on in that parking lot?"

"It doesn't concern you, Alexander," Robert stated simply.

Furiously, Alex continued, "The hell it doesn't. You could have been killed!"

"Hardly," Robert said arrogantly.

"You could have at least told someone where you were going," Alex stated before adding, "I would have gone with you."

"It's not your fight, Alexander," Robert replied matter-of-factly.

"It's not yours either," Alex stated raising his voice. "You went there with one thing on your mind—revenge."

"You're damn right I did," Robert answered furiously. "Those bastards were waiting there for Mitch to return. What do you think they would have done to him if he went back there? Huh? Do you think they would have shook his hand and apologized? No, they would have killed him the next time, and there is no way in hell that I am going to sit back and let that happen."

"So you decide to go there alone and nearly kill them all," Alex said scornfully.

"I had no intention of killing them," Robert replied angrily, "But I did want them to suffer like they made Mitch suffer."

"Well you did a damn good job of that," Alex replied indignantly. "But you went beyond vengeance, didn't you? They hurt Mitchell badly, but his injuries were nowhere near as extensive as the ones you inflicted on those men."

"They deserved worse than what they got," Robert replied irritably.

"Those men did not deserve to be beaten half to death. Mitchell is recovering, and soon he'll be back to one hundred percent," Alex stated as he stared angrily at Robert. "What you did to them was for your own need for revenge."

"You don't know what the hell you're talking about," Robert replied as he turned to walk away.

"I know those men didn't deserve to be beaten like they were," Alex responded without looking away from Robert.

With lightning fast quickness, Robert grabbed Alexander by the collar and slammed him against the wall, and with all the hurt and pain within him, Robert verbally exploded in anger, "They raped him." Robert tightened his grip before continuing. "After they nearly beat him to death, they threw him over the hood of his car and took turns raping him. After they finished, they finished drinking a fifth of whiskey, and then they," Robert swallowed hard before continuing, "Used the bottle. They tore him so badly inside that he needed surgery."

Alex, with his eyes wide from being thrown up against the wall and the story that he was hearing, spoke sternly, "I didn't know."

"You speak about those animals and their feelings. What about Mitch's? How do you think he's going to feel in three months when he has to go for a blood test to see if those bastards gave him a disease that could kill him? And then in six months and every six months after that for the next two years? How is that going to affect him? How would you like to live in fear for the next two years?" Robert yelled.

"I'm sorry that happened to Mitchell, but it still doesn't excuse you from what you did. Obviously you wanted them to suffer. What were you going to do if we didn't show up? Rape each of them to make up for what they did to Mitchell?" Alex asked condescendingly.

Robert shook his head in disbelief as he loosened his grip on Alex's collar, "What kind of person do you think I am?" Robert looked away for a brief moment before adding, "I'm not an animal like them."

"Maybe not, but you certainly aren't the person that I thought you were," Alex said heatedly.

Robert shook his head in disbelief and sudden understanding, "Oh, I get it now." Robert suddenly grabbed Alex's shirt tightly and slammed him against the wall again as he said, "In your eyes, Mitch must have enjoyed them raping him since he's a faggot." Robert let go of Alex and walked away.

"I didn't say that," Alex yelled.

Robert threw his hands in the air as he was walking out the door, "You didn't have to."

Before Robert made it to the hallway, Dr. Hamilton called out, "Robert, please wait."

Robert turned and glared at both men in his study. "Just leave us alone," Robert said irately as he turned and walked out of sight.

Dr. Hamilton stared angrily at Alex before he started walking toward the door. Alex took a deep breath and straightened his shirt before speaking to Dr. Hamilton. "What?"

"Nothing," Dr. Hamilton replied angrily as he was leaving.

"Wait," Alex called out to him. "Tell me what you're thinking, please?"

"Trust me, Alex. You don't want me to tell you right now," Dr. Hamilton answered irritably.

"Yes I do," Alex responded.

"Fine," Dr. Hamilton replied as he turned to face Alex. "You just basically told your father that the person he loves most in this world isn't worth protecting and that Mitchell's well-being isn't as important as the men's well-being who attacked him."

"I didn't say that," Alex protested.

"Right," the doctor said sarcastically. "Like Robert said as he was leaving, 'you didn't have to.'"

"You can't believe that what he did was right," Alex interjected.

"Who am I to judge him?" Dr. Hamilton said sarcastically. "What I do know is that male rape victims are usually extremely traumatized. And Mitchell is not the only one who was victimized—Robert was as well, as the person who loves Mitchell and who sees how Mitchell is suffering everyday, and how he will continue to suffer, as your father has said, for the next two years."

"I guess I didn't think of it like that, but you can't believe that I would ever think that he enjoyed being raped," Alex offered hoping to win over Dr. Hamilton.

"It doesn't matter what I believe. What I know is that you made it clear to your father that he's not any better than the bastards who brutalized Mitchell, and that Mitchell's life isn't worth a damn," the doctor explained. "Not only does Robert have to deal with the things that led him to try to commit suicide mere months ago, but now he has to deal with the impact that this assault has had on Mitchell and their relationship, and now add to that your chastisement of his actions and your feelings that Mitchell's life isn't worth a damn."

"I never said Mitchell's life isn't worth a damn," Alex stated defensively.

"Whether you like it or not, Robert loves Mitchell. You heard him say that he loves Mitchell only a few minutes ago when they were in the bedroom," the doctor explained. "I thought that you put aside your bigoted attitude, but apparently I was wrong, and the most unfortunate part of all this is that your father felt the brunt of all your hatred."

"I don't hate my father," Alex stated fiercely.

"From where I was standing, it sure did appear that you hated who he was, and who he loves," the doctor added as he walked out the door, leaving Alex standing in the study dumbfounded.

# CHAPTER 38

▼

Robert pushed the door to his bedroom open slowly as he walked in with despair and pain written all over his face. Mitchell, who was once again watching television, turned the television off when he caught a glimpse of Robert's face.

"What happened, Honey?" Mitchell asked with alarm as he stood up and slowly walked over to stand in front of Robert, who had stopped after only taking a few steps into his room.

Robert looked up at Mitchell and started to cry, "I'm so sorry, Mitch."

"You have nothing to be sorry for," Mitchell softly reprimanded as he wrapped his non-injured arm around Robert's back and held him tight.

"I told them," Robert said through his tears as he put his head on Mitchell's shoulder, "I'm so sorry."

"You told who, what?" Mitch asked gently.

"Alexander was yelling at me for dealing with those animals, and I just grabbed him by the collar and threw him against the wall and blurted out what they did to you." Robert buried his head and wept, "Can you ever forgive me?"

Mitchell gently lifted Robert face to look into his own. Mitchell smiled at him and then kissed him on the forehead, "There's nothing to forgive, Sweetie. It was only a matter of time before I came out and told everyone what happened to me that morning." Mitchell once again pulled Robert into a tender embrace as Robert's tears continued to flow. "It's okay, really," Mitchell added as he gently lead Robert over to the sofa and sat down with him still resting his head on Mitchell's shoulder.

"He hasn't changed," Robert said sadly.

"Who hasn't changed?" Mitchell asked.

"Alexander," Robert answered as he softly pulled away to look into Mitchell's eyes. "In his mind, those animals did nothing wrong. He thinks that you enjoyed what they did to you," Robert said sorrowfully through the tears.

"I'm sorry Robert," Mitchell said as he wiped Robert's tears away with his left hand. "I thought that he had changed, and I prayed that he had, for your sake."

"He'll never change, Mitch," Robert said as the tears started to subside. "Deep down inside, you and me disgust him, and nothing is ever going to change that."

"Well you know what?" Mitchell said as he smiled at Robert. "It's his loss."

"You're right," Robert replied my forcefully. "Everything that I want and need is right here beside me."

Mitchell leaned over and kissed Robert on the cheek, "The same for me, Sweetie. If Alex doesn't want to be a part of our lives, that's his loss, especially when he'll miss out on what a wonderful person you are."

"And you are as well," Robert added to Mitchell's thought. "I love you, Mitch, and I'm sorry for blurting out what happened to you."

"I love you too, Sweetie, and please stop apologizing," Mitchell flashed Robert a smile and pulled Robert into an embrace. As Robert held Mitchell close, Mitchell turned slightly and the two of them laid down on the sofa with Robert still embracing Mitchell. "Let's just forget about everything that happened today, okay?"

"Fine with me," Robert added as he snuggled even closer to Mitchell as Mitchell reached for the remote control and turned on one of their favorite CD's. As they were relaxing comfortably on the sofa, a loud knock came at the door. Robert muttered, "Don't answer that. Maybe they'll go away."

Robert's hopes were quickly dashed as Dr. Hamilton gingerly pushed the door open and looked around the room. When he spotted the men on the sofa, Dr. Hamilton went over to stand in front of them. "I'm sorry to barge in here like this," the doctor started.

"Doctor, please go away," Robert pleaded without looking at the doctor or without moving out of his embrace with Mitchell on the sofa.

"I will, I promise, but there's something that I want to say, but first I want to say how sorry I am for what happened to you, Mitchell," the doctor offered sincerely.

"Thank you," Mitchell replied.

"Robert, what I was going to say downstairs in your study was … that I thought Alex was completely out of line with what he said and how he treated you," the doctor explained.

Robert nodded without looking up, but the doctor continued, "My wife is the person I love most in this world, and if she were attacked and the men waited for her to attack her again, I would have done the same thing you did … with one major exception," Dr. Hamilton paused. "I would have probably gotten my ass kicked, but watching you deal with them, I saw first hand that you knew what you were doing."

"It's too bad that Alex doesn't see it like that," Mitchell replied angrily.

"Speaking to you as my friend, I have to say that you were amazing out there today, Robert," the doctor complimented. "It was like I was watching a karate movie happening live right in front of me."

"Thank you," Robert replied stoically without moving from his position on the sofa, or even looking in the doctor's direction.

"I told Alex that he had no right talking to you the way he did," the doctor continued.

"It doesn't matter," Robert replied. "I have what I need right here in my arms."

"Now, speaking to you as a doctor, I see that your knuckles are busted. Does it feel like there is anything broken?" Dr. Hamilton asked gently.

"I'm fine, doctor," Robert replied, still without looking away from Mitchell.

"Okay, but you need to wash your knuckles thoroughly to prevent any type of infection," the doctor instructed.

"Doctor, please forgive my rudeness, but could you please excuse us," Robert replied. "It's been a long day."

"Yeah, I'd agree with that. If you need to talk, call my anytime—day or night, okay?" the doctor offered.

"Thank you," Robert replied tiredly.

"Mitchell," Dr. Hamilton started, "I'm truly sorry about what happened to you."

"Thank you," Mitchell replied graciously.

"If there's anything I can do for you, please let me know," the doctor explained.

"Thank you again, doctor," Mitchell replied. "We'll be fine."

"I know you will. Take care," Dr. Hamilton said as he walked toward the door.

Robert called out to Dr. Hamilton before he opened the door, "Could you please lock our bedroom door on your way out?"

"Sure," the doctor replied as he locked the door and pulled it shut gently.

Mitchell shifted slightly and kissed Robert on the cheek. "Well, at least everyone isn't as prejudiced against us as Alex," Mitchell stated.

"That may be so, but from now on, I'm looking at our life as being you and me against the world," Robert said solemnly.

"Always and forever, my love," Mitchell replied.

"Always and forever," repeated Robert.

"What do you say I run you a nice hot bath so that you can relax and soothe your weary soul?" Mitchell said semi-teasingly.

"Weary soul?" Robert repeated. "You can say that again."

"Plus, you need to clean your hands carefully," Mitchell added.

"Yes doctor," Robert teased as he carefully rolled off the sofa to let Mitchell up.

Mitchell stood up slowly and extended his left hand to Robert, who took Mitchell's hand and held it lovingly. Mitchell led Robert into the bathroom and started to run the water for Robert's bath. When Mitchell turned to look back at Robert, Robert was staring at him sadly. Mitchell asked, "What's wrong?"

"You're the one that's injured. I'm supposed to be taking care of you, and here I am letting you take care of me," Robert answered sadly.

"Let's just say we're taking care of each other," Mitchell responded with a smile. "Besides, all I'm doing is running you a bath. I owe you so much more," he paused. "After all, I wasn't here when you needed me the most."

"Please don't say that," Robert said sorrowfully. "All that matters is that you are here now, and hopefully will be here forever."

"What's with the 'hopefully'? You're stuck with me forever, Bobby," Mitchell said with a beaming smile.

"Well, then, that makes me the happiest man alive," Robert said honestly. With a glint in his eye, he added, "And what a future we are going to have, Mr. Rains."

"I can't wait, Sweetie," Mitchell replied with a smile.

"I think it's a safe bet that this past year has been the worst for both of us. It's going to be blue skies and sunny days ahead, Mitch. I promise," Robert responded as he pulled Mitchell into a tender embrace.

"Amen to that," Mitchell answered.

# CHAPTER 39

▼

As Alex walked out of his father's study, Emily came rushing toward him, "What's going on, Alex?"

"What do you mean?" Alex asked still slightly dumbfounded from his conversation with Dr. Hamilton.

"What do I mean?" she repeated. "Robert comes home with busted knuckles. You and Dr. Hamilton come home a few minutes later, with you looking pissed and looking like you wanted to fight with someone, and then I hear you and Robert yelling at each other. Then I hear Robert leave the room, but then I hear more yelling, and next thing I know Dr. Hamilton is heading back toward Robert's room." Emily stood directly in front of Alex as she spoke sternly, "Now tell me what the hell is going on!"

With his anger returning, Alex stared at his wife as he spoke, "Dad went and confronted the men who attacked Mitchell."

Emily looked at Alex with shock and disbelief, "What?"

"Yeah," Alex answered. "He went to Mitchell's office and confronted them."

"What happened?" Emily asked.

"Robert nearly killed all three men," Alex related with latent anger.

"What? How did he do that?" Emily asked with continuing disbelief.

"It seems that Robert is some kind of karate expert, and he nearly beat those three men to death," Alex said with disgust.

Emily visibly relaxed, "Karate expert?"

"Yeah, that's what I said," Alex said arrogantly.

Emily glared at Alex as she continued, "Well, I can see why he did it. Nobody deserves to be beaten like Mitchell was, especially for just being who he is."

"Nobody deserves to be beaten like Robert beat those men either," Alex shouted. "Those men will be in the ICU for weeks."

"Why are you so pissed?" Emily asked with building anger.

"Because Robert did this for revenge, pure and simple. I can understand him being upset and furious about them raping Mitchell, but that still doesn't give him the right to do what he did," Alex yelled.

Emily shouted, "What did you just say? Did you say that those men raped Mitchell?"

"Yes," Alex yelled back.

"Then how the hell could you not see that Robert was justified in what he did?" Emily's face turned scarlet as she shouted at her husband.

"Oh for God's sake, not you too," Alex replied furiously as he turned and walked away from Emily.

Emily stood in the center of the room as her anger toward her husband continued to build. She was about to go after him when Dr. Hamilton walked quickly through the room toward the front door, without even seeing Emily.

"Dr. Hamilton," Emily called out.

Dr. Hamilton stopped abruptly, "Yes."

"Did you see Robert?" she asked as her anger started to dissipate.

"Yes, I did," Dr. Hamilton replied without further reply.

"Please tell me he's okay?" Emily asked sincerely.

Dr. Hamilton melted a bit, "I truly don't know, Emily."

With her anger returning, she asked, "What did Alex say to him?"

Dr. Hamilton closed his eyes and shook his head in anger, "Do you really want to know?"

"Yes, please. Me and Alex just had it out over the little information that he told me, but I know there's a lot he left out," Emily answered.

"He basically told Robert that he's no better than the bastards who traumatized Mitchell, and he even went so far as to suggest that Robert would have raped all those men to get revenge for them gang raping Mitchell," Dr. Hamilton replied angrily.

Emily's hand flew up to her mouth in disbelief, "Oh my God. Is Robert all right?"

"Alex couldn't have hurt him any worse if he had stuck a knife through Robert's heart," Dr. Hamilton replied sadly. "He wouldn't talk to me when I went upstairs, or even look at me. I told him that I told Alex how wrong Alex was, and that he had no right treating Robert like that, but Robert didn't care."

"What was he doing when you were talking to him?" Emily asked sorrowfully.

"They were lying on the couch. Robert had his head resting on Mitchell's chest and his arms wrapped around Mitchell like he was holding on to the only person he could trust to love him," Dr. Hamilton related sadly.

"How could Alex treat him like that?" Emily asked rhetorically before adding angrily, "Damn him!"

"I know, Emily," Dr. Hamilton replied in mutual understanding and compassion. "Alex hasn't changed, and Robert pointed it out accurately."

"What do you mean?" Emily questioned.

"Robert told Alex that in Alex's eyes, Mitchell enjoyed being raped because, as Robert put it, he's a faggot," the doctor explained.

"Damn him!" Emily repeated angrily. "How could he treat his father like that after all he's been through? I thought he had changed too, but I guess we were all wrong."

"The unfortunate part of all this is that Robert had to get hurt," Dr. Hamilton added.

Emily started to cry softly, "How could he treat him like that? Robert and Mitchell are two of the sweetest, kindest men that I have ever known."

Dr. Hamilton hugged Emily gently, "I know."

Emily hugged the doctor back as she asked, "What can we do to help him?"

"I think right now Robert just needs to be with Mitchell," Dr. Hamilton replied.

Emily pulled out of the embrace as she looked up questioningly at Dr. Hamilton, "Is Robert going to be okay?"

"I don't know, Emily," the doctor answered honestly. "He wouldn't talk to me, but maybe in a few days he'll feel like talking. Keep a close eye on him, okay?"

"You know I will," Emily replied. "I love Robert, and I love Mitchell as well. It tears me apart to know how he must be hurting."

"I know it does. Robert and Mitchell are both lucky to have you in their lives," the doctor said as he smiled at a tearful Emily.

"No, Doctor, I'm the lucky one," Emily responded with a sad smile.

"Keep an eye on Robert, and if something seems amiss, call me," Dr. Hamilton instructed.

"I will," Emily replied.

"I'll call tomorrow to see how he is, and hopefully I'll be able to get him to talk to me," Dr. Hamilton explained.

"I'll check in on them tomorrow morning after Alex takes the kids to school," Emily replied.

"Good," the doctor said. "Like I said, if something seems amiss, call me immediately and I'll come out."

Emily hugged the doctor, "Thank you."

"Good night," Dr. Hamilton said as he pulled gently out of the embrace and walked toward the door.

Emily waited for Dr. Hamilton to disappear out the front door before she sat down on the arm of the sofa and wept. As the tears flowed uninterrupted, Alex pushed the glass back door open to come into the living room and immediately saw his wife sobbing uncontrollably. With sadness in his eyes, Alex quietly walked over to the sofa and softly touched Emily's cheek. Emily looked up with rage emanating from her eyes as she pulled away violently and stormed out of the room.

# CHAPTER 40

▼

The next morning Emily characteristically got Stevie and Steffi up and ready for school. Alex came into the dining room earlier than usual to be greeted by his wife with a frosty reception that even the five year olds noticed. The twins exchanged glances and then went about eating their breakfast.

Alex kissed each child on top of the head as he absentmindedly tried to pour a glass of milk. As he looked up at Emily for some sign of hope that he would be forgiven, or at least spoken to, he spilled the milk across the table and onto the floor. Emily looked at him disgustedly as the twins scattered to avoid the flood of milk that was washing across the table. Emily gathered the children and motioned them out of the dining room and back to their rooms to finish getting ready for the day ahead at school. After assuring them that she would be right behind them to help them with last minute tasks, Emily walked back into the dining room to find Alex on his knees with a towel cleaning up the mess that he had created.

Alex looked at Emily sadly as he stood and straightened his suit, "I'm sorry."

Emily stared at him for a moment before speaking, "The kids should be ready in a few minutes."

"Em," Alex called out. "Wait. Please."

"The kids need my help," she said with words laced with anger.

"Em, please!" Alex pleaded. "Can we talk?"

Emily glared at her husband before she responded with open hostility, "I have nothing to say to you right now."

"I'm sorry," Alex apologized again.

Emily walked out of the room as she spoke back to him once again, "The kids will be ready in a few minutes."

"Do they know anything about last night?" Alex asked with fear and dread.

"Know what?" Emily asked bitterly as she turned back to face her husband. "That you think their grandfather is some kind of perverted homicidal animal?"

"Come on, Em," Alex said sadly. "I don't think that."

"You could have fooled me," Emily replied as she stormed out of the room to leave Alex standing alone and dejected in the dining room.

A few minutes later, the twins came back to the dining room laughing and giggling like most five year olds living a normal life. Emily helped each child put on his or her coats and backpacks before kissing and hugging them as they went out the door without a care in the world. Alex looked back at his wife as he was walking out the door, "Can you meet me for lunch?"

"No," she said shortly. "I have plans."

"Please," he asked with pleading in his voice. "I hate the way things are between us."

"You should have thought about that last night when you went off on your father," Emily answered nastily as she pushed the door shut. After waiting to hear Alex's car pull out of the driveway, Emily rushed upstairs to Robert's room. She tapped on the door lightly and waited.

After a few moments, a faint voice asked, "Who's there?"

"Mitchell? It's me—Emily," she replied.

Mitchell gently opened the door and quickly put his index finger to his lips to silence Emily as he nodded in the direction of a sleeping Robert.

"How is he?" Emily asked sadly.

"He's been up all night," Mitchell replied wearily. "He just fell asleep a little while ago."

Emily reached out and hugged Mitchell firmly, causing him to wince. "Oh, I'm sorry," Emily apologized, realizing that she was squeezing his injured ribs.

Mitchell returned the hug as he whispered, "That's all right. I'm still just a little sore."

Emily pulled back slightly as she looked at Mitchell with tears in her eyes, "I'm so sorry about what happened to you."

"You heard then?" Mitchell responded with melancholy.

Emily nodded in affirmation, "Are you okay?"

"I will be," Mitchell replied. "I didn't tell you because …"

Emily interrupted softly, "I understand. You don't owe anyone an explanation."

"Who told you?" Mitchell asked calmly and without any hint of anger.

Emily took Mitchell's hand and held it gently, "Alex told me … well, that's not true. He shouted it at me, but then I stopped Dr. Hamilton before he left last night."

"So you know what happened last night?" Mitchell questioned.

"Unfortunately—yes," Emily replied angrily. "I am so mad at Alex that I can't even look at him."

"Well, that makes two of us," Mitchell replied with growing anger.

"I can't understand how he could treat his father that way," Emily stated with still obvious disbelief.

"I know, Emily," Mitchell said as he squeezed her hand and continued on angrily, "Alex can say anything he wants to about me. I don't much care, but when he hurts Robert, he crosses the line."

Emily peeked in at Robert, who was sleeping peacefully, "How is he? I couldn't sleep last night worrying about him."

"Alex hurt him deeply," Mitchell replied as he sadly smiled at the man sleeping quietly in the king size bed.

"Damn him!" Emily snapped. "Robert should have knocked him on his ass last night."

Mitchell laughed softly, "I agree."

"Dr. Hamilton was really worried about him last night, and he said that he's going to call today to see how he's doing," Emily explained.

Mitchell frowned, "I don't think Robert is going to talk to him."

"Why? Did Dr. Hamilton say or do something that upset him?" Emily questioned.

"No. He actually said he understood why Robert did what he did, but I don't think Robert wants to talk to him—probably because he was there," Mitchell answered.

"Why would that make a difference if he was there or not?" Emily asked slightly perplexed.

"Don't you see? Robert hates what he did. You know him, he's the most gentle man alive," Mitchell paused. "But he needed to do this—for me, and to a lesser extent, for himself."

"And he doesn't want to be reminded of it," Emily replied in understanding.

Mitchell shrugged, "We're both living with this everyday, and I sure as hell wouldn't want any more reminders of what happened, so I understand how he could feel that way." Mitchell paused before continuing, "He sees Dr. Hamilton and relives what happened last night between him and Alex, so if he doesn't want to see or talk to Dr. Hamilton, I'm not going to push it."

"Damn," Emily said as a single tear trickled down her cheek. "I hate this, Mitchell."

Mitchell put his arm around Emily's shoulder and pulled her close, "I know."

"I love you," Emily said as she leaned against Mitchell.

"I love you too," Mitchell replied as he held her tight.

"Do you think it would be all right if I come back when Robert wakes up?" Emily asked.

"Of course," Mitchell replied truthfully as he continued to console her with his arm around her shoulder. "Robert loves you, Emily."

"I love him too. He means the world to me," Emily said as she sadly peeked in once again at Robert. "Is there anything I can do for you?"

Mitchell looked down at Emily and smiled, "No, I'm fine. I'm just going to lie back down so that I know when Robert wakes up."

"I'll be back later, okay?" Emily returned his smile.

"Yeah, that's fine."

"If you need me, for anything, I'll be here," Emily explained.

"Thank you," Mitchell replied gratefully. Seeing Emily's concern, he tried to alleviate her anxiety by adding, "Don't worry Emily. We'll be fine."

"Promise me that," she implored.

"As long as we're together, we can take on the world," Mitchell replied more willfully.

Emily stretched and gently kissed Mitchell on the cheek before turning and walking toward the stairs.

*       *       *       *

A few hours after Emily checked in on Robert and commiserated with Mitchell over Alex's vile treatment of his father, Robert awakened to find Mitchell quietly napping at his side. Robert carefully leaned over and kissed Mitchell on the forehead, causing Mitchell to stir and slowly open his eyes. When he saw Robert, Mitchell smiled broadly, "Hi handsome."

Robert smiled as he kissed Mitchell once again, but this time on the cheek. When Robert pulled away, concern was evident on his handsome face.

"What's wrong, Bobby?" Mitchell asked equally concerned.

Robert laid the back of his hand gently against Mitchell's forehead, "You feel warm. Are you feeling okay?"

Mitchell smiled tiredly, "I'm fine."

"I think you may have a slight fever," Robert replied as he gently and lovingly trailed his fingers down Mitchell's cheek.

Mitchell winked and smiled seductively, "Of course I feel warm. That's what happens when I awaken to my sexy man kissing me!"

Robert laughed, "Oh, is that why?"

"You bet, and in a few weeks when these damn wires come off my teeth, I'll have a fever that skyrockets right off the scale," Mitchell explained.

Robert leaned in and kissed Mitchell tenderly on the lips, "Honey, I promise you that when your jaw is unwired, I'm going to give you the longest, deepest, most passionate kiss of your life."

Mitchell smiled broadly, "I can't wait." As Mitchell sat up and stretched gingerly, his tone turned serious, "How are you doing, Bobby?"

Robert tried to hide his hurt from Mitchell, but Mitchell knew him too well. "I'm fine, Mitch. All I need in my life is here with me on this bed."

"I feel the same way, Honey, but you know that you don't have to hide your hurt from me. Alex hurt you deeply last night, and it's okay to be sad because of that. Just know that I love you no matter what," Mitchell said genuinely.

"I love you too," Robert replied as the sadness started to seep into his mahogany eyes. "I should have listened to you all along."

Mitchell teased, "Well, that's a first. What should you have listened to me about?"

Robert smiled sadly, "About Alexander. You've been right about him all along, but I've been too blind and stupid all my life to see it."

"You're not stupid, Bobby. I don't ever want to hear you say that. You just love with every ounce of your being, and you put those you love above everything else," Mitchell stated strongly. "But you know what?" Mitchell asked.

"What?" Robert asked intrigued.

"I never want you to change. I love you for the way you love. You're the toughest man I've ever known, but you have the most tender of hearts, and I'll spend the rest of my life making sure no one ever hurts you again," Mitchell said from his heart.

Robert gently pulled Mitchell into an embrace and held him as he whispered, "I love you."

Mitchell held Robert as he lovingly rubbed Robert's shoulders, "I love you too."

After a few minutes of cuddling, Mitchell broke the silence, "Emily stopped by this morning to see you. She was worried about you."

"Why was she worried?" Robert asked before he remembered the events of the previous night. "Does she know what happened?"

"Yeah, she knows everything, and as it stands right now, she is so pissed at Alex that she can't even stand to look at him," Mitchell explained.

"How did she find out?" Robert asked slightly upset.

"She asked Alex, but when she told him that she agreed with your way of handling things, he got all pissed and stormed off, so Emily asked Dr. Hamilton as he was leaving," Mitchell continued.

Robert closed his eyes tightly as he asked, "You said that Emily knew everything. Does that mean that she ..."

Mitchell interrupted calmly, "Yeah, Honey, she knows what happened to me."

Robert buried his head in his hands, "Me and my big mouth. I'm so sorry Mitch."

Mitchell put his hand under Robert's chin and lifted until Robert was looking directly into Mitchell's eyes, "There's no need to apologize, Bobby. The truth is I should have told Emily weeks ago." Mitchell hugged Robert as he continued, "She's my best friend, and I should have trusted her."

Robert hugged Mitchell affectionately, "She's my best friend too. I just wish that she wasn't stuck in the middle of all this."

Mitchell chuckled lightly, "Can you believe that Emily actually asked me if it'd be okay for her to come back to talk to you this afternoon? She's definitely one of a kind."

Robert laughed, "Yes, she is, and I'm so glad that we both have her in our lives."

"She loves us, Bobby," Mitchell replied. With a twinkle in his eye, Mitchell added, "But then again, what isn't there to love?"

Robert laughed out loud as he pulled Mitchell close, "Absolutely nothing. We're the most lovable guys alive!"

Mitchell laughed, "It's getting warm in here. Must be all the hot air."

"Yeah, there's a lot of that," Robert added with a smile.

"Can you help me out to the balcony, Honey?" Mitchell asked.

Robert stood and pulled Mitchell to his feet, "Sure."

As Robert guided Mitchell to the balcony with a strong arm around Mitchell's waist, a faint knock came from the bedroom door. Mitchell stopped as Robert opened the door leading to the balcony and smiled, "I can manage from here. That's Emily at the door."

Robert smiled mischievously, "Oh, and now you have ESP?"

"Yeah, I've been taking an online course," Mitchell added with equal mischief in his eyes.

"You sure you can make it the rest of the way?" Robert asked with loving concern.

"Bobby, I only have to go about four more feet," exclaimed Mitchell. "Now stop worrying about me and go see what Emily wants."

Robert crossed the room and opened the door. As the door fully opened, Emily threw her arms around Robert and hugged him tightly. When Robert recovered from the surprise of Emily diving into his arms, Robert returned the tender embrace. When Emily pulled slowly out of the embrace, her eyes scrutinized Robert from head to toe to make sure he was okay.... at least physically okay.

Emily reached a soft hand and let it trail down Robert's unshaven face, "Are you okay?"

Robert smiled wearily, "I'm fine."

"Robert, I'm so sorry for the way Alex treated you last night. He had no right," Emily said with a building anger.

"It doesn't matter, Emily," Robert replied.

"It does matter," Emily exclaimed. "Who the hell does he think he is?"

"Honestly Em, it doesn't matter. Mitch and I are happy, and no one is going to interfere in our lives. Alexander made it clear last night that he'll never accept Mitch and me for who we are, so that's his problem—not ours," Robert explained matter-of-factly.

"How can he be so bigoted?" Emily asked rhetorically.

"I don't know, but I do know that I lost Mitch before because of Alexander, and I'll be damned if I ever let that happen again," Robert explained.

"Robert," Emily paused a moment before she spoke. "Do you want us to move out?"

"No. Absolutely not. You're welcome here until your house is built," Robert spoke honestly. "You don't want to move out, do you?" Robert asked apprehensively.

"No, of course not. I just thought that maybe you didn't want to be so close to Alex right now."

"Honestly, I don't want to see Alexander right now, but this is a big house, and it shouldn't be a problem to avoid him. Besides, you don't want to disrupt the kids' lives while they're in school, do you?" Robert asked.

"No, of course not. I hadn't even thought of that," Emily confessed.

"Then I take it you'll stay?" Robert asked softly.

Emily pulled Robert toward her while she kissed him on the cheek, "Yeah, we'll stay."

"That's the best news I've heard all day," Robert replied with a smile.

Emily looked around the room, "Where's Mitchell?"

"On the balcony, which reminds me, I need to check to see if he's okay or needs something. I'll be right back," Robert said as he crossed the room to the balcony.

In a matter of moments, Robert returned to the bedroom where Emily was waiting on the sofa. When Emily glimpsed the look on Robert's face, she became alarmed, "What's wrong?"

Robert sat down beside Emily on the sofa, "Mitch feels hot. I think he may have a fever."

Emily's eyes grew wide with concern and fear, "What?"

"I think Mitch has a fever. I know he's not feeling well, but he won't admit that he's feeling bad because he doesn't want me to worry," Robert explained.

"Did you take his temperature?" Emily asked.

"No, I haven't," Robert replied.

"Why not?" Emily questioned.

"Think of the locations of his injuries, and then tell me how I'm supposed to take his temperature," Robert stated matter-of-factly.

Emily frowned, "Oh, that is a problem." Emily took Robert's hand and held it lovingly, "What are you going to do?"

"After he has his protein shake, I'm going to call his doctor," Robert explained.

Emily reached around Robert's back and pulled him into an embrace, "If you need me for anything, I'll be here."

With gratitude and love, Robert replied, "Thanks Em. I don't know what Mitch and I would do without you."

"I love you both," Emily stated tenderly. "And I'll always be here for both of you, no matter what."

# CHAPTER 41

▼

The following morning while the twins were finishing getting ready for school, Alex gently confronted Emily in the hallway outside the twins' bedrooms. "Can we talk?" he asked politely.

"No. I need to help the kids finish getting ready," Emily replied, devoid of all emotions.

"Can you just answer me one question, and then I'll let you alone?" Alex asked.

"What?" Emily said abruptly.

"Have you seen Dad?" Alex asked sincerely.

"Yes, I have," Emily answered.

"Well?" Alex asked, hoping for further information.

"Well what?" Emily countered.

"Is he okay?" Alex asked with genuine concern.

Emily shook her head in disbelief, "You lost the right to ask such a question when you went off on your Dad."

"Em," Alex paused. "You can't honestly say that what Dad did was right."

"Listen to me, Mr. Self-righteous. If Robert had asked me to go with him, I would have taken a ball bat and helped him with those thugs," Emily answered defiantly.

Alex's eyes went wide, "What?"

"You heard me. I'd do whatever I had to do to keep the one's I love safe, and I count Mitchell as one of those that I love," Emily continued caustically.

"But Emily, beating those thugs didn't solve anything," Alex argued.

"Let me ask you something," Emily replied.

"Sure, go ahead," Alex answered.

"If it had been me who was beaten and gang-raped in that parking lot, and the animals who attacked me were set free because of a damn police error, and then those animals were waiting for me again in the same parking lot, to do God knows what to me, what would you do?" Emily asked angrily.

Before Alex had a chance to answer, the twins came out of their bedrooms and announced that they were ready for school. Emily smugly looked at Alex, "Think about that."

After Alex left with the twins, Emily went up to Robert's room to see how her best pals were getting along. As she gently knocked on the door, Robert quickly opened it, "Hi Em."

"Hi Robert, what's going on?" she asked as she looked around the room.

"I'm taking Mitch to the doctor," Robert answered.

"What's wrong?" Emily asked as she sat down on the bed where Mitchell was lying in his faded blue jeans, white button-down shirt, and running shoes.

"His fever hasn't gone down, even after the over-the-counter stuff the doctor suggested yesterday evening," Robert replied, the anxiety in his voice evident.

Emily touched Mitchell's forehead, "You are hot. How do you feel?" Emily asked with concern.

"Lousy," Mitchell replied.

"I called his doctor this morning, and he said to bring him right in," Robert explained.

"Is there anything I can do?" Emily asked.

"Can you stay with Mitch while I get the car?" Robert replied.

"Yeah, no problem," Emily responded.

While Robert was retrieving the car, Emily pulled Mitchell closer to her and held him in her arms like a mother holds a child. She gently kissed Mitchell on the forehead, "You're going to be okay."

Mitchell reached for Emily's hand and held it tightly, as if not wanting to let go, "I feel bad, Emily. I think this is more than a simple cold."

Emily, trying to hide her fear that Mitchell was right, replied, "Well, I'm sure your doctor will get you feeling better. Robert will make sure of that."

Mitchell laughed, but a spasm of pain in his chest stopped him, "You're right. Bobby will make sure I get better, even if it kills him."

Emily laughed, knowing that Robert would do everything humanly possible to make Mitchell feel better, even to the detriment of his own health. "Well, Mitchell, I'm going to make sure that you both are healthy and well when this is all over."

Mitchell brought Emily's hand to his lips and kissed it softly, "Thank you."

"No need to thank me, Mitchell. After all, that's what friends are for," Emily replied.

Mitchell painfully laughed again, "You're not going to break out in song now, are you?"

Emily tousled Mitchell's hair, "I thought Robert was the smart ass?"

"He is, but I'm learning from the master," Mitchell teased.

Emily laughed, "God help us. Two smart asses in the family."

Mitchell smiled at Emily, "I love you, Emily. You're the best friend I've ever had."

Emily hugged Mitchell and kissed him on the cheek, "I love you too, Mitchell."

Robert walked in the bedroom and smiled when he saw Mitchell and Emily embracing, "Are you ready to go, Mitch?" Robert asked softly.

"Yeah, I'm ready," Mitchell responded as Emily kissed him on the forehead.

Robert went to the bed and helped Mitchell to stand. Once Mitchell was upright, Robert placed his strong arm around Mitchell's back to support him. As they were nearing the hallway, Mitchell stopped briefly to catch his breath. He winked at Emily, "Thanks, Em."

Emily got on the other side of Mitchell and placed her arm around his back, slightly lower than where Robert's arm was placed, "You're going to be fine, Mitchell," Emily stated. "And, if you're good, maybe you'll get a lollipop," she teased.

Robert laughed, "Yeah, Mitch, maybe you'll get a lollipop from the doctor."

"He can give me anything he wants, just as long as he makes me feel better," Mitchell replied as Robert and Emily helped him into Robert's Jaguar.

After Mitchell was seat-belted in the car, Robert shut the passenger side door and faced Emily, "See you later."

Emily, hearing the fear in Robert's voice, tried to alleviate his anxiety, "He's going to be fine, Robert. He's a tough guy—just like you."

"I know he's a strong man, Em, but how much can one person take?" Robert asked fearfully.

"He'll be fine. Love is the strongest of medicines, and he has plenty of love," Emily stated sincerely.

"Thanks Em," Robert replied gratefully.

"If there's anything I can do," Emily stated before being interrupted.

"Pray," Robert instructed.

"I will," Emily answered. "I love you, Robert."
"I love you too, Emily," Robert replied as he got into his car and drove away.

# CHAPTER 42

▼

Around lunchtime, after replaying Emily's words over and over again in his mind, Alex left the office to go home. As he entered his father's stately mansion, Alex found the place eerily quiet. He searched various rooms on the ground level of the home, but no one was to be found. As he neared the family room, located by the kitchen, he heard noises and was glad to find Emily sitting in the family room watching her soap opera and eating a sandwich.

"Hi Em," Alex said.

Emily looked away briefly from her show, "What are you doing here?"

"I couldn't concentrate at work," Alex admitted.

Emily continued to watch her show as she instructed, "There's meat in the refrigerator if you want a sandwich."

"No, I'm fine," Alex replied. "Aren't you curious why I couldn't concentrate at work?"

"Not really, but if it'll get you to be quiet so that I can hear my show, go ahead and enlighten me," Emily said bitterly.

"I couldn't concentrate because I kept replaying our conversation over and over in my head," Alex explained.

"What conversation?" Emily asked impatiently.

Alex sat down opposite Emily as he continued, "The conversation we had this morning. The one which you said I should imagine you in Mitchell's place."

"And?" Emily asked.

"I was wrong to treat Dad the way I did, so that's why I came home early. I want to apologize to him," Alex explained sincerely.

"How very noble," Emily mocked. "You think that saying 'I'm sorry' will fix everything, but let me tell you something. You hurt Robert deeply, and your contrite apology isn't going to alleviate the pain that you caused him."

"I know I need to make up for my judgment of him. That's why I came home. I want to take that first step," Alex replied.

"Well then, you came home for nothing," Emily stated matter-of-factly.

Alex looked at Emily with a confused expression, "Why do you say that?"

"Your Dad's not home," Emily replied.

Caught off guard, Alex asked, "Where is he? Do you know?"

"Yes, I know where he's at," Emily answered sarcastically.

"Please tell me. I really need to talk to him," Alex pleaded.

Emily melted a bit as she answered, "He took Mitchell to the doctor this morning."

"I wasn't aware Mitchell had any appointments, at least not for the next few weeks," Alex stated.

"He didn't have an appointment. Mitchell wasn't feeling well yesterday afternoon, and this morning he was feeling worse, so Robert called Mitchell's doctor and took him in this morning," Emily explained.

"How long ago did they leave?" Alex asked as he looked at his watch.

"Right after you left with the kids," Emily replied.

"Em, that was four hours ago," Alex stated with growing concern.

Emily nodded, "I know."

As Alex and Emily talked in the family room, Emily heard a noise coming from the front door. "I think they're back," she told Alex. "I don't want you to confront your Dad until I see if he's in the right frame of mind to deal with it, you understand?"

"Yeah, I understand," Alex replied a bit annoyed.

Emily and Alex walked out through the hallway and stopped near the living room when they saw the door come open. The image before them made them seriously concerned. Robert had Mitchell in his arms carrying him, along with a small tank of oxygen hung over his shoulder. Mitchell, barely conscious, had a full oxygen mask covering his nose and mouth. As Robert kicked the front door shut behind him, Mitchell awakened suddenly with a fright, but Robert eased his mind, "It's okay, honey. We're home now."

"I'm sorry I'm so sleepy, Bobby," Mitchell said weakly.

"Shhhhhhh, it's okay, Mitch. The doctor said that the medicine would make you sleepy. Plus, it means it's working if you're sleepy," Robert explained tenderly as he carried Mitchell toward the stairs.

Emily gently pushed Alex into the study so that Robert would not see either of them. "Stay out of sight, Alex. The last thing your father needs right now is to see you," Emily stated with great concern.

The fear in Alex's eyes penetrated Emily's soul, "Em, what's wrong with Mitchell?"

"I don't know," Emily replied in a shaky voice, "But I'm going to find out." Alex followed Emily out of the study and through the hallway to the stairs. Emily turned to Alex, "I think you better stay out of sight."

"I will," Alex replied.

Emily climbed the stairs and quickly went to Robert's bedroom. The door was left open, and she peeked inside. Robert had Mitchell in his arms as he walked to the side of the bed, "Honey, do you want to lay on your side or propped up?"

Mitchell answered groggily, "On my side."

Robert gently laid Mitchell on the bed on his side. Robert took the portable oxygen tank off of his shoulder and sat it next to the bed. "Are you comfortable like that on your side?" Robert asked tenderly.

Mitchell nodded groggily, "Yeah."

Robert kissed Mitchell on the forehead as he started to unbutton his jeans. Robert carefully pulled Mitchell's jeans off and unbuttoned his shirt. With Mitchell only in his underwear and socks, Robert went to the dresser and pulled out a pair of flannel pants and a tee shirt. Robert very carefully dressed Mitchell and then lifted him to put him under the blankets. To make sure that Mitchell did not accidentally role over onto his back, Robert stacked the other bed pillows behind Mitchell's back. As Robert sat gently beside Mitchell on the bed, Robert glanced over and noticed Emily standing in the doorway.

Robert gingerly stood so as not to disturb Mitchell's rest, and went quickly to the door. As he approached Emily, she opened her arms and they embraced each other desperately. Alex witnessed the embrace, but he was carefully concealed so that his father would not see him. As Robert slowly backed out of the embrace, Emily saw the fear in his eyes, "Robert, what's wrong with Mitchell?"

Robert closed his eyes tightly for a brief moment before answering, "He has pneumonia."

The tears welled up in Emily's eyes, "What?"

"He has pneumonia, Em," Robert said sadly.

"That's terribly serious, isn't it?" Emily asked as the tears flowed down her cheeks.

Robert hugged Emily as he responded, "The doctor said that it could kill him."

Emily broke down and cried in Robert arms, "He can't die, Robert."

Robert held Emily as she cried, and then he addressed her, "He's not going to die, Em. He can't. I told him that we are going to get through this together." Robert touched Emily softly on the cheek, "I told him that this is going to be the hardest battle of our lives, but we can get through it together if he fights and doesn't give up."

"He can't give up, Robert," Emily replied.

"He won't Em. Not as long as we keep things positive. We have to believe that he's going to get better, no matter what." Robert paused a moment to collect his thoughts, "Can you do that?"

As tears continued to flow down Emily's face, she replied emotionally, "Yeah, I'll do anything to make him better."

"Good," Robert replied as he hugged Emily.

"Is there anything I can do?" Emily asked.

"As a matter of fact, yes there is. The pharmacy is going to deliver some medication this afternoon. Can you sign for it for me? It's already paid for. All you have to do is sign for it."

"Yeah, that's no problem," Emily replied.

"Good. I don't know what I'd do without you, Em," Robert stated tiredly.

"I'll do anything in this world for you and Mitchell," Emily stated as she looked into Robert's tired eyes.

"I know you would, and that means the world to both of us," Robert explained.

"You look exhausted, Robert. Why don't you go lie down next to Mitchell and rest for awhile?" Emily instructed.

"I'm fine, Em," Robert replied.

"No, you're not. You look like you're ready to fall over." Emily paused. "Robert, Mitchell needs you, and if you don't take care of yourself, how will you be able to help him?"

Robert closed his eyes and acquiesced, "You're right. A little nap would help."

"Good. Now if you need me, just hit the intercom, okay?" Emily stated.

"I will. Thanks Emily," Robert said as he kissed Emily on the cheek.

"I'll bring the medicine up whenever it gets here," Emily replied.

"Okay," Robert answered.

"Robert," Emily said as Robert was walking back into the bedroom. "He's going to be okay. He has too many people who love him and need him, and I know Mitchell won't let us down."

Robert wiped away a stray tear, "Thanks Emily."

Emily walked dumbfounded down the hallway when an arm reached out and pulled her into another bedroom, "What's going on, Em?" Alex asked hurriedly.

Emily took a moment to try to clear her head, "Mitchell is quite ill."

"What's wrong with him?" Alex asked impatiently.

Emily stared harshly at Alex, "He has pneumonia."

"Oh," Alex said relieved. "That's not too bad."

Emily snapped, "No, it's not too bad, Einstein. It can only kill him."

Alex's eyes grew wide, "What?"

"It can kill him. The doctor informed him of the severity, and he told Mitchell that it could be fatal," Emily replied as tears formed in her eyes at the thought of losing Mitchell.

"I had no idea," Alex responded sincerely, serving only to anger Emily.

"This news should make your day. You wanted Mitchell out of your Dad's life, and now you may just get your wish," she said with hostility.

Alex took Emily's hands in his as he spoke, "I don't want Mitchell to die either. What can we do?"

"WE," Emily emphasized, "Can't do anything." She glared at Alex for a moment before continuing, "I'll help however I can." Emily pulled her hands away as she added, "Stay away from your Dad. The last thing he needs to deal with right now is you."

# CHAPTER 43

▼

As Alex wondered aimlessly around the lower level of his Dad's stately home, he kept replaying in his mind the scene of Robert carrying Mitchell through the front door and the sound of fear in his wife's voice as she informed him of Mitchell's condition.

Alex walked over to the sliding door that led out toward the pool and sat down. The thought of Mitchell dying was causing his knees to give out on him. "How could they think that I want Mitchell to die?" he asked himself. Granted, he thought, up until that morning and his eye-opening conversation with Emily, he did believe that Robert was better off without Mitchell, but that had nothing to do with Mitchell. Alex finally accepted that it was because of his deep-rooted homophobia. Alex hung his head, "I don't want him to die."

As the full impact of what was happening descended upon him, Alex decided he had to do something. "I just can't sit here and let him die," Alex said to himself sadly. As he was heading toward the living room, with hopes of finding Emily, he heard the doorbell ring. Going to the main door, Alex saw that Emily had beaten him to it. He stood and watched as a pharmacy deliveryman handed Emily a large bag of medication and waited for her signature. After signing, Emily saw Alex and asked him to hold the bag for a moment. As he and the deliveryman waited for her to return, Alex looked inside at the various medications and took a mental inventory of the names of the prescriptions. Emily returned quickly and handed the deliveryman a twenty dollar bill and thanked him.

Closing the door gently, Emily turned and took the bag of medications from Alex. Alex put his hand on her shoulder to briefly stop her, "I have to go back to the office for a little while, and then I'll pick up the kids from school."

Emily nodded, "Thank you."

"Em," Alex said as he looked sincerely into her eyes. "I don't want Mitchell to die."

Emily melted slightly, "I genuinely hope you mean that."

"I do," Alex replied. "If anyone needs me for anything, call me on my cell phone. I'll help anyway I can."

"Thanks Alex," Emily responded.

"I'll do whatever I can, and I promise I'll stay away from Dad," Alex informed.

"It's for the best," Emily replied as she turned and headed for the stairs.

✴     ✴     ✴     ✴

Alex's car just seemed to automatically steer in the direction he needed to go. Within a half an hour, Alex was walking through the revolving doors of the hospital. A few moments later, he was standing outside the very familiar office. In a daze-like state, Alex pushed the office door open and went to the receptionist's window.

"I need to see Dr. Hamilton right away," Alex stated.

"Oh," the receptionist replied as she saw Alex and recognized him. "Hi, Mr. Petrovic. How are you?"

Alex anxiously repeated, "I need to see Dr. Hamilton. Tell him it's urgent."

As the receptionist was about to pick up the phone to buzz the doctor, Dr. Hamilton appeared in the hallway outside his office door. When he saw Alex, he could tell something was wrong, "What's going on, Alex?"

Alex mumbled anxiously, "Mitchell's dying."

Dr. Hamilton frowned as he came around to escort Alex into his office, "What did you say?"

Alex reiterated, "Mitchell's dying."

Dr. Hamilton guided Alex over to a chair in his private office and had him sit. "Alex," the doctor said, "I just saw Mitchell a few days ago and he was fine then, or at least he looked fine."

"I know, Doc. The last time I saw him was the same time you did, but he's really sick now and I'm afraid he's going to die," Alex explained sadly.

"What's supposed to be wrong with him?" Dr. Hamilton asked skeptically.

Alex closed his eyes tightly, as if doing so would change reality, "He has pneumonia."

Dr. Hamilton could not conceal his shock, "What? Do you know for sure?"

"Yeah, I know for sure. Emily told me after we saw Dad carrying Mitchell through the front door. Mitchell's doctor told him he has pneumonia, and that it could be fatal."

Dr. Hamilton tried to hide his sadness and concern, "Tell me what happened—from the beginning."

Alex took a deep breath and complied, "Like I said, I hadn't seen Mitchell, or Dad for that matter, since our blow-up the other night. I was smug in my self-righteousness, but Emily finally brought me down to Earth."

"How'd she do that?" the doctor inquired.

"Well, after a few days of the cold shoulder, and no adult communication from anyone in the house, I began to worry. Not about whether I was right, for I felt that I was, but worry about whether I could lose my family over such a thing," Alex explained.

"Being totally selfish?" the doctor said rhetorically.

"Yes, I was being selfish, but then I genuinely began to worry about Dad, so I asked Emily if he was okay, but she went off on me as usual."

"Can you understand why she felt that way?" Dr. Hamilton asked.

"I can now. After a few more times of knocking me down, Emily made me think about something, and it was then that I realized how wrong I was and have been," Alex stated.

"What did she make you think about?" Dr. Hamilton inquired.

Alex looked at the doctor sadly, "She had me substitute her for Mitchell in everything that happened to him."

Dr. Hamilton nodded, "And you finally saw things from Robert's perspective."

"Yeah, and I hated myself for the way I treated him, so I left early from work to go home to apologize to Dad and beg for his forgiveness, but he wasn't home."

"He had taken Mitchell to see his doctor?" the doctor interjected.

"Yes. Emily said that Mitchell hadn't been feeling well yesterday, and this morning he was worse, so Dad called his doctor and took him in," Alex answered.

"And he was diagnosed with pneumonia?" Dr. Hamilton asked again for clarification.

"Yes," Alex replied sadly. "The pharmacy delivered several medications before I left. I remembered the names."

"What are they?" Dr. Hamilton asked.

"Give me a piece of paper and I'll write them down. I can't pronounce them," Alex replied.

Dr. Hamilton handed Alex a small notepad and Alex scribbled the names on the notepad and handed it back to the doctor. Dr. Hamilton looked at the names of the medications and responded optimistically, "These are the strongest drugs on the market. His doctor seems to be treating him aggressively."

"Will those drugs make him better?" Alex asked solemnly.

"They should. They're the best available," Dr. Hamilton answered.

"Which means if they don't work, there's nothing better to give him?" Alex asked rhetorically. Sadly he already knew the answer.

"You have to think positively, Alex," Dr. Hamilton advised.

"How do I do that? Emily is distraught, and I can only imagine what Dad is going through right now."

"Can you?" Dr. Hamilton asked.

"Yes Doc, I finally get it that Dad loves Mitchell. The thing that scares me to death is what is going to happen to Dad if Mitchell doesn't make it?"

"Let's just hope that it doesn't get to that point," Dr. Hamilton replied.

"Would you talk to Dad and see how he's doing?" Alex asked.

"I could stop out in a few days. Right now, Alex, I think he needs to focus on Mitchell, and Mitchell alone. If I went to see him today, he wouldn't see me. And worse yet, he'd probably throw me out," Dr. Hamilton explained.

"Damn," Alex replied. "I feel so helpless. What can I do to help?" Alex asked, hoping for some useful wisdom from the doctor.

"To start with, stay away from your Dad. The last thing he needs is to be reminded of what happened between the two of you," Dr. Hamilton instructed.

"I will. Emily already told me the same thing," Alex answered.

"The other thing that you can do, and it's an important thing, is to be there for Emily. You need to be her support system. I know that Robert is taking care of Mitchell, but I also know that he and Mitchell rely on Emily. If you can keep Emily strong and focused, it will allow her to support Robert in his care of Mitchell. Do you understand what I'm saying?" Dr. Hamilton asked.

"Yes, I understand. I'll do whatever it takes," Alex replied sincerely.

"Good. In a few days I'll stop out and try to get your Dad to talk to me," Dr. Hamilton offered.

"Doc," Alex paused. "It's never been personal with Mitchell. It was just my homophobia."

"Has that changed?" Dr. Hamilton asked skeptically.

"Yes. To be honest with you, I like Mitchell," Alex answered truthfully.

"Good. Make sure you remember that when he gets well," Dr. Hamilton instructed.

"I will," Alex replied. "Thanks for everything, Doc."

"No problem. I'll be here if anyone needs me," Dr. Hamilton responded sincerely.

Alex got up and walked toward the door, "Bye Doc. Thanks again."

"Bye Alex. I'll pray for Mitchell," Dr. Hamilton added.

"Thanks."

# CHAPTER 44

▼

Four days passed and Mitchell slowly began to feel better. His fever broke the day after he visited the doctor, and Robert was there every second to take care of him. As Mitchell awoke to the bright sunlight coming through the large window in their bedroom, he noticed Robert sitting on the sofa absently staring out the window. Mitchell sat up slowly in bed, and with a gruff voice he spoke to Robert, "Good morning."

Robert instantly smiled when he heard Mitchell's voice, "Good morning. How are you feeling?"

"I'm not sure," Mitchell replied with a hint of mischief. "I haven't been up long enough to know."

Robert came over and sat down on the bed beside him, "You're looking better."

"Thanks," Mitchell replied.

"Can I get you anything?" Robert asked as he leaned over and kissed Mitchell on the cheek.

"Not right now, but there is something you can do for me," Mitchell replied.

Robert smiled, "Anything. Your wish is my command."

"Good. I'm glad you feel that way because I want you to go outside today, or at least out of this room," Mitchell said seriously.

Robert stared at Mitchell with a slightly hurt expression, "Why? Are you getting tired of having me around?"

Mitchell took Robert's hand and brought it to his lips and kissed it, "No, not at all, but you've been looking after me twenty-four hours a day for the past four days. I know you need a break."

"I'm fine, Mitch," Robert replied as he continued to hold Mitchell's hand.

"Honey, it's a beautiful day, and you've been stuck inside for too long. Please just go and take a break from it all. Go for a run, or take Sebastian for some exercise, okay?" Mitchell responded matter-of-factly.

"I'm not going to leave you here alone," Robert responded sternly, but lovingly.

Mitchell smiled, "I'm sure if I ask Emily she'll come up and sit with me for awhile. Would that ease your mind?"

Robert reluctantly replied, "Well ... I guess so."

"So you'll take a break later today?" Mitchell asked hopefully.

Robert nodded, "As long as Emily stays with you."

Mitchell pulled Robert close and kissed him tenderly on the cheek, "Thank you, Bobby." Mitchell paused a moment, "You know ... I worry about you too."

Robert winked, "I know you do, and I love you for it."

"I love you too," Mitchell said softly. "Would you call Emily on the intercom and see if she can come up and see us for a minute so that I can ask her?"

Robert leaned over and kissed Mitchell on the forehead, "Sure."

Robert walked over to the phone by the sofa and started pushing the buttons to the various rooms that he thought Emily might be in. When he spoke into the intercom that was connected in the kitchen, he got a response, "She's in the living room, Dad."

Robert unemotionally replied, "Thank you." When he pushed the intercom for the living room, he got the voice for which he was hoping.

"Good morning, Robert." Emily replied amiably. "Everything okay?"

"Yes, everything's fine, but can you stop up when you get a free minute?" Robert asked.

Emily quickly replied, "I'm on my way."

Within a few minutes Emily was knocking on Robert and Mitchell's bedroom door. When Robert opened the door, Emily characteristically smiled and hugged him affectionately. She walked in and went over and kissed Mitchell on the cheek. As she sat down on the bed beside Mitchell, Robert joined her by sitting at the bottom of the bed.

"What's up, guys?" Emily asked optimistically after seeing that Mitchell was looking better than the day before.

Mitchell asked sincerely, "Could you spare about an hour this afternoon to sit with me?"

"Sure, no problem," Emily replied with a smile.

"He's kicking me out this afternoon with instructions to go outside," Robert replied as Emily laughed.

Mitchell shook his head slightly and smiled, "I'm not kicking you out, Bobby. I just made a request, and you accepted."

Robert laughed, "A request that I was intimidated into accepting."

They all shared a well deserved and long overdue laugh together. Mitchell still was not completely out of danger, but his prognosis was getting better. Robert was overprotective, but Mitchell felt like he needed to be a little overprotective as well when it came to Robert.

"What time did you have in mind?" Emily asked.

"Whenever you decide," Mitchell replied.

"Well, I have to drop the kids off at their friend's house around noon, and then I'll have the entire afternoon."

"That sounds great," Mitchell replied.

Robert winked at Emily as he teased Mitchell, "Nothing like trying to get rid of me. You really make me feel wanted."

"Awwwww," Mitchell cooed as he opened his arms as an invitation for Robert to hug him. "I love you, Bobby, but you need to get out of this damn room for awhile."

Emily laughed as she watched Robert and Mitchell playfully embrace, "I think he's right, Robert."

Robert looked down in mock defeat, "Well then, I guess I'll go. No use arguing with the two of you."

Emily playfully pulled Robert toward her and hugged him, "I love you too, and I think Mitchell's right, so go this afternoon and relax."

Robert kissed Emily on the cheek, "Yes Ma'am."

$$\ast \qquad \ast \qquad \ast \qquad \ast$$

Alex conspicuously tried to look busy as he waited for Emily to return from Robert's bedroom. He did not want to look overly anxious, but he desperately wanted to know why Robert was looking for Emily. Alex's first thought was that something bad had happened to Mitchell, but he quickly dismissed that recurring obtrusive thought. After all, Robert did not sound worried or panicked when he called on the intercom. As Alex was trying to figure out what was going on, Emily walked into the room. "Where are the kids?" she asked amiably.

Alex, relieved at her demeanor, answered with a smile, "They're playing videogames." He paused a moment to hide his anxiousness, "Did Dad find you?"

Surprised, Emily responded, "Yes, he did. How did you know he was looking for me?"

"He called on the intercom, and I told him you were in the living room," Alex answered honestly. "Is everything okay?"

"Everything's fine. Mitchell just wanted to know if I could sit with him sometime this afternoon," Emily explained.

Alex became visibly alarmed, "Why? Isn't Dad feeling well?"

"Robert is fine. Mitchell just thought that it would do him good to go outside for a little while today," Emily replied.

"Oh," Alex responded with relief before asking, "Is Dad going to do it?"

"Do what? Go outside?" Emily asked.

"Yeah."

Emily smiled as she remembered Mitchell and Robert playfully hugging on the bed, "Yes, your Dad agreed, but only after Mitchell and I strong-armed him."

Alex stared at Emily strangely until Emily burst out laughing, causing Alex to break out in laughter as well. The thought of anyone strong-arming Robert had them both in fits of laughter. As they had learned only a few days prior, Robert could hold his own with anyone, and even with more than one.

About an hour later Alex again waited anxiously for Emily, but this time for her to leave. After watching her car disappear through the front gate, Alex sprinted into the study and locked the door behind him. He quickly picked up the telephone and started dialing. When he heard the voice on the other end of the line, he smiled with relief. "Hi Doc, this is Alex Petrovic," Alex said calmly.

"Hi Alex, how are you?" the doctor asked.

"I'm fine. I hope I'm not bothering you?" Alex asked.

"Of course not. What can I do for you?" Dr. Hamilton inquired.

Alex closed his eyes and took a deep breath before continuing, "Would it be possible for you to come out to the house in about an hour or so?"

"Did something happen? Are Robert and Mitchell okay?" Dr. Hamilton asked with great concern.

"Nothing bad happened. Actually I'm hoping something positive can be gained today," Alex replied.

"Okay, you've lost me," the doctor responded with a low laugh. "What's going on?"

Alex explained, "Mitchell asked Emily if she could sit with him this afternoon so that Dad could go outside and relax for awhile. From what I gathered, this wasn't Dad's idea, but he agreed, so I was hoping you could drop by and talk with him."

"Just an impromptu visit to say hello?" Dr. Hamilton asked rhetorically.

Alex laughed, "Yeah, something like that."

Dr. Hamilton asked, "What time?"

"Well, Emily just left to drop the kids off in town, so she won't be back for at least an hour," Alex explained as he looked at his watch. "It's noon now, so how about 1:30?"

"I can do that," the doctor replied.

"Thank you so much," Alex responded gratefully. "I'll be waiting for you."

"Alex," the doctor continued, "Try not to set your hopes too high about what may come out of my visit."

"It can't hurt, so I'm optimistic," Alex offered.

"Okay then. I'll see you at 1:30," the doctor replied.

"Thanks again, Doc. I'll see you soon."

✳     ✳     ✳     ✳

When Emily returned from dropping off the children, she immediately went to Robert and Mitchell's room, where she found Mitchell lying on the bed, and Robert sitting anxiously on the sofa in his jogging shorts and his running shoes. She went over and draped her arms around Robert's neck and hugged him.

Robert sighed, "I guess my reprieve is up."

"You know we're only doing this for your own good," Emily said with a laugh.

Mitchell rolled over slowly to face Robert and Emily, "She's right, Bobby."

"How come I'm feeling like I'm only five years old?" Robert said with a grin.

"Sometimes even big boys need to be looked after," Emily answered.

Mitchell laughed, "That's true, and for today you need to get some fresh air."

Robert stood up and kissed Emily softly on the cheek before going over to the bed to sit beside Mitchell. He leaned down and tenderly kissed Mitchell on the lips. As he pulled away, Robert smiled mischievously, "Well, I guess it's time for this five year old to go outside to find some trouble."

Emily winked at Robert, "Behave yourself."

Mitchell caught Robert's hand as Robert was about to leave, "I love you, Bobby."

"I love you too," Robert replied.

"Have a good time," Mitchell added as Robert walked toward the door.

# CHAPTER 45

▼

After a long, invigorating run that meandered along the pond and through the lush row of trees, Robert returned to the house. With a rejuvenated spirit flowing through his veins, Robert decided to continue his workout in the gym.

Robert pushed his limits and was feeling great as he mentally made a note to thank Mitchell for insisting on this free time. After pulling on his sparring gloves and pushing the play button on the CD stereo in the gym, Robert started punching the heavy bag. When a high tempo song began to play, Robert increased the intensity as he punched and kicked the bag as if it were a person. After landing a particularly hard spinning roundhouse kick, Robert detected motion out of the corner of his eye. He turned around to see what was there, and he glared angrily at what he saw standing in the doorway. Robert continued his sparring workout without uttering a word.

"Hello Robert," the man in the doorway said.

Robert punched the bag with a variety of combinations without looking away, "What are you doing here, doctor?"

"I was in the neighborhood, so I thought I'd drop by to see how you're doing," Dr. Hamilton replied.

Robert punched the bag again before turning toward Dr. Hamilton. "Really," he said sarcastically. "Now why don't you tell me the truth?"

"What makes you think I'm lying?" Dr. Hamilton asked.

Annoyed, Robert replied, "Don't try to play your mind games on me."

"I'm not playing any mind games, Robert. I'm just concerned about you," Dr. Hamilton said sincerely.

Robert spun around and kicked the bag fiercely, "If you're concerned about anyone, it should be for Mitchell, not me."

"I'm concerned about you both," Dr. Hamilton admitted.

Robert punched the bag a few more times before asking sarcastically, "So how did you know I'd be alone this afternoon?"

Dr. Hamilton asked, "Does it matter?"

"No," Robert replied before adding, "Because I have nothing to say to you."

"That's your decision, but I'd like to know why?" Dr. Hamilton responded.

Robert started to pull off his sparring gloves as he sarcastically replied, "This was supposed to be a relaxing afternoon."

"Talk to me, Robert," Dr. Hamilton gently implored.

Robert turned off the stereo and headed for the door, "I have to check on Mitch."

"Robert!" Dr. Hamilton said sternly.

Robert turned and stared the doctor down, "What the hell do you want from me?"

Dr. Hamilton spoke more softly, "I want you to talk to me."

"I already told you. I have nothing to say to you," Robert replied forcefully.

"Please Robert. I see all these stressful things happening to you, and I see you carrying that stress on your shoulders, and the last time you had those burdens, you tried to end your life," the doctor explained.

Robert shook his head from side to side in angry disbelief, "So that's it? You think I'm going to off myself?"

"Are you?" the doctor asked.

Robert glared at Dr. Hamilton, "You don't know a damn thing about me."

"I just asked a simple question," the doctor responded.

Robert walked to the door, "Fine. You want an answer. NO. I have no intentions of killing myself."

"I'm glad to hear that," Dr. Hamilton replied with obvious relief.

"Good. Now you can show yourself out," Robert stated caustically as he walked out of the gym.

✳     ✳     ✳     ✳

Robert involuntarily stomped through the hallway on the way to his bedroom as the anger coursed through his veins like molten lava. As he came to stand outside the bedroom door, Robert leaned back heavily against the wall as he tried to calm himself. "Damn him," Robert said silently to himself. After a few deep breaths, Robert opened the door to the bedroom and walked in.

Mitchell, being able to read Robert better than anyone, instantly knew that something was wrong. "Bobby, what's wrong?"

Trying to smile through his anger, Robert replied stoically, "Nothing's wrong. I had a great run."

Mitchell sat up in bed and motioned Robert to come join him on the bed, but Robert walked toward the bathroom as he added, "I need to take a shower."

Unwilling to let things go, Mitchell threw his legs over the edge of the bed and was about to stand up when Robert swooped over and gently placed him back in bed as he reprimanded, "What do you think you're doing getting out of bed? You know your doctor's orders."

"Fuck my doctor's orders," Mitchell said strongly.

Completely in the dark about what was happening between Robert and Mitchell, Emily stepped in, "What's going on?"

"Nothing," Robert added quickly.

"The hell there isn't," Emily replied. "I've never heard Mitchell use such language, and I'm pretty damn sure that something provoked it."

"You're right Emily," Mitchell replied as his breathing began to become labored. "Something happened this afternoon—something that upset Bobby, but he's trying to hide it."

Seeing Mitchell's growing breathing difficulties, Robert put the full mask oxygen gently over Mitchell's nose and mouth, and turned the oxygen up to an appropriate level. Robert did not want to upset Mitchell by telling him about his encounter with Dr. Hamilton, but Robert had no idea that Mitchell would get this upset by his reluctance to elaborate about the afternoon. Robert gently helped Mitchell lie back against the pillows that Emily instinctively stacked up behind him while Robert administered the oxygen.

"Lie back and relax, Honey. Let the oxygen help," Robert instructed.

Mitchell did as Robert instructed, but he reached over and took Robert's hand and held it firmly while he implored him for the truth with his eyes.

"I'm okay, Mitch. I had a wonderful time outside," Robert explained.

Emily sat down next to Mitchell on the bed opposite Robert. For Mitchell to react so strongly, Emily believed that his instincts were right and something did happen earlier while Robert was enjoying his free time. She smiled sadly at Robert before asking, "Did Alex do something to upset you?"

"What makes you think that?" Robert questioned.

"Because I trust Mitchell's instincts that something happened earlier," Emily explained calmly.

Robert stood up and was about to launch into an angry defense, but his anger dissipated when he looked at Emily and Mitchell's faces. All he saw in their eyes were love and concern. Robert took a deep breath and sat back down. "I'm sorry," Robert said sadly as he looked deeply into each of their eyes.

Emily reached over and took Robert's hand, "What happened?"

Mitchell gently took Robert's other hand and held it lovingly, "Bobby?"

Robert pulled his hand away for a second and held up his finger to Mitchell to stop him from speaking, "Shhhhh, Honey. Save your breath." Robert paused for a moment to collect his thoughts. "Something did happen downstairs, but I didn't want … I didn't know …" Robert searched for his words before just saying what happened. "Dr. Hamilton showed up while I was working out in the gym."

"How did he know you'd be alone in the gym?" Emily asked before she realized the answer. "Damn him!" Emily added.

"What did he …?" Mitchell tried to ask through the oxygen mask before Robert finished the question for him.

"What did he want?" Robert repeated. "He thinks I'm going to try to kill myself," Robert angrily answered.

"What?" Mitchell and Emily responded at the same time.

"Yeah, he sees the stress I'm under and he thinks I'm going to end it all," Robert explained sarcastically. "Just goes to show how well he knows me."

Emily walked over to Robert and hugged him, "I am so sorry, Robert. I had no idea Alex would stoop this low."

Robert affectionately embraced Emily, "It's okay, Em. I didn't want to say anything because I didn't want to upset either of you, but now I've gone and done just that. I'm the one who's sorry."

"Bobby," Mitchell mumbled through the oxygen mask.

"Yeah, honey," Robert said warmly as he sat back down next to Mitchell.

"It's okay to be upset. Just don't keep us in the dark, okay? We both love you, and we both know you're not going to try to commit suicide," Mitchell explained as he lifted the oxygen mask from his nose and mouth so that Robert could hear and understand him.

"I love both of you too," Robert replied as he gently replaced Mitchell's oxygen mask back over Mitchell's nose and mouth. "I know you both believe in me, and that's all I need. I'm just sorry that I upset you both."

Emily smiled broadly as she winked at Mitchell, "It's okay Robert. We're tough. We can take it!"

All three of them laughed as they embraced each other in a group hug on the bed.

Mitchell teasingly pulled slightly back from the group hug and remarked with a sly grin, "Honey, I think maybe you should hit the shower."

Robert tapped Mitchell on the head playfully, "You're a genius, Mitch. I never would have thought of that on my own."

"Glad I can help," Mitchell added as he laid back against his pillows.

"Now that's what I like to hear! My two best friends teasing each other," Emily offered with a bright smile.

"Here," Robert said as he put Mitchell's oxygen mask back on him properly. "Emily, can you stick around for a few more minutes?"

"Certainly," Emily replied as she sat back down beside Mitchell on the bed. "Go take a long, relaxing shower."

"Yeah," Mitchell mumbled through the mask. He was about to continue until Robert put his index finger to Mitchell's oxygen mask.

Robert pulled out some casual clothing and disappeared into the bathroom. As he was undressing, the anger started to return as he remembered the day's events. Robert turned the water on and stood in the middle of the six different spray jets, as the anger bubbled up all over again.

Robert closed his eyes and tried to relax with the hot water cascading down over his head and all areas of his body, but the anger would not vanish. As the sound and vision of Mitchell struggling to breath crept into his head, Robert knew he had to do something. Anything. Mitchell was priority number one, and Robert was not about to allow anyone to derail his care of the man he loved.

Robert leaned heavily against the shower wall as he allowed his mind to wonder. Suddenly his mahogany eyes popped open. A plan was born.

# CHAPTER 46

▼

Later in the evening, after snuggling together to watch the news, Robert tucked Mitchell into bed and gave him his medication. Within a few minutes, Mitchell was sleeping soundly. Robert stayed beside Mitchell in the bed for a few more moments, and then it was time to put his plan into action.

Robert took a medium-size black duffel bag out of his closet and started to pack some essentials. He quickly filled it with his and Mitchell's socks, tee shirts and underwear. After the duffel bag was filled, Robert pulled out a small Pullman suitcase. He scavenged through his closet for shorts, swim trunks and polo shirts. Mitchell had swim trunks and polo shirts at Robert's, but Robert was going to have to go to Mitchell's condo to pick up some shorts, especially since Mitchell lost weight. After neatly folding his clothing, Robert packed all he and Mitchell would need from the bathroom. Throwing in a spare pair of Raybans and a baseball hat, Robert zipped the Pullman shut and wheeled it quietly to the door.

After midnight, Robert opened the bedroom door and checked the hallway for any movement. Satisfied that everyone was in bed and soundly sleeping, Robert threw the duffel bag over his shoulder and quietly pushed the Pullman through the hallway and down the stairs. He took a set of keys out of his pocket and unlocked an inconspicuous closet off the study. Dropping the duffel bag and setting aside the Pullman, Robert quickly closed the closet door and locked it. Satisfied that no one heard him, Robert returned to bed with a determined attitude.

After awakening early in the morning, Mitchell groaned as he looked at the desktop calendar beside the bed.

Robert rolled over and smiled, "Someone seems grumpy this morning."

Mitchell nodded as he wiped the sleep from his eyes, "Yeah, I forgot about the damn doctor's appointment this morning."

Robert softly ran his fingers through Mitchell's hair, "It's not until eleven, so why don't you try to go back to sleep for awhile?"

Mitchell frowned, "I'll never be able to fall back asleep now. Especially knowing that I have to get another shot today."

"Another one today and then you should be done with them," Robert explained.

"I hope so. My ass is still bruised from the last time," Mitchell added grumpily.

"I think you'll be done with them. You're looking a hundred percent better," Robert replied as he leaned over and kissed Mitchell's forehead.

"I feel a hundred percent better as well," Mitchell added.

"That's great Honey, but we're still going to tell your doctor about your trouble breathing yesterday."

Mitchell started to pout, "Do we have to?"

Robert firmly answered, "Yes."

"Why?" Mitchell asked in a semi-whine.

"Because we're not taking any chances with your health," Robert answered.

Mitchell tried to reason with Robert, "But yesterday was just a fluke. It was because I was upset."

"Regardless of why it happened, it happened, and we're telling the doctor about it," Robert replied firmly.

"Damn," Mitchell responded in concession.

Robert pulled Mitchell close and kissed him gently on the lips, "I'm never going to lose you, Honey. I love you more than life itself, so I'm not going to take chances or short cuts on your health, okay?"

Mitchell nodded and snuggled against Robert's muscular chest, "You're never going to lose me, Bobby. You're my reason for living."

Robert closed his eyes and savored the moment of having Mitchell holding him tight. "We got through this, Sweetie. Together we can get through anything."

Mitchell squeezed Robert a little tighter as he whispered, "Always and forever."

"Always and forever," Robert repeated softly as he heard Mitchell starting to cry softly. "What's wrong, Sweetie?"

Mitchell buried his head in Robert's chest as his emotions spilled out, "I was so scared, Bobby."

Robert blinked back a tear, "I was scared too, Mitch, but I knew you'd be okay."

"How'd you know?" Mitchell asked as he looked up at Robert with eyes brimming with tears.

"Because I know deep down you are a fighter, and you promised me that we would fight this battle together, and we did. I know it would've been so much easier and a lot less painful for you to give up, but you fought for us, Sweetie, and I have never been prouder in my life," Robert explained emotionally.

Mitchell embraced Robert as the tears cascaded down his battered face, "Thank you, Bobby."

"No, Mitch. Thank you," Robert whispered as a single tear trickled down his unshaven face.

After lying in each other's arms for quite some time, Robert rolled over and looked at the clock. "I'm going to take a shower. Do you want something to drink before I go?"

Mitchell smiled, "No, I'm fine. Hurry back, okay?"

A mischievous smile crept onto Robert's handsome face, "You know, you're going to need a shower too."

Before Mitchell could say anything, Robert had him in his arms carrying him to the bathroom. Mitchell playfully asked, "What are you doing?"

Robert laughed merrily, "Conserving water!"

# CHAPTER 47

▼

After showering and putting Mitchell temporarily back to bed, Robert dressed quickly and looked at his watch. It was still early and he was still on schedule.

"Where are you running off to?" Mitchell asked amiably.

"I have to take care of something important," Robert answered as he leaned down and kissed Mitchell on the cheek. "I won't be long, and I'll tell you all about it later, okay?"

"Okay, but Emily can't stay with me too long this morning, remember?" Mitchell asked before continuing. "She has a meeting at the kids' school."

"Yeah, I remember," Robert replied. "I'll be back before she has to leave." Robert picked up the phone and hit the intercom, and Emily answered almost immediately. Within a few minutes, Emily was at Robert and Mitchell's bedroom door.

Robert opened the door and Emily characteristically hugged him and then moved on to hug Mitchell as he was lying in bed. "What can I do for my best buddies today?" she asked warmly.

"Can you stay with Mitch for a little while?" Robert asked.

Emily pretended to study Robert's appearance, "You're looking rather dapper this morning."

Mitchell chimed in grinning, "My man *is* looking debonair this morning, isn't he?"

Robert looked away, embarrassed. He was just dressed in his normal clothing. Nothing he considered special.

Emily stopped the teasing as she replied, "Of course I can stay with Mitchell, but I have to leave about ten thirty."

"I know. The kids have their track and field day today," Robert replied. "I won't be long."

"That's fine," Emily replied. "So, where are you running off to so early in the morning dressed so handsomely?"

Robert blushed at the compliment, "I just have to take care of some business." Robert added, "By the way, tell the kids 'good luck' at the events today."

"I will," Emily replied.

"Do they understand why we haven't been able to see them?" Robert asked.

"They understand. They know that Mr. Mitch is sick and that you have to take care of him," Emily explained to Robert softly, easing his worry.

"Tell them it won't be much longer until I'm better," Mitchell added.

Emily laughed, "You may regret wanting me to tell them that."

"Why?" Mitchell asked curiously.

"Because they can't wait until Mr. Mitch can teach them how to play soccer."

Robert kissed Mitchell on the cheek, "That's good, Sweetie. It'll give you something to look forward to."

Mitchell smiled devilishly as Robert was walking toward the door, "Among other things."

"Behave," Robert added with a twinkle in his eyes.

"Yes dear," Mitchell responded playfully.

Emily laughed, "We'll be fine. You just make sure you behave dressed so handsomely."

Robert shook his head as he closed the door behind him. Once down the hallway, Robert sneaked off to his study to retrieve the bags that he had packed the night before. Emily and Mitchell were on the opposite side of Robert's huge estate, so there was no worry of Robert being spotted.

After throwing the bags in the trunk of his Jaguar, Robert sped off to his meeting with Mitchell's doctor that he had arranged the previous night. If his plan was going to work, Robert needed the approval of Mitchell's doctor.

After convincing Mitchell's doctor that Mitchell would be fine and well-looked after, the doctor relented, but only after having Robert's assurance that a doctor and medical facility would be nearby at all times. During the short drive to Mitchell's condominium, Robert called the caretaker of the place where he and Mitchell would be spending their time. After giving the caretaker his instructions, Robert phoned the county airport to make sure the private jet Robert frequently used was available. As he pulled into the condo parking lot, Robert shut his cell phone, satisfied that everything was taken care of and on schedule.

After packing some of Mitchell's shorts, Robert grabbed the bag and headed for home.

*        *        *        *

Robert arrived back home in plenty of time to see Emily off to the school, and to get Mitchell up and ready to go. Mitchell grumbled and complained as he was getting ready, thoroughly not wanting any parts of going to the doctor.

Robert smiled to himself the entire time that Mitchell was complaining, fully knowing that in a short time, Mitchell would be having the time of his life. When Mitchell was completely ready, Robert placed his arm around Mitchell's back and helped him to the driveway. When Mitchell walked through the door to the driveway, his eyes went wide in surprise. Waiting in the driveway was a large black limousine, complete with a chauffeur.

"What's this?" Mitchell asked in wide-eyed disbelief.

"It's a limousine, Sweetie," Robert said teasingly.

Mitchell turned and looked at Robert, "I know it's a limo, but why's it here?"

Robert smiled, "I thought that after your appointment we could go for a ride. I sorta think we need a change of scenery, so I thought why not get a limo so I could snuggle with my Sweetie in the back." Robert paused, "Unless you don't feel up to staying out for a few hours?"

Mitchell laughed, "Are you kidding? I'm ecstatic that we can get out of the house for awhile. I just wish we could skip the doctor's appointment."

Robert hugged Mitchell affectionately as Manny, the chauffeur, opened the back door for them. "No such luck, Mitch. First to the doctor, and then we can go anywhere you want."

As Robert and Mitchell were being chauffeured, Robert kept Mitchell occupied and engaged in conversation in the back so that Mitchell would not see where they were going. When the limousine stopped and the door opened, Mitchell could not believe his eyes. "Honey, why are we at the airport?"

Robert stepped out of the car and could not hold back the beaming smile that lit up his handsome face. "We're going on vacation for a few weeks."

Mitchell suddenly became terrified, "Oh God, I'm going to die. That's why you're taking me away, so that I can die peacefully."

Robert stifled a laugh, "Honey, I swear you aren't going to die. You aren't going to heaven, but we are going to paradise."

Mitchell stared at Robert, his confusion apparent, "What?"

Robert put his arm around Mitchell's shoulders, "We're going to the island."

Mitchell could not hide his excitement, "We're going to your private island?"

"Well, it's not *my* private island," Robert answered playfully.

"Yeah it is. Yours and two other people," Mitchell added. "I can't believe you're finally taking me there."

"It was the best change of scenery that I could think of. Plus it's a perfect place for you to finish your recovery." Robert replied.

Mitchell excitedly kissed Robert on the lips, "Thank you, Honey."

\*　　　\*　　　\*　　　\*

Mitchell usually abhorred airplanes, but this flight was something that he gladly anticipated as they boarded the private jet that Robert always chartered for his flights. Even though he was not fully recovered from his pneumonia, Mitchell felt wonderful as he peered out the window on take-off, with the gleeful knowledge that the man he loved with every ounce of his being was taking him to a secret hideaway known only to a few people—the owners and the pilot who flies them there. Robert only divulged the information that he co-owned a small island to Mitchell once, and when Mitchell asked the whereabouts of this island paradise, Robert jokingly replied, "I could tell you, but then I would have to kill you!"

Several hours into the flight, Robert tapped Mitchell on the shoulder. Mitchell briefly turned his attention away from the window, but the smile that adorned his face remained.

Robert teased, "I've never seen you so happy to be going to a doctor."

With a playful mock-frown, Mitchell replied, "I guess going to some island witch doctor is a small price to pay."

Robert continued the playfulness by acting hurt, "Sweetie? Do you really think that I'd take you to an island witch doctor?"

Mitchell, suddenly fearing that he had offended his lover, reached for Robert's hand as he replied seriously, "I'm sorry, Sweetie. I was just teasing you."

Robert's eyes were downcast as he replied, "I would never take you to a witch doctor." Robert's eyes suddenly sparkled as he continued, "I found a young doctor from a small village, and he has a degree in medicine. I think he may be a veterinarian, but what the hell! Medicine is medicine, right?"

Mitchell shook his head as a smile brightened his serious face, knowing fully that he had been had. Robert continued as he failed to withhold his laughter, "I'm sure he'll have all the latest technology, and his waiting room should be a blast." Robert ducked to avoid the playful slap that Mitchell had intended.

"The latest technology? What? Technology from the 1940's?" Mitchell asked with a jovial sneer. "Do they even know what penicillin is?"

"Of course they know what penicillin is! They make it in-house from home-made moldy cheese!" Robert could barely get the words out from all the laughter that inhabited his entire body. He grasped Mitchell's shoulders lovingly, "And just think, Sweetie, you might even make some new friends in the waiting room."

Mitchell could not hold back his laughter any longer, as he hugged Robert with complete and total love. It had been quite a long time since they could laugh so freely, and it had been even longer since Mitchell heard Robert laugh with such openness and pure affection. The Robert he had fallen in love with so long ago was back and better than ever. Mitchell knew at that moment, as he hugged his lover, that the two of them could weather any storm together. The past was in the past, Mitchell felt it in his heart and soul, and his future with Robert was going to be beautiful. He had escaped the icy grip of death with Robert by his side, and nothing was going to stand in the way of their happiness if Mitchell had anything to say about it.

As they continued to laugh in their warm embrace, Robert pulled back slightly, and with deeply felt appreciation and sincerity, he gazed deeply into Mitchell's crystal blue eyes as he whispered softly, "I love you, Mitch."

Mitchell sought Robert's lips and kissed him softly, "I love you too, Bobby. Always and forever."

Robert gently kissed Mitchell and pulled him close, with Mitchell's head resting on Robert's shoulder, and Mitchell lovingly nuzzling his neck. Even though it was an exceedingly warm day, the air conditioner was making it increasingly cooler in the cabin. Instinctively, Robert reached for a thin blanket and covered Mitchell inconspicuously. Robert knew that Mitchell was exhausted, despite his consummate enthusiasm. He held Mitchell with Mitchell's head resting comfortably at the nape of Robert's neck, and they snuggled for several hours in the privacy of the small jet as Mitchell lightly dozed. Sleep overtook him after only a few moments of being snuggled tightly in Robert's strong arms.

As the small jet approached the biggest and closest island to Robert's island paradise, Robert gently awakened his snoozing lover with a soft kiss to the forehead. Mitchell's eyes sparkled when he looked into Robert's eyes.

"Are you ready?" Robert asked softly. He knew that Mitchell hated to go to doctors, and that Mitchell particularly wanted to avoid this appointment, but Robert would not jeopardize Mitchell's health for any reason. Robert had playfully teased Mitchell earlier about going to the doctor, but now as the time drew nearer, Robert was protectively supportive without being judgmental.

"I guess so," Mitchell replied as a brief flash of dread and anxiety registered on his handsome face.

Robert pulled Mitchell to him and hugged him, as he reassured, "It's okay, Sweetie. This won't take long, and I promise I won't leave your side."

Mitchell nodded before pulling slightly away so that he could see Robert's face. A tiny smile crooked the corner of Mitchell's mouth as he replied, "You better not leave me—not even for a second. Since this guy's a vet, he might try to euthanize me."

Robert laughed, "Never, Sweetie. He'd have to kill me first, and I have no intention of letting anyone screw up our vacation."

Mitchell smiled, "Good."

"By the way, Mitch," Robert paused.

"Yeah?"

"This doctor isn't really a veterinarian. Your doctor recommended this doctor, and even called him this morning to explain your condition and to explain how he intended to treat you today. This guy we're going to see now is just going to do the same thing Dr. Wagner would have done. Okay?" Robert explained.

Mitchell nodded, fully appreciating the length Robert went through to make sure that he was okay, "Yeah, I'll be fine, Bobby."

"I know," Robert replied.

A car and driver awaited the men at the small island airport. As Mitchell and Robert stepped off the plane, they were greeted by two very tanned young men in white coveralls, and a middle-aged, blue jean clad man wearing a Panama hat. The middle-aged man's effervescent smile was contagious as Mitchell felt himself returning the smile, despite his apprehension regarding his appointment.

Robert hugged the middle-aged man as if he had known him a lifetime, "Carlos, my friend, how are you?"

Carlos squeezed Robert and lifted Robert slightly off the ground as he returned the hug, "Wonderful! It's been too long since you were here last, Roberto!"

Robert clasped him on the shoulders, "I have someone I want you to meet." Robert put his arm around Mitchell's waist and pulled him close. "Carlos, this is my sweetheart, Mitchell."

Mitchell smiled broadly as he held out his undamaged left hand, expecting an awkward handshake. Carlos took Mitchell's proffered hand and pulled him into a friendly embrace, "It is so good to finally meet you, Mitchell. I've heard so much about you!"

"Really?" Mitchell replied surprised.

"Oh yes, my friend. Roberto's told me all about you," Carlos answered jovially.

"Hmm," Mitchell uttered as he glanced over at Robert briefly with a smile before returning his attention to Carlos. "It's funny, but Robert somehow forgot to tell me about you."

Carlos winked at Mitchell, "That's probably because Roberto wanted to surprise you on your first trip to his island paradise. You see, I'm the guy who'll be flying you there shortly, and the only person—besides Roberto—who you'll see for the next few weeks."

Mitchell grinned his own effervescent smile at the prospect of being alone in paradise with the man of his dreams. "Oh, okay! It's nice meeting you, Carlos."

"The same here, my friend. It's wonderful to meet the man who puts wind in Roberto's sails, and it's so great to see him so happy," Carlos added.

# CHAPTER 48

▼

After an extremely hectic morning of dealing with a hostile client, Alex rushed home to get some lunch and some peace and quiet. Alex knew that Emily was away at the kids' school, and that Robert would be busy taking care of Mitchell in their upstairs bedroom. A half an hour of relaxation was what he hoped for, and from the sound of silence permeating through the mansion, he thought he had hit the jackpot.

As he walked into the living room, throwing his car keys on the sofa, Alex noticed an ivory-colored envelope propped up on the coffee table. Alex picked it up and examined it. On the front, in a steady and elegant handwriting, was the name "Emily." It was undeniably Robert's handwriting. Alex studied the envelope, held it up to the light, and tried to guess its content. After a few moments of frustration, Alex set the envelope aside and walked to the kitchen.

As Alex opened the refrigerator, a flash of panic smacked him hard in the chest. "Oh God," Alex uttered as he ran toward the stairs. Taking the stairs two at a time, he reached Robert's bedroom door breathless. Alex took a deep breath and started knocking loudly. No answer. "Dad?" Alex yelled, panic filling his voice. "Mitchell?" Still no answer. As the anxiety rose even higher, Alex raced back down the stairs to the envelope. "That envelope holds all the answers," Alex thought.

Alex sat down on the sofa and ripped the envelope open. "Emily is already pissed at me, so what's a little more anger?" Alex said aloud. He unfolded the stationary and began to read the letter Robert wrote to Emily.

*Dearest Emily,*

*I apologize for not telling you in person, but it had to be this way. I hope that you can forgive me. Mitch and I are going away for awhile. He doesn't know my plans, so this is a surprise to him as well. We need a change of scenery, and a place to rest and relax without any turmoil. I don't know when we'll be back. Please tell the kids that Grandpa loves them.*

*Thank you, Emily, for all that you've done for us. We both love you more than any words can say. Tell Alexander that I made arrangements for my upcoming meetings at work. He has nothing to worry about—I took care of what needed to be done. Don't worry about us, okay? We're fine. We just need some time to ourselves. I don't know when we'll see you, but please take care of everyone, and let them know that we love them.*

*Love,*
*Robert*

With frightened disbelief, Alex stared at the words on the stationary as he reached for his cell phone. In two rings, Emily's voice came through the cell phone.

"What is it, Alex?" Emily asked hostilely.

"Come home. It's really important," Alex answered as he continued to stare at the contents of the envelope.

Hearing a hint of fear in his voice, Emily replied, "Okay, I'm almost done here, so I should be there in about twenty minutes."

"Thank you," were the only two words that escaped his lips.

After twenty-five agonizing minutes of waiting, Alex saw Emily's car pull up to the garage. He could not wait for her to come into the house, so he rushed out to meet her.

Seeing the anxiety etched on Alex's face, Emily asked, "Alex, what's wrong?"

"Did you see Dad or Mitchell today?" he asked anxiously.

Emily nodded, "Yes. I saw them both this morning. Why?"

Alex hurried Emily in the door and closed it behind them. "They're gone," he replied apprehensively.

"Of course they're gone," Emily replied as she relaxed at the meaning of Alex's questions. "Mitchell had a doctor's appointment this afternoon."

"No Emily," Alex said nervously. "They're gone." He handed the already opened envelope to her. "I'm sorry I opened it, but I was worried."

Emily pulled the stationary out of the envelope and began to read the contents. For a brief moment, Alex saw Emily blanch, but she recovered quickly. "They went on vacation," she offered with all the confidence she could muster.

"Em, you don't just run off on the spur of the moment when you are in the condition Mitchell is in, and definitely not for an unspecified amount of time with no contact with your family," Alex offered.

"Is that what this is about … Robert not letting you know where they are going?" Emily asked with a hint of anger evident in her tone.

"Of course not," Alex replied defensively.

"Good, because that stunt you pulled yesterday is probably the reason they left," Emily explained.

"Why do you say that?" Alex asked nervously.

"Didn't you get a full report from your partner, Dr. Hamilton?" Emily asked sarcastically.

Alex diverted his eyes from Emily's accusing stare, and stated softly, "He just said that Dad refused to speak with him."

"Your little stunt caused Robert and Mitchell to get into an argument, and ending with Mitchell gasping for breath and needing oxygen," Emily explained angrily.

Alex's face was a mixture of horror and surprise, "What? Why? Was Mitchell okay after getting the oxygen?"

"Yes, the oxygen helped, but I think it was mostly Robert's love that calmed him enough to get his breathing under control," Emily replied, thinking back to the previous afternoon.

"Why did they argue?" Alex asked.

Emily replied smugly, "I don't break my friends' confidences."

"Emily … Please!" he implored.

Emily stared coldly at her husband for a few moments. "Why are you so worried?" she finally asked.

"Don't you get it?" Alex replied apprehensively. "Mitchell was on the verge of death, and from what you've just said, he was still very ill yesterday afternoon, and they left," Alex explained.

"So?" Emily stated.

Alex took the note Robert left and waved it in front of Emily. "What if this was some type of suicide note?"

"You're crazy," Emily stated disdainfully.

"Am I?" he asked as he took her hand and held it gently. Looking deeply into her eyes, Alex continued, "What if Dad took Mitchell somewhere peaceful to die?"

"Mitchell isn't going to die," she said defiantly.

"What if he was dying and Dad sensed it? That could be why he didn't tell anyone, including Mitchell," Alex explained.

"Well then, if that's a suicide note, I don't think Robert would be arrogant enough to write it for Mitchell," Emily countered.

Alex gently took Emily's other hand in his, "What if he wasn't writing it for Mitchell but ..."

Emily looked at him in horror, "You think Robert's going to wait for Mitchell to die and then kill himself?"

Alex's silence answered her question.

Emily violently pulled her hands away, "Neither you nor Dr. Hamilton have any clue about Robert." She turned and walked back out to her car and left, leaving Alex standing dumbfounded in the foyer.

Alex paced briskly back and forth for several interminable minutes trying to think of something—anything—he could do. Suddenly he grabbed his car keys off the sofa and headed for his car. As he was pulling out of the driveway, he hit the speed dial button for the only person he thought could help.

After several rings, a man's voice came through, "Hello, this is Dr. Hamilton."

Relieved, Alex spoke quickly, "Hi Doc, it's Alex Petrovic."

"Hi Alex. Everything okay?" Dr. Hamilton inquired.

"No, not at all," Alex replied nervously. "Can you meet me somewhere, or can I come to your office?"

"I have a patient, but after that I'll be going out to lunch. Do you want to join me?" Dr. Hamilton asked.

"Yeah, that'd be great. Where and when?" Alex inquired.

"I don't know how much longer I'll be, so why don't you stop by my office and we'll go from here?"

"I'm on my way as we speak. See you in a few minutes," Alex replied with a sigh of relief.

\*        \*        \*        \*

Alex and Dr. Hamilton sat down in a booth at an old-fashioned diner and gave the lanky, red-haired waitress their orders. When the waitress left, Dr. Hamilton started his questioning. "Alex, what's wrong?"

Without uttering a word, Alex handed the letter to Dr. Hamilton. As Dr. Hamilton read the letter, all his attempts to keep a blank, emotionless expression failed. He looked across the table with understanding as to why Alex was so worried.

"Where did you get this?" Dr. Hamilton inquired.

Alex ran his hand through his hair nervously, "I came home from work early to have a quiet lunch, and I found this envelope addressed to Emily on the coffee table. I knew immediately that it was Dad's handwriting, but I didn't bother with it because it was addressed to Emily."

"So how did you find out what the letter said?" Dr. Hamilton asked.

"I went to make a sandwich, but something flashed in my mind, and I suddenly felt like I did when I found Dad out in the barn," Alex explained.

"What did you do?"

"I ran upstairs and started pounding on Dad's bedroom door. I called out for Dad, with no answer, and then I called out for Mitchell, and he didn't answer either," Alex continued. "So I raced back down to the living room and ripped open the letter."

"Have you talked to Emily about it?" Dr. Hamilton asked.

"Yes, of course. After I read the letter, I called her and told her to come home," Alex replied.

"And what did she say about the letter?" Dr. Hamilton asked curiously.

Alex massaged his temples before answering. "She thinks nothing's wrong ... that they just went on vacation," Alex answered.

"But you don't believe that, do you?" Dr. Hamilton asked.

"Do you?" Alex asked annoyed.

"I'm not sure, but I'd like to hear your theory," Dr. Hamilton offered.

With growing annoyance and fear, Alex answered, "Isn't it obvious? It sounds like a suicide note."

"What makes you think that?"

"Mitchell's dying, and Dad took him away somewhere instead of taking him for his scheduled doctor's appointment, and it sounds as if Dad's saying goodbye." Alex explained.

"That's true about saying goodbye, but it might be just that—goodbye—until they get back," Dr. Hamilton offered.

"So you don't think it's a final goodbye?" Alex asked slightly more optimistically.

"I'm not sure, but we do have a few things to go on. First off, Robert didn't leave a note when he tried to kill himself. Secondly, he promised you that he'd never do that again. Thirdly, he told me yesterday that he wasn't going to kill himself, and ..." Dr. Hamilton explained before being interrupted.

"What?" Alex asked surprised.

"What?" Dr. Hamilton repeated.

"Dad told you he wasn't going to kill himself?" Alex asked.

"Yes, that's right," Dr. Hamilton answered, somewhat confused about the question.

"I thought you said Dad refused to talk with you?"

"He did, but I sorta pressed him on it, and he answered very vehemently 'NO.'" Dr. Hamilton explained.

"Hmm," Alex murmured. "Maybe that's why Emily is pissed with you and me both."

"What? Why would Emily be mad at me?" Dr. Hamilton asked confused.

"I don't know the specifics, but Emily referred to you as my partner in causing an argument between Dad and Mitchell," Alex explained.

"You've really lost me now," Dr. Hamilton replied. "How did we cause an argument between the two of them?"

"Like I said, I don't know the specifics, but Emily hinted that our 'little stunt' may be the reason they left," Alex continued.

"What were they arguing about?" Dr. Hamilton asked.

"Emily wouldn't tell me, but she did say that it ended with Mitchell gasping for breath and needing oxygen."

"Is Emily at home now?" Dr. Hamilton asked.

"No, she was upset with me and left," Alex explained.

Dr. Hamilton thought for a moment before speaking, "Can you call her and ask her to meet us?"

"I can call her, but don't be surprised if she refuses," Alex said as he took out his cell phone.

"When you get her on the line, let me talk to her, okay?" Dr. Hamilton added as Alex pressed the speed dial button.

In a matter of moments, Emily answered her cell phone with a disgusted tone when she saw Alex's number come across her caller ID. "What do you want, Alex?"

"I'm here with Dr. Hamilton, and he wants to talk to you. It's really important," Alex said before handing the phone over to Dr. Hamilton without waiting for Emily to speak.

"Hello Emily, this is Erik Hamilton," he said in a concerned, but friendly tone.

"Yes Doctor, what is it?" Emily said impatiently.

"Alex told me what happened and showed me Robert's note to you. Would it be possible for you to meet us? We're at the Spurs Diner," Dr. Hamilton spoke with a tone of quiet despair, hoping that she would pick up on the seriousness of what was happening.

Emily hesitated a few moments and looked at her watch. "I guess I can drop by, but I can't stay long. The kids get out of school in a couple of hours."

"Thank you, Emily. We'll be waiting," Dr. Hamilton added before he shut the cell phone and handed it back to Alex.

"She's coming?" Alex asked surprised, just as their food was brought out and set on the table.

Dr. Hamilton waited for the waitress to leave before answering. "Yes, she's coming, but she said she can't stay long because your kids get out of school soon."

Alex dropped his head and massaged his temples. "Damn, I forgot about someone having to pick up the kids. Dammit!"

Dr. Hamilton reached across the table and put his hand on Alex's arm as he spoke gently, "Alex, get yourself together. Getting overly stressed isn't going to help anyone, and if your kids see you so stressed out, they're going to begin to worry and ask questions."

Alex took a moment before looking up at Dr. Hamilton, and when he did his eyes brimmed with unshed tears, "This is all my fault. I did this, and now they might be gone forever."

Dr. Hamilton, ever the pragmatist, replied in a calming voice, "You can't keep thinking that they are gone forever. What you need to do is think about how you can change your behavior so that you don't hurt either of them anymore. Do you think you can do that?"

Alex nodded slowly, "I have to. I love my dad, and I care about Mitchell. I don't want to ever hurt them again. They've both been through enough … they don't need me to keep adding to their problems."

"Good, then you need to get started on changing yourself before they get back," Dr. Hamilton explained.

Alex looked at Dr. Hamilton with hope in his eyes, "Do you think I can change?"

"Of course you can change. If you need my help with anything, you know I'll be here," Dr. Hamilton answered with a reassuring smile.

The two men sat quietly, lost in their own thoughts while they finished their lunches and waited for Emily. It took Emily a few minutes to get to the Diner, and when she arrived she found the two men waiting in a booth for her. She walked over coldly and sat down. As she slid in next to Alex, the waitress came over and asked what she wanted to drink. Emily ordered a coffee and waited for Dr. Hamilton to begin his questioning.

"Thanks for coming," Dr. Hamilton gratefully said to Emily.

"Why did you want to see me?" Emily asked with impatience.

Dr. Hamilton picked up the envelope, "Alex showed me the note from Robert."

"Did he? That's awfully nice of him, especially since it wasn't even addressed to him!" Emily replied with growing annoyance.

"You don't think that there's anything to this note?" Dr. Hamilton questioned.

"It's just a note. They went on vacation. What's the big deal?" Emily stated sarcastically.

"Alex thinks it has a deeper meaning to it. Are you sure his assumptions aren't correct?" Dr. Hamilton continued.

"Yes, I'm sure of it. Mitchell isn't going to die, and Robert isn't going to kill himself," Emily said vehemently.

"How can you be so sure?" Dr. Hamilton asked.

"Because I know Robert better than you and Alex put together," Emily replied smugly. "And if I were a betting person, I'd say that you and Alex are the reason that they left!"

"Why do you say that? Alex mentioned something about Robert and Mitchell arguing."

"Oh yes, they argued briefly, and it was all because of your visit yesterday," Emily replied angrily.

"Alex said that you were angry with us both. Is that the reason?" Dr. Hamilton inquired.

"Yes, of course it is. My best friends were arguing, with it ending in Mitchell struggling to breathe, and it was all because of the two of you," Emily replied as her anger continued to build.

"Please tell us what happened, Em," Alex implored.

"Why should I? You both think you know Robert so well, and from the sounds of it, you already have him in the grave. Why the hell should I tell either of you anything?" Emily stated heatedly.

Dr. Hamilton interrupted, "Because it could be very important. From what I know so far, I agree with you Emily. I don't think that Robert is going to kill himself, but I need to know all the facts. Please tell me what happened yesterday."

Emily took a slow sip of her coffee and tried to decide if she should tell Dr. Hamilton what he wanted to know. As she set her coffee cup aside, she spoke with anger-laced words. "Fine, I'll tell you. When Robert came back to the bedroom, he immediately tried to go take a shower, but Mitchell could see that something was bothering him. When Robert tried to deny it, Mitchell tried to get out of bed and go after Robert, but Robert saw what he was doing and picked him up and put him back in bed. Mitchell started having problems breathing, but he wouldn't let Robert off without telling him what was wrong."

"And did Dad tell him?" Alex interrupted.

Emily fixed Alex with an icy glare before continuing. "Robert continued to deny that anything was wrong, but Mitchell knew that something was going on. He could see it on Robert's face. As Mitchell started to gasp for breath, Robert put the oxygen mask over his face and I stacked up the pillows so that Mitchell would be more comfortable, but Mitchell still wasn't giving up."

"Please continue," Dr. Hamilton stated softly as he listened to the story.

"It wasn't until Mitchell started to use some language that I have never heard him use before, that I became involved," Emily explained.

"How so?" Dr. Hamilton inquired.

"I took Robert's hand and held it while Mitchell held his other hand, and we both implored him to tell us what was wrong. Finally, after a few moments, he told us what happened. More specifically that you thought that he was going to kill himself," Emily stated as she glared across the table at Dr. Hamilton.

"I didn't think that he was going to kill himself," Dr. Hamilton meekly tried to explain before being interrupted by Emily.

"You asked him point blank whether he was going to kill himself. Robert is the most honest person I know, so are you going to try to deny that you asked him that?"

"No, of course not. I did ask him that, but I didn't intend for him to get upset about it," Dr. Hamilton explained.

Emily nearly exploded, "How the hell couldn't he have been upset?"

"Emily, I was worried about him. What I did was out of concern, and the reason for me asking you here is also out of concern," Dr. Hamilton explained.

"You don't have a reason to be worried about him killing himself. You upset him greatly yesterday by your questions, and because of that, Robert and Mitchell both ended up suffering," Emily replied more calmly.

"Was Mitchell okay after he got the oxygen?" Dr. Hamilton asked, genuinely concerned.

Emily got her anger under control and replied calmly, "Yes. After Robert told us what happened, Robert calmed Mitchell down, and with that and the oxygen, Mitchell got his breathing under control."

"So Robert knew that me being there yesterday was a setup?" Dr. Hamilton asked after a few moments of reflection.

"Of course he knew. He's not stupid," Emily replied irritably.

Dr. Hamilton looked across the table apologetically, "I know he's not stupid."

"Neither one of you have any clue about who Robert really is, and he even said that yesterday about you, Dr. Hamilton," Emily explained.

"Why did he say that?" Dr. Hamilton inquired.

"Because if you really knew him, you'd know that he would never try to take his own life again," Emily answered.

Alex interrupted, "We just want to make sure that's true."

"That's your problem, Alex. You don't know him. Of course he loves Mitchell more than anyone else in the world, and if he lost him, he'd be devastated. But he'd continue on because he has other people in his life that he knows loves him and needs him. That's why he's not going to kill himself," Emily explained with a mixture of impatience and conviction.

Alex looked across the table at Dr. Hamilton, "What do you think?"

"Emily makes a very convincing argument," Dr. Hamilton replied.

Alex continued, "So you don't think that he's going to kill himself?"

"Honestly, no I don't," Dr. Hamilton replied.

"And Mitchell isn't going to die!" Emily emphatically chimed in. "That's something else that neither of you obviously understand about Robert ... he'd move heaven and earth to get Mitchell well. How could you think that he'd just give up and take him away somewhere to die?

"I agree, Emily," Dr. Hamilton admitted. He reached across and touched Emily's hand, "And I'm sorry that I caused you and your dearest friends any pain yesterday. That wasn't my intention, and when they get back I'll apologize to both of them for my actions."

Emily softened at Dr. Hamilton's heartfelt words, "Thank you." She looked at her watch and stood gracefully, "I have to go. It's time to pick up the kids."

"Thanks Em," Alex said as Emily walked away.

# CHAPTER 49

▼

After spending two full days resting and relaxing, Mitchell was well on his way to fully recovering from his brush with death. Mitchell's breathing was back to normal, and most of his strength had returned. As a precaution, Robert made him take it easy and not do too much. On the third day of being on the beautiful, tropical island, Mitchell was finally permitted to walk with Robert to the lagoon to sunbathe on a comfortable chaise lounge. The warm wind coming off the water and the sun relaxed Mitchell and Robert so much that they both briefly fell asleep on the beach.

After his little nap, Mitchell looked over at Robert and smiled, "Thank you, Bobby."

Robert returned his smile, but questioned, "Why are you thanking me?"

"For bringing me to paradise. For getting me well," Mitchell answered appreciatively.

"We both needed some relaxation, Mitch, and I couldn't think of a better place than this. And as for getting you well, you did all the work. I was just your cheerleader," Robert said with love in his eyes.

"You were more than a cheerleader, Bobby. If it weren't for you, I'm sure I wouldn't be alive right now," Mitchell explained gratefully.

"Yes you would. You're a strong guy, Mitch," Robert replied.

"I'm not that strong on my own. I'm here today because you're my reason for living," Mitchell clarified.

Robert reached over and took Mitchell's hand in his, clearly touched by Mitchell's words, "And you're mine as well."

Mitchell winked at Robert, "Can you put some suntan lotion on my back, Sweetie?"

Robert smiled devilishly, "Absolutely." Robert took the lotion bottle out from under his lounge chair and moved to sit beside Mitchell. He squeezed the lotion into his hand and rubbed his hands together briskly before rubbing Mitchell's shoulders gently. As Robert moved his hands sensually down Mitchell's back and legs, Mitchell moaned in appreciation. When Robert finally stopped massaging the lotion onto Mitchell's smooth, toned body, Mitchell pulled Robert toward him for a gentle kiss.

"That was nice," Mitchell cooed.

Robert winked, "I aim to please."

"You've definitely succeeded," Mitchell replied as he glanced down. "In more ways than one."

Robert looked down as well, but chose to remain silent about the effect that his massage had on Mitchell. Instead he reached into the cooler for a bottle of water. After taking a long drink, Robert turned serious as he took Mitchell's left hand in his. "Mitch," he started.

"What is it, babe?" Mitchell asked as he looked lovingly into Robert's eyes.

"Over the past few weeks I've come to see something so clearly. Even though these weeks have been fraught with fear and terror and anger and despair, they've also been the happiest time of my life," Robert paused. "I know that sounds crazy, but it's true."

Mitchell gently squeezed Robert's hand, "How so?"

Robert's face lit up with a beaming smile, "It's because you and I are together everyday."

"I feel the same way," Mitchell replied with a smile that equaled Robert's.

"I'm glad you feel that way," Robert stated as he gazed lovingly into Mitchell's crystal blue eyes. "Because I have something I want to ask you."

Mitchell held Robert's gaze as he held his hand, "What?"

"You don't have to answer right now, okay, but I'd like you to think about it," Robert explained.

"Think about what?" Mitchell questioned with anticipation.

"I told you when you were in the hospital that my place was your home, so," he paused, "I want you to move into *our* home ... permanently," Robert explained sincerely.

Mitchell beamed as he pulled Robert forward to embrace him, "Are you sure?"

Robert hugged Mitchell tenderly as he replied honestly, "I've never been more sure of anything in my life." Robert pulled back slightly so that they were gazing into each other's eyes, "I never want to spend another day or night without you by my side."

"And I want to be beside you for eternity," Mitchell said with heartfelt emotion that washed over him like the waves of the ocean.

"Is that a yes?" Robert asked anxiously, not wanting to jump to conclusions.

"YES," Mitchell happily yelled as he once again pulled Robert into an embrace.

Robert smiled mischievously as he returned the embrace, "Well you don't have to yell." Robert pulled back and winked at Mitchell, "I know I'm an old guy, but I can still hear okay."

Mitchell playfully swatted Robert on the shoulder as they both burst out laughing, "Smart ass!"

# CHAPTER 50

▼

Days of silence passed as Alex and Emily went about doing their business. Alex wanted desperately to talk to Emily, but he knew that it was a bad idea because of the way they had left things the afternoon when he called her to meet with him and Dr. Hamilton. Alex tried to put things in perspective, but he could not shake the feeling that he would never see his dad again.

After a late dinner with Emily and the kids at Robert's stately mansion, Alex excused himself and went for a walk. He meandered around the backyard, beyond the tennis court, and stopped at the hillside that Robert fell down the night he regained his memory. Alex carefully slid down the steep slope to the bottom and sat down on the warm grass. Memories came flooding back like a raging river. He remembered Robert's soft cry, the grass stains on his shorts, and the look of concern on Dr. Hamilton's face as he tried to get Robert to respond. As he stood up, he remembered helping Dr. Hamilton carry Robert back to the house after he had been sedated. Alex tried to shake the memories as he climbed back up the hillside, but they continued to follow him relentlessly.

As the sun was setting, Alex felt himself being pulled in the direction of the barns. He walked past the first barn and heard one of Robert's thoroughbred horses moving about. He continued to walk toward the farthest barn on the property. Alex stopped at the door, realizing where he was at, and hesitated. This was where it all began. A force stronger than himself pulled him toward the door, and he opened it hesitantly. He felt goosebumps running down his arms as he stepped inside. It was different from the last time he was there, that dreadful afternoon, but somehow it was still the same. The broken remnants of an old wooden chair no longer lay in the center of the barn under the rafter. Alex closed his eyes and the images came rushing back. He could smell the freshly mowed grass that he had smelled that afternoon, and he could see his father's limp, lifeless body dangling from a thick rope from the center rafter.

Alex fell to his knees and began to sob as he tried to block out those haunting images, but his efforts were fruitless. He rolled onto his side as sob after sob wracked his entire body and soul. "How could I have been so cruel?" Alex cried out into the evening air. Alex sobbed until he was physically ill and completely fatigued. After finally being able to garner the strength to pull himself into a sitting position, Alex reached for his handkerchief and wiped his eyes and nose. At that moment, sitting alone in the barn where his father tried to end his own life, Alex never felt so alone and isolated.

Exhausted and forlorn, Alex picked himself up and walked back to the house. As he walked through the foyer, he noticed Emily sitting on the sofa reading the newspaper. He kept far enough away so that she would not see his miserable appearance, but Emily heard him enter, "The kids wanted me to tell you goodnight."

"Thanks," Alex replied despondently as he headed toward his bedroom.

"Wait," Emily called out as he was near the stairs.

Alex stopped, but did not turn around, "What?"

Emily's voice was tender, "Are you okay?"

Alex tried hard to keep it together as he started to go up the stairs, "No."

"Alex wait," Emily said as she walked over to her husband. When she put her hand on his shoulder to turn him around, she noticed that his eyes were red and puffy from crying. "What's going on?" she questioned with a soft voice that he had not heard for a long time.

Alex looked away from Emily, but she gently ran her soft fingers down the side of his cheek, breaking through the fragile veneer that Alex was hiding behind. The tears trickled down his face as he buried his head in Emily's shoulder, "I don't want to lose him."

Emily remained silent as she comforted Alex and allowed him to bare his soul. The tears flowed freely and turned into sobs once again as Alex poured out his feelings to his wife, "They have to come back, Em."

Emily guided Alex over to the sofa and sat down with him still clinging helplessly to her. Alex pulled away briefly to search Emily's eyes, "They are coming back, aren't they? Please tell me they are?"

Emily's heart was breaking seeing her husband so miserable and pitiful, but she knew that he deserved to feel that way. She tried to ease his fears, "I do believe, without a doubt, that they will be back."

Alex put his head back on Emily's shoulder, "I'm so sorry, Em."

Emily held him tightly against her as she spoke tenderly to him, "I'm not the one you should be apologizing to."

"I know I have to apologize to Dad, but I don't know how he could ever forgive me for how I treated him," Alex said as the tears were washing down his face and soaking into Emily's blouse.

"You'll have to prove to him that you're sincere," Emily replied before adding, "Are you sincere?"

Alex nodded his head up and down on Emily's shoulder, "Yes, I swear to you I am." Alex pulled away again as he searched Emily's face for understanding. "I also owe Mitchell an apology as well."

Emily smiled at her husband's newfound tolerance, "Yes, you most certainly do."

"Em, I can't lose him. I need my dad, and I love him," Alex explained as the sadness in his eyes penetrated Emily's soul.

"What made you come to that conclusion?" Emily asked with concern and without accusation.

Alex wiped his eyes with his handkerchief, "I went out to the barn for the first time."

Suddenly, Emily realized where all the emotions were coming from. Alex was reliving the day he found Robert hanging in the barn. "Alex, your dad loves you and always will, but he has his own life and you have to accept that."

"I know," Alex replied softly as he fought back the urge to cry. "I don't know why I said the things I said to him."

"I do," Emily replied. "You've bought into thinking the way your friends think. I think that sometimes you substitute their thinking for your own."

"You mean my political colleagues?" Alex conceded. "You're right. I wanted to fit in, and it didn't matter who I hurt in the process of fitting in."

"Do you feel that way now?" Emily inquired.

"No," Alex answered honestly. "I'm going to spend the rest of my life making up for all the times I hurt Dad and Mitchell."

"I hope you do. I love Robert and Mitchell both … it hurts me tremendously to see how your behavior hurts them," Emily explained.

"I promise you, Em, that I'll never hurt either of them ever again," Alex replied.

"I'm going to hold you to that," Emily said as she smiled at her husband. "I want you to think about something while your dad and Mitchell are away."

"What?" Alex asked intrigued.

"If you didn't know that your dad and Mitchell were gay, would either of them be someone that you would want Stevie and Steffi to look up to as role models?" Emily asked.

Alex answered instantly, "Of course."

"Which one?" Emily quizzed.

It dawned on Alex where Emily was going with this, and he was glad that she asked. "Both of them," Alex responded honestly.

"Are you being totally honest?" Emily asked.

"Yes," Alex answered. "I see where you're coming from, Em, and you're right as always. Dad and Mitchell are both wonderful human beings, and we're lucky that the kids have them in their lives to look up to."

"I don't think that the kids are the only ones who can look up to them," Emily said with a smile.

"I agree," Alex replied. "Dad was always there for me no matter what. He was always there to catch me when I'd fall," Alex said as his voice broke and the tears threatened to fall once again. "And now I may never see him again, and it's all my fault. I drove him away." Alex covered his face with his hands, "How could I have done that?"

Emily rubbed Alex's shoulders gently, "They'll be back, Alex. I know they will, but by the time they come back, you have to be a new man ... a better man. Will you do that?"

Alex tried to form the words, but nothing escaped his lips. He nodded his head up and down in acknowledgement. After a few moments, Alex got his emotions under control, "I swear I'll change, Em."

"Then I think everything will work out fine," Emily replied softly as she stood and pulled Alex toward the stairs. "Let's go to bed. When you wake up tomorrow, you can start working on becoming a new man."

Alex put his arm around Emily as the two ascended the stairs to their bedroom. It was the first night in a long time that they had gone to bed on speaking terms, and Alex vowed to himself that that night was the first night of his new life.

▼

# CHAPTER 51

After cleaning up the kitchen in the early evening, Robert went to the computer and slumped into the comfortable desk chair. This was the part of the day that Robert disliked the most … having to make contact with the outside world. He promised Mitchell's doctor that he would keep him updated frequently on Mitchell's condition, and then there were two businesses that needed his guidance. Robert arranged to keep updated about his business by emailing his secretary, Helen, at her private email account that she only accessed at home, so as to prevent Alexander from knowing anything about his father's absence. Robert also kept things running smoothly at MER Technology, Mitchell's computer company, by keeping in contact with Mitchell's secretary, Katherine.

"What are you doing?" Mitchell asked casually as he sipped his fresh strawberry smoothie.

"Checking in," Robert answered as he logged onto the computer. "Nothing to worry about."

Mitchell knew what Robert was doing, and he loved Robert so much for taking the burden of his business off Mitchell's shoulders as he recovered. Mitchell acted disinterested as he walked toward the door, "I'll be down at the lagoon."

Robert looked over his shoulder and smiled, "Okay, I won't be too long."

Mitchell nodded as he walked out the front door and toward the white sand of the lagoon. The evening was warm as a light breeze swept across the majestic blue water, wafting a light smell of saltwater over the creamy white sand. The sun began to tip into the ocean on the horizon as Mitchell sat down and gently grasped a handful of warm sand in his left hand. With a handful of sand, Mitchell opened his hand and watched the white sand trickle through his tanned fingers.

After a few moments of sifting absently through the sand, Mitchell was completely lost in his thoughts.

Robert strolled relaxingly along the sand until he was standing at Mitchell's side. Mitchell, lost in the past, failed to hear Robert approach. Robert cleared his throat, trying not to startle his lover, "A penny for your thoughts."

Mitchell continued to stare out at the orange horizon, "They're not worth a penny."

Robert felt a cloud of melancholy descend upon his lover, "What's wrong, Sweetie?"

Mitchell stroked his fingers through his sandy blonde hair, "Nothing."

Robert sat down next to Mitchell and draped his arm over Mitchell's shoulder, "Are you thinking about the past?"

Mitchell, astounded by Robert's guess and insight, turned and looked at Robert in surprise, "What makes you think that?"

"I recognize the stare," Robert answered softly. "I've been there," he continued as he looked lovingly and knowingly into Mitchell's blue eyes. "And I'm here for you whenever you need me."

Mitchell squeezed Robert's hand and continued staring out at the glorious tropical sunset. After a few moments of companionable silence, Mitchell started to speak in a voice that was barely a whisper, "They took so much from me. From us." Robert massaged Mitchell's taut shoulders as he allowed Mitchell to open up without interruption. Mitchell fought back the lump that was rapidly forming in his throat, "I'm scared, Bobby."

Robert put his strong arms around Mitchell as he asked tenderly, "Of what, Sweetie?"

Mitchell's voice cracked as he battled with his emotions, "Everything. Being attacked again, but mostly of losing me."

Robert turned Mitchell's face by gently stroking the side of his smooth cheek, "Sweetie," Robert said seriously. "Those bastards broke your bones, but they couldn't break your spirit. You're still you. You're still the same wonderful, warm, kindhearted, loving, funny, handsome man that I fell in love with all those years ago."

A single tear trickled slowly down Mitchell's face, "Do you really think so?"

Robert answered confidently, "I most certainly do." Robert wiped Mitchell's tear as he continued, "It's okay to be afraid, Mitch. You were a victim of a violent crime, and it's natural to feel that way."

Mitchell leaned into Robert and rested his head on Robert's shoulder, "Will this fear ever go away?"

Robert held Mitchell to him, "It'll go away, Mitch, but it's going to take some time." Robert paused before continuing, "I've actually read that victims of violent crimes often suffer from Post Traumatic Stress Disorder."

"Really?" Mitchell replied softly before pulling away to look into Robert's loving eyes. "Do you think that's why I've been having nightmares?"

Robert nodded his head in acknowledgement, "It's very possible." Robert looked soulfully into Mitchell's teary eyes, "Are you still having them?"

"Not since we've been here," Mitchell replied before adding, "But that's probably only because I feel completely safe here."

"But you think that'll change when we get back?" Robert inquired.

Mitchell contemplated the question a moment, "Unfortunately, yes, and that scares the hell out of me."

"I understand, Sweetie," Robert said from experience. Robert stared out at the rapidly setting sun as he collected his thoughts. "Mitch?" he finally said.

"Yeah," Mitchell answered absently.

"When we get back, maybe it'd be a good idea for us to look for a therapist that you can talk to," Robert explained softly.

Mitchell thought about what Robert's comments meant and replied honestly, "I think that'd be a good idea, as long as it's someone who I feel comfortable with, and someone who won't judge me."

"Of course," Robert responded. "We'll search until we find the right one."

"That might be quite time-consuming and difficult," Mitchell replied jokingly.

"You think?" Robert joked back. "Seriously Sweetie, we'll find someone. When we get back, I can call Dr. Hamilton and ask him for a referral, if you'd like?"

Astounded, Mitchell asked, "You'd do that?"

"What?"

"Call Dr. Hamilton," Mitchell replied.

Robert smiled, "I'd do anything for you, Sweetie."

"You'd call him even after the way he treated you?" Mitchell asked.

"Yes, of course. If he can tell us the name of someone who can make things easier for you, I'll gladly forget our last meeting," Robert answered sincerely.

"Aren't you still angry with him?" Mitchell inquired.

"Yeah, but he's the best doctor I've ever met," Robert replied.

"Okay then," Mitchell said with resolve. "When we get back, we'll contact Dr. Hamilton and ask him for his help."

"I've also been thinking," Robert added. "That when we get back, I'm going to start back to therapy as well."

"With Dr. Hamilton?" Mitchell asked surprised.

"I don't know. It depends," Robert answered vaguely.

Mitchell did not want to pressure Robert on the subject, but his relief was evident, "I think it's a good thing that you want to go back to therapy."

Robert smiled teasingly, "Why? Do you think I'm on the verge of snapping?"

Mitchell understood Robert's teasing nature, but he remained serious, "No, but you were doing so well in therapy until all this happened, and now you're under a ton of stress because of what happened to me."

"Mitch," Robert admonished. "None of this is your fault, and my reason for stopping therapy had nothing to do with what happened to you. You know that!"

"It's because of Alex, right?" Mitchell asked with uncertainty.

Robert closed his eyes momentarily and took a deep breath, "Mostly because of Alexander, but also because of Dr. Hamilton. I didn't want to have to explain to him, in a therapy session, what I did that night."

Now Mitchell felt the need to admonish, "Bobby, you did nothing wrong, and you owed no one an explanation."

"I owed you an explanation," Robert corrected.

"Okay," Mitchell replied. "And you gave it and I understood. Just because he's your doctor doesn't mean you have to share every detail of your life with him."

"It does when he witnesses my actions," Robert replied with latent guilt.

"Robert," Mitchell said forcefully, but compassionately. "What you did that night gave me a huge sense of relief and security, and Dr. Hamilton even told you himself that he didn't condemn your actions, so how can you think that what you did was wrong?"

"I don't think I was wrong, but I'd feel a lot better if I was the only one who saw what I did that night," Robert tried to explain.

"Babe, you're just letting Alex get into your head. Stop, okay? You did what you did for me, and I'm thankful. Knowing that those bastards were laid up in the hospital suffering gave me a feeling of peace, if only temporarily," Mitchell explained.

"Mitch, I promise you those bastards will never bother you again," Robert said trying to ease Mitchell's fear.

"I know that with the beating you gave them that they'll think twice before bothering me again, but I still can't shake this fear," Mitchell replied.

"It'll take time, but it will get easier ... I promise," Robert said from experience.

"What am I going to do about work?" Mitchell asked.

This was a question that Robert had thought of, and he was prepared to give some options. "Well, Mitch, I don't think you'll be able to work for awhile yet, but when you're ready to make a decision, you have several options."

"Like what?" Mitchell asked curiously.

"Well, first of all, if you don't want to work, that's fine. I make enough to keep us comfortable for the rest of our lives. But, if you want to work again, there are a few options. You can go back to work at your office—with some new security measures. Or, you can move your office to a new location. Or ..." Robert paused.

"What?" Mitchell asked inquisitively.

"You can work from home. We can take a room or two and make it into an office for you," Robert explained.

"That's something that I would have never thought of," Mitchell confessed. "But, maybe that would be the best option, at least in the beginning."

"It's your decision, Mitch," Robert replied. "I'll support any decision that you make."

"I like the idea of working from home," Mitchell admitted.

Robert smiled, "That's good, but don't worry about that now. You have plenty of time to make a decision."

"Yes dear," Mitchell said playfully.

Robert pulled Mitchell close and hugged him playfully. After a few moments of embracing, as the moonlight reflected off the mirror-like water, Mitchell kissed Robert tenderly. When they pulled away reluctantly, Robert glimpsed the tears brimming in Mitchell's eyes. "What's wrong, Sweetie?" Robert asked.

The tears cascaded down Mitchell's cheeks as all his defenses over the past few weeks dissolved, "Those bastards took away our intimacy."

Robert felt the tears forming in his own eyes, but he remained focused, "Mitch, I promise you that when the doctor says that you are one hundred percent healthy, I'm going to make passionate love to you all night long."

"But they took away our time together now. Here we are in a tropical paradise, and all we can do is hold each other," Mitchell cried. "It's not fair."

Robert agreed, "I know, Mitch. It's not fair, but we'll make up for lost time, I promise you."

"I know, but I hate that we can't make love. I need you so much," Mitch explained emotionally.

Robert felt a twinge of guilt, "I need you too, Sweetie, but I won't risk hurting you any further. We need the doctor's go-ahead before I make love to you." Robert sighed deeply, "You know, I'm also to blame for our lack of intimacy."

"How so?" Mitchell asked confused.

"All those months we could have been sharing our lives and our beds, but I put our sex life on the backburner," Robert explained. "I'm sorry about that."

"Bobby, you were dealing with a lot of heavy issues, not to mention a lot of medication," Mitchell replied sternly.

"Yeah, but that's not an excuse. I could have dealt with the medication, and found a way to get around the side effects."

"Sweetie, if memory serves me, the first time we did make love after our reconciliation—it was amazing," Mitchell clarified. "Not to mention well worth the wait," Mitchell added with a smile.

Robert acquiesced. He knew that to continue this line of conversation would serve no purpose. He took Mitchell's hand and brought it to his lips as he kissed it tenderly, "I love you, Mitch."

Mitchell smiled and wrapped his arms around Robert's neck, "I love you too."

"Mitch?" Robert said as he returned the embrace.

"Yeah," Mitchell replied.

Robert took a deep breath before speaking, causing Mitchell to pull back slightly from the embrace to look into Robert's eyes. Robert smiled shyly as he gathered his nerve.

"What is it, Bobby?" Mitchell asked with concern.

Robert touched Mitchell's cheek with the back of his fingers and traced the outline of Mitchell's broken jaw. He took another deep breath, and with love and passion dancing in his eyes, he asked boldly, "Make love to me."

Mitchell, caught completely off guard, looked at Robert with unsuppressed surprise, "What?"

"Make love to me," Robert repeated softly.

Mitchell took a moment to collect his thoughts before responding, "I didn't think you wanted to bottom."

"I never trusted anyone before," Robert replied honestly.

Mitchell looked confused, "You don't want to make love to me anymore?"

Robert smiled, "Of course I do. I can't wait for the day when I can make love to you again." Robert looked deeply into Mitchell's eyes once again, "I just thought that this would be a way for us to regain some of our intimacy, and no it's not because of our conversation a moment ago. I've been thinking about this for a few days."

"But we'd go back to our old way of doing things when I'm well?" Mitchell questioned hesitantly.

"Most definitely," Robert replied confidently.

Mitchell battled with his conflicting emotions. Robert could sense the battle he was waging, and he hung his head slightly. Mitchell touched Robert under the chin and lifted until Robert was eye to eye with him, "Bobby, I'm not rejecting you."

"It's okay, Mitch," Robert said disappointedly. "I understand."

"No, I don't think you do," Mitchell replied with a shy smile. "I love you, but it's just that I've never topped before."

"Well, I've never bottomed before," Robert responded with a glint of hope. "Maybe we can learn together."

Mitchell smiled bashfully, "We'd have to use a condom."

"I know," Robert answered. He knew that using a condom would be part of their routine for the next two years, but he did not mind. When he saw Mitchell smiling, Robert repeated, "Mitch, make love to me."

"Okay," Mitch replied nervously but anxiously. "Let's go, handsome."

Robert stood up and pulled Mitchell with him. They wrapped their arms around each other and walked up the moonlit beach to the beach house.

"I love you, Bobby." Mitchell said passionately as he snuggled close to Robert.

"I love you too, Mitch."

# CHAPTER 52

▼

Days passed and Alex's attitude changed dramatically. As he walked into the kitchen to have lunch with his wife and children on a Saturday afternoon, he groaned when he heard the telephone ring. Emily motioned for him to sit down with the twins while she answered the telephone. After picking up the receiver, she tried to hide her concern when she heard the voice on the other end. After the normal greetings, she called to Alex, "Honey, it's for you."

Alex went to the phone, "Hello." He immediately recognized the gruff voice. "How are you, Leyland?" After a few moments of pleasantries, Alex smiled and hung up the phone.

"What was that about?" Emily inquired.

Alex returned to his seat next to the twins, "Leyland wants me to give a speech next weekend for a fundraiser for the Party."

Emily tried to read Alex's face, but she could not get a fix on his feelings about the phone call. She asked anxiously, "Are you going to do it?"

"Yes," Alex said.

Emily's concern was evident, "Do you think that's a good idea?"

Alex smiled, "Yes, I do."

"Alex, I think you should reconsider. Remember what we talked about a few days ago about their influence over you." Emily paused briefly to give gravity to her comment. "I thought you wanted to change?"

"I do, Em, and I have changed. That's why I'm going to give the speech," Alex replied mysteriously. "I'll let you read it when I'm finished writing it, and if you object to something, then I'll change it. Okay?"

Emily stared at Alex skeptically, "I guess so."

As the family ate their lunch in relative silence as Alex and Emily both contemplated the implications of the speech, Steffi broached the silence with her tiny voice, "Mommy?"

"Yeah Sweetie," Emily replied.

"When's Grandpa and Mr. Mitch coming home?" Steffi asked innocently. "I miss them."

Emily smiled sadly, "I know you do, and I miss them too. Honestly Stef, I don't know when they'll be home, but I'm hoping it's soon."

"I miss them too," Stevie chimed in. "Why did they go away?"

Alex felt an overwhelming pang of guilt in his soul as he answered, "Grandpa and Mr. Mitch went away because I did something really stupid."

The twins looked at their father in surprise, before Stevie asked, "What did you do, Daddy?"

"I said some mean, hurtful things to Grandpa," Alex explained guiltily.

"Why didn't you apologize to Grandpa?" Steffi asked simply.

Alex smiled sadly at his daughter, "They left before I got the chance to apologize, but I promise you that I'm going to apologize as soon as they get home. I just hope that Grandpa can forgive me."

Stevie got up from the table and went over and patted his father on the back, "Grandpa will forgive you, Daddy."

Alex smiled at his son, "Do you think so?"

"Yeah," Stevie said. "Grandpa told me before that you'll always be his little boy, no matter how old you are."

Alex bit his lip to stem the tears that were building, "Grandpa told you that?"

Stevie nodded up and down, "Yeah. He told me that he loves you like you love me and Steffi, and that he'll always love you, no matter what."

Alex hugged his son and pulled Steffi into the embrace as well so that the twins would not see the tears brimming in his eyes. Emily locked eyes with Alex, smiled, and said approvingly, "Nice."

After hugging the twins for several long moments, Alex pulled back and looked them both in the eyes, "Thanks, kids. I swear to you that I'll make it up to Grandpa and Mr. Mitch so that they never feel like they have to go away ever again."

"Good idea, Daddy. Grandpa and Mr. Mitch are cool," Stevie said with a wide smile.

"You love them both, don't you?" Alex inquired.

"Yeah," Stevie replied simply.

"Me too," Steffi added.

Alex smiled at his children, "I'll tell you both a little secret, but you can't tell Grandpa or Mr. Mitch, okay?"

Both kids answered eagerly, "Okay."

"I think that they're both pretty cool, too," Alex revealed.

Emily beamed proudly at her husband. As the kids excused themselves to go play outside, Emily scooted her chair over to Alex's, "That was really nice."

"I owe, not only Dad and Mitchell, but my kids as well to change my behavior. That was never more clear than right now," Alex explained matter-of-factly. "I will never be someone who my kids, my dad, or you won't be able to be proud of."

"I'm proud of you right now, Alex. You've changed a lot in just a matter of days, and I'm sure that if you keep committed to this, that you'll be the person you want to be in no time at all," Emily said lovingly.

"I swear to you, Em, that I'll never be the person that Dad last spoke to," Alex replied sincerely.

"Good," Emily responded. "Just don't forget what I said about your political 'friends.'"

"I won't," Alex answered as he got up and cleaned off the dining room table. As he finished, he smiled at Emily, "Do you mind if I go out for awhile?"

"Where ya going?" she asked.

"I want to go somewhere that I think will inspire me to write a great speech," Alex answered enigmatically.

"Okay, have a good time," Emily replied curiously.

"Oh, I'm sure it will be quite enlightening," Alex said as he walked out of the dining room. "See you later."

"Bye Honey. Be careful," Emily said automatically.

"Always," Alex shouted back as he headed for the front door.

\*　　　\*　　　\*　　　\*

Alex drove the long curvy road to the outskirts of town to the one place he knew would provide the necessary inspiration for the speech he had to perfect before the weekend. After driving for about thirty minutes, Alex pulled into the dirt parking lot of the bar that sat conspicuously to the side of the lonely two-lane country road. He locked the doors of his car, took out a small notepad from the glove compartment, and headed into the bar. As he walked into the bar, he was greeted jovially by the bartender.

"Hello, what can I get you?" the familiar bartender asked.

"Well," Alex paused. "I have an important speech to write, so I better stick with a ginger ale."

"A speech?" the bartender asked curiously. "Are you some kind of professor?"

Alex laughed, "No, not at all. I've been asked by my political party to give a speech at an upcoming fundraiser."

"Wow, you must be some sort of VIP," the bartender exclaimed.

"No, not really. I used to be a ranking member, but I've since moved into the private sector," Alex explained.

The bartender handed the ginger ale to Alex, "Well, it's an honor to meet such a distinguished member of the party."

Alex looked at the bartender curiously, "Are you a Conservative?"

"Since I was a little bitty kid," the bartender said proudly.

Alex smiled amiably, "How much do I owe you?"

The bartender smiled, "It's on the house. It's not often that we get a high-ranking, card-carrying member of the best political party on the planet."

"Thank you," Alex said politely.

"No sir, thank you. It's because of people like you that our party is flourishing. Without our conservative views, what would our country be like today?"

Alex shook his head, "I don't know."

"Well, I do. It'd be going to hell in a hand basket. We need young people like you who believe in self-responsibility. People who believe that having God in our lives is a good thing. And most of all, people who believe that a traditional family is the only way to save our children from the evils of the world. Without a good foundation, people's souls crumble," the bartender said passionately.

Alex took a long sip of his drink before responding, "What do you mean by a traditional family?"

The bartender stared at Alex curiously, "I shouldn't have to tell you."

Alex smiled, "I know what it means to me, but even within the Party there is some dissention."

"Okay, a tradition family to me means a man and a woman who are married and have children. None of this living in sin and having kids to several different men, and definitely not fags living together and pretending that they are equal to the rest of us," the bartender said adamantly.

Alex bit his lip to keep from losing his temper. Through gritted teeth, he replied, "Well, it's nice to know the different views of our members. Now, if you'll excuse me, I have to start writing my speech."

"Sure, and if there's anything I can get you, just let me know. My name's Jimmy," the bartender replied.

"Thank you, Jimmy," Alex said as he walked away with his blood pressure rapidly rising.

As he sat down and opened his notepad, Alex closed his eyes and remembered the last time that he was in this bar. He shook his head to wipe away the image from his mind. With a renewed zealousness that he had not felt since his days in Washington, Alex put pen to paper and wrote his speech. Within a few minutes, the notepad was practically filled with Alex's passionate words. After rereading his speech, Alex smiled to himself as he flipped open his cell phone and pushed the speed dial.

"Hello," a young woman's voice said.

"Hi, is Dr. Hamilton there?" Alex asked.

"Who's calling please?" the pleasant voice asked.

"Alex Petrovic," Alex replied.

"Hold on a moment," the lady responded. Alex listened as the feminine voice called out, "Erik, there's an Alex Petrovic on the phone."

Within a few seconds, Dr. Hamilton's voice came on the line, "Hi Alex, how are you? Have you heard anything from your dad?"

"Hi Doc. No, I haven't heard anything from Dad, but I think I'm making progress in what we discussed last week," Alex explained.

"Really?" Dr. Hamilton asked. "How so?"

"Are you busy right now?" Alex asked.

Dr. Hamilton looked at his watch, "No, not at the moment."

"Can you meet me? There's something that I want you to see," Alex said eagerly.

"Sure," Dr. Hamilton answered. "Where?"

"I'm at the bar on Highway 21, just outside of town," Alex replied with a smile, imagining the look that he knew was undoubtedly on Dr. Hamilton's face.

"Okay," Dr. Hamilton said skeptically. "I'll be there in about twenty minutes."

"Thanks Doc," Alex said.

As Alex was waiting for Dr. Hamilton to arrive, he put his notepad in his pocket and went into the restroom. After looking at himself in the mirror for a few long minutes, he smiled at the man looking back at him. He knew he had come a long way. As he left the restroom, he stopped at the bar, "Hey Jimmy, I'll take another ginger ale."

"Coming up," Jimmy replied as he poured the drink from the tap. "How's the speech going?"

Alex smiled, "It's going well."

"I sure wish I could be there to hear it," Jimmy replied as he handed Alex the drink.

Alex handed Jimmy a five dollar bill, "Well, I'm sure that you can still get tickets to the fundraiser."

Jimmy laughed, "Hey, I'm just a working-class guy. I can't afford those five-hundred-dollar-a-plate dinners."

"Well then, I guess you should count your lucky stars because one of the local television stations is going to cover the fundraiser. It will be on television from start to finish," Alex explained.

"That's great," Jimmy replied enthusiastically. "I'll be sure to watch it, and I'll make sure my kids watch it as well."

"That's good. It's never too early to get the kids involved," Alex said with a wicked smile as he spotted Dr. Hamilton's car pulling into the parking lot.

Alex waited at the bar until Dr. Hamilton made his way through the front door. When Dr. Hamilton entered, he looked around the bar cautiously, and nodded his greeting when he saw Alex talking casually with the bartender. Dr. Hamilton shook hands with Alex, "How are you?"

"I'm doing great," Alex replied with a mischievous grin.

Jimmy, the bartender, interrupted politely, "What can I get you, sir?"

Dr. Hamilton stared down at the drink in Alex's hand, "I'll have what he's having."

"One ginger ale coming up," Jimmy said amused as he filled the glass with ice and ginger ale. He handed the drink to Dr. Hamilton with a smile, "There you go."

As Dr. Hamilton reached for his wallet, Alex handed Jimmy the money for the drink. "It's on me, Doc."

Dr. Hamilton looked curiously at Alex, "Thank you."

Alex motioned for Dr. Hamilton to join him at a table, "Let's go sit down. I'm sure you're curious as to why I asked you here."

"That's the understatement of the year," Dr. Hamilton replied.

Alex smirked, "Well, I wanted to come somewhere that would give me inspiration, and this was the best place that I could think of."

"Inspiration for what?" Dr. Hamilton asked disdainfully.

Alex was bemused by Dr. Hamilton's anxiety, "Earlier today I got a phone call from an old colleague from the Party in Washington. He asked me if I would give a speech next weekend for a fundraiser for the Party."

Dr. Hamilton's voice was full of disbelief, "And you agreed?"

"Yes," Alex said playfully. "I couldn't pass up an opportunity like this."

"An opportunity like what?" Dr. Hamilton asked in disbelief.

Alex took the small notepad out of his pocket and handed it to Dr. Hamilton, "I think you'll understand after you read the speech I intend to give next weekend."

Dr. Hamilton took the small notepad and started reading inquisitively. His eyes widened as he read paragraph after paragraph. As he read the last page, he flipped the notepad shut and handed it back to Alex. "Are you serious about this?" he asked with a mixture of disbelief and hope.

"As serious as a heart attack," Alex answered.

Dr. Hamilton looked at Alex with a perplexed gaze, "Why did you come here?"

"Like I said, I needed some inspiration," Alex answered with a bemused smile.

Dr. Hamilton shook his head in confusion, "How could this place possibly give you inspiration?"

Alex answered matter-of-factly, "It's the place that started a chain of events that lead to me finding my dad hanging from a rope tied around his neck out in the barn."

Understanding was finally setting in for Dr. Hamilton. "Is that what made you write that speech?"

"Not entirely," Alex answered honestly. "Something happened today that opened my eyes completely."

"What's that?" Dr. Hamilton inquired.

Alex swallowed hard and took a deep breath, "Stevie told me that Dad would forgive me because Dad told Stevie I'll always be his little boy, no matter how old I get."

"Why did he say that?" Dr. Hamilton asked.

"Steffi asked when Grandpa and Mr. Mitch were coming home because she missed them, and Emily told her that she didn't know. Stevie then said that he missed them as well," Alex said guiltily.

"They don't know why your dad and Mitchell left?" Dr. Hamilton asked.

"They hadn't up until that time, and Emily wasn't going to tell them, but I felt the need to come clean and tell the truth," Alex said honestly.

"What did you tell them?"

"I told them that I said something mean and hurtful to their grandpa, and that's why Grandpa and Mr. Mitch left," Alex replied painfully.

"What did your kids say?" Dr. Hamilton solicited.

Alex closed his eyes for a moment as he remembered their conversation, "They asked why I didn't apologize, and I told them that Grandpa and Mr. Mitch left before I could tell them that I was sorry, but that I would apologize to them as soon as they returned."

"So is that when Stevie told you what his grandpa had said?"

"Yeah," Alex answered sadly. "He told me that Grandpa would forgive me because I'll always be his little boy, and that Grandpa loves me just like I love him and Steffi."

Dr. Hamilton smiled, "It sounds like you have two very bright children."

Alex beamed through his sadness, "Yes, I most certainly do, and that's one of the main reasons I wrote this speech."

"Really?" Dr. Hamilton asked.

"Absolutely. I want my kids to be proud of me, so I plan to do everything in my power to achieve that," Alex replied seriously. "And the man I was a few days ago wasn't a man who they could be proud of."

"It sounds like you're on the right path, Alex," Dr. Hamilton said sincerely.

"I am, Doc. I've changed a lot since the other night," Alex related.

"What happened the other night?" Dr. Hamilton inquired.

Alex took a sip of his ginger ale before explaining, "Well, after spending an eternity in the doghouse with Emily, I decided to go for a walk around Dad's estate. For some reason I ended up down over the hillside where Dad fell the night before regaining his memory. After reliving that night, I started to walk back to the house, but I felt drawn to the barn area. It was like a magnet was pulling me toward the barn and I couldn't resist."

"Did you go to the barn?"

"Yeah, I couldn't stop myself. It was the first time I was in the barn since I found Dad hanging from the rope, and it made me physically ill to be in there. I fell on the floor and sobbed like I had never sobbed before," Alex explained stoically.

"Why were you crying?" Dr. Hamilton probed.

"That's the place where I almost lost my dad forever, and I was at least partly to blame for him hanging there from the rope," Alex said emotionally.

"And that's what forced you to accept the reality that you played a part in your father's suicide attempt?" Dr. Hamilton asked perceptively.

"Yes. Finally, after all this time, I realized that I was hurting my father so much that I almost caused him to kill himself. And now my behavior has caused him to go away without any word of how he or Mitchell is doing. What the hell was I thinking?" Alex said regretfully.

"I don't think you were thinking, Alex. At least not about anyone but yourself," Dr. Hamilton said with delicate scolding.

Alex nodded, "You're right. Emily said the same thing. She said that I was only concerned about fitting in with my political friends, and to hell with how my actions may have hurt my dad."

"I think Emily hit the nail right on the head," Dr. Hamilton said. "The question now is how you're going to handle how your colleagues react to your speech."

"Frankly, I don't really care. They came to me regarding making this speech; I didn't go to them. I wrote that speech from my heart, and that's the speech I'm going to deliver next weekend," Alex said with resolve.

Dr. Hamilton beamed proudly, "You've come a long way Alex, and in just a matter of days. Without sounding condescending, I want you to know how proud I am of you."

"Thanks Doc," Alex said with heartfelt gratefulness. "Your opinion means a lot to me."

Dr. Hamilton lightened the mood, "Deep down inside you're a really good guy, Alex, even though you try to hide it."

Alex laughed and put his notepad back in his pocket before he turned serious again, "Doc? Can I ask you something?"

"Sure," Dr. Hamilton replied truthfully.

"Why do you care so much about Dad?" Alex asked delicately.

Dr. Hamilton answered instantaneously, "Because I admire him."

"Really?" Alex asked surprised.

"Why should that surprise you? Your dad is an admirable man. He's overcome a lot in his life, and he lives his life with dignity and integrity, regardless of how others might treat him," Dr. Hamilton answered candidly. "I see your dad, and your family as well, as my friends. I know that doctors are supposed to keep doctor-patient relationships purely professional, but I couldn't help but be drawn to your family. Robert is as real as they come, and I'm honored to know him. I just hope that he'll accept my apology when he gets back."

Alex smiled proudly, "Dad is an admirable man. I swear to you, Doc, that from this day forward I'll never forget that."

"And don't forget Mitchell. He's been through a lot as well, and I admire and respect his courage and determination, but most of all his love for Robert," Dr. Hamilton related.

"I agree," Alex said honestly. "I have a lot of bridges to rebuild in my family, and I promise you I'll spend the rest of my life doing just that."

"I believe you," Dr. Hamilton said. "Honestly, this is the first time I truly believe that you are sincere in changing your preconceived ideas. I'm glad that you realized what you have to lose by your intolerance and ignorance."

"Oh, I understand completely," Alex replied. "As I told Emily earlier, I'll never again be the man I was who last spoke to Dad. I love my dad, and I want my children to grow up with Dad and Mitchell in their lives."

Dr. Hamilton smiled widely, "I'm truly glad to hear that. Your children will benefit greatly from having them both in their lives."

"I couldn't agree more," Alex replied.

Dr. Hamilton looked around the bar in overt disgust, "Now that you've been inspired, what do you say we get out of this place?"

Alex stood up from his chair, "I couldn't agree with you more. Let's get the hell out of this place. If my dad's not welcome here, then neither am I."

"Bravo," Dr. Hamilton said as he followed Alex out of the bar.

# CHAPTER 53

▼

The following days on the island dawned and set with unfathomable bliss for both Robert and Mitchell. The island had cast its spell and worked its magic. Mitchell glowed from the happiness that Robert loved him so much that Robert would forever change the dynamic of their relationship by giving himself, body and soul, to Mitchell. Previous to that magical night, Robert obstinately defined his role in their relationship, much to Mitchell's happiness. Mitchell never desired to make love to anyone. He was more than content to have Robert make love to him. That is until that night when Robert asked Mitchell to make love to him. At first Mitchell was shy, and more than a little frightened at the prospect of making love to someone for the first time, but Robert's confidence and unconditional love gave Mitchell the strength and encouragement that he needed. That night, after learning pleasurably from each other during their lovemaking, Mitchell fell asleep with his head on Robert's muscular chest, completely intoxicated by Robert's warm body entwined with his on the king-size bed.

Even though their new union was for only one night, an all encompassing smile never abandoned Robert's handsome face. He had vulnerably reached out to Mitchell that night, wearing his huge heart on his sleeve, and Mitchell did not reject him. On the contrary. They both glimpsed a side of each other that had always been hidden—from each other and from themselves. The more they learned from each other, the more they fell in love with each other ... if it were possible for either of them to love the other more than they already had. That magical night, Robert showed a vulnerability that no one had ever seen, and Mitchell showed a tenderness that made Robert's breath catch in his throat.

Robert and Mitchell relaxed lazily each day under the hot rays of the cloudless skies. Mitchell's pulse pounded every time Robert removed his shirt on the beach or to go swimming in the pool. Robert's dark brown hair had lightened considerably from the omnipresent sun, and his ever-darkening skin made his taut muscles highlight his sophisticated masculinity even more. Mitchell's gaze frequently wandered involuntarily to his sexy lover, and Robert would smile seductively each time he felt Mitchell's eyes gazing at his body, causing Mitchell to blush.

After taking Mitchell for an exhilarating cruise around the island on the two-seat personal watercraft, Robert parked the craft next to the dock and helped Mitchell safely out onto the dry wood of the peer. Robert proceeded to tie the craft securely to a wooden post on the peer, and joined Mitchell for the walk back to the beach house. Mitchell reached for Robert's hand as they strolled leisurely on the white sand to the path which would take them to the heavenly paradise they called home for the past fortnight.

"Thank you Mitch," Robert said unexpectedly.

Mitchell grinned curiously, "For what?"

Robert stopped and faced him, "For making this the best two weeks of my life."

Mitchell winked, "What are you talking about? You're the one who made this happen, and I might also add that you not only saved my life, but renewed my spirit as well. These last two weeks were a dream come true for me, Bobby."

"For me too, Sweetie," Robert said appreciatively before turning serious. "I wish our time here didn't have to end, but unfortunately it does. We're going to have to go back soon."

"That's fine with me, Bobby. Your love and our solitude here has rejuvenated me and has given me the strength to go back and face what happened to me," Mitchell explained with his blue eyes emanating gratefulness and love.

Robert gently pulled Mitchell into an all enveloping embrace, "That's more than I could have ever asked for."

Mitchell relished the warmness of Robert's body and the distinct masculine smell of Robert's cologne for several moments before he pulled back to look into Robert's loving eyes, "When do we have to leave?"

Robert looked pained, "Maybe tomorrow afternoon?"

Mitchell tried to lighten the mood, "We better get moving then. You know how long it takes me to pack."

Robert's lips turned up into a radiant smile, "Yeah, you don't have to remind me."

"Well then, we need to make our last night in paradise something that neither of us will forget for a very long time," Mitchell explained with lust-filled eyes.

Robert's smile rivaled the sun in its brilliance, "I'm open to all suggestions."

With a confidence that Robert had not witnessed in weeks, Mitchell grinned, "Trust me, Bobby. I'm up for any and all things."

Robert tenderly kissed Mitchell on his warm, soft lips. "I'm glad to hear that. What do you say we get an early start on the evening?"

With a voice filled with passion, Mitchell answered seductively, "I thought you'd never ask." He wrapped his arm around Robert's waist and let his hand slide down to rest in Robert's back pocket as they briskly walked back to the beach house.

# CHAPTER 54

▼

As Robert and Mitchell waited for Carlos to come to the island to take them to the airport, Mitchell sprawled out on the hammock where he would usually find Robert napping every afternoon. Mitchell stared heavenward into the cloudless, baby blue colored sky and smiled. Only two weeks prior, he had feared that he would die. What a difference two weeks could make. After leaving Robert's home two weeks earlier, Robert had told him at the airport that he was taking Mitchell to paradise, and in Mitchell's eyes that is exactly what he did. In two short weeks, Mitchell went from being at death's door to being ecstatically happy and healthy, and it was all because of Robert's consummate love for him.

After rechecking the beach house and locking up one last time, Robert joined Mitchell on the hammock. Mitchell snuggled close to Robert and laid his head on Robert's chest, being careful not to wrinkle Robert's shirt, and draped his arm around Robert's waist. Mitchell immediately sensed sadness emanating from his lover, "Bobby, what's wrong?"

Robert sighed, "Nothing really. I'm just going to miss this place."

Mitchell leaned back so that he could see Robert's face, "Me too, but we'll come back, and the next time will be even better."

"I don't know if anything will ever be able to top this trip for me, Mitch. This has been the best two weeks of my life," Robert explained with heartfelt emotion.

"For me too, but just think?" Mitchell said mischievously.

"What?" Robert asked.

Mitchell smiled seductively as he teasingly caressed Robert's chest, "The next time we come we'll both be one hundred percent healthy."

Robert pulled Mitchell to him and kissed him on the lips, "Yeah, I'm already counting the days."

Mitchell snuggled tighter against Robert, "I can't wait, Bobby."

Robert started to laugh, causing Mitchell to stare at him curiously. Robert answered his curiosity by joking, "I better start taking my vitamins now."

Mitchell laughed, "Don't worry, Sweetie. You'll be fine. I'm sure you'll have no problem rising to the occasion."

Robert hugged Mitchell to him, "That's true. The old guy still has a lot of life left in him and is still up to putting a smile on your face."

Mitchell continued to teasingly caress Robert's chest, "I like the sound of that."

Robert let out a soft groan at Mitchell's caresses, "Ah, Sweetie, if you keep that up I'm going to rise to the occasion sooner than I have to!"

Mitchell laughed lovingly, "Okay, I'll stop, but just remember that it should only be a few more weeks before we can resume our usual 'play' time."

"How could I forget! I can't wait for that day," Robert replied with unsuppressed lust in his voice.

As they relaxed on the hammock and basked in their love for each other, the sound of a small airplane grew nearer, and within moments Carlos was landing on the small runway about a half mile from the beach house.

"Are you ready?" Robert asked as he rose from the hammock and extended his hand to Mitchell.

"Yeah," Mitchell replied with a smile. "Let's go home."

✳    ✳    ✳    ✳

On a cool, autumn Saturday afternoon, Alex mentally practiced his speech one last time before going into Robert's study. He sat down at his father's desk and dialed the telephone. After several rings, a man's voice came over the line, "Hello."

"Dr. Hamilton?" Alex inquired.

"Yes," Dr. Hamilton answered.

"Hi Doc, It's Alex Petrovic. How are you?"

Dr. Hamilton's voice lightened, "I'm fine, and you?"

"I'm doing well, but I could use some help," Alex replied.

"What do you need?" Dr. Hamilton asked.

"I have about an hour before I have to leave to give my speech, and I could really use some feedback. Are you busy?" Alex asked anxiously.

"No, I was just watching a ball game," Dr. Hamilton answered honestly.

"Could you possibly come out to the house?" Alex asked.

Dr. Hamilton looked down at his watch, "Sure, I don't see why not. My wife is out shopping with her mom, so I'm free for the afternoon."

"Great. So I'll see you in a little while?" Alex inquired.

"Yeah, I should be there in about twenty minutes," Dr. Hamilton answered.

"Thanks Doc."

"No problem. I'm glad you called," Dr. Hamilton said sincerely. "See you in a few minutes."

Alex let out a sigh of relief as he hung up the phone and stared momentarily at a photograph of the twins that adorned his father's cherry desk. He took a deep breath and felt the enormity of what he was about to do by giving his speech. He smiled at the photograph and the thought that he was about to finally stand up for a man who had sacrificed so much for his family over his lifetime. Alex stood up and walked to the kitchen to find his wife and children having lunch. He walked over to Emily and kissed her on the cheek.

"Would you like some lunch?" Emily asked.

Alex shook his head in the negative, "No, I'm too wired to eat."

"Where were you?" Emily inquired.

Alex sat down next to the twins, "I was going over my speech, and then I went to Dad's study to call Dr. Hamilton."

Emily looked at her husband quizzically, "Why?"

"I just needed someone else to listen—to give me his opinion," Alex replied.

"To give you some moral support?" Emily asked perceptively.

"That too," Alex admitted. "Although I know, without a doubt, that I'm doing the right thing."

Emily beamed with pride, "I'm really proud of you, Alex. You've come a long way in the past week."

"Thanks Em," Alex said appreciatively.

Steffi looked up from her plate, "You'll do great, Daddy."

Alex smiled at his daughter, "You think so?"

Steffi and Stevie both answered in unison, "Yeah. You're the best."

Alex pulled his children to him and hugged them tightly, "Thanks kids. You are the best two kids in the world."

As Alex and his family sat at the table and chatted, the front doorbell rang, and Alex got up from the table to go answer it. A few moments later, he was greeting Dr. Hamilton and leading him into the living room.

"So Alex, are you nervous?" Dr. Hamilton asked.

Alex looked pensive for a moment before answering, "Not really nervous because I know what I'm doing is right, and it's been a long time coming. I want everyone to know that I love my dad, and after today, they'll all know."

"You're not concerned about the fallout?" Dr. Hamilton asked.

"No," Alex answered honestly. "The only person's opinion I care about regarding this speech is my dad's."

"Are you videotaping it?" Dr. Hamilton asked.

"Yeah, the tape's in the VCR. I know he won't be able to see it live, but I'm hoping that Dad and Mitchell will watch it when they get back … if they come back," Alex said apprehensively at the thought that his father might not be coming home.

"Don't think that way, Alex. You need to keep focused on your speech," Dr. Hamilton instructed.

"Yeah, I know. I have to believe that Dad and Mitchell will be back soon, and I've been praying everyday that they'll forgive me, and if they don't, I'll spend the rest of my life trying to prove to them that I changed," Alex explained.

"You have changed, Alex, and I'm sure that your dad and Mitchell will realize that, but it may take time before they can forgive you. After all, you hurt them both, so your actions are going to have to speak louder than your words," Dr. Hamilton expounded.

"I hope that this speech is the first step in proving to them that I'm sincere," Alex replied.

"You're on the right track, without a doubt," Dr. Hamilton offered. "So, can I be one of the first to hear your speech?" Dr. Hamilton asked as he looked down at his watch.

"Absolutely," Alex replied. "I've changed a few things since you first read it, but the gist is still the same."

"Well, I liked the first version a lot," Dr. Hamilton said with a smile. "What did Emily say about it?"

"She said she's never been more proud of me," Alex answered modestly.

Dr. Hamilton put his hand on Alex's shoulder, "Well then, I'm sure I'll approve of it as well."

"Have a seat, sit back and relax, and enjoy," Alex said assuredly.

Several minutes later, after Alex finished presenting his speech to his one-man audience, Dr. Hamilton stood up and shook Alex's hand. "Let me be the first to say how wonderful it is to meet the real Alex Petrovic."

"Do you mean that?" Alex asked hesitantly.

"Without a doubt," Dr. Hamilton answered confidently. "You're now the kind of man that a father can be proud to call a son."

"From your mouth to God's ear," Alex said with hope.

As Alex and Dr. Hamilton stood talking in the living room, Emily came in and smiled at Dr. Hamilton, "Hi Doctor, how are you?"

"I'm quite well, and you?" Dr. Hamilton replied.

"I'm fine, especially after hearing the speech that my husband is about to give," Emily said proudly.

"I agree. It's a great speech," Dr. Hamilton admitted honestly.

"Thanks guys. I couldn't have done it without either of you. You've both helped me so much, and for that I'll always be grateful," Alex said humbly.

Emily looked at the clock on the wall, "You better get going."

Alex glanced at his watch, "Yeah, you're right." Alex folded the paper his speech was typed on and tucked it into the pocket of his suit coat. "Doc?"

"Yeah."

"Could you stick around until I get back?" Alex asked with hope ringing in his voice.

"Sure. No problem. Just give 'em hell today," Dr. Hamilton instructed.

"I will," Alex said with newfound courage. He kissed Emily on the cheek and shook hands firmly with Dr. Hamilton. "Bye guys. Wish me luck."

"Good luck," Emily replied.

"Good luck, Alex, although I know you don't need it," Dr. Hamilton said with a reassuring smile.

Alex took a long deep breath and walked toward the door. Dr. Hamilton and Emily stared momentarily at each other before Emily smiled, "Can I get you anything?"

"No thanks, I'm fine," Dr. Hamilton replied amiably.

As Emily and Dr. Hamilton made small talk in the living room, the twins came in and ran around the room playing tag. After several minutes of the twins' chaos and the idle laughter from Dr. Hamilton playing along with their games, a sound came from the foyer. The twins ran in the direction of the front door with Emily tailing behind them. As the twins came around the corner, they squealed with delight at what stood before them. The kids ran full speed to the open door, "Mr. Mitch!"

Mitchell gently closed the door behind him and knelt down to greet the kids jovially, "Hi kids!"

"Hi," they said in unison. When the twins saw what Mitchell held under his left arm, they jumped up and down with uncontained joy, "You got a puppy."

Mitchell smiled as he set the puppy on the floor, "Yeah, your grandpa got him for me. His name's Phantom."

"Cool," Stevie exclaimed.

"He's so cute," Steffi added before looking back at Mitchell. "Mr. Mitch?"

"Yeah Steffi," Mitchell replied.

"Where's Grandpa?" she asked.

Dr. Hamilton and Emily stood in the corner of the room and listened to the conversation, with Emily barely able to contain her enthusiasm at seeing her dear friend.

"He's talking to the driver," Mitchell answered as he smiled at Emily. "He'll be in in a few minutes. And now, kids, could you do something for me?"

"Sure," the twins answered eagerly.

"Could you watch Phantom for a little while?" he asked.

"Yeah," Stevie and Steffi answered.

Mitchell stood up and Emily came running to him and practically dove into his arms. She hugged Mitchell to her, "It's so good to see you."

Mitchell embraced Emily affectionately, "It's great to see you too."

Emily clung to her friend for a few moments before pulling back to look into Mitchell's blue eyes, "How are you?"

Mitchell beamed, "I'm wonderful, Em. I've never been better."

"You look so good," Emily added.

"I am good, Em. Actually, I'm great. I've never been happier in my life," Mitchell replied sincerely. He looked over at Dr. Hamilton and smiled, "Hi Dr. Hamilton, how are you?"

Dr. Hamilton returned his smile, "I'm fine, especially seeing you doing so well."

"Thanks, I am doing well," Mitchell replied.

As the three walked further into the foyer, Emily squeezed Mitchell's hand, "Where have you been?"

"We were on the island," Mitchell answered in a relaxed tone.

"You were in Hawaii?" Emily asked surprised.

Mitchell laughed, "No, we were on Robert's private island."

Dr. Hamilton and Emily both stared in disbelief before Emily chuckled, "Robert's private island? I guess I shouldn't be surprised."

"Well, it's not just Robert's private island. He's actually a co-owner of the island, but it was just the two of us in that tropical paradise," Mitchell elaborated.

"So you're completely healthy?" Dr. Hamilton asked optimistically.

"Completely," Mitchell answered gleefully.

"I'm so glad to hear that," Dr. Hamilton said.

"Thanks."

Dr. Hamilton came to stand in front of Mitchell, "Mitchell, I have something to say."

"Sure, go ahead," Mitchell replied.

"I want to apologize to you," Dr. Hamilton said humbly.

Mitchell stared at Dr. Hamilton in astonishment, "For what?"

Dr. Hamilton explained genuinely, "For upsetting Robert before you left. Emily told me that because of me, you and Robert argued, and you ended up having a difficult time breathing."

Mitchell dismissed Dr. Hamilton gently, "It's in the past. Forget about it."

As Dr. Hamilton was about to speak, the front door opened and Robert walked in and was jovially attacked by his grandchildren. Robert gleefully knelt down and pulled the twins to him and hugged them, "Hi kiddoes."

"Hi Grandpa," Stevie said as he continued to hold the puppy against him. "You got Mr. Mitch a puppy?"

"Yeah," Robert laughed. "And I got something for the two of you as well," Robert said as he caught the sight of Emily and Dr. Hamilton and smiled. "Wait here and I'll go get your surprise."

Robert walked back out the front door, and the twins waited anxiously as Mitchell put his arm around Emily's shoulder. Mitchell whispered in Emily's ear, "Get ready." Before Emily could respond to Mitchell's playful warning, Robert reentered the house and at his feet walked a beautiful little black and tan Doberman Pinscher puppy. The twins' faces lit up like the north star as Robert explained, "This is Shadow. He's Phantom's brother, and he needed someone to love him and play with him, and I thought and thought and thought of someone who might be able to love him, and you know, I finally decided that the two of you were the best two people for the job."

Stevie and Steffi's smiles radiated throughout the foyer, "Thanks Grandpa."

"Do you think you can love him and play with him like he needs?" Robert asked.

"Yeah," the kids answered in harmony.

Robert looked over at Emily as he handed the leash to Steffi, "Okay then, he now belongs to the two of you. Mitchell and I will help you train him, but you have to promise to always love him."

"We promise," the kids answered with unsuppressed joy as they took the puppies and ran into the living room.

Robert smiled mischievously at Emily who was walking toward him, "Before you throw something at me, let me ..."

Emily interrupted Robert's words by diving into his arms. Robert wrapped his arms around Emily and hugged her tight as he teased, "This is definitely better than having something thrown at me."

"I missed you," Emily said softly into the front of his shirt.

Robert's voice turned serious, "I missed you too. I'm sorry that I left like I did."

Emily softly reprimanded him as she pulled out of the embrace, "No, don't apologize. You did what you had to do, and after seeing the two of you look so damn good, I'd say that your plan was flawless."

"It was the best two weeks of my life," Robert replied with a heartfelt smile. "But before I go any further, I have to tell you about the puppy. When you move into your new house, if you don't want to take the puppy, he can stay here with us."

Emily smiled at Robert's last words and looked at him quizzically, "Us?"

Robert's smile lit up his face as he put his arm around Mitchell, "Yeah. I asked Mitch to move in with me permanently, and he agreed."

Emily wrapped her arms around Robert and Mitchell and hugged them, "I'm so happy for you both."

"Thanks Em," Robert said, and Mitchell echoed his words. As Robert pulled out of the embrace, he noticed Dr. Hamilton standing to the side uncomfortably. Robert smiled, "Hi Doc. How are you?"

"Hi Robert," Dr. Hamilton replied. "I'm fine. It's great to see you, and to see Mitchell looking so well."

Robert laughed, "Yeah, a suntan does him a world of good, doesn't it?"

"Hey!" Mitchell chimed in.

"You both look great," Dr. Hamilton added.

"Thanks," Robert replied as he looked around the room. "Where's Alexander?"

Emily glanced knowingly at Dr. Hamilton, "He left a little while ago to give a political speech. It's going to be televised in about a half an hour."

"Okay," Robert said nonchalantly.

Dr. Hamilton looked down uncomfortably before addressing Emily, "I guess I should go."

"No, you don't have to go," Robert offered. "In fact, could I talk to you privately for a moment?"

Dr. Hamilton looked surprised, "Sure."

"Let's take a walk outside," Robert said as he walked to the front door with Dr. Hamilton following him.

Dr. Hamilton walked outside and stopped momentarily. He laughed nervously, "You're not going to kick my butt, are you?"

Robert laughed, "Would I have a reason to kick your butt?"

Dr. Hamilton sighed loudly, "Unfortunately for me, yeah."

"And what reason would that be?" Robert teased.

Dr. Hamilton failed to notice the playfulness in Robert's voice, "For the way I treated you the last time I saw you. Robert, I want to apologize to you."

"It's not necessary," Robert replied seriously.

"Yes, it is. I upset you that day, and because of that, Emily told me that you and Mitchell argued. I never intended to upset you, Robert."

"Honestly, Doc, it's in the past. Forget it, okay? I have," Robert instructed sincerely.

Dr. Hamilton smiled at Robert, "It's so great to see you and Mitchell looking so well."

Robert smiled gratefully, "Yeah, it was the best time of my life. Mitch and I connected in a way that neither of us had ever thought possible."

"I'm glad to hear that," Dr. Hamilton offered genuinely.

"Thanks Doc," Robert said as he stopped walking. "Doc, I want to apologize to you for the way I treated you that day in the gym."

Dr. Hamilton interrupted, "No Robert, please don't apologize."

"I owe you an apology. I was worried about Mitch, and I was angry with Alexander, and I took that all out on you. You've only ever tried to help me, and for that I treated you badly. I'm truly sorry, Doc."

"Like you said, Robert. It's in the past, and it's forgotten," Dr. Hamilton replied sincerely.

"Thanks," Robert said gratefully. "Can I ask you something?"

"Sure," Dr. Hamilton said.

"Can you recommend a therapist for Mitch? Someone who is sensitive to what happened to him," Robert asked.

"Yeah, sure. There are two that immediately come to mind, but give me a couple of days so that I can talk to them and see which one I think would be best suited for Mitchell, okay?"

"That's fine," Robert replied. "Thanks Doc."

"Is Mitchell having problems?" Dr. Hamilton asked sensitively.

Robert nodded, "He was having nightmares before we left for the island, but he didn't have any while we were away."

"But you think that'll change since you're back home?" Dr. Hamilton asked perceptively.

"Unfortunately yes. Once we get back into the routine of everyday life, I'm afraid the nightmares will return," Robert answered.

"Has he talked to you about the nightmares?" Dr. Hamilton asked.

"While we were on the island, he did open up to me a little about the rapes," Robert answered.

"That's a good start," Dr. Hamilton added.

"We talked about everything while we were gone … our hopes, our dreams, our fears," Robert explained.

"It sounds like you had a very productive vacation," Dr. Hamilton replied.

"We did. As I said, we talked about everything, and Mitch thinks it'd be a good idea if I started back to therapy as well," Robert said before adding, "And I think it's a good idea as well, that is if you'll have me back?"

Dr. Hamilton was slightly taken aback, but he quickly replied, "Of course. Whenever you're ready, just call my secretary." Dr. Hamilton paused before asking, "Can I ask you why?"

"Mitch deserves to have me at my best, and right now I'm not at my best, and I think the only way for me to get to that point is with your help," Robert explained simply.

"I think you made the right choice to continue therapy," Dr. Hamilton said warmly. "And I'll do my best to get you to that point."

"Thanks," Robert said.

"Can I ask where things stand regarding Alex?" Dr. Hamilton asked.

Robert answered matter-of-factly, "I'm living my life the way I want to live it, and if he can't accept that, then that's his problem."

"I think you'll be pleasantly surprised at how much Alex has changed in your absence," Dr. Hamilton added with a smile.

"Regardless of how much he's changed or hasn't changed, I'm not going to allow him to derail my happiness," Robert replied seriously.

"I'm glad to hear that," Dr. Hamilton said. "Alex has changed, Robert. He's realized how much he needs his dad in his life."

"I've always been here," Robert interjected.

"I know, but it didn't hit home for Alex until he read your note to Emily," Dr. Hamilton replied.

"How so?" Robert questioned.

"Well, that note scared the hell out of him."

"Why?" Robert asked.

Dr. Hamilton answered seriously, "He thought that note was a final goodbye
…"

"He thought I was going to kill myself?" Robert asked incredulously.

"Yeah, he did," Dr. Hamilton answered matter-of-factly.

"Why? And what about Mitch?" Robert asked disbelievingly.

Dr. Hamilton sighed, "He thought that Mitchell was going to die from his illness, and that you were taking him away somewhere to die, and then you were
going to kill yourself."

Robert looked at Dr. Hamilton skeptically, "And did you agree with him?"

"I honestly didn't think you'd kill yourself, but I would be lying if I said I
wasn't worried," Dr. Hamilton answered honestly.

"So what made you change your mind?" Robert asked.

"In a word—Emily," Dr. Hamilton responded.

"Emily?" Robert repeated.

Dr. Hamilton smiled, "Yeah. She made it crystal clear to Alex and me that we
didn't know anything about you."

"Really?" Robert replied.

"Yeah," Dr. Hamilton responded with a wry smile. "She called us both on the
carpet."

Robert laughed at the image of Emily taking the two men to task for doubting
him. "I would have liked to have seen that."

Dr. Hamilton laughed, "She is definitely yours and Mitchell's staunchest
defender, and she put us both in our places for thinking the way we were."

"Well, Emily is the best friend that Mitchell or I have ever had," Robert said
warmly. "What's interesting is that you and Alexander both entertained the
thought that I would take Mitch away while he was so sick to just die."

"That's what made me skeptical about the note you left. I honestly didn't
think that you would jeopardize Mitchell's health," Dr. Hamilton explained.

"Never," Robert said strongly. "I made arrangements for his medical care
before we left, and there were always protocols in place in case his condition
changed."

Dr. Hamilton smiled sadly, "I'm sorry that I doubted you for even a moment.
I know how much you love Mitchell."

"Let me ask you something," Robert said earnestly.

"Sure."

"Would you take your wife somewhere you knew she could relax, but not take
precautions if she were ill?" Robert asked.

"Of course not," Dr. Hamilton answered.

"Why?" Robert asked.

"Because I love her and want what's best for her," Dr. Hamilton responded sincerely.

"So why would you think I'd do anything differently for Mitch?" Robert inquired.

Dr. Hamilton nodded his understanding, "I shouldn't have doubted your love for Mitchell."

"I took him to the island because I knew that the warm weather and sea air would do him good. We both needed to get out of this house for awhile, but I never would have considered it if safeguards weren't in place and I didn't have the go-ahead from his doctor," Robert explained matter-of-factly.

"I understand," Dr. Hamilton replied. He looked down at his watch, "It's almost time for Alex's speech."

"We better head back then," Robert said as they walked back to the house. "I don't want this to come out the wrong way, but why are you here?"

Dr. Hamilton laughed, "I was wondering when you were going to ask that. Alex called a couple of hours ago to ask if I would be a sounding board for him before he went to the fundraiser."

"That makes sense," Robert replied as they walked through the front door.

Dr. Hamilton smiled to himself, "It's quite an interesting speech."

"I'm sure it is," Robert responded nonchalantly. "Alexander is quite a talented politician."

*    *    *    *

Alex milled around the lobby of the hotel mentally going over his speech while political colleagues came up to him and shook his hand and patted him on the back. All of them told him how much they missed his presence in the party hierarchy, and they all tried to persuade him to come back into the fold. Alex smiled at their comments, but he reiterated to them that his family came first and that is the reason he left. They told him that they understood, but hoped that he would someday change his mind. The door, they said, would always be open for him.

As the fundraising attendants took their seats, the head of the County Party walked to the podium and welcomed everyone before introducing Alex. The Party head beamed as he shook Alex's hand at the podium, "Ladies and Gentlemen, one of the youngest and most influential members of our prestigious Party, and no doubt a force to be reckoned with in the future—Alex Petrovic."

Alex smiled at the warm applause and soaked it in for a moment. He took his speech out of his pocket and placed it on the lectern. He took a deep, silent breath and began with a steady, forceful voice …

*Good afternoon ladies and gentlemen, and welcome to this year's state Conservative Political Party fundraiser. As some of you may know, my name is Alexander Petrovic, and I'm a former party leader at the national party level. I was graciously asked to be here this afternoon to deliver the keynote address for this most important fundraiser for the incumbents and our new Conservative candidates in the upcoming election, and I could not pass up the opportunity to speak directly to my former colleagues and fellow party members.*

*A lot has happened in my life since I resigned from my position approximately ten months ago, and I'd like to tell you about it if I may. First I'd like to tell you the stories of two men.*

*The first man I'd like to tell you about was born fifty years ago in a rural state adjacent to our illustrious state. Both of his parents were first generation Americans. His mother stayed home and raised him while his father went off to work each and every day in the steel mills. Life in that little rural town was tough, and the family struggled to make ends meet. Work in the steel mills was exhausting and dangerous, and because of the working conditions and health hazards, the father of this man I'm telling you about died and left behind his wife and fifteen year old son. Times were tough, but life had to go on.*

*Shortly after his father's death, with the bank threatening foreclosure, this fifteen year old boy went to work in the same steel mill where his father had worked. He would not turn sixteen for another several months, but the boss at the steel mill knew that this young man and his mother would be thrown out into the street if he did not hire him, so he ignored the regulations and put him to work on the afternoon shift. This young man was brilliant in school, always making straight A's, and he was a gifted athlete as well. In his freshman year of high school, he lettered in basketball, but by his sophomore year, he was working forty hours a week in the steel mills. He would go to school everyday, keeping his grades as perfect as always, and then go directly to work after school.*

*At the beginning of his senior year in high school, he was offered a full-tuition scholarship to a prestigious ivy league university. The scholarship paid both tuition and room and board. For most high school kids, this would be a dream come true, but this young man turned the school down. You're probably wondering why he would turn down an offer to leave the grueling, back-breaking work at the steel mills, but he had a good reason. He passed on the offer because he had to take care of his mother. You see, he had made a promise to his dying father that he would always take care of his mother, and he couldn't have done that several hundred miles away. Sure, his college and room and board were going to be paid for, but who was going to make the mortgage payments at home if he wasn't working? How would his mother afford to eat? These were some of the basic questions that he asked himself, and the answer, for him, was simple—he couldn't accept the scholarship. He needed to stay home to take care of things there, but his dream of college was still very much alive.*

*The summer following graduation, he decided to supplement his income by working a construction job during the day, and then going to his regular job at the steel mill in the afternoon. The money he made during the summer was set aside for future college classes.*

*Now you're probably thinking, that with his kind of schedule that he wouldn't have time for a social life, and you'd be right. He didn't, but he did fall in love with his high school sweetheart, and they married when they were only nineteen. The girl's family disapproved. They were from the "better" side of town, and they didn't think their daughter's new husband would amount to anything, but the daughter was stubborn and married the man she loved. After the wedding, she moved in with her new husband and her mother-in-law, and she could not have been happier. A year later, the young couple welcomed a baby boy into their home, and even though money was tight, they were happy.*

*The following year, after working and saving for two summers, the young man started fall classes at a local university. Mind you it wasn't an ivy league, but it was a respectable school that he could afford. He attended classes during the day, and worked in the afternoons at the mill. Four years later he graduated Magna Cum Laude with a degree in business.*

*After graduation, the president of the construction company offered him a full-time position as a foreman, and the young man jumped at the opportunity. He would no longer have to work in the unbearable conditions in the steel mill, and his new job would pay double what he made in the steel mill. The only problem was that after only a few months, he grew restless with the new job, and he disapproved of some of the building techniques that his superiors ordered. The question at this particular time in his life was what to do. He had a wife, young son, and a mother who he was responsible for, so he couldn't just walk away from responsibility. After many long conversations with his wife and best friend, a guy who he worked with since he started working summers at the construction company, he came up with a plan that changed his life. He decided to start his own construction company.*

*With a small amount of money he had saved, and a handful of guys he worked with at the construction company, he started his own business. With business savvy, integrity, and hard work, his business flourished. Now, some twenty-five years later, this guy's endeavor is a multimillion dollar business. The name of this multimillion dollar business is Petrovic Construction, and the man is my father—Robert Petrovic.*

*Two of the hallmarks of our Party, in my eyes, are family values and self-responsibility. Another is being tough on crime, but I'll talk about that later. Back to family values and self-responsibility. Robert Petrovic personifies them both. He went to work at fifteen to support himself and his mother. He turned down an ivy league scholarship to stay at home to continue to work. He put himself through college while working and caring for his family and his mother. He started his own business and soon after put his wife through school so that she could fulfill her dream of becoming a school teacher. He did all those things on his own, without any government handouts. If ever there were a poster child for our Party, I think you'd all agree that my dad would be it.*

*There is another man I'd like to tell you about. He left his family's home on the West Coast after graduating from college, and came to our state for employment. He worked at a major corporation for many years, but realizing that he needed a change, he ventured out on his own and started his own business. Because of his expert knowledge and people skills, his business took off rapidly. He was an instant success.*

*He lived and worked in this region for many years, and almost everyone he ever met immediately liked him. Almost everyone. A couple of months ago, he got in his car one morning and drove to his office like he had done thousands of times before, but when he got out of his car, he was attacked by three thugs. They beat him nearly to death, and left him bloody and broken in his office parking lot. His injuries were severe, and because of complications related to the attack, he almost died. The police arrested the three attackers several hours after the attack and charged them with robbery and aggravated assault, but no robbery occurred. The thugs didn't take any of his possessions, even though he carried several hundred dollars in his wallet and wore an expensive gold watch and ring. They didn't attack him for his valuables; they attacked him to brutalize and intimidate him. All three were released on technicalities, and are free roaming our streets right now.*

*We, as a Party, have always been tough on crime, and I'd guess from the facts that I've just told you that you'd want to know why and how those thugs were allowed to go free. Well, my friends, I'll tell you why. The arresting officer knew all three subjects, having dated one of their cousins, and he didn't agree that what they did was wrong, so he conveniently forgot to read them their Miranda Rights. As you all know, such a glaring omission would be grounds for throwing out the charges, and that's exactly what happened. Was the arresting officer fired or reprimanded? Not to my knowledge. Why did this decorated officer, with a clean and stellar record, condone the actions of the attackers and be willing to blatantly ignore procedure? Because the man attacked in his parking lot was attacked because he's gay. Those three thugs successfully carried out a gay bashing, in broad daylight, and got away with it.*

*How do I know about this? I know because the man's name is Mitchell Rains, and he's my dad's boyfriend. Yes, you heard me right. I said he's my dad's boyfriend. My dad told me he was gay about ten years ago, and I completely disowned him. After he told me he was gay, my father was dead to me. I went off to college and immersed myself in building my own life. One day, after signing up for a political science class, an upperclassman told me about a conservative political party meeting that was going to be held the next day. I went, and it forever changed my life. I found a home among others who thought just like I did. We had the same values and the same outlook on life. All the while, I told most of my conservative political party friends that my father was dead, and in my mind, he really was. Every time I thought of my father, it sickened me to know he was gay, so I just put him completely out of my mind.*

*I became president of my campus's Conservative Political Club, and that opened many doors for me. While I was expounding the virtues of self-responsibility, nobody knew that I was going to school on money that was provided by my father in a trust fund. At the time of my father's college graduation, he had already worked almost ten years. Here I was living off of money that he provided, and foregone working myself. You see, in my eyes, my job was to further the ideas of my Party, and that was a full-time job.*

*After graduation, I was offered a prestigious job in Washington, and I accepted it immediately. Shortly after arriving in D.C., I made friends with many of you sitting here this afternoon, and those are friendships that have helped me greatly through the years. A few years later, I married my college sweetheart and we had the perfect yuppie life. A year later, we were blessed with twins, who are now five years old. As my life was moving ahead and my family was growing, I still was revolted by my father's homosexuality. I told my wife about it, but no one else. When we married, I didn't even invite my father to my wedding, nor did I let him know that he had twin grandchildren. I guess my family values were a bit lacking at the time.*

*As some of you may know, I had been testing the waters regarding a possible run for Congress. After long consideration and countless conversations with my wife, I have decided to forego that possibility. You see, almost a year ago, I found what I was truly meant to do, and that is work side by side with my dad. It took almost losing him for real to get me to see that I needed him in my life. And not only did I need him in my life, but I wanted him there as well. I still don't completely understand his homosexuality, but I accept it. That acceptance only came a couple of weeks ago. I did something incredibly stupid, and drove my father away, possibly for good. I just hope that when he gets back that he and Mitchell will forgive me for what I did. After reflecting long and hard on what I had done, I realized that I was the type of person that I never wanted my children to see. I was a bigot, and my hatred nearly cost me my family.*

*Now, I see many of you rolling your eyes and looking disgusted by my comments, and I know I'm going to hear from many of you that homosexuality is a sin. Well, my friends, so is adultery. As is stealing and taking the Lord's name in vain. Those sins made the top ten, and as I look out at this crowd today, I see many of you who have committed one or more of the sins that I just mentioned. Several of you broke up your families by divorce, and many of the divorces were brought on by your adulterous acts. Others have embezzled money and got away with it because you were friends or colleagues with the judges. I know for a fact that many of you owe back taxes and cheat on your income taxes. That my friends, is stealing, and it's a sin. After a lot of soul searching, I realized that I was a hypocrite regarding sin. I condoned many of my colleagues' sins, but I could not accept my father for who he is. That changed a few weeks ago, and I'm going to spend the rest of my life living in a way that my children will be proud of me.*

*Think about what I've said, my friends. Who would you want your children to look up to as role models? Men who play by the rules and work hard to take care of their families, or politicians who are intolerant of those who are different? I know who I want my children to look up to—my dad and Mitchell Rains.*

*Thank you everyone, and please have an enjoyable afternoon.*

Alex gathered his papers and walked away from the podium with a satisfied smile adorning his face. Several former colleagues scowled and uttered sardonic remarks, but Alex held his head up high as he walked out of the hotel conference room. He knew he had done the right thing, and he never felt better about himself.

$$* \qquad * \qquad * \qquad *$$

Robert, Mitchell, Emily and Dr. Hamilton sat in Robert's living room attentively watching the big screen television as Alex delivered his speech on a local cable channel. Emily and Dr. Hamilton sneaked glances at Robert and Mitchell to gauge their reactions, but Robert and Mitchell sat stoically listening to Alex's speech.

As Alex brought his speech to a close, Mitchell turned and looked at Robert, "Did we come back to some sort of alternate universe?"

"I'm not sure," Robert said disbelieving.

"Did I just hear what I thought I heard?" Mitchell asked his lover.

"I don't know what to think," Robert admitted. He turned to Emily and asked, "What's going on?"

Emily smiled, "Alex has finally grown up and accepted reality."

"It sounds as though he burnt a lot of bridges amongst his friends," Robert replied.

Emily reached for Robert's hand, "The only bridge that Alex cares about is the bridge he needs to rebuild to lead him back to you. He loves you Robert."

"I don't know what to think," Robert admitted. "He's made gestures like this before …"

"Yeah," Dr. Hamilton interjected, "But he finally realized this time that he could lose you forever, and that thought scared the hell out of him."

"Dr. Hamilton's right," Emily offered. "Alex has changed so much since you left."

Robert was still skeptical, "But why? What brought about these immense changes?"

Emily smiled sadly at Robert, "He went out to the barn for the first time, and he realized that he was at least partially responsible for your suicide attempt, and if you had gone off this time and contemplated suicide, he would have been the cause of that as well."

"I've told everyone before that I chose to try to kill myself, and no one else is responsible. I will never try that again, and I thought that everyone would know that was true," Robert replied indignantly.

"I know that Robert," Emily said.

Robert melted a bit, "I know you do."

"Robert?" Dr. Hamilton said. "I know that to be true as well. I honestly don't know why I ever doubted it for a moment."

Robert relaxed, "Forget about it."

Mitchell entered the conversation, "So Em, from your heart of hearts, do you truly believe that Alex has changed for good?"

"Yeah Mitchell, I do. I saw him after he returned from the barn that night. He was a sobbing mess," Emily answered sincerely.

"I sure hope he has for Bobby's sake," Mitchell added.

"It's true, Mitchell. And he hasn't just changed his view of his dad. He's also seen you in a new light," Emily explained.

Mitchell looked intrigued, "What do you mean?"

"Well," she started. "He finally admitted that he likes you, and that you're good for his dad."

Mitchell laughed, "Okay, ice water is now being served in hell."

Emily laughed, "It's true. Seriously Mitchell, when he saw Robert carrying you in from the car after you went to the doctor, he was greatly concerned ."

"It's true, Mitchell," Dr. Hamilton interjected. "He came to my office right after seeing how sick you were, and he was scared that you were going to die."

"Really?" Mitchell asked disbelieving.

"Yes," Dr. Hamilton answered. "He actually remembered the names of the drugs that your doctor prescribed so that he could ask me if they were the best treatment options."

"What?" Robert asked. "How did he know what prescriptions Mitch was given?"

"He took the prescriptions from the deliveryman," Emily remembered. "He must have glanced inside the bag. I'm sorry Robert."

"Don't be," Robert offered warmly. "You didn't do anything wrong."

"Anyways," Dr. Hamilton continued, "Alex came to my office and was distraught. He kept saying that he didn't want Mitchell to die."

"What did you do?" Robert asked.

"I told him that the drugs were the best available, and that he should think positively. Worrying wasn't going to solve anything, and it could have adversely affected him," Dr. Hamilton paused. "I also told him to give you some space, Robert. I told him that you needed to focus on Mitchell, and not be reminded of your fight."

"So it took seeing Mitch gravely ill for him to realize all this?" Robert asked rhetorically.

"I guess so," Emily answered. "Alex had come home early that day to apologize to you for the way he treated you, but I told him that you were at the doctor's office with Mitchell. He was concerned, so he waited, and then he saw you carrying Mitchell into the house with oxygen."

"What made him want to apologize that day?" Mitchell asked.

Emily answered, "I hadn't talked to him since the night he attacked Robert. He pleaded with me to talk to him, and finally I exploded and I made him reverse the situation and put me in your place, Mitchell. I wanted him to see things from Robert's perspective of having the person he loved most in danger."

"And it worked?" Robert asked.

"Apparently it did. He came home at lunch feeling awfully guilty," Emily remembered with a smile.

Robert shook his head, "This is all hard to believe."

"I know where you're coming from, Robert, but I think you'll meet a brand new Alex when he gets home," Dr. Hamilton said knowingly.

Mitchell grasped Robert's hand, "I hope he has changed, Bobby."

"So do I, but forgive me for not getting my hopes up," Robert responded pragmatically.

"I don't blame you for being skeptical," Emily replied. "I was too."

"So was I," Dr. Hamilton added. "But, over the past several days, I've seen a changed man."

Robert stood up, but continued to hold onto Mitchell's hand as he addressed his lover, "Do you mind if I go outside for a little while?"

Mitchell smiled, knowing fully that Robert needed time to think before Alex returned home, "No, I don't mind."

Robert leaned down and kissed Mitchell on the lips before turning toEmily and Dr. Hamilton, "I'll be back in a little while."

"Okay," Emily and Dr. Hamilton both replied as Robert walked out of the living room.

Robert walked out the front door and proceeded to walk to the small pond on his vast estate. He picked up a few stones and skipped them absentmindedly across the pond, causing several ripples in the murky water. He tried to focus his thoughts, but the overwhelming implications of Alex's speech kept intruding on his thought process. He did not want to get his hopes up, as he had told the others in the living room, but a flame of hope was igniting within him. If only it were true he kept telling himself. After a few minutes of restless thought at the pond, Robert walked to the front of the house. As he stared out at his lush acreage, he heard a car coming up his long driveway. He waited silently as Alex pulled his car to the front of the house and got out. Alex instantly saw his father standing on the front lawn.

"Dad," Alex said hurriedly as he ran toward his father. "You're back?"

Robert nodded, "Yes."

Alex smiled with obvious relief, "It's so great to see you." Before he could continue, Alex had a terrifying flash in his mind. His features turned suddenly pale, "Oh my God, where's Mitchell? Please tell me he's okay."

Robert answered stoically, "He's fine. He's inside with Emily and Dr. Hamilton."

Alex let out an audible sigh of relief, "Thank God." He paused a moment, "You look great, Dad."

"Thank you," Robert replied coldly.

"Dad," Alex started. "I'm so sorry for how I treated you, and I swear to you I'm going to make it up to you."

"I don't need anything from you, Alexander," Robert responded as the hurt came rushing over him like a tidal wave.

Alex felt his heart breaking, "I know I've apologized in the past, Dad. But I swear to you that this time I'm sincere." Alex looked away as tears formed in his eyes, "I don't want to ever lose you."

"I've always been here for you, Alexander. You're the one who didn't want me," Robert said aloofly.

Tears cascaded down Alex's face, "I'm sorry, Dad. I was so wrong, and I want to prove to you that I want you—need you—in my life."

"I love Mitchell, Alexander, and I've asked him to move in with me permanently. You have to accept that, but more importantly, you have to accept Mitchell. And honestly, from your past actions, I don't know if you'll ever be able to do that," Robert replied honestly.

"I can Dad. I swear I can," Alex answered as he sniffled. "Please just give me a chance to prove myself to both you and Mitchell."

"Swear to me that you'll never hurt him," Robert said forcefully.

"I swear, Dad. Please just give me a chance," Alex pleaded.

"I think you have someone to apologize to inside," Robert responded non-committally.

Alex took his handkerchief out of his pocket and wiped away his tears, "I know I do. I have a lot of fences to mend, and I'll spend the rest of my life mending them if that's what it takes." Robert put his hand on Alex's shoulder, "I'm glad to hear that."

Alex threw his arms around his father's neck and hugged him tightly, "I'm so glad you're okay."

"I'm better than okay," Robert replied stiffly as he returned the embrace.

"Mitchell is really okay too?" Alex asked as he continued to hold his father.

"He's fine, Alexander," Robert responded as he pulled out of the embrace.

"That's the best thing I've heard in a long time," Alex replied honestly.

Robert stared briefly at his son before finally asking, "Did you really mean what you said in your speech?"

Alex beamed, "Every word. I swear on my children's lives."

"You burnt a lot of bridges today, Alexander," Robert stated.

"Well," Alex smiled. "I'm in the construction business, so I thought I'd try rebuilding some of the bridges that I burnt in the past."

Robert could not help but smile, "Finally, you're learning."

Alex smiled wryly, "I'm a slow learner, but I'm an overachiever once I put my mind to something."

"That's for sure," Robert replied with a smile.

"Do you mind if we go inside now? I'd really like to talk to Mitchell. That is if he'll see me?" Alex stated seriously.

"We'll have to go inside and find out," Robert said as he started walking to the door.

Alex followed behind, but stopped his father before he opened the door, "Really Dad, I'm glad you're home. I missed you."

"Thanks son," Robert replied warmly.

As Robert and Alex made their way through the foyer to the living room, Stevie and Steffi ran out holding Shadow and Phantom in their arms. "Look what Grandpa brought back for us, Daddy."

Robert laughed, "Are you sure you're glad we're back now?"

Alex looked slightly confused, "You brought the kids back two Dobermans?"

"No," Robert replied with mock-seriousness. "I only brought them back one. The other one is Mitchell's."

Alex laughed, "Oh, I'm glad you cleared that up." He bent down to pet the puppies, "They're beautiful, kids."

"Yeah," the twins replied. "Grandpa is the coolest."

Alex looked up at his Dad, "Yeah, I agree with you on that."

"Why don't you take the puppies out on the patio?" Robert instructed.

"Okay," the twins responded as they scooped up the puppies in their arms and carried them to the patio.

Alex stood up and continued on into the living room. Emily came over to him and hugged him, "Hi Honey."

"Hi Em," Alex said affectionately as he returned the embrace.

"Great job, Alex," Dr. Hamilton said as he extended his hand to shake Alex's hand.

"Thanks Doc," Alex said affably as he firmly shook the doctor's hand. Alex looked over at Mitchell sitting silently on the sofa before he faced Emily and Dr. Hamilton, "Can you give us a few minutes alone, if that's all right with Mitchell?"

Mitchell nodded his agreement, and Emily, Dr. Hamilton and Robert left the living room to join the twins on the patio. Alex walked over and sat opposite of Mitchell, "Hi Mitchell, how are you?"

"Fine," Mitchell answered shortly.

"You look great," Alex offered genially.

"Thank you," Mitchell replied, determined to make Alex lay all his cards on the table.

"Mitchell," Alex started. "I owe you a humongous apology for the way I've treated you, but especially for the way I've treated Dad. I'm truly sorry, and I hope that someday you'll forgive me."

"You think that by saying you're sorry that everything will be forgotten?" Mitchell asked stubbornly.

"No, I want to prove to you and Dad that I'm sincere. I want my actions to speak louder than my words—that is if you'll give me the chance?" Alex asked.

"I hope for Robert's sake that you're sincere. You've hurt him tremendously," Mitchell explained.

"I know I have, and I know that saying I'm sorry isn't going to suffice. But, I hope that you can give me the chance to prove to you that I've changed," Alex replied respectfully.

"Honestly Alex, in the past I've never cared what you thought of me. I would have liked for us to have gotten along for Robert's sake, but it was never that important to me," Mitchell explained. "Your opinion of me didn't mean a thing, but when you hurt Robert, it ripped my heart out to see him suffer."

"I'm sorry, Mitchell," Alex said meekly.

"You know, if I hadn't been injured that night you hurt him, I would have done more to you than throw you up against the wall," Mitchell said seriously.

"I wish you would have," Alex replied sadly.

"I can't stand to see him hurt like that," Mitchell said strongly.

"I swear to you that I'll never hurt him again," Alex offered emotionally. "I know you don't have any reason to believe anything that I'm saying, but I swear to you on my children's lives that I'm telling you the truth."

"Honestly, I hope you are Alex," Mitchell responded. "Robert is the finest human being I've ever known, and he deserves to be treated with dignity and respect, especially from his family."

"I agree. Please give me another chance," Alex gently implored.

"If you ever hurt him, you'll answer to me," Mitchell answered.

"I'll hold you to that," Alex replied. "Does that mean you'll give me another chance?"

Mitchell stared intently at Alex before speaking, "Yeah, I guess it does."

Alex beamed as he held out his hand to Mitchell, "Thanks Mitchell."

"Just remember what I said," Mitchell replied with a sincere threat evident in his voice.

"I'll never forget. I promise," Alex said. "Now, for my first act as a normal son, can I take you and Dad out for dinner?"

"I'd like that," Mitchell answered truthfully.

"Good," Alex said as they walked toward the patio to join the others. "By the way," Alex stated.

"Yeah?" Mitchell replied.

Alex smiled warmly as he put his hand on Mitchell's shoulder, "Welcome to the family."

Mitchell stared curiously at Alex before a smile grew on his face. The two men walked shoulder to shoulder out to greet their family on the patio.

# THE END

978-0-595-44405-2
0-595-44405-9

Printed in the United States
82555LV00004B/34